Hearthstones III:
Glowing Embers

By MaryLee Marilee
and
Sheryl Drake Lawrence

Paper Bridges
Books

Hearthstones III: Glowing Embers
A Paper Bridges book/February, 2013
Published by Paper Bridges
www.Hearthstones.net

Disclaimer:

This is a work of fiction. Names, characters, places and incidents are either the products of the authors' imaginations or used fictitiously. Any resemblance to actual people, living, dead (or otherwise incarnate), or to events or locales is entirely coincidental. If you think you recognize someone within these pages, all we can say (as our old, writing professor used to say) is that "it's all grist for the mill!"

ISBN 978-0-9831765-5-8
Print Book

Scripture references taken from King James Version of the Holy Bible.

Paper **Bridges**
Linking Author
P.O. Box 142
Loudonville, OH 44842
To Reader
email: Publisher@paper-bridges.com

DEDICATION

MaryLee Marilee: To the welcoming people of Edisto Island, South Carolina, thank you from the bottom of my heart for all your help in my research. From the first moment I crossed the bridge onto Edisto, I felt as though I'd come home.

ALSO BY THE AUTHORS:

(MaryLee Marilee & Sheryl Drake Lawrence)

The Hearthstones Series

Book I
Keep the Home Fires Burning

Book II
Let the Sparks Fly!

PROLOGUE
(February 1818)

"What's the meaning of all this dying business, pray tell? Don't you know you have Bently blood coursing through your veins, Amanda Jane? True Bentlys never give up without a fight."

"But, it's been so hard Grandmother! So many terrible things have happened. I can't go on... I just can't!"

"Nonsense. You underestimate yourself, my girl. You can survive, and you shall. You simply must, you see. It's in the blood."

"But how will I ever manage, after... after–"

"Do you think you alone have suffered the greatest of insults at the hands of men?"

"How can you ever know what it was like," she whimpered.

"I know, because I lived through the very same anguish, my dear."

"You?"

"Yes, me."

"Who?"

"Suffice it to say that Chickasaw blood still imparts a great strength to the blend of your life's vital flow."

"Redskins?"

"A chieftain's son, himself a great leader. Bent Leaf," she said with a regretful smile. "Our first meeting may have been far from agreeable, but I came to bear him great respect, as well as a son."

"You?"

"Me."

"But how did you endure the disgrace?"

"With dignity, and with fortitude," she said. "And so shall you, Amanda Jane. So shall you."

"But how can I, Grandmother? How can I go on?"

"Take a deep breath, put one foot in front of the other, and keep yourself moving forward," she said. "And Amanda..."

"Yes, Grandmother?"

"Never, never look back."

"Yes, Grandmother."

"If ever you should come to doubt yourself again, just remember the brooch—this one, the one I gave you before," she said, placing the treasured heirloom in Amanda's hand once again. "Remember?"

"I remember, Grandmother."

"Pin it on, right over your heart, close to that which pumps your life force. It will remind you whose strength drives your spirit."

"I will, Grandmother," she said, holding tight the pearl-surrounded, cameo brooch.

"The blood runs weak in your father—my grandson. The wife my son took for himself brought a regrettable failing that defiles the lineage yet. And with the taint of your mother's pompous mediocrity, those feather-brained sisters of yours don't stand a chance. But in you, Amanda—in you, and in your daughters, and in the boy you now carry—Bent Leaf's noble strength flows yet, strong and true." She took her great-granddaughter by the chin and raised her head high, tilting it slightly to reveal the small birth mark hidden behind her right ear. "Remember this, Amanda Jane: nothing can stand in the way that you, or they, cannot surmount. Do you believe me?"

"Yes, Grandmother. I believe you."

"Then rise from your bed and look after your daughters like the noble, Bently woman you are. You must teach them whom they, also, shall someday become. Listen to me now, Amanda. Be careful for your son. Heed my words, for I cannot come to you again. Up, now. To the day!"

Chapter 1

Letter from the Solicitor
October 1820, Justice, Ohio

Last Will and Testament
Dated February 27, 1818

I, Olympia Lillian Wallingsford Bently, of the Borough of Charleston, in the great State of South Carolina of these United States of America, do make, publish and declare this to be my Last Will and Testament, hereby revoking and annulling any and all wills and codicils by me, heretofore disposed in any way, shape or form...

Amanda Jane looked up from the official-looking document she held, giving Michael a puzzled expression. "They sent me Grandmother Bently's will? What do you suppose it means?"

"We'll never find out, if you don't keep reading."

She held the page more closely to the cabin's south-facing window, squinting to make sure she didn't miss a single word in the fading, late-afternoon light of autumn.

ITEM I: RESIDUARY ESTATE

At the time of my demise, I leave the entire estate and legacy—real, personal and exceptional—which I now own, to Amanda Jane Bently r.e. Harrison, lineal descendant of afore designated personage, hereby circumventing any and all descendants of the first and second degrees to this previously named grantor who are living at the date of execution of this will.

To Amanda Jane, I entrust all things connected with Wallingsford Plantation and Orchard, both earthly and ethereal, practicable and unexpected.

ITEM II: STIPULATION

I specifically make no provision in this my Last Will and Testament for Joseph Alexander Bently (lately designated III), nor for either one of the younger, empty-headed fruit of his loins. They no doubt will make suitable enough matches to please their social-climbing mother and be adequately looked after for the duration of their inconsequential lives.

To the only true descendant carrying the soul-marker of the great Chickasaw, Bent Leaf, I leave the key to his birthright. Although at present this may appear unusually perplexing to most, in due time, Amanda Jane, and only she, will have the necessary insight and fortitude to understand the full scope of this bequest.

"I certainly don't understand any of this," Amanda said, waving the document in the air. "What did Grandmother mean? What key is she talking about? And why on earth did this take so long to reach me?" she asked, turning the document over and over again in her hand.

"What else does it say?" Michael asked.

"Only a little more legal doubletalk before all the signatures... grandmother's and the people who witnessed for her."

...In witness whereof, I have heretofore set my hand to this, my Last Will and Testament, cast at Wallingsford Plantation and Orchard, Edisto Island, South Carolina, this 27th day of February, the One Thousand Eight Hundred and Eighteenth year of our Lord.

Signed by Olympia Lillian Wallingsford Bently, a.k.a. Woman Who Sings to Bent Leaf, and by her acknowledged to be her Last Will and Testament, before us and in our presence, by us subscribed as attesting witnesses in her presence and at her request.

2

"Oh my Lord, that was the day before I saw her... in my dream!" Amanda dropped the document to her lap and her hand flew to the oversized, heirloom brooch she constantly wore at her throat—the treasure Great Grandmother Bently had pressed upon her when Amanda left the only life she'd ever known in Charleston, on her way North to marry a stranger.

Michael picked up the paper and examined it carefully, reading all the way through once again, slowly. "These people who signed... this Winston Horatio Applebaum, a Douglas B. Hornsby and Pitney Doubleday Bower. Who are they? Do you know them?"

"Winston is Grandmother's plantation manager. He's run Wallingsford for years," she said. "Mr. Hornsby's her barrister. He has an office in Charleston. He's always taken care of Grandmother's legal dealings. Lord knows, she had enough of those over the years. But I can't believe Pitney Bower ever signed a thing! As far as I know, she never learned to read or write." Amanda rose from the bench under the window and walked over to check the baby, beginning to stir in his bentwood crib beside the hearth. "Three or four years before I left home, Grandmother brought Pitney in the house to ease her workload. As I recall, Pitney threw a hissy fit about having to give up her work in the orchard. That woman had to be nearly 90 back then. No one left alive knows how old she is for sure."

"A woman? Isn't that peculiar? I didn't think women could sign anything legal."

"As a rule they don't. Especially not Negro women."

"She's a slave, then."

"Grandmother never kept slaves. She freed all the people who came to her when she inherited Wallingsford from her father. It caused quite a stir in the low country, I can tell you that. Grandmother didn't believe in slavery, after being kept in servitude herself."

"Your Grandmother, a slave? How?"

3

"She was 14 when Redskins took her from her father. After a time of hard work, she acquired a place of high standing among them. She used to tell me stories about her time with the 'People of the Forest,' as they called themselves. Other folks call them Chickasaws."

The baby began to fuss, and Amanda lifted him to cuddle as he came fully awake, rooting for his next meal. Little Jems. Jeremiah's last child. What would his daddy think of this precious boy? If only her husband could be here to see his namesake grow. But no, she dare not let herself go down that road. It still brought too many tears.

Keep moving forward. Never look back.

"Do you want me to read this other letter while you feed Jems?" Michael asked, waving the second paper from the packet. "Maybe it'll give some explanation."

"Go ahead. I'll sit by the fire," Amanda said, taking her place in the rocker Jeremiah had made for her three, short years ago—years that held a lifetime. She put the baby to her breast, discretely covering herself from view with a receiving blanket while he nursed.

Michael unfolded the document. "It's from that Hornsby fella, written last winter…"

29 February, 18 and 20

To Amanda Jane Bently, r.e. Harrison:

As you no doubt surmise by the inclusion of your great-grandmother's Last Will and Testament in this posting, Olympia Bently made her exit from our earthly sphere on the last day of February, 18 and 18. The day before she died, she called me to her bedside to execute this most recent of changes to her Will, naming you sole beneficiary of her entire estate. Heretofore, you had been named as beneficiary with your father appointed as acting trustee, to deal with all matters of legal import.

I forewarned that it would undoubtedly cause a rift among the living relatives, knowing that her grandson, your father, would contest such a last-minute change completely removing him from the line of inheritance. To that warning she made reply, but being a gentleman born and bred, I shall not pass along her retort, to you, a lady —and now one of considerable means, I might add. In all her years your grandmother never claimed the status of gentle woman. She was, however, a formidable person without equal—one far advanced for her time.

Joseph Alexander Bently, your father, has done exactly as predicted, forcing the execution of this Last Will and Testament into such a legal dispute, that it has delayed notification to you of your bequest, to the point of complete ignorance on your part that your grandmother had even died. Only recently have I been given leave by the Judge overseeing this case to notify you of her demise. By the time you do receive this missive, she will have been gone more than two years.

"I don't understand," Michael scratched his head. "If they just now sent word your grandmother died, how did you know already?"

"From the dream. I saw her on the very day she died," Amanda said. "Some things may have gotten muddled in my head over the past two years, *Brother*, but never that. I'll remember it to my dying day. Grandmother came to give me her last words of wisdom before she left this earth. To tell me goodbye." Amanda put Jems over her shoulder, patting softly to dislodge a burp. "Does the letter contain anything more?"

"Just a few paragraphs…"

Let me be the first to offer you my sincere condolences, Miss Amanda Jane. And at the same time, may I offer my services as barrister in the battle you now face in settling the estate of your great grandmother Olympia. I am afraid there is nothing else for it than to request you make the trip back to Charleston in order to see to the administration of our current legal dispute with Joseph Alexander Bently III. Without your presence, there can be no resolution to this dilemma, which keeps all assets tied up ad infinitum, causing undue distress— most especially for the free people of color currently employed on Wallingsford.

Since Olympia's demise, Winston H. Applebaum has continued to oversee the management of afore- mentioned plantation in your stead. On her death bed, Olympia empowered me to continue handling all banking and financial affairs for the plantation, as I have done for the past fifteen years, with her blessing, I might add. She also requested that Winston remain in charge of any and all details pertaining to the supervision and safeguarding of the workers at Wallingsford, until you should take over in her stead.

I hope to hear from you as soon as is humanly possible, Mrs. Harrison. Until such time as you make your wishes otherwise known, Winston and I shall carry on with plantation business as usual, to the best of our combined abilities, insofar as these legal entanglements allow us so to do.

Most sincerely,
Douglas B. Hornsby,
Barrister of the 1st Degree

"Well, Sister. Looks like you're making a trip to Charleston."

"How on earth can I be expected to travel in the cold of winter with a tiny infant?" She cradled the two-month old closer in a protective embrace. "I flatly refuse to lose another boy! I will NOT put Jeremiah's only son at risk over some legal wrangle I care nothing about." She set her chin and stomped her tiny foot.

"Wait a minute. Let me get this straight," Michael said. "You mean to tell me you don't care about inheriting a plantation, lock, stock and peach pits?"

"That's not what I said, *Brother*." Her voice had a decided edge to it. "I don't want to even think about getting involved in litigation of any kind. Especially with my own family."

"I've got news for you, *Sister*, you're already involved. Wanna be or not."

"Oh *horsefeathers*!" At her agitation, the baby began to fuss in Amanda's arms. She rose from her rocker to pace the floor in an effort to quiet them both.

"You'd better listen to that boy," Michael said, nodding toward the baby. "He knows land is worth fighting for."

"Well, what in the world am I supposed to do about it?"

"Send word you'll come after spring thaw. Once Jems makes it through his first winter, you'll feel better about taking him on a trip."

"Do I really need to go?"

"You really need to go."

"Couldn't you go for me?"

"You know I would if I could, Mandy," he said, gently touching her arm. "I'd do anything for you."

She blushed at the change in his tone of voice and flinched at his touch. Quickly he pulled his hand back to his side. "They wouldn't let me represent you, anyway... seein' as we're not married. I'm just your dead husband's brother. No way any judge will take my word for anything concerning you and yours... not until you marry me."

"I know that. I'm just having trouble thinking about marriage so soon after... well, Jeremiah's only been gone for three months! I still expect to hear his footsteps on the porch and see him walk through that door after milking time–" she caught her breath in an involuntary sob that took her by surprise; tears slid down her cheeks unchecked.

"We'll always miss him," Michael said, pulling her into his arms and holding her and the baby to himself while she cried softly onto his shoulder. "We don't have to rush into anything, Mandy. Not until you're good and ready."

"I just need some time," she sniffled, wiping her nose with the edge of the baby blanket. "Time to grieve. And time to heal, before I can move on."

"I don't plan on going anywhere. I promised Jeremy I'd take care of you and the girls, and that's exactly what I intend to do. Nothing short of dying myself will keep me from it."

"Don't you even joke about a thing like that!"

"I'm not joking! I won't leave you, Mandy, not unless you send me away or the Lord sees fit to take me away. So until you're ready to have me as husband, I'll just have to be content being Brother to you... Uncle Mikey to the children." He took his handkerchief and wiped her tear-streaked cheeks. "Now blow," he instructed. She blew. "And when you're ready to head to Charleston, I'll make sure you get down there safe and sound."

"Thank you, *Brother*."

"Don't mention it, *Sister* of mine."

Chapter 2

Lucy
December 1820

December dawned rainy and cold. Although she'd lived in this northern clime for five years now, tiny, Southern-bred Amanda Jane Bently Harrison had still not adjusted to winter's bone-chilling conditions. She huddled closer to the fire while giving their noon-time soup another stir. When the door banged open behind her, she jumped in fright. "My Lord! You liked to scare the wits right out of me!"

"Sorry. Door got away from me," said Michael, dropping an armload of firewood into the wood box. "It's fixin' to blow up quite a gale out there."

"I'll never get used to this climate," Amanda growled, pulling her shawl tighter around her slight shoulders.

"It must be hard for someone who grew up where it's warm all the time," Michael commiserated. "But just think about this. Next spring you'll be back down there. An' then you'll probably grouse about the heat."

"Ohhhh! *Thhhhhhh!*" Amanda stuck her tongue out at Michael.

"I seem to bring out the best in you, don't I, Sister."

"You are *so* exasperating!"

"Guess that's my lot in life. Keep you stirred up enough so you never get bored."

"How could anything be boring around you?"

"Mama! Mama! Jems rolled over in his crib!" Three-year-old identical twins, Camellia and Lillian, came running into the kitchen addition from their play place in the main cabin. "He's laughing, Mama! Jems is *laughing*! Come see! *Quick*!"

Amanda handed her wooden spoon to Michael and hurried to the other room.

"What in blue blazes am I supposed to do with this?" he hollered after her.

"Use your imagination," Amanda called back. She hurried over to the bent-twig crib where her cherished son lay kicking on his back, waving little fists and giggling.

"He has a funny laugh, Mama," Millie said, pulling on Amanda's skirt.

"That laugh has a tickle in it, just like your Papa's," Amanda said, patting Camellia's head softly.

The other twin peeked out from underneath the crib, bringing on a fresh set of giggles from her baby brother.

"Lillian Jane, what on earth are you doing?"

"Making him laugh! He likes peek-a-boo."

"Come out from under there this instant!"

"Yes, Mama." Lilly scooted out and hopped to her feet.

"Straighten your dress. Little girls should not crawl around on the floor so. Do you hear me, young lady?"

"Yes, Mama," Lilly said, tugging at the sides of her pinafore to untwist it.

Amanda pulled the cover back over Jems, tucking it securely on each side. "You girls stay over in your play area and occupy yourselves quietly so Jems can go to sleep."

"Yes, Mama."

As soon as Amanda disappeared into the kitchen, Lilly scooted back underneath the crib and began her peek-a-boo game all over again, this time in a whisper.

"Everything all right over there?" Michael asked, handing back the spoon.

"He's growing so fast," she said, moving to the pantry cupboard and laying the spoon aside. Amanda took a bowl down from the shelf, put it on the fold-out counter of the sideboard Jeremy had built, and began to measure ingredients for biscuits. "I can hardly believe Jeremiah's been gone five months already. How can time go by so quickly?"

A knock at the door startled them both.

"Who on earth could be out in weather like this?" Amanda wiped floury hands on her apron as Michael headed over to open the door.

"Mornin'," said lanky neighbor Jonathan Johansen, standing beside Lucy, who braced herself against the doorway as she held the sides of her swollen belly.

"Lucy! Are you all right?" Michael helped her inside.

"Give me a minute. I'll be fine," she said in a heavy breath.

With little Hank sitting atop his shoulders, Jonathan took Lucy's other arm and helped her inside, ducking down as he did so to avoid hitting the boy's head on the doorpost. "Looks like we got a baby comin'," he said nonchalantly.

"Why on *earth* didn't you send for me?" Amanda fussed at her soft-spoken neighbor, helping his wife out of his own greatcoat, after standing little Hank upon his feet. The three-year-old shrugged out of his coat and immediately ran to the twins.

"I asked Jonathan to bring me here instead," Lucy said. "You have no business taking Jems out on a day like this. He's too little to expose to so much wind and cold," she said, taking a deep breath as another pain gripped her. "You couldn't very well leave him behind to come help me, now, could you?"

"I suppose you're right on that account. But look at you, Lucy! You're in labor! You shouldn't be traveling anywhere in such a condition!"

"Wasn't that far across the woods from Jonathan's. He took it slow and easy," she said. "I believe I had better lie down, though. Things seem to be moving right along."

"Here, come over to the bed in the main cabin—no, wait... the children are playing in there. Do you think you can climb stairs?"

"Of course I can. Just give me a minute till this pain eases off." Lucy leaned into Jonathan a few moments, then straightened to her full, six-foot height.

"It's colder up there, but I don't imagine that should be an issue for a while."

"I'll stoke up the fire," Michael said, nervous for something productive to do. He still felt panicky when it came to human births, after losing his own wife and child in their bloody ordeal. Later delivering Amanda's healthy son for his deceased brother did precious little to alleviate his fear.

"We'll need plenty of hot water," Amanda said, doffing her apron and stretching as high as she could to hang it on the pantry peg. Even on tiptoe she could barely reach it. She took Lucy's arm in her own, looking up at her tall friend—the two quite a contrast standing side by side. "We'll get through this just fine, you'll see," she said, clucking at her friend.

"I have no doubt." Lucy patted Amanda's hand. "Between us we've done this enough times to know the worst childbed has to offer. I say it's high time we get to see the best of it, don't you?"

The two women started for the steps in the corner of the kitchen, Amanda holding tight to Lucy's arm to steady her. "Bring hot water up as soon as you get a pot boiling, would you Brother?" A knowing look shot between the two.

"I'll go check on the youngens," Jonathan said, disappearing into the main cabin.

Lucy leaned in to whisper, "You're still calling him *brother* I see."

"We'll talk later," Amanda stood on tiptoe to whisper back. "I believe we have enough to keep us occupied for the time being." She pulled the stairway door shut behind them. "Not really much to tell, in that department, anyhow."

* * * * *

"Good vittles, Mike. Thanks." Jonathan sopped up the dregs of his soup with the last buttermilk biscuit. Michael had taken over lunch preparations after the women went upstairs. "You do a right decent job of biscuit makin'."

"I don't know how you can eat at a time like this. I'm a nervous wreck, and she's not even my wife!"

"Not a dern thing I can do about what's transpirin' up yonder," Jonathan nodded toward the steps. "Don't know as worryin' about it ever helped ary a thing."

"I've lost too many females I loved at a time like this—my mother, my wife, my daughter, my niece—I have no choice but to worry."

"Can't say as I blame ya' there," Jonathan pushed away his bowl. "You check on them youngens recent?"

"Not since we shooed 'em back over to play after they ate."

"I'll go make sure that boy ain't into somethin' he ought'nt be." Jonathan pushed his long legs back from the table and sauntered into the main cabin. At his entrance through the doorway, a scurry of little feet skittered across the floor to the other side of the room. Three toddlers stood behind the big bed in the corner, hands over eyes, trying to hide. Jonathan began to play along with their hide-and-seek game. "Now where h've our youngens got to," he said making a show of looking beside the fireplace and below the baby's bed. Little Jems lay sound asleep, unaware of the activity around him. "Reckon we'll just have to throw that extra shortbread out to the hogs, Mike," he said, raising his voice enough to make his point, but not so loud as to disturb the babe.

At the mention of shortbread, all three children ran out to grab Jonathan's legs. "Give us shortbread! We eat treats! Don't give it to the hogs!" they called altogether.

Jonathan couldn't help but laugh when he looked down at the soot-smeared faces peering up at him. "You childr'n been right busy, I see." All three sported black finger marks across their eyes, like three little raccoons.

Millie, always at the ready to tattle on her sister, took up her opportunity. "Lilly did it! She drawed pictures first!" Millie

13

pointed toward the hearthstone, where Jonathan could make out sooty shapes drawn with a charred stick.

"You been playin' in that fire?" he asked Hank directly.

"No, sir," said the solemn little boy.

"How 'bout you?" he asked Millie.

"Nope. Not me! I'm a good girl, I am."

"Lilly?"

Lilly kicked her feet and tried to hide her sooty hands behind her back.

"Miss Lilly, you sure do make purty pi'tchers, honey. But you daren't fool with fire."

"I only used that cold stick. The one Uncle Mikey lights to puff up his pipe!"

"You didn't play in the fire?"

"No sir. Mama would tan my hide if I played in fire."

"Good. Nothin' for a arteest like you to fuss with, no how."

"No sir. What is arteest?"

"Someone who draws purty pi'tchers."

"I'm a arteest?"

"Sure enough. Anybody worth his salt can see that," he patted her head. "Come on back over to the kitchen now, an' wash up real good 'fore your mamas come back down here an' find youens in such a unclean state."

The children dutifully marched back to the kitchen, where Michael stood washing lunch dishes in the graniteware basin sitting in the dry sink. One by one, he lifted the three-year-olds up and washed off hands and faces, before sitting them back at the table with a mug of cold milk and a chunk of shortbread each.

"Sure has been a goodly while since we heerd anythin' from up yonder," mentioned Jonathan all casual like.

"You beginning to worry a bit, are you?"

"T'ain't worried. A mite *concerned*, is all," Jonathan admitted.

14

"Want me to go and find out what's holding things up?"

"Naw. Don't bother. They got enough to keep 'em occupied."

As the men sat back down with cups of hot chicory coffee and shortbread of their own, the unmistakable cry of a newborn pierced the afternoon stillness.

"Reckon we can stop our worryin' now, Mike."

"S'pect so," he agreed. "You wouldn't care for a splash of celebration in that coffee of yours, would you?"

"Don't mind if I do, neighbor. Don't mind if I do."

* * * * *

"You have a beautiful daughter!" Amanda wrapped the warm receiving blanket securely around the newborn babe she'd just cleaned up. "She has quite the shock of curly, black hair!"

"Just like Henry," Lucy said, with tears streaking down her bony cheeks.

"God bless his well-meaning soul," Amanda said, intending comfort.

"I don't doubt even God has trouble knowing what to do with Henry's soul," Lucy said, wiping her eyes and extending her man-sized hands to take her dead husband's last child. "I can tell you for certain, Henry wouldn't have had any idea what to do with a little girl," she said, those hands of hers nearly engulfing the tiny bundle. She cuddled the babe to her breast. "Poor man barely knew what to do with a wife."

"I don't know how you stood such bossy ignorance, Lucy."

"Henry wasn't so bad, really," she backpedaled. "He didn't begin to understand a thing that had to do with the female persuasion, is all."

"Then maybe it's a good thing he's left this little angel in Jonathan's care."

Lucy choked back a fresh wave of tears. She took a big breath. "I don't know how I came to be so blessed… to have such a wonderful man step up for me after Henry died."

"He knew Henry long before you and I came out here. I'm not a bit surprised."

"Jonathan always did have a way of showing up just when I needed help the most," Lucy said, "like he did when Henry and Jeremy got trapped under that tree." She caught her breath as an afterbirth twang tightened its grip. "Sorry. My, I wasn't expecting such hard pains once the baby got here... after everything's all over with."

"I hate to tell you, but they seem to get worse at every birth."

"Well, the prize is still worth the agony," Lucy smiled, cuddling the newborn as she suckled. "You know, when you think about it, we both ended up out here with total strangers for husbands. Both of us at the mercy of the luck of the draw."

"I never gave it much thought before."

"Difference is, you didn't have a whole lot of choice in your situation. I did."

"I don't know how you ever found the courage to come to this wilderness all by yourself. Not knowing what kind of man you'd find waiting to claim you, what kind of life you'd have."

"When you come right down to it, no matter how long you might know a man beforehand, it's totally different once you start livin' with him," Lucy observed. "So I guess moving in with a stranger wasn't all that remarkable. But, tell me... how is it *really* going for you, living with Jeremy's brother now?" Lucy asked. "Doesn't it seem strange, having someone who looks so much like your dead husband sitting across the table from you every day?"

"It's funny, but I don't see that much of Jeremiah in Michael at all," Amanda said, straightening the bed and gathering up soiled linens. "Their personalities were always so different."

"Are you two ever going to 'tie the knot'?"

"I imagine it will come to that...," Amanda said, stopping and turning to face Lucy, "...eventually. To tell you the truth, I'm just not ready to think about Michael *that* way. Know what I mean?"

"'Course I do. I had trouble with that, myself. It being so soon after Henry died, and all. But Jonathan's so tender and loving. I never knew such depth of feeling was possible from any man," Lucy said, "thinking so much of someone other than himself."

"Jeremiah put others' happiness before his own, too. I never knew another man like him."

"I don't mean to sound critical of the dead—and mind you, I did love my husband the best I could manage—but for all of Henry's professed faith, he sure did have trouble practicing what he preached."

"Far as I'm concerned, you deserve all the happiness you can find with Jonathan," Amanda said, giving her bony friend a big hug. "It's about time you have a man who treasures you."

"Thank you, my friend," Lucy said. "And thank you for helping me bring this sweet little bundle into the world."

"What are you going to name her?"

"I think I'd like to name her after my mother... Alice Francine."

"You never mentioned your mother before. I bet she'd love to see her new granddaughter... especially one named for her."

"She'd be overjoyed," Lucy said with a sad smile. "But she's been gone quite a few years. Died shortly before I came out here, matter of fact."

"I'm sorry. I didn't know."

"She raised me on her own, after my Pa drank himself to death. Never knew anything but hard work and abuse at his hand." Lucy heaved a big sigh. "That's why I decided to come out here. No men back home would even look at a big-boned girl like me. I took after my Pa in that regard. Ma always told me I was made of the kind of grit that would make for a good settler's wife. So when I saw Henry's advertisement, something just clicked inside. I had nothing to keep me in New York. So, out I came to start a family and new life of my own."

17

"I'm so glad you're here. I don't know what I'd have done these last months without you to lean on, Lucy."

"You got that all wrong. I'm the one who's been leaning on you!"

"Maybe we hold each other up."

"I like that. I truly do," Lucy said, running her finger over Alice's fuzzy brow.

"I'll go down and send Jonathan up... if you're ready to see him."

"I'm ready. This little girl will belong more to him than Henry, anyhow."

Amanda headed down the steps, glancing back at Lucy, basking in the afterglow of new life.

Mid-September 1820
Tuesday Forenoon
Riverstop on the Clear Fork
From your friend Ellie Mae

Dear Libby,

I can not thank you enough for comin to help my Katrina birth her boy. Our little Simon. Seein as I could not help her my own self. Over Jerometown way helpin Mary Sue birth her own babe like I was. It is fittin you were the one to be here. Now that we are grandmaws to the same pup.

Well, I have spent these last weeks stewing about my Johannah. That letter you spoke of that was waiting for me back here at Riverstop turned out to be from her. My middle girl who run off West with that stranger. Our Katrina guessed it rightly. Making out her older sister's hand. I opened it happy enough when I got home from son Jason and Mary Sue's. After her confinement with chick number four. I was careful with it too. Seeing as how that letter was over a year old and wrinkled up so. It was in better shape than that other one Johannah sent two years back. Ink smeared so bad I barely could make out that first one. Wetted through so many times it looked to be.

What I read in the pages of this letter kept me sitting straight up all the next night. I can not even make to write it down here. It was that bad. What that poor girl went through is too much to think on. Took me back to how I felt that day when I kilt Theodore on accident. Harvey's boy. The boy I raised as my own.

Another thing was like a goose walking over my grave. Knives. Both her and me killing fellas who attacked us with a knife.

She is out there somewheres. Alone. Thinking we do not want her for things that was not her doing. Mayhap she is in some worse way by now. Or even dead. As it has been more than a year since she wrote this. And her not even knowing we would be glad to see her turn up on the doorstep. No matter what happened. Lib I hardly can stand it. I do not know where

19

she headed. She wrote from near the Missouri River. Fixing to move on. I recollect your boy Christian wanted to go off West after his sister gets hitched. That wedding what took you back home so quick after our grandpup got borned. Libby, you got to tell him to keep his eye out for the girl if he heads off that-a-way. I know it ain't likely he can find her. But it is all I have to go on.

I will put her letter in here so you can see for your own self what she suffered. Keep it safe for me, friend. It is all I have left of my girl if your Christian can not find her.

(Johannah's Letter)

Spring 1819

Dear Mother,

I have missed you and my home since I left. All went well with me that first year, hardship being part of the adventure. The horseman I ran off with on that big bay, Jake Sullivan as I told you in my other letter, was kind to me. I hope that letter found you. The fella I sent it with said he would hand it to you himself, so I have to believe that he did.

Jake and I had a wonderful love, though we had no wedding of the proper sort. He was my man and I his woman. You know we had us a child, Mae, named for you, Mother. She was born beside the Missouri River in a lean-to of tree branches Jake fashioned for us that summer of '18. He was out hunting when my time come, which is about the only thing a man does in these wild parts besides some trapping. I remembered you telling once how the Injun women just squat down and pop out their babes, so that is what I did.

She was a fine, pretty little girl, but my milk never did come in good enough, as she did not grow proper. She could barely hold up her head. Did not make it through the winter, my little Mae. Maybe we was eating a mite lean, but we did have us a cabin before the snow fell. Measured 12x12. With the ground so frozen, we thought to bury Mae after the thaw.

20

Then one day in deep winter them devils come, just as I was about to call Jake in for our evening meal. Killed my man for his horse, they did. I saw him shot down by the pen out there, bleeding onto the snow. I grabbed my butcher knife and thought to kill them varmints myself, but they took it as a great joke. I always figured myself for a strong girl, till them 3 men showed me how weak I was.

They hurt me, Mother. Used me bad. But worse than that was Jake out in that winter night, and me pinned down, not knowing if he had any life left in him or not. If he did, it would not last for long. And nary a thing I could do about it.

I acted like I took on a fit and fainted. It was so hard to lay still. Hardest thing I ever done. Even that did not stop them for a time. But I guess by not putting up a fight, it did take some of the fun out of it for them. They finally let me be and commenced to eating the dinner I made for me and Jake a hundred years before. They found Jake's jug of whiskey and drained that, too. Then with full bellies and swimming heads, at last they fell to sleep.

What happened then, I seen as from above. Like I watched myself, but it weren't me doing it. I got that knife back and crept to the only one who did not stink of drink, the one who slept quiet like, not snorting and snuffing and carrying on like the others in their sleep. I slit his throat real quick. It is strange, but I wasted a thought about the mess his blood was making on my floor, dirt though it be. Then I did the same to those other two. I did not give them another thought as I ran out to Jake. He was froze stiff.

I dragged him in, stoked up a big blaze, and thawed him out. I saw what looked like all the blood his body could hold out there in the snow. But I had to try it. See if any life spark might be left in him. I hate to think of that time right after. When I come to know he was gone for good. Think I musta been crazed for a bit, screaming and slapping him and myself for the fix I was in. Then I picked up that knife from the floor where I had dropped it and went back to them devils who caused it all. I'll leave that part be.

21

All was dead but me in that cabin, filled with a smell like iron and something else that liked to make me gag. I barely had a path I could walk without stepping in blood. I thought to get on that bay and just ride. Ride till I was stiff as Jake had been. But I could not even dare to leave in that weather. I had a husband and child who needed burying in spring. There was nothing else for it.

One at a time, I dragged them polecats out into the night, far away from the cabin as I could manage without the frostbite getting me. Left them for the wolves, I did.

Now we had put Mae right outside the front door in a tiny coffin Jake made for her. But I had no wood or trunk, nothing decent to put him in to lie at rest. The planks we used as our table were too short by half. And only two of them. Then my eyes rested on the big barrel that served as the bottom for that plank table. That barrel was the best I could do. I did put our pillow in and tried to see he was comfortable as possible in that doubled up state. Then I banged the lid down tight with the back of his hatchet and wrestled the thing out the door, to sit beside Mae till spring.

I set the place to rights, boiled up some snow, and washed myself up. That water turned pink and needed changing more than once. I had to even wash blood from my shift, as it had soaked through all my clothing. Dried my things over our only chair there by the fire. I sat and watched the fire all that next day. Fire became the only thing in my life for a time. I would feed it and watch it burn, feed and watch. I think a few days went by thataway, doing nothing else.

At the times I went out for wood I did see the bay horse wandering loose, trying to dig through snow looking for grasses. He never went too far away. We lived through the winter, that bay and I. Them human animals had rode in on two nags and a mule. I shot one of the nags right off and had meat the rest of the winter. The other ran off, but the mule stayed around.

I aim to ride out of this place on the morrow atop that bay horse. Pack out what few belongings I have on the mule. Make my way alone for a time, maybe for all time. I have our rifle plus those varmints' side arms carried in my bag and on my person. I know how to use them all. Practiced on and off all winter. I leave my girl and my man, resting side by side. The hole I dug for that barrel sure did look a mighty strange grave.

I want to come home, Mother, but I do not think I am fit to be around regular folks no more. I am sullied and there is blood on these hands. I do not know how you will feel about me after this telling. But I had to tell someone what I have suffered. Someone who used to care.

I hope you are well, dear Mother.

I am still your daughter Johannah, like it or not.

Still September 18 and 20
Tuesday evening

Lib,

I got to try and turn my mind to other things. If I keep thinking of the fix my girl has got herself into it will make me daft. I got side tracked from writing this here letter. Had to serve noon time meals to these rivermen. Then get vittles on to cook for supper.

I have to say I was right glad to see this new grandpup of ours when I got back here to Riverstop. Little Simon sure is a looker. Just like his daddy. You can be proud of your Simeon. He dotes on his son like a proud papa should. And he clucks after my Katrina like no man I ever saw. Makes sure she never lifts a thing heavy. Fetches and totes for her like she can not do for herself. I never saw the like.

Katrina has took to motherhood fine. A body would think she has a passel of pups the way she handles this first one. She hauls him around on her back just like a Injun papoose. Pouring coffee to these rivermen we feed round here. They sure get a kick out of that babe. He smiles at everyone. Being just two months you would not believe it of him. But there it is.

Simeon thinks he will take to the water. Being born right here on the bank of the Clear Fork like he was. Become a riverman when he grows up. I say he is too sweet to ever turn into one of those crusty river rats I earn my living from feeding. But Simeon smiles and shakes his head. Says, Just you wait and see, Mother Ellie. He will have him a whole fleet of ships. And paddle wheelers to boot!

I told him he better keep his trap shut about paddle wheelers when Zeke comes round. Hates those churning wonders does Zeke MacTavish. That river-runner bears no ill feelings toward ary a living soul. But he does get powerful worked up over paddle wheelers!

You were right about him, Lib. Zeke hangs round here more and more since we got back from that trip down New Orleens way. When we went to look for your boy Levi. But I can not even think about getting mixed up with any kind of male critter ever again. After all I went through on account of my first man Tobias who left me for that red-headed floozy. Then going off to the whooscow on account of Harvey. Him out to kill me after his Theodore got kilt falling on that knife like he done when he come at me with that same knife. And there is my poor Johannah off in the wilds thinking she done so bad. All the time she has a jailbird for a Ma with no way even to know it.

Zeke tells me not to fret so. But there is no help for it. He does keep a spark alive for me, Lib. But I will not hold my breath to see if it lights up any fires. That kind can burn a gal bad. And I already been singed a-plenty.

Write me back, Lib. I know I have sounded strange and all with worry about my girl. Please tell me if that wandering boy of yours travels West. He is my only hope to track any word of her.

Your friend for always. And now grandmaw to the same pup as you.

just plain Ellie Mae
No more men's last names for me.

Dear Ellie,

I have read your letter from Johannah and know not what to make of it, friend. I am sorry to report that Christian has already removed himself from the environs of these Fire Lands just this week past, before I received your distressing missive asking him to look for your girl. He told me to send any news to him in care of general delivery at the post office in St. Louis. So I shall send a dispatch to inform him of your request, and to let him know of Johannah's last whereabouts. We can only hope he receives it before too many moons pass by.

We must keep the faith, Ellie, that our chicks are alive and well in the midst of their own adventures. You, with your Johannah, and me, with my trouble-magnet, Levi, and now new wanderer, Christian, who is so much like my foot-loose Da. It never is easy to let our fledglings fly from the nest. But let them go, we must. It continues to mystify me, that if one has been a good mother to her children and trained them up in the way they should go, she works herself right out of her life-long job!

At least for a time, I still have two of my seven chicks left me. After Lizzle took to married life, she and Kit, who is properly known as Christopher Lavengood, I discovered when they were wed, moved in with us and have been living here since their nuptials on September third. They were loath to wait even a week after my return from our Katrina's confinement, let alone a whole month.

But as this is the only daughter I will ever give in marriage, with my sweet Leesha so recently gone on to her reward and my Lucy never having lived past the cradle, I would not be gainsaid. I insisted upon doing this wedding up in proper style.

It was a beautiful church ceremony, and as much like my own as I could possibly manage, even though they married in autumn while Zach and I had tied the knot in spring. Kit and Lizzie did agree to wait the length of time it would take for a dress to be made, but they balked at a supply trip to the Great Lake for imported laces and finery, which Christian was more than willing to undertake on his sister's behalf. With hard money a bit more plentiful in the recent year, now that Zach has the mill up and running, it would have come as no great hardship for us. But the lovebirds' eagerness dictated we make do with what supplies we could find in local environs.

Ivy donated the wedding dress material that she never used, since, as you recall, she surprised everyone by claiming our Nate in her green taffeta when her sister left him standing at the altar. Ivy had a goodly amount of white tulle and organdy laid by for her own use, which, under the impromptu circumstance, she never did have opportunity to sew up for herself. So she gladly donated those yard goods to Lizzie.

We also had not yet exhausted our own supply of lawn, sent out by my sister Abby for little Buddy's layette. The thing wanting was lace, and none of that anywhere to be had. I worked myself into quite a state, until I recollected the lace hankie, which I had carried in my own wedding. Carefully cut, corner to corner, I had a nice-sized piece to insert into the bodice at the throat. Then, with the other piece cut in half again, I made small triangles of lace for the bottom edge of each sleeve. It looked wonderful!

Now Lizzie maintained that a many-flounced gown would make her look the plainer, so I restrained myself to two flounces only, but nothing could have kept her inner beauty from shining through on that special day of days. Ivy fashioned a very attracttive headpiece with tulle and flowers bunched in here and there, and she did Lizzie's hair up in a very formal style reminiscent of that famous Martha Washington coiffure of yore. She looked such a vision that I grow misty eyed even in remembrance. It turned out I had need of that lace hankie on her wedding day, even though it served a much nobler purpose by then.

We have quartered the newlyweds in the wing Zach built onto our cabin when the size of our family grew to include my niece Caitlin, her passenger little Buddy, and my sister Suzannah, back in 1817.

Christian and little Elijah (though no longer dare I call him "little" as he is all of six years and a "big boy" in his own eyes) those two being the only others in residence, slept up in the loft, which accorded my husband and I the most privacy we have ever known under this roof. This arrangement seemed to suit everyone. And Elijah felt so proud to spend time with his older brother that he took to imitating Christian both in speech and in gait. My baby now is bereft at his brother's departure to explore western environs.

Needs must I bring this long epistle to a close, dear friend. Take care of yourself and give our new, little Simon lots of hugs for us both. The good Lord only knows when I might see that cherubic face again. Zach does not foresee any trips south for some time, with the mill work so time consuming at present and only he and our new son-in-law, Kit, to see to the farm.

So for now I must satisfy myself with news from you and Katrina. Write soon, Ellie. I hardly can stand missing out on so much of our grandson's early growth and development. Report every little detail to me, please!

Until again I hear from you, your faithful friend,
Olivia Lane Howard (Libby to you)

P.S. I am sending along some daffodil bulbs for you, Ellie. These make beautiful, double flowers. I had never seen the like, until Ivy gave me some last fall. I know you will love them, too. Think of me when they bloom next spring, dear friend!

Dear Lib,

Hope youens all wintered fair up there in them Fire Lands. We made it through bad weather in fine fettle. We have not closed up Riverstop for winter since your Simeon come down to claim my Katrina. I got to say it is right handy to have a man cut and tote wood for us. Every year that task gets harder and harder for creeky knees like mine. Course Katrina is young and full of pep. She straps little Simon on her back and helps her man with what ever he is doing at the time.

I can tell you that grandbabe of ours does not miss a thing. Watches like a hawk, that one. He is smart for no more than eight months. You mark my word. He will be talking before he makes a year. You can see him try to say words already. Course no one but his mama can make out too many of em.

That boy has the biggest shock of red hair you ever did see. It is something to behold. We try to puzzle out where that carrot top might-a come from. Katrina and Simeon both have such dark hair. We all are stumped.

You would not know this place now. What with all that Simeon has built round here since last fall. We have a new chicken coop that holds twice as many laying hens. Need em to keep these hungry river men fed. And that son of yours has built us a bridge over the river. If you can credit that. Stood right there in the water hammering away. Never saw the like of it myself.

That bridge makes it right handy to travel Perrysville way for supplies. I can make the trip in half the time now on Lucifer. My old mule. Do not have to go the long way round no more. Mind, I could go in to Loudonville, as it is some closer. But then I could not get to see my brand new grandbaby. Another girl.

Flora Jean had her first little babe last month. Flora is oldest of my girls as you recall. She and Wheatly named their babe Virginia. Like the state. They call her Ginny. She is a pretty little thing. Tiny face like a sprite. But Flora has some funny idees about how to raise a baby. Reckon she learned em from my citified mother when Flora spent time back east with her. Before she took up keeping school by the Coulters. And now here she is. A Coulter herself.

Flora has took to motherhood right well. In spite of not letting that babe cry one bit. I say a child needs to stretch its lungs. Does em good. Makes em strong. But Flora will not let Ginny make one little peep. Spoiled rotten is that child. At no more than 6 weeks of age.

We have us quite the crop of baby girls round abouts this spring. You should tell your Lizzie. Show her how many other women come through their confinement just fine. By now I reckon she likely could find herself in the same fix. Tell her we need us some boy babies to tip back the balance.

Netta Bailey has her a third child. Of course another little girl. Name of Rebecca. Luther calls her Buttons. And he is right about it. Cute as a button is this one. Netta's cousin from back east is still with the Baileys. So at least Netta has help. You know how Luther takes off to the woods for long spells. It is nice she has Luella with her to help times he is gone. I hear tell my nephew Harmon now pays court to Luella after his mail runs. He is the footloose one of sister Edie's boys. Mayhap he is about to get his foot stuck in Luella's door!

Over in Petersburg them Simpsons also had em a tiny girl. Named her Ella Marie. That makes 8 living offspring for them folks. The Missus had children every year or two. If I ain't mistaken. I hear tell she lost two or three along the way afore they moved out here. Then she had this tag along babe after a rite long spell since her last boy. Come as quite a shock after 8 years. Already that youngest boy makes barrels at his papa's side, learnin the trade of cooper. Lordy, I think that Simpson woman must be close of an age to me! I can not begin to think on raising babes again at this late stage in life. Got to say I have to admire her spunk.

Sadie Hawkins delivered all three of them new baby girls. You recall she is my nephew Willie's wife. Edie's youngest boy that would be. Edie give up tending births after losing her own grandbabe way she done last summer. Sadie's little Nell that was. Born and died on the same night as Jeremy Harrison died. After he broke his back under that big oak tree. So sad.

If you do not remember he was Sadie's brother.

Now Sadie has took to the task of delivering babes in Edie's stead. She says the girl promises to make a good midwife. Has a light touch. Level head. Steady nerves. Edie still goes along to give advice now and again. But she will not get in there and work no more. Says that task should fall to younger hands. Someone more sturdy and spry.

Last of all brother Jonathan's new wife Lucy also had her a girl. Name of Alice after Lucy's dead Mama. She give birth afore Christmas over at the Harrison place. Amanda herself helped bring that curly haired tyke into the world. Who could guess that frail little Southern gal would turn into such a steadfast woman. Bout time I say. After all she put her dead husband through. But that opinion goes no farther than betwixt you and me and this hearthstone here. I heard Lucy and the babe and little Hank stayed on with Amanda till after Christmas. Jonathan took em back home during a warm spell right after New Years.

I still hardly can believe that little brother of mine. Getting his self hitched up after all these years living single. No one but his hogs and old dog Rip for company. Him and Lucy had a quiet little service nigh onto a month after Henry got his head smashed in by that same tree what broke Jeremy Harrison's back. Sure is strange. Two young wives left in the family way. Both with small children to raise. And now them gals with new babes leftover from dead husbands. I knew Jonathan would step up to help Lucy out. He has been sweet on her for years. Jeremy's brother Michael looks after Amanda and her youngens. But there is no word of any wedding for them. Not yet.

Funny how life can work itself out.

I reckon this letter has got way too long by half. Harmon comes by for supper now and again here at Riverstop. So I will have him tote it up there to youens in them Fire Lands.

Hope you all have made spring in fine spirits. I think of you every time I pick my double daffydills. Never saw the like! Thank you again for sending me bulbs last fall.

Write when you can, Lib. Hope you get news from that foot loose son of yours with some word about my Johannah. I pray he has found sign that tells she is alive and well. That might lead him to her.

Your friend as always,
Ellie Mae

April 10, 1821
Cranberry Corners, The Fire Lands

My Dear Ellie,

How good to have word from you after so long a cold winter. We have survived to spring as snug as we have ever come through winter in these environs heretofore.

I welcomed the news about our own little Simon. It surprises me not in the least that he tries to speak at such a young age. Simeon spoke volumes before he reached his first year. No one could believe the words pouring forth from that tiny boy. Having his son do the same brings smiles of remembrance to my countenance.

As for Simon's shock of red hair, I can solve your puzzle. My Da, Shaun McNally of the Irish, was he, had exactly such a head of fiery hair. Since he disappeared before any of my children's births, Simeon had no way of knowing such fact. Though his sister's hair does have a reddish-brown tint to it in the sunshine, I doubt he ever took notice of such thing himself. So now the source of our red-headed babe need remain a mystery no longer.

I did share your news about all the latest babies with Lizzie, since she, too, as you so astutely surmised, finds herself in the family way. Lizzie kept her own council until Christmas when she gave Kit a small package, which he opened to reveal baby garments made by her own hand, I know not when. She kept them a secret from everyone.

The young man grabbed her up and kept her awhirl until she begged him to stop, so dizzy and nauseous had she become. Nate ran up to clap Kit on the back at our Christmas gathering and placed a shy peck on his sister's cheek, while Elijah pulled at Kit asking could he take a turn as well (at the twirling, not the kissing). Nate's Ivy and I hugged one another and Lizzie until all had been squeezed so thoroughly that Lizzie pleaded for mercy.

It turned out quite the festive affair altogether, with Nate and Ivy's little Annabelle taking center stage most of the day. We had celebrated her first birthday shortly before the Nativity Holidays, so she dutifully entertained us all by taking her very first steps.

All passed well enough throughout the winter, as Lizzie's middle began to bulge and this new life began to make itself known. But of late, I discern a sense of panic behind her brittle smile. When mention is made of the coming confinement, too much white shows in Lizzie's eyes. Though content with her condition thus far, she would fain prolong it, never to reach the end of this particular journey, I fear. I have tried to point out nature's inevitable course, in this and all other things. But she bolts from me whenever she hears.

It puts me in mind of something I saw as a child: a barn on fire having horses within, terrified, shrieking, dashing back and forth pointlessly, rearing up to strike out, fighting the very people who would rescue them. I believe that Lizzie, usually so calm and sensible, is now a high-strung horse who smells smoke.

You know how a woman in her condition can take a notion. Why, when I was expecting Simeon, I became convinced that I would fall in a river. In dreams would I look down at swirling, dark water and in horror feel the overwhelming certainty that my child would never breathe sweet air but drown with me under that current. I find it particularly curious, still, that Simeon turned out to be such a water-loving child.

We must help her, Ellie, this high-strung daughter of mine. All I can think to do is send for you. With such an experienced person in residence, she could not help but feel reassured. And whatever is bothering you on Johannah's account, we can talk it through, you and I, to see how her situation may be set to rights.

Please come, Ellie. It has been so long since we have spent any time together to have one of our good, long talks. Not since Zach and I came to help fix up your Riverstop. Three years ago! How can we have let so much time pass us by without coming together?

I have asked Zach if he would speed this message to you and assist in your arrival, but with all his sons, save the youngest, spread out over the territory—mayhap the world— he says he must continue on here running the mill, as well as overseeing Kit's work on our farm. He cannot be spared.

Were but Christian here, I have no doubt he would jump at the opportunity to travel.

As always, we deal in the way of things, not the wish of things. Please come soon, El. Lizzie's passenger looks to arrive sometime in early June. That does not give you much time to make preparations for Riverstop and arrange for someone to escort you up here to us. Oh, Ellie, I can hardly stand thinking about going through this birth without you beside me. I become too easily upset these days, and you always maintain such a calm, cool head during any crisis. I need you, friend!

Make every effort to come to us, will you? I hold my breath awaiting your speedy reply.

Yours, Lib

Chapter 3

Letter from Mother
Early April 1821
Vermillion Township

Michael Harrison heard the bugling of a horn in the distance. "Hallelujah! I sure hope he brought it." He headed out the lane to meet Harmon Hawkins before he reached the cabin. Busy stripping beds inside, Amanda hadn't yet heard the mail horn's blast.

"'Lo, neighbor. Good to see ya this forenoon," stocky Harmon greeted.

"Any deliveries for us today?" Michael reached up and gave Harmon's hand a hearty shake.

"Rit'chere in this poke," he said, patting a bag tied on behind the saddle. The sack wiggled at his touch. "Ortta grow into a right good mouser. Gar-uhn-teed." He leaned to the side of his horse and spat a stream of tobacco juice.

"I sure hope so. Amanda's driving me crazy with these cleaning fits every time she finds a mouse. After her Lucky cat disappeared last fall, she fusses about mice in the cabin most every day. She's at it again in there... boiling up bedding for the second time this week. Never saw the like in all my born days!"

"Never can tell what's apt to set off a female. Hell, I once knowed a gal, got herself so worked up over a snake, she liked to trample her own youngens tryin' to run off when she seen that thing come a-crawlin' out from underneath of her bed. Refused to sleep in that bed ever again, too, she did."

"Fear of snakes I can understand. Especially the timber rattlers we have in these parts. But a mouse? It doesn't make a bit of sense."

"Since when do a woman's notions have to make sense?"

"Ride on up to the cabin, Harmon. I'll be right behind you."

"Think mebbe I should give another honk on this 'ere tooter?"

"Better make it a loud one, so she's sure to hear."

At another long blast of his mail horn, Amanda appeared in the doorway, with a wiggly babe on one hip, and two, four-year-olds peeking out from behind her skirts.

"'Lo, Mrs." Harmon tipped his hat as his horse trotted up to the stoop. "Girls."

"Why Mr. Hawkins, it's so good to see you!" she said.

"Got a dee-livery here." Harmon reached into his vest pocket and pulled out a wrinkled post. "Come all the way from Carolina. For Mrs. Amanda Jane Bently Harrison," he read, smoothing the letter out as best he could. "Been journeyin' a far piece, by the look of it."

She reached up to accept the crumpled letter and stuck it into her apron pocket to keep Jems from grabbing it.

"Come certified to Mt. Vernon. Tom Parsons handed off to me. He carries official mails outta state. I only carry local, or-din-arily." Harmon leaned back to spit a stream of tobacco juice away from the porch. "Federal dee-liveries come postage due, ya know. Two bits for this 'un here, seein's it come such a far distance."

"Oh my. I don't know if I have enough hard cash in my emergency jar to pay you that much right now. Will you take something in trade?"

"T'would suit me fine, Missus. But them gova'mint agents don't take none to barter."

"What do you suggest?"

"I can wait," Harmon said. "No skin off my nose. 'Sides, far's it concerns me, them revenuers don't need to know if'n that post ever got dee-livered to its rightful end or not. Could be at the bottom of the Black Swamp for all they know," he winked.

Little Jems kicked and wiggled trying to reach for Harmon's horse. Michael stepped onto the porch beside Amanda just as the babe pitched sideways, almost making Amanda lose her balance. Michael caught the boy and swooped him up, over his head, sending him into a fit of giggles.

36

Millie and Lilly joined in the laughter, jumping out from behind Amanda's skirts and chasing one another round and round Uncle Mikey.

"You two! Off the porch if you're going to race around," Amanda directed.

"Welp, I best be off. Got to make Uniontown 'fore the sun sets." Harmon turned his horse, then stopped. "Oh, uh. Almost forgot this 'ere special order for the lady of the house." He unfastened the wiggling sack from behind the saddle and held it out.

"It's moving!"

"Shore enough, it's movin.' I'd let it out of that poke right quick, if I was you. Ain't none too happy about bein' stuck in that thing so long."

"What on earth?"

"Take it," Michael smiled. "Harmon's not gonna sit there all day waiting."

Amanda took the bag with two fingers, holding it as far away from herself as she could.

"Ain't gonna hurt ya' none, Ma'am. Fact is, you'll be happy with this 'ere special order mouse trap. Gar-uhn-teed." He spat a last stream of tobacco juice, gave his horse a jab with his heel, and took off at a trot, waving his hat as he headed out the lane.

"Well, aren't you gonna open it?"

"*You* do it." She shoved the bag toward Michael, almost dropping it before he rescued the squirming sack with a quick grab of his empty hand.

"All right, all right. Take Jems. I'll open the pouch." Michael began to untie the bag, but before he got it open more than a few inches, a fuzzy, calico head popped up and gave a pathetic, little 'mew.'

"A kitten? Oh, it's a *kitten!*"

She scooped it up with her free hand. "Did you know about this?"

37

"Could be. Could also not be."

"You did," she said, nuzzling the kitten to her cheek. "Thank you, Michael. This is so thoughtful." For the first time in months she'd actually used his first name.

Little Jems made a grab for the kitten. "Be careful. It's a baby, just like you. Mustn't hurt the baby." She put it down on the ground and watched as it scampered around her feet, tickling her when it licked at her ankles.

"They say calicoes make the best mousers," Michael offered.

"I sure hope he grows up fast."

"She."

"She?"

"Yup, she. Calicoes 'most always turn out female, you know."

"I didn't know, "Amanda said. "She looks a lot like the Lucky cat Jeremiah gave me that first year we came here." Jems waved his arms and legs and giggled as he watched the kitten at play. He leaned so far reaching for it again, that his weight made Amanda totter off balance. She sat him down on the ground next to the kitten. It jumped onto his lap and began to lick at the milk-soaked collar of his shirt. Jems laughed so hard, he got the hiccups.

"You sat him down on the ground?"

"Humm?"

"You sat him in the dirt!" Michael couldn't believe his eyes, so thoroughly did she always work to keep the cabin spotless and everyone in it squeaky clean.

"Well, maybe Jeremiah was right. He always did say a little bit of dirt now and again helped to keep a child healthy."

* * * * *

By the time Amanda got everyone fed, the noontime meal cleaned up, and all the dishes put away, she'd nearly forgotten about her letter. Little Jems played in his crib, and the girls sat underneath, dressing and undressing the doll babies Aunt Sadie

38

had made for them Christmas before last. After two years of constant play, those dolls looked very well loved.

Michael pushed back from the table, puffing on his afternoon pipe. He'd taken to smoking Jeremy's old pipe last fall, after his brother's death. Made him feel more "connected" to him, using something so personal, he said. He blew a smoke ring toward Amanda. "You gonna read that letter of yours, or just carry it around all day?"

"I'll get to it when I'm good and ready," she answered back with a snip.

"Never knew you to hold off readin' mail before."

"I never received a letter from my Mother before. I'm not entirely certain I want to read it at all."

"You'll never find out what's in it, less'n you do."

"Oh, horsefeathers! Here." She tossed the letter onto the table in front of him. "*You* read it if you're so curious!"

"You sure?"

"Read it for me, won't you?" she pleaded. "I don't think I can face it by myself."

"All right " He tore open the seal and unfolded the wrinkled paper..."

19 February, 18 and 21

Amanda Jane:

Joseph has informed me that you plan to make a trip back to South Carolina. He received word of it from Olympia's Solicitor, Douglas B. Hornsby, who has kept her estate in litigation ever since her demise.

Your father has declined to share any of the details with me, but I can assure you, the entire affair has him most dreadfully upset. Frankly, it surprises me not that you have become ensconced at the center of a family dispute. Leave it to Olympia to create such an unseemly situation among her progeny.

39

> In view of the fact that you will be coming this
> summer (and I assume the only reason you're coming
> has to do with these unfortunate legal entanglements),
> I have a deathbed request to make of you...

"Deathbed! She's on her *deathbed*?"

"That's what it says, 'deathbed request.' You gonna let me continue?"

"Oh, please... *do* go on."

"Thank you." He shook the paper with a flourish and resettled himself to read on..."

> ...I have a deathbed request to make of you, should
> I be so fortunate as to remain on this earth long enough
> to experience the momentous occasion of your return.
> When you arrive in Charleston, I have need of your
> presence in my bedchambers as soon as is humanly
> possible, for I fear I have precious little time left to make
> any attempt at rectifying matters as they stand between
> us—to settle my affairs, as it were.
> Come with all haste. I remain,
> Evangeline Louise Tedrow Bently, a.k.a. your mother

"She don't sound all that ready to expire, if she plans to wait around four months until you get down there," Michael said. "Hell, she wrote this thing clear back in February!"

"You'd have to know my mother to appreciate her colossal gestures. She never fails to make a major production out of anything," said Amanda. "I expect nothing less at her final demise... *whenever* that event may happen to occur."

"What do you suppose this is really about?"

"It's a ploy to get her way with Father. It must be something of considerable consequence, or I'm certain she'd never resort to writing me."

"Reckon we can leave none too soon for her taste, then."

"I've got the children's things about all ready to go," Amanda said, wringing her hands. "There's just so much to think about... so many things to prepare!"

"I'll make sure the wagon's stocked with feed and supplies for Freddie," Michael said. "I'm glad Willie agreed to trade horses with us for this undertaking. I don't think old Patsy has another big trip left in her. Especially not through the mountains again."

"Will it be safe to board him so long in Philadelphia?"

"Jonathan said his brother Jason'd see to anything we need, once we make it that far. Gave me good directions to find him, too. So don't fret yourself over Freddie. He'll be well looked after for as long as we're down South."

"Do you think we'll reach the coast in time? I certainly don't want to miss our ship's sailing."

"We have plenty of time to make the coast," Michael said. "'Specially if we leave this week, way we planned. That gives us an extra week for trouble along the way."

"Bite your tongue! We will think of no such thing!" Amanda fussed at him.

"I'll make a last supply run up to Uniontown tomorrow."

"I have a list," she said, taking a paper down from the side of the pantry where she had it tacked. "I need fresh meal to make up a pile of journey cakes before we go. And enough really fine meal for making Little Jems' pap along the way. I'll need more molasses for that, too," she instructed.

"If you can find any dried fruit left at this time of year, that would make good travel fare for all of us. We already ate up everything I dried for the winter." Amanda tacked the list back on the pantry. "I'll keep this up here till you go, just in case I think of anything else to add."

"Fine with me." Michael rose from his chair and sauntered to the fireplace.

"You're sure you can talk Mr. Tucker into more credit until we get back?"

41

"Don't worry your head over Tucker," he said, tapping spent tobacco from the bowl of his brother's pipe. "I can be very convincing when I need to be."

Amanda rolled her eyes as she shook her head. "You're hopeless, you know."

"I know."

"Would you ring the necks of those three young roosters before you leave in the morning? I want to pluck and roast them for our trip. It'll give us fresh meat for the first week, at least. I'll boil up the last of the eggs, too."

"Sounds like you have travel provisions well in hand," Michael acknowledged. "Jonathan should be here in a couple days to go over the chores. I'll show him what needs doing while we're away. No sense taking up his time planting any corn here this year. Not knowing when we're apt to come back home," Michael mused. "We can make do with the winter wheat I put down last fall. That'll be enough for him to fool with harvesting while we're gone. He may as well take Bertha on home with him, too, till she dries up—save him coming over here twice a day to milk a cow. That way he'll only need to check on the hogs and chickens once a week or so. They oughtta fend for themselves just fine, running loose."

"I think we should send our new kitten over for Lucy. Till we get back home," Amanda suggested.

"You think up a name for her yet?"

"The girls have come up with all manner of far-fetched ideas. But I'd like to call her Hope."

* * * * *

"We're gonna miss you," Lucy said, giving Amanda a hug. "I'll have no one close by to visit, except Netta. And you know how she can be. Getting a word in edgewise is always a challenge."

"I do wish you were going with us. It'd sure make this trip more fun," Amanda whined to her best friend.

"Fun? You don't think *I'm* fun?" Michael asked, looking stricken at her comment.

"Just don't forget us simple folk, once youens get down to all them fancy parties an' dances an' such," Jonathan said. "I hear tell them South'rn bucks can charm the socks off'n a gal, when they set their minds to it."

"I have no intention of letting any man charm me out of my socks... nor any *other* piece of my attire," Amanda said with authority.

"Don't you know a comely young widow makes prime pickin's for them kind of wolves?" Jonathan mentioned.

"There'll be no wolves sniffing around this family," Michael bristled. "I aim to keep the two-legged variety far away from *all* my girls."

"I won't have time for any such tomfoolery," Amanda said. "I have a job to do, setting Grandmother's estate to rights. After that, I intend coming straight back home."

"Just remember that, when them charmers start sweet-talkin' ya." Jonathan gave Amanda an impulsive hug, which surprised them both. "We'll look after things till youens get back." He help- ed Amanda step up into the wagon.

"Write me Lucy, won't you? Tell me all the news?" Amanda asked, handing her the address for Grandmother's Orchard.

"I'll write." She stood beside Jonathan, holding Alice in a sling-like carrier made from a shawl hung across her shoulder. Hank stood solemnly holding Jonathan's hand.

"Thank you for your good cup-cheese, Lucy. And for the pocket soup. We'll enjoy them both on the trip." Amanda waved, as Michael clicked his tongue to get the horse underway.

"Bye-bye, Hank! Bye!" the twins called, waving from their spot at the back opening of the wagon's cover. Inside, securely tied trunks of clothing lined both sides of the wagon; bedding lay stacked in the center, making a small nest at the ready for sleepy heads to lie on. Jems lay kicking in the large basket fastened right behind Amanda's seat, where she could easily turn to tend him whenever necessary. Between the seat and the trunks, several crates of foodstuffs and miscellaneous supplies filled the remainder of the space. Outside the wagon hung a large barrel of water; pots, pans, and buckets; and a few other sacks holding the rest of their dry provisions.

"Don't forget us, Hank! Take care of Hopper!" the twins waved and called.

"Hopper?" Michael asked with a puzzled look.

"They decided Hope sounded too grown up a name for such a little kitten," Amanda explained. "Lillian liked 'Hopper' better."

"Hopper." Michael repeated.

"You two be careful back there," instructed Amanda. "Do not lean over so far you fall out."

"Yes, Mama." They continued waving and hollering to Hank, who got smaller and smaller in the distance.

May 3, 18 and 21, Thursday Forenoon,
Riverstop

Dear Libby,

I have some news will no doubt make you happy to hear.
Your Simeon and my Katrina plan to travel up north to visit
youens with their little Simon. When they heerd you asked me
to come help Lizzie whelp her babe, Katrina got all excited to
come her own self. Please Mother, she said, let me go for you!

I studied on the notion and I have to agree with the girl. She
says it is high time this boy of theirs meets his Grandpap. What
better time to come than now. With nice weather on us. You will
see a big change in Simon, Lib. You only saw him as a brand
new pup. Now he is nearly a year. You need time to get to know
this grandbaby for your own self.

We can not all up and leave Riverstop at the same time.
Not during spring with so much boat traffic running the river this
season. So I aim to stay here and tend to business. Let them two
lovebirds head north to you. I believe it may turn out best for a
gal her own age to give Lizzie a good pep talk. By now Katrina
has seen both ends of this birthing business. I have no doubt she
can do a good job of gettin Lizzie through her confinement.

I have to say I am awful let down that you and me can not
have us a visit at this time. But I think you will agree it is more fit
that babe gets to meet his Grandpap than two old crows have a
good gab fest.

Now for a piece of worrisome news. Zeke come round last
week. But that ain't the worrisome part. Though it does concern
me that I get right happy to see the likes of that scraggly face
show up now and again. What he told me is what has me fretful.
He saw a man down Cincinnati way who looked a lot like Harvey.
Give me a jolt for a minute when he spoke the name Harvey and
the word alive in the same breath. All I can say is I hope he
keeps far away from here. As I have no wish to see that man
ever again.

I can not get out of my head how he tried to harm you in my
stead. Mixing you up for me when you had on my own bed gown.

45

Him hiding out there in the dark like he done. I am so glad your Zach has a good swing that knocked Harvey right into the drink. I reckon Harvey musta washed clean down river. Sounds like he ended up living to tell the tale.

I only hope he stays way down there in Cinci. Or farther down river still. I can tell you Zeke has stuck right close to shore since he brought me the news. Does not want me fending alone. For fear that hot head might take a notion to show up here again. Try to finish what he started before. Namely kill me.

I told Zeke not to worry about me. I can shoot straight when I have to. I would not give a second thought to blasting that varmint to his just reward. I can tell you it would not be to them Pearly Gates, neither! So I aim to waste no more worry over the likes of him.

Harmon will likely show up in the next day or two. So I best get this letter ready to post. I will send along two Cana bulbs for you with the children. Do you know Canas? My Mother sent them out to me. Make a big show of red color in summer. Just like her, truth be told. The flowers last nice and long. But they are tender. Ain't hardy like them daffydills. You have to lift the bulbs in fall. Store em in a dry place for winter. Like up in the loft or some such. I hope they grow strong for you, Lib. Think of me when they bloom.

Have a good visit with our children. I reckon they will turn up on your doorstep before May's end. Send word when Lizzie is delivered. Tell her we must all make ourselves think on the best. More likely will come to pass that-a-way.

Your always friend, Ellie
though I am right sorry I can not see you my own self

Dearest Lucy,

I hope this finds you all well and happy. Though we have been away but a few, short weeks, I am missing you terribly, as are the girls. Little Jems knows not that he is anywhere out of the ordinary, as long as he remains with me, although he does seem to take an interest in the new sights and sounds around him. The girls, however, have had quite an unsettling time being thrust into such unfamiliar surroundings.

We have enjoyed seeing new people and places. But the noise and activity of a big, port city has come as quite a shock to two, sheltered, country girls. They cling to Michael and I at every juncture. If we are not directly at hand, they cling to each other. Since we boarded this steam packet three days ago, they have begun to relax and explore their environs a bit more thoroughly and are making friends with a few of the other passengers. Over the last day, their usual, spirited personalities have begun to shine through, once more. Lillian has even managed to track down the shipboard cat and smuggle it into our stateroom on more than one occasion.

We managed to get all our possessions settled aboard ship with little trouble and found our assigned seats in the dining room. The girls are quite fascinated with the fancy table linens and shiny silver table service, not to mention waiters bringing all manner of foodstuffs they have never seen before.

I must say travel aboard this ship is beyond anything I ever expected. Mr. Hornsby reserved the best accommodation for us, which took me quite by surprise. He must believe we have extra money to burn! I fussed at Michael about throwing away precious funds on such extravagance, but he became so irritated with me, I have kept my peace ever since. He asked me why did I worry so, now that I owned an entire plantation?

I think the reality of this inheritance just now begins to dawn on me.

We have had quite pleasant days since leaving the port of Philadelphia and heading south. We did find Jonathan's brother and left Freddie with him to board for the summer. So now with no horse to tend, nor any campsite to establish each night, no meals to prepare, nor the stress of hurried wagon travel to reach our ship in time, we can now relax and enjoy ourselves, as we watch coastline scenery glide along beside us.

I hardly know what to do with so much leisure.

Even though I was raised in such luxury, I had quite forgotten what it feels like to be pampered and waited upon so. I now have a great deal of trouble letting someone else pour the cream into my coffee, not to mention stir it in, as do these waiters, they so anticipate each person's needs. It is <u>real</u> coffee, too, Lucy! Not chicory cut with dandelion roots. Can you believe it? I feel as though I've died and gone to heaven, it has been so long since I had a taste of the real thing.

I shall be sure to bring home a big bagful of coffee beans for you. And a big sack of real, white sugar, straight off the ship from Barbados. There's nothing else like it in the world! I would love to bring some fresh seafood home for you, too. But I honestly don't know how I would ever transport such a thing so far a distance.

I wonder if a person can dry shrimp? I'll be sure to ask Mother's servants if that is possible. No one else would know. We girls were never taught how to do anything practical. We only received instruction on how to plan the menus, order the correct wines, and arrange flowers for a dinner party. No one ever dreamed of showing us the way to make a pie, or a loaf of bread, nor—heaven forbid—how to clean a chicken!

I can honestly say everything I learned in my early life turned out to be completely useless in the Ohio wilderness. I guarantee these daughters of mine shall not only learn how to manage and run a proper household, but they shall also become skilled in the practical tasks necessary to accomplish it. Grandmother Bently was right: No human being able to do an honest day's work has the right to expect anyone else to do it for him.

Listen to me, lecturing so. If I had a soapbox to stand upon I should mayhap run for political office, were I dressed in frockcoat and trousers. HA! Can you imagine a woman so attired? She could never undertake such a task, lest she masquerade as a man in order to do it. I wonder, has a woman ever tried such a thing, do you think?

I hope I will not have the need to be directly involved in too many legal proceedings, in order to get Grandmother's bequest properly settled. I certainly am thankful Michael is along to help me manage the puffed up men with whom I shall undoubtedly be confronted—the ones who think they control all the crucial matters of government and commerce. Grandmother was right in that regard, as well: Men only think they run the machinery of this world. It truly is the women who must keep the wheels greased!

I'd best bring this missive to a close, Lucy. Dinner will be served shortly, and Little Jems needs nursing before we leave our stateroom for the dining room. I shall post this letter at the Purser's desk on our way. It will no doubt be put to shore at tomorrow's stop in Virginia, where it can begin to make its way back to you.

You must be sure to show Jeannette the Virginia postmark, as I am sure it will give her quite a thrill and keep her talking about her home state for hours without end! Poor Luther. It will no doubt drive him to the woods again, just to escape her enthusiasm.

Please give each other big hugs for us, and think of us in your prayers. The girls say a prayer for Hank and Alice every night. They also say one for Hopper the kitten!

With lasting affection,
Your friend, Amanda Jane

Chapter 4

Charleston Harbor
May 26, 1821

Michael heard the bell ring, signaling the ship's final approach into Charleston Harbor. "We're almost there! Let's go up on deck to watch the Captain park this barge."

"He'd be terribly offended if he heard you refer to his ship a barge," Amanda said. "Girls, you need to put your hats on. The sun gets very hot here in the low country."

"Yes, Mama." They dutifully donned their bonnets, Amanda methodically tying the strings of each one in turn.

"Would you hand me Little Jems' cap? His sensitive skin will burn to a crisp without proper covering."

Michael dug through the basket of baby things, searching for the hat she wanted. "Here," he said. "Sure don't know why you fret so much about a little bit of sun."

"You'll understand soon enough," Amanda said, fussing to wrap the baby sufficiently to protect his tender skin. "There. I think we're ready."

"'Bout time."

"Oh, stop your grousing."

"Yes, *Ma'am!*" he saluted.

Amanda gave Michael's shoulder a poke. "Come on, girls. Take your uncle's hands so you won't get lost. I'm sure we'll run into quite a crowd on deck," she said. "Charleston Harbor is the most wonderful sight in the world!" She had just begun to let her own excitement show through. "Nothing else on earth can quite compare!"

By the time they reached a place along the railing where the girls could see, they'd already sailed through the harbor's entry. A panoramic view opened before them revealing townhouses, St. Michael's steeple, and the unmistakable Exchange building dominating the shoreline of Charleston.

"Such a gorgeous view! I've never seen it look more welcoming!"

"Missed home, didn't you," Michael said.

Tears stung her eyes. "I didn't realize how much, till this very moment."

Michael put his arm around her shoulder, hugging her to his side; the girls clung to the rail, squealing as they watched porpoises circling the ship. In a short time *The Harpster* eased into its assigned berth, and deck hands threw lines ashore to men who secured them to huge piers at the water's edge.

"Did you lock our trunks?" Amanda asked.

"Locked up tight. Everything's ready to unload."

"You're sure they're properly marked? We don't want to lose anything."

"Will you quit your fussing, already? They'll be fine," Michael said. "That Hornsby fella has everything so well organized, I don't doubt those trunks will make it off this ship before we do!"

They watched as the crew extended a gangplank onto the wharf, and men on shore worked with haste to secure it. Passengers surged toward the ship's exit, but the First Officer held back the crowd for what felt like an eternity.

"What are they waiting for?" Michael asked.

"Probably official permission from the Harbor Master to disembark." Amanda nervously scanned the gathering crowd on shore. "Do you think Father will be here?"

"I'd be surprised if you found him down there," Michael answered, eyeing the milling crowd below. "But I'd bet my eye teeth that fella waving a flag over there is your Hornsby character," he said, pointing to the far side of the wharf where a portly man in spectacles waved a sign with the name "Harrison" printed on it.

"Stick close to me," Amanda beseeched, as people elbowed and shoved at one another in an effort to push to the head of the line. No one seemed to have the inclination to wait.

"Unka Mikey! I dropped Dolly!" Millie began to panic, pulling at his arm.

"Hold on to your mother's skirts, you two. I'll go find dolly."

"Don't get lost!" Amanda shouted to his disappearing back. "Oh, Camellia, why didn't you pack that doll in the trunk with the rest of your belongings as I told you to?"

"It's dark in that trunk, Mama. Dolly's *scared* of the dark!"

"Lillian Jane. Come out from there this instant!" Amanda ordered the other twin, who squatted underneath the lifeboat, beside which they'd stopped. "What on earth do you think you're doing down there?"

"Hiding from that bad man." She pointed to a black man carrying a trunk up from the lower deck.

"What makes you think he's bad?"

"He's all dirty," Lilly said in her simple, no-nonsense manner.

"What are you talking about?"

"It's bad to get dirty. You told us so!" she insisted. "Look at him. He's so dirty, he's black all over!"

"That's not dirt, dear. He was born that way. His skin *is* that color," she explained. "Many people that color live down here."

"Really?"

"Yes, really. He's a Negro. They have darker skin than white people do."

"Are we white people?" Lillian asked.

"Yes, dear. We're white."

Camellia scrutinized her arm. "I'm not white, Mother. See? I look pink." She held it out so Amanda could look for herself. "I'm pink people."

"We'll talk about this later, girls. Come out from under there, now, Lillian. No bad man is going to hurt you."

Amanda switched Jems into her other arm, then leaned down to take Lillian's hand and pull her out from under the lifeboat. But the baby pitched sideways toward his sister, just as Amanda shifted her balance in an effort to reach Lilly, and she began to stumble sideways. Before she fell to the deck, a strong hand grabbed her elbow, guiding her back into balance.

"Hello, Mandy."

"Father?" She stood, stunned at the surprise of his massive presence. "*FATHER!*" She threw herself into his arms, weeping, squashing Jems between them. At his mother's apparent distress, he began crying, too. The girls, frightened at the huge man standing beside them and bewildered by their mother's unusual behavior, clung tightly to her skirts, as well as to each other, close to tears themselves. Amanda mastered her emotions, and straightened up to quiet the babe in her arms. "How did you find us so quickly?"

"I boarded with the Harbor Master. Bertram's a friend of mine."

"Father, I–"

"Before you say anther word, there's something I need to tell you," he said, holding her shoulders and looking deeply into her eyes. "No matter what happens with this legal mess we find ourselves entangled in, don't ever forget that I love you, Mandy."

"But Father–"

"Complex matters are afoot here. Much of it beyond anything you could possibly imagine. But that doesn't mean it has to affect anything between you and me. Do you understand?"

"You know I've always loved you, Papa. Nothing could ever change that."

He leaned down to kiss her brow, then felt a tug at his waistcoat.

"Only my Papa kisses Mama like that," Lilly declared protectively.

"Well, I kissed your Mama long before your Papa ever knew her, darlin'," he said with a wry smile. "And just who might you be?"

"I'm Lilly."

"And I'm Millie," her twin spoke up, not to be outdone in making herself known.

"Father, these are my twin daughters. Camellia Jane and Lillian Jane," she said, touching each one in turn. "Girls, this is your Grandfather Bently."

"We have a... a *Grandfather?*" they squeaked together, one beginning the sentence as the other finished it.

"Pleased to make your acquaintance, my lovely little blossoms." He extended his hand in a formal manner, bowing to the little ladies as he kissed the hand of each. They looked at one another and giggled.

"And I take it this must be your newest addition?" Joseph said, putting his finger into Jems' fist.

"Jeremiah Junior. We call him Jems for short."

Joseph Alexander Bently, III, nodded his approval. "I must make myself scarce before Hornsby finds me talking to you, my dear," he said, donning his hat. "I know you won't be able to come home until the judge brings a conclusion to this regrettable situation. Hornsby's had him declare that we are to have no *'official'* communication until such circumstance should come to pass." He gave her another big hug, "We'll talk soon." He disappeared into the crowd.

"Who was that?" Michael asked, catching up to Amanda and the children from the other direction, as he held on to a bedraggled-looking rag doll.

"You found Dolly!" Millie retrieved her prized possession from Uncle Mikey.

"That was my father!" Amanda said, still stunned by their surprising interlude.

"He's leavin' already? I never even got to say 'Hello'."

* * * * *

Douglas B. Hornsby stood at the bottom of the gangplank, shifting from one foot to the other, impatient to claim his charges and see them safely to The Kingston Hotel, where he knew they'd be sheltered from any meddling interference.

He watched a stocky man, holding a little girl in each arm, walk down the gangway followed by a petite, brown-eyed woman carrying a wiggling babe. He recognized Amanda immediately, from the striking resemblance she bore to her mother, Evangeline Louise. He heaved a great sigh and stepped forward. Doffing his bowler hat, he made a sweeping bow. "Douglas B. Hornsby, at your service, Mizz Bently."

"Pleased to make your acquaintance," she said, making a half curtsey. "You look familiar to me. Have we met before?"

"It's quite possible. I've known your parents for years," Hornsby said. He turned to address Michael. "You're Mr. Harrison, I presume. Come with me, I have a carriage waiting to take you all to The Kingston. Best accommodation in town."

"But I thought we'd be staying at my parents' townhou–"

"There's one thing you need to be made aware of immediately, Mizz Bently," he said, donning his hat. "The Judge has placed a restraining order against your family to keep them from exerting undue influence over you, until this inheritance dilemma has been rectified to his satisfaction," he instructed. "In the meantime, you'll be stayin' at the Kingston, or out at Wallingsford."

"Oh," she sighed. "Then I'm afraid we'll need to change the addresses on all our trunks. I hope we can stop them before they get picked up."

"Not to worry. I've already taken care of it," he said. "Your luggage has been rerouted to The Kingston. So we have nothing further to detain us." He ushered them toward the waiting coach, scanning the crowd with apprehension. His eye fell upon Joseph Alexander Bently, III, standing in his most imposing manner, deep in conversation with the Harbor Master. Bently looked up to make eye contact with Hornsby, giving a half-salute, before resuming his intense discussion.

By the time the coach driver deposited the Harrison party at their hotel, the girls and baby Jems were all becoming cranky.

"It's past their dinner time," Amanda explained to Hornsby. "They tend to get irritable when they haven't eaten in a timely manner."

"Then we'd best get some food in 'em," he said. "Would y'all like to change out of your travelin' clothes before you eat? Clean up? Maybe put on something a bit more... ah, suitable for the dining room?"

"We're already wearing our best duds," Michael pointed out. "Anything we'd change into might be cleaner, but it won't look any better than these."

"In that case, come right this way," he motioned toward the dining room. "I'll have the Maître-D seat us in a spot with a bit of privacy. We must keep these little people happy, now, mustn't we," he said, condescendingly patting the head of each little girl.

They both gave him exasperated looks, until their mother glared them into submission. They dropped their eyes and followed along behind her, with Uncle Mikey bringing up the rear. Hornsby made a grand show of seating Amanda, who still held Jems in her lap. "Would you like a chair for the baby?"

"I don't know that he'd stay put in one," Amanda said. "We can try."

Hornsby signaled to the black waiter. "Roland... we need a chair for the baby."

"Yass'suh."

Michael put both girls in seats, helping them remove their hats and tie them to their chair backs. They fidgeted, trying very hard to sit still.

"Order whatever your little hearts desire," Hornsby addressed the girls. "You, too, Mizz Amanda. I don't su'pose you have much seafood in that wilderness of yours," he said. "May I recommend the sea bass? Came in fresh this morning."

"We had opportunity to eat a good deal of fish on the ship coming down here, Mr. Hornsby," Amanda pointed out. "I must say, I've never had anything that tasted quite so wonderful, after going so many years without any seafood whatsoever. I sorely missed the fresh selections available here on the coast."

"We eat deer meat," Camellia declared. "I like it in stew."

"*I want chicken!*" Lilly hollered to be heard over the din of so many diners enjoying their evening meal.

"Keep your voice down, Pipsqueak," Michael held his hand over her mouth, then released it. "We can hear you just fine using your quiet voice."

"I want chicken," Lilly whispered.

"You may have chicken, dear," Amanda said. "And Camellia, we'll ask if they have any stew. But I doubt you'll get venison. It'll more likely be a gumbo here."

"Gumbo? That's a funny word. What's gumbo?"

"Gumbo, gumbo, mumbo, bumbo—"

"Lillian, mind your manners," Amanda corrected. "Gumbo is a stew, Camellia, made with fish and sausage and vegetables."

"Oh," she sounded a bit disappointed. "Will I like it?"

"You won't know until you try it, now, will you."

The waiter brought over a tall chair for the baby, and Amanda got Jems settled, using the restraining ties to fasten him in securely. "I think I'd like some grits for Jems, and maybe some custard pudding, if you have it," she told the waiter.

"Yass'um. And for the young lay-dies?"

"Chicken for one. A stew of some kind for the other, if you have it."

"Yass'um. Today we have us a fine, pork stew wi' dumplin's. An' nice, juicy roastin' chicken."

"That'll do nicely," Amanda instructed. "I'd appreciate it if you could bring the children's food as quickly as possible."

"Yass'um. I bring it out di-rek-ly."

Hornsby butted into the conversation. "Bring the daily special for the lady, Roland. An' I'll have the creek shrimp." He pointed to a heaping plate full, going by on another waiter's silver, serving tray. "Nothing in the world like our creek shrimp, Mr. Harrison. You should try some."

"I'd rather have a steak," Michael said with certainty. "Rare, if you don't mind."

"Like it served up with the 'moo', do you?"

"You just eat them glorified crawdads your way, and I'll eat a good ol' beefsteak the way I like it, thanks."

The waiter brought the children's food in a matter of minutes, along with a bottle of Claret for the adults, whose meals would take a bit longer to prepare. He poured a small splash for Hornsby to taste, then, at the lawyer's nod of approval, continued pouring glasses all around.

"A toast!" Hornsby said, raising his glass. "Here's to making this lovely little lady the richest woman in the low country!"

Amanda looked at him with a stunned expression.

"You really don't have any idea how well off your grand-mother was, do you."

"I haven't given it all that much thought," Amanda admitted. "Till now, I've focused only on my responsibilities to Wallings-ford's people. It's up to me to see they're treated fairly," she said. "Grandmother Bently entrusted that obligation to me."

"Not if your father has anything to say about it."

"I'd rather we talk about all this *after* our dinner, Mr. Horns-by. I prefer not to discuss business matters around little ears, if you don't mind."

"Certainly, my dear. I understand completely." He took an-other sip of his wine and leaned back in his chair. "By the way, I've taken the liberty of arranging for a nursemaid to mind the children, while you're here at The Kingston... since a good deal of your time will be otherwise occupied with business matters, Mizz Bently."

"I'm not sure I like that idea, sir. I look after my own children. You realize, I am the only one who feeds Little Jems."

"We can talk about that later, too, my dear. Here comes our dinner," he said, pointing toward Roland, just exiting the kitchen.

They worked through their meals with light conversation peppered between courses, then finished up with hot coffee for the adults and cambric tea for the girls.

"Would y'all have a taste for afta' dinner sweets?" the waiter asked.

"Yes, Mama!", "Please, Mama?" the girls begged at once.

"Just a small taste of something. Perhaps some benne wafers, if you have any?"

"Yass'um."

"I'll have a piece of pecan pie," Hornsby cut in.

"What is bennie wafer?" Camellia asked.

"It's a special kind of crunchy, sweet, sesame-biscuit, sweetheart. You won't find them anywhere up north," Amanda said. "I used to love them as a child."

"Can Jems have one too?"

"He hasn't grown enough teeth for hard biscuits yet."

"When will he have enough teeth, Mama?"

"Soon, darling. Very soon."

By the time the Harrisons finished up dessert, the girls sat yawning.

"We'd best get these children to bed," Amanda told Michael. "Would you direct us to our rooms, Mr. Hornsby?"

"I'll get the manager to escort you. I have some work to finish up in my office before I can retire for the evening. I'm sure you're all done in after such a long trip," he said, pushing himself away from the table. "Shall we meet in the morning to discuss our modus operandi?"

"Our what?" Michael asked.

"Our main course of action, our approach to the legal complications we face."

"Perhaps you should call after breakfast," Amanda suggested. "We'll no doubt have a much fresher outlook by then."

"Very well, Mizz Bently. I'll see you in the forenoon, say around nine?"

"Mr. Hornsby, I do prefer that you call me by my proper name, 'Mrs. Harrison,' if you don't mind, sir."

"Oh, by all means. I just thought it more expedient to use your maiden name here in Charleston, since people do recognize that name more readily," he said, beginning to rise.

"I'm proud of the name I bear, Mr. Hornsby. And out of respect for my deceased husband, I shall continue to use it, even though he's no longer with us."

Hornsby sat back down, looking confused. "Wait a minute. I thought this man was your husband. " He gave Michael a perplexing look. "You mean to tell me you two are not husband and wife? Aren't you Mr. Harrison?"

"He is. But I'm afraid you didn't give us opportunity to introduce him properly at the ship. You simply assumed he was my husband and hurried us off. This is my brother-in-law. *Michael* Harrison," Amanda said in a snippy tone, beginning to sound rather miffed at Hornsby. "My husband Jeremiah met an untimely demise less than a year ago," she said with a catch in her voice, as she struggled to master sudden emotion. "His brother Michael promised to look after us, and see us safely down here."

"Let me get this straight then," Hornsby said. "You two are not married."

"No, we are not," she said. "I'm too newly bereaved to even consider remarriage so quickly. Not to mention completely occupied caring for young twins and an infant."

"I see," Hornsby said. "I had assumed you wore mourning for your grandmother, not for a husband." He turned his hat round and round in his hands. "Well, this does put a new light on our dilemma. You do realize, that as a woman, you cannot sign any official documentation and have it accepted in a court of law," he mused. "Under normal circumstances, a woman facing litigation and the forthcoming inheritance of such a sizeable estate would be represented by her husband in any and all matters of legal concern," he said. "The responsibility of signing all said documenttation falls to him."

"Mama! Lilly pushed me!"

"Lillian, stop that this instant," Amanda directed, separating the girls by removing Lilly from her chair and pulling the child to one side.

"We cannot sit here and discuss anything more tonight, Mr. Hornsby. If you'll excuse us, I must tend to the children. We'll see you in the morning." She dismissed him with a nod, then rose to shepherd her girls out of the dining room toward the stairs, while Michael extricated Jems from his high chair and followed along behind.

"This is going to be a *l-o-n-g* ordeal, I can see that clear," he said to the baby.

Jems stared at Uncle Mikey as if he could understand every word.

June 8, 1821
Cranberry Corners, Fire Lands

Dear Ellie,

My dearest friend, I cannot begin to tell you how excited I was to receive your last missive telling me of Simeon and Katrina's plan to come to us. As you can imagine, I flew into a flurry of activity, cleaning the cabin, preparing special foodstuffs, and washing fresh bedding to have accommodation ready for our little family's imminent arrival.

Your prediction that my Simeon and his loved ones would "turn up on our doorstep" before the end of May proved accurate. They pulled in on May 25, to be exact. What a thrill to see that little Simon, smiling his cherubic smile and stretching his arms out to his Grandmama and Grandpapa. Not a bit strange, was he! Just like his Daddy at that age. Simeon would happily go to anyone without a bit of fussing. Other than that bright shock of red hair, Simon is so like his Daddy, it takes me quite aback.

During the happy arrival, Lizzie and Kit made a big fuss over Simeon's family. Katrina and Lizzie took to one another immediately, leaving me feeling completely ignored by them a good deal of the time. But I didn't mind one bit, since Zach and I took that chubby babe aside for our exclusive entertainment. Of course, Simeon and Kit renewed old acquaintance and spent hours conversing over pot after pot of steaming chicory coffee and some of Lizzie's sweet maple buns, thinking they could no doubt solve all the state's economic problems between them.

What a buzzing household this has become! It feels so wonderful to have excited young people filling our days with energy again. Lizzie and Katrina assumed most of the kitchen duties to themselves, giving me the luxury of time to play with our precious boy. Would that you could see these two young women together, Ellie. They remind me so much of you and I, it truly is uncanny. Even gives me goose bumps on occasion, when I hear nearly identical conversations to some of ours, coming now from their mouths!

The only drawback to this domestic harmony has been my own Elijah. He feels quite left out of the excitement, with no one of an age to engage his attention. I have tried to entice him into playing with the baby, but at seven years, he feels himself much too "grown up" to stoop to playing with infants. He sees it as far beneath his station of "oldest child in residence" to wallow on the floor like a babe. I find it most interesting that he considers not his own sister as competition for his place of honor as eldest, since she now is a married woman, therefore no longer regarded as his contemporary, even though she does still reside under the same roof.

Oh, Ellie, the joy of having a houseful of loved ones here! I cherish every moment, as I know this time will fly by much too quickly.

Now to the news of Lizzie's confinement. As you know, this high-strung daughter of mine has been more than a little panicky over the impending arrival of her own babe. I cannot say as I find fault with such fear, knowing the bloody birth spectacle she witnesssed when we lost our precious Zannah and her web-footed babe. But with all the hubbub of Katrina and Simeon's arrival, she became so thoroughly distracted, that the initial stages of labor sneaked up on her without her immediate knowledge.

One morning while the girls were preparing a special lunch of pot pies for the entire household, she began to feel a bit "unsettled" while peeling onions for their project. Katrina distracted her with so much chit-chat about curious rivermen, a hilarious incident involving a chicken, and her own aversion to onions, that when the first contraction tightened, it took Lizzie completely by surprise. "Oh, I think something's happening, here!" she said of a sudden, when water began to rush down her limbs.

Katrina took over the whole birthing process so efficiently, one would believe she's handled this sort of thing countless times before. She turned meal preparations over to me, ushering Lizzie to bed so smoothly, Lizzie had not even time to think, let alone

63

panic over the coming drama, so intently did Katrina keep up their conversation. She sidetracked Lizzie time and time again, until those very last stages of labor when total concentration needs be focused on none else. By that time, Lizzie had become so completely involved in the process, she barely realized she already had overcome her fears concerning the matter.

When Katrina placed her precious, little daughter into Lizzie's arms, after just five, short hours of labor (can you believe such of a first birth?), tears flowed freely among all women of the household. The men and Elijah, who had excused themselves to the barn early on in the process, returned to a late dinner of pot pies and found a contented, though thoroughly spent, Lizzie holding her beautiful, new daughter. She named the babe Liberty Lane Lavengood. I felt completely overwhelmed, when she gave her girl my own middle name.

Thank you so much, Ellie, for sending us Katrina. The girl is a gem. Would that she and Simeon might consent to stay on the remainder of the summer. But I hesitate even to broach the subject, lest it spur them into leaving that much sooner. So I keep my peace, enjoying these grandbabies, hopeful that time will stand still for a trice longer to allow me this fleeting joy.

Before I close my missive, I must pass on a bit of news to you concerning your own Johannah. I received a post from Christian, dated February last, mailed from St. Louis, which has taken these past four months to make its way to us. Apparently he did receive the letter I sent to him in care of the St. Louis Post Office, for in a return dispatch he related that when he treated himself to a warm meal at the hotel in that city and complimented the manager upon its excellence, aforementioned manager told Christian that a hard-working widow girl by the name of Johannah Sullivan would be the one to compliment for the recipe. Unfortunately, she no longer worked at his establishment.

Apparently she had cooked meals and cleaned rooms for him that previous summer and fall. But in October of 18 and 19, she moved on, which made her trail more than one year old for Christian to follow. He said he would do his best to glean more information concerning her whereabouts and send it on to us as he can discover such.

That means your girl was doing fine, Ellie Mae! Earning her way after she left the scene of her tragedy. That should warm your heart considerably, even though we still have no clue as to where she may be at the moment. The fact that she was working in an honorable fashion, taking the name of her lost love to protect herself as best she could as a widow, comes as wonderful news! You are right, El, we must think on the best that could happen, so as to make it that much more likely to come to pass.

As for your news of Harvey, I say the less you think on that rogue, the better.

Oh, I nearly neglected to relate another wonderful tidbit of news: When Nate and Ivy came to visit after Liberty's birth, they told us that Ivy would be expecting their second child sometime near the Christmas Holidays. What wondrous tidings! Then, this next you will hardly credit, but I swear it happened exactly this way. When Nate and Ivy told of their coming addition, Simeon and Katrina looked at one another and burst into laughter. Before Nate and Ivy could take offense, Katrina hastened to tell the assembled company that they, too, expect their own little Christmas bundle!

Who would have guessed it, Ellie? But we are to have another grandchild between us, which means two Christmas babies for me to love and spoil! That will make five grandchildren for Zach and I. Hardly could I guess this grandparent business would bring us so much joy. And so quickly! I thought nothing else could ever compare to having babies of our own. But Ellie, I can barely hold the delight these precious grandchildren bestow.

And, as if the day had not already brought enough good news, our little Simon decided to make the occasion even more momentous by taking his first steps! I am sorry you could not see them. But since we have missed out on so many of his other "firsts" Zach thinks it fitting that we are the ones who had opportunity to witness those initial, wobbly steps. Thank you so much for sending these loved ones to us, dear Ellie.

I hope the good news in this missive brings as much joy to you as it has to us. I wish I could be there to give it to you in person. Perhaps we can arrange to meet for the holidays, do you suppose? Both be present when these children give us more grandchildren?

Think on it, Ellie. We must make a way to give one another a real hug again. Such fun we could have together at Christmas time!

Yours, Lib

P.S. I did plant the Cana bulbs. Thank you so much for sending them. And yes, I am familiar with Canas, as I had some growing in my flower garden back in Connecticutt. Unfortunately, I had to leave them behind, as needs must I left so many things. So I was especially thankful to receive the ones you sent. I shall, indeed, think of you when they raise their lovely, red heads. Thank you, again, my friend.

Chapter 5

Pitney sat rocking on the expansive porch, gnarled hands busy shelling sweet peas into the bowl on her lap. She picked out another handful from the sweetgrass bushel-basket sitting at her feet, as she watched the youngsters play beneath the sprawling, live oak tree, hanging low with Spanish moss. Older children continued to pick more peas out in the expansive garden, where their mothers hoped such a task would keep them occupied and out of trouble—for the time being, at least.

Pitney loved to hear the littlest ones' laughter, as they chased each another through the yard, then round and round the large, flat stone that looked like a giant mushroom standing in the central turnabout. No one knew who'd put the stone there, for it had obviously been shaped by human hands and set upon a granite pedestal for some mysterious purpose, long since forgotten.

"Keep 'em babes to hand," Pitney called to the older, coffee-colored girl, who bore high cheek bones like her own. The girl, supposedly minding a bevy of toddlers, stood lost in thought, staring at the north orchard where wiry youths climbed among the trees, trimming off smaller, misshapen peaches, so that too much weight wouldn't end up breaking down the branches when the largest fruits swelled and ripened during the coming weeks.

Pitney watched over her progeny and took great pains in making sure no child got lost in the daily shuffle. For in one way or another, most everyone on Wallingsford had blood ties to Pitney Doubleday Bower. Her own children, save one, had already crossed the great divide between this world and the next, but her continued interest in the expanding number of youngsters came as no surprise to anyone. The group, playing happily within shouting distance of her wrinkled smile and nappy, white head, represented a small number of the great, great grandchildren she claimed as her own.

To observe Pitney, one would guess her somewhere near the age of 75 or 80. But the most accurate estimate anyone could calculate put her well over 100 years old. Perhaps closer to 110, according to some. No doubt, even that number fell short, for nary a living soul could remember Wallingsford without Pitney Bower here, attending to her domain.

It stood to reason that if she didn't know how that mushroom stone in the front yard came to stand there, no one in living memory possibly could.

A tall, striking man stepped up, onto the porch. "Afternoon, Pitney," he said, tipping his hat. Winston Horatio Applebaum stood well over six feet tall. The green, cat-like eyes missed nothing within his range of sight, which happened to stretch much further than the average person could begin to see.

When Winston came to work at Wallingsford eighteen years before, Pitney had put him through his paces before she approved Olympia's selection for plantation manager. Unlike other plantations in the South, her people worked freely to earn their daily wage—slaves to nary a soul. Winston relied on his charismatic charm, not to mention a handy system of rewards and incentives, to insure that the workers at Wallingsford accomplished their tasks without feeling put-upon to do so. They knew what needed to be done, and they had a say in divvying up the jobs necessary to keep Wallingsford a prosperous enterprise benefitting all—in effect a type of share-cropping, long before such a term became common in the South.

Wallingsford's people had the freedom to learn and ply a trade, as well as keep the earnings involved in such industry. Some had even managed to purchase freedom for extended family members from agreeable owners on other plantations. More often than not, they'd bring them to join this ever-growing community of freedmen living on Wallingsford, here on Edisto Island. For to remain in the south, they had few other choices, free or no.

Over the last ten years of her life, Olympia Bently had relied heavily upon Winston's tactful handling of her people, as well as his razor-sharp business acumen to stay on top of ever-changing market conditions and government regulations. Knowing that her time grew short in this world, Olympia extracted a promise from Winston, before she changed her will leaving everything to her great-granddaughter without her grandson's supervision: "See that my people remain free and protected until Amanda Jane lays claim her inheritance."

Olympia had come to believe that if Joseph Bently, a slave trader for the greater part of his adult life, managed to overturn her last wishes and gain control of the estate, her people would undoubtedly find themselves on the auction block, regardless of valid manumission papers drawn up years ago. Her barrister suspected it would take only one, troublesome incident to convince Joseph that her people did not have entitlement to handle their own freedom, and she reluctantly came to agree with him.

Pitney maintained enough influence among her extended family to keep her finger on the pulse of all the plantation's workers. She knew the people most apt to cause trouble, and she always knew whom to call upon to prevent it. Winston recognized that such knowledge and unquestioned authority made her as integral a part in managing Wallingsford as was he.

So, he made it his ongoing business to remain in Pitney's good graces. He'd invested far too much at Wallingsford to risk losing this plum position now. With nearly total control of the plantation's day-to-day operations already in hand, he didn't aim to jeopardize his long-term strategy to take over this venture by making a single misstep now. Winston knew that if he offended Pitney Doubleday Bower, he may as well kiss Wallingsford Plantation goodbye.

Besides, as he saw it, he need only bide his time, and wait. Surely she could not live forever.

The reverse, however, also held true: Pitney knew she must rely on Winston's strength and position in the world of white businessmen to keep Wallingsford flourishing. She aimed to see uninterrupted prosperity continue for her people. Yet she, more than anyone, understood that she now lived on borrowed time. If Amanda Jane didn't assume the reins of authority soon, she feared for the continued freedom of her people.

Pitney only hoped that Amanda Jane had finally gained enough maturity to take her rightful place at Wallingsford's helm and guard what she and Olympia had so carefully orchestrated here.

"Winston." Pitney acknowledged the manager's cordial greeting. "Nice breeze."

"Certainly is a lovely day," he said. "You feelin' fit?"

"Tol'able," she said, stiff fingers flying, as she tended to her pea-shelling task.

"I assume you have household operations well in hand."

"Ada Mae keepin' our gals workin' fine," she said. "Dinner 'most all set."

"Excellent." He pulled the watch fob from his vest pocket and checked the time. "I'll give the orchard workers another half hour before I ring everybody in for dinner."

"Might wait a bit mo'," Pitney said, nodding toward the northeast road down from the wharf. "Comp'ny comin'."

"I wasn't informed of any visitors expected today," he said, beginning to sound testy. "Hornsby would have notified me, had he made plans to come out to the island."

"Just tellin' what I know," Pitney stated.

"Your soothsaying powers at work again, I take it?"

Pitney kept her peace, rocking, smiling, shelling peas.

"I'll give your sup-*po*-sed company forty-five minutes. If they haven't arrived by then, we carry on as is customary," he said, replacing the watch fob and scanning the road to the north. His sharp eyes caught a wisp of dust on the horizon. "*Lucky guess,*" he muttered to himself. "I'll tell Ada Mae to bring some wine in from the cold house."

"No need," Pitney said. "Already been done."

Winston stepped off the porch and headed at a swift pace toward his office behind the main dwelling. "That reprobate should have sent word," he grumbled. Over the last several months, Winston had begun to suspect treachery in Hornsby's actions, and he'd started to question the barrister's long-term intentions concerning Wallingsford. In his estimation an unannounced visit could indicate nothing fortuitous.

Twenty minutes later, a carriage loaded with trunks pulled up to the front portico, the driver reining the horse to a stop.

"Run 'at step over, Buzzy," Pitney directed the black-eyed boy sitting on a box stool beside the steps. "Help Mizz 'Manda down proper." Pitney grunted upright, leaning heavily on the rocking chair's sturdy arms. Though it took her a moment to gain firm footing, she stood tall, steadying herself against the porch rail.

A wiry stable boy came forward to take the horse's head, while Buzzy placed his step beside the carriage, precisely between front and back wheels, making sure it sat solid and level on the crushed, oyster-shell lane. He stood proud, ready to help the beautiful lady step down. She reached her tiny hand out to his small one, placed her booted foot cautiously on the box, then stepped onto the crunchy pathway.

Amanda took a big breath and sighed it out slowly, surveying long-familiar surroundings. *"Ohhhh, Pitney!"* She hurried up the steps to embrace the old woman. "I've missed you all so! I didn't know how much till we made the turn in from the landing, and I saw the boys up in the trees, just like old times!"

"I knew you was comin' Manny," Pitney said, hugging her best friend's most cherished grandchild. "Had me a sure sign last evenin'."

"You and your premonitions," Amanda said, hugging her back. "That's why you already had the carriage waiting for us at the dock, isn't it." She turned and motioned to her girls, whom Michael had helped down from their seats. They scuttled up the impressive steps grabbing their mother's skirts, one on either side, each wide-eyed with wonder.

"What have we here?" Pitney asked, looking from one to the other. "Two peas in a pod!"

"Pitney, my girls, Camellia Jane and Lillian Jane," she tapped each one in turn as she introduced them. "Twins, as you surmise."

"Lillian," Pitney nodded. "Your gran'mama'd be proud a piece o' her name livin' on."

Michael picked Jems out of his basket, lifted him up against his shoulder, and strolled up the steps to stand behind Amanda.

"And this be your man." A statement. Not a question.

"This is my brother-in-law, Michael Harrison. I don't know how I could have managed everything without his help," Amanda babbled nervously.

"Ma'am," Michael said, tipping his hat.

"He's my husband's brother," Amanda said. "Last summer Jeremiah…" she took a deep breath and started again. "My husband died last summer, Pitney," she said, in simple explanation. "Michael promised Jeremiah he'd look after us."

"That be what *you* say," Pitney chucked the baby under his chin. "Me, I know what I know," she said with a nod of her head toward Michael.

"And this," Amanda took the baby from Michael, "is my son, Jeremiah Junior." Jems leaned in, reaching for her bodice. "I'm afraid it's long past time for him to eat."

"Praise be! You nu'sin' that babe yo' own self! Well, bring him on up to the nu's'ry. Get settled in," Pitney directed. "Been long time sin' we have us any babies up there."

"I'll go see to the baggage." Michael turned toward the carriage to unload their luggage, but the house staff already had the trunks out of the wagon and half way up the steps. Michael shrugged his shoulders and walked over to take hold of the horse instead, see to its needs.

"I's ta look after yo' hoss, suh," said the gangly stable boy.

"Well, it looks like I'm not needed at all then," he said, smacking his legs.

"Unka Mikey! Unka Mikey!" the girls called, nervous at their new surroundings and the uncharacteristic shift they'd sensed in their mother. Craving the familiar security their uncle represent-ted, they ran to him and clung to his legs.

Before Amanda entered the house, Winston appeared from the far side of the porch. "Mizz Amanda Jane, how wonderful to see you again," he said, removing his hat as he stepped forward to make a gracious bow. "You are even more lovely than I remem-ber." He took her hand in a gesture of welcome. "Motherhood definitely becomes you."

"Thank you, Winston. It's good to see you." Amanda pulled her hand back and shifted the baby to her other arm. "If you'll excuse me, I need to tend to Jems. But I do hope we can catch up on Wallingsford later on."

"It will be my distinct pleasure," he bowed again. "I am at your service, as always." He made a hasty retreat in the same di-rection from whence he'd come.

"Who was that?" Michael asked, taking the last step up, onto the porch, with little girls holding his hands.

"Grandmother's manager, Winston," Amanda answered.

"Don't waste words, does he."

"Winston can talk your ear off, if you get him started on the right topic."

"And what might that be?"

"Wallingsford."

Michael nodded and walked through the front door into a small vestibule that led to a sitting room on one side, and a dining room on the other. Directly in front, a set of stairs ascended to the nursery and bedrooms above.

On most plantations, the "Big House" had come to reflect the affluent grandeur of the Southern planter class, with imported fineries making opulent statements as to the taste and wealth of those living within. However, the manor house at Wallingsford presented quite a different face—more like a hunting lodge than a grand residence. Smaller rooms, furnished in a casual style, created a more relaxed, informal feeling.

To Michael, raised on a rustic, Pennsylvania farm, it all seemed a veritable palace.

A large, fireplace stood center stage at the end of the sitting room, the stone-work of which gained his immediate attention. It was flanked by two, walnut chairs with deep-green, overstuffed cushions and faced by a masculine looking, leather settee with a table stationed at either end. Each table held an assortment of ancient stone relics. Michael expected to see cigar smoke rising from the other side of the settee, this room indicated such a strong presence of a man. Nothing feminine about it. Yet for years a woman had stood at the helm of this plantation. Curious. Quite curious, indeed.

* * * * *

Pitney postponed dinner until the travelers had a chance to sufficiently gather themselves and settle into their upstairs bedrooms: the girls and Jems in the nursery, with Amanda in the adjoining bedroom, and Michael occupying another room across the hall. When the Harrisons descended the staircase half an hour later, Winston stood at its foot. Both girls held their mother's hands as they came down the flight of stairs, and Michael carried Jems. When Amanda took the last step onto the main floor, Winston offered up his arm.

"May I have the honor of escorting you in to dinner?"

Amanda put the girls' hands into one another's grasp, instructted them to follow along, then took the well-turned arm. The twins looked at each other and burst out giggling. This unexpected formal side of their mother came as something altogether new.

Amanda stopped and turned to her girls. "Do you two have a problem?"

"No, Mama." Both immediately snapped to attention.

"Then follow along quietly, and act like company," she said, turning back to Winston as he guided her toward the dining room.

"I beg to differ, Miss Amanda," Winston said, making every effort to charm his new employer, "but y'all are definitely not company here. You own this place, now."

Amanda stopped dead in her tracks. "Oh, my." She stood a moment, trying to let that thought sink in, as she took a good look around. "I really do, don't I."

"That's what your Grandmother intended." Winston pulled out the chair at the head of the table and seated her, then proceeded to seat both girls in the same, formal manner. Michael followed along with Jems.

"Looks like it's you and me again, champ," Michael said to the baby. Jems took hold of his uncle's ear and pulled. "All right, pal. Time to get something solid for you to chew on," he said, easing the baby into the child's chair conveniently placed beside Amanda's place at the head of the table. A crusty biscuit sat at the ready, and Jems picked it right up and began to gnaw. Michael sat in the empty seat beside the twins, since Winston had already taken the spot directly adjacent to Amanda Jane's, in order to have opportunity for uninterrupted conversation.

The girls kicked at each other under the table and giggled, only this time more quietly, so as not to disturb their mother, who at that moment was closely scrutinizing the serving girl just entering the room.

"Effie Lou? Is that you?" Amanda asked the tall, comely woman advancing with a soup tureen. "You grew up!"

"It's me, in the flesh, Mizz 'Manda!" she bubbled, setting the large serving bowl on the sideboard near her old friend. "An' look at you, gal? Sittin' head table, just like yo' own Gran'mama!" She proceeded to ladle bowls of gumbo all around. "I can see de years away kep' you rite busy," she said, eyeing the girls and Jems.

"You don't know the half of it."

"We catch up later, Manny. You a grand lady, now," she said in a low voice, meaning no one else to hear but knowing they took in every word.

75

"There's one thing I want understood before we go any further," Amanda said, clearing her throat. "We will have no stomach-churning business discussions over the dinner table. Is that quite clear?" she said, looking directly at Winston. "I refuse to have my children's meals upset with talk of market prices and orchard problems."

She shook out her napkin and laid it primly across her lap, nodding at her girls to indicate they do the same. They promptly complied, unaccustomed though they be to these new matters of etiquette, which they'd only begun to learn on-board ship and at the fancy hotel.

"The boss has spoken!" Michael said with a smirk, taking his own napkin and making a grand show of shaking it out and tucking it into the shirt beneath his chin.

The girls giggled again, and Amanda gave him a squint-eyed glare.

"We'll have ample opportunity to discuss your grandmother's vision for Wallingsford," Winston acquiesced, pouring glasses of champagne for the three adults. "Meanwhile, may I propose a toast?" He lifted his goblet. "To a new beginning!"

"Here, here," Amanda said, clinking her crystal glass against Winston's. They took a taste of their champagne while Michael sat holding his up—no other glass anywhere near "clinking" distance of his own. He shrugged, then took his first sip of the nose-tickling vintage.

It made him sneeze.

"Bless you," Amanda said, giving her brother-in-law a smirk. "Told you."

Michael said not a word, but took another sip, this time knowing better what to expect from the unfamiliar effervescence. The wide-eyed girls took in everything: fancy silver serving dishes, ruby colored damask linens draping the dining and side tables, and long, sweeping, golden velvets festooned with fringe, framing the tall, arched windows. This room definitely reflected the stylish grace of a sophisticated woman. Nothing rustic about it.

Once they finished with the gumbo, Effie Lou busied herself gathering up soup bowls. Then Pitney entered from the kitchen, carrying a huge tray covered with tiny birds smothered in onions and gravy.

"Pitney! You fixed your famous potted quail!" Amanda gushed.

"Had to cook my Manny's fav'rite tucker, when she come home like the prodigal."

"You give that platter to Effie Lou and come sit right down here!" Amanda fussed. "What on earth ever possessed you to carry such a heavy thing in here all by yourself?"

"Nary a soul touches my birds 'ceptin' me!" she stated with solemnity. Pitney glared at Effie Lou, then set her tray on the sideboard. She stood a minute to straighten her back before painfully lowering herself into the chair at the foot of the table, opposite Amanda Jane. To see a person of color sit at a formal dining table with the white folk came as quite a shock to most people—not to mention one sitting in a place of prominence. Being unfamiliar with Southern ways, Michael never flinched.

"Pitney's raised her birds for as long as I can remember," Amanda informed Michael. "Up to now, she only prepared them for *special* occasions."

"What be more special than my Manny comin' home?"

"Perhaps Miss Amanda's return with three, lovely progeny in tow," Winston schmoozed, nodding toward the girls and Jems. "Effie Lou, why don't you serve these little ladies their dinner?"

"My lands, I hardly can get over those two lookin' 'zackly alike!" Effie said. She put a split bird on every plate (two for the men), then dished generous portions of green peas, chainey briar and Carolina Gold rice along side, covering the rice with rich, brown gravy and onions from the quail platter.

Taking his knife and fork in hand, Michael looked his little birds over from neck to tail, then plunged the knife into a miniscule joint between the tiny thigh and drumstick.

"Like this, Michael," Amanda demonstrated. She picked up a leg in one hand and a wing with the other, then bit into the juicy breast meat between.

"Don't mess with 'em bony parts," Pitney explained. "Breast meat's onliest part worth eatin'."

"Whatever you say." Michael did as instructed, chewing the tender meat and swallowing in a swift motion. "Tastes like chicken," he said with a smirk.

"Chicken never come outta no pot this tender!" Pitney took umbrage.

"By that I *meant* this is right tasty," he said. "No insult intended, Ma'am."

Pitney nodded her head in acknowledgement of his assessment.

When everyone had finished eating the main course, and Effie Lou had cleared away the remains, Ada Mae entered carrying a flaming pudding.

"Mama! It's on *fire!*" Millie shouted, as she took a nose-dive under the table. Lillian sat mesmerized by the flames.

"Come out, dear. It's all right," Amanda said to her cowering daughter. "Ada Mae's brought us an extra-special dessert."

"But it's burning!" Camellia insisted from underneath her mother's skirts.

"It's *supposed* to be on fire, darling. Now sit back up in your chair like a big girl."

Camellia peeked out from under the tablecloth with a bewildered expression, then slowly slithered back up to her place at the table. "Does it taste good?"

"It tastes divine," Amanda reassured. Sit like a lady, now, please. Put your napkin back on your lap." Camellia did as instructed. "Ada Mae, what a lovely surprise! You made your specialty for us, too!"

"Fo' true, Manny. Fo' true." The pudgy cook placed the pudding in front of Amanda Jane, flames now extinguished after all

78

the brandy had burned itself off. "I got sweet cream an' rum sauce to cover it, too!"

"How can I be so fortunate as to have all my favorite dishes at one meal?" Amanda raved.

"Obviously *someone* expected you today, my dear," Winston said, giving Pitney a hard look.

"Tol' you onc't. Had me a sign," Pitney responded. "Someone special always comin' when the Ol' Shaman 'pears by my bed."

"And *no* one argues with the prophetic visions of Pitney Doubleday Bower," he stressed, leaning in to touch Amanda's arm.

"Well I don't know about you folks, but I sure would like a taste of that puddin', if you don't mind," Michael spoke up.

Effie Lou busied herself dishing portions all around, smothering each bowl with a generous ladle-full of sweet cream, then covering the whole thing with warm rum sauce.

Jems sat banging on the tray of his chair.

"Let me feed dat boy, Manny," Effie Lou beseeched.

"I suppose he could have a small taste," Amanda consented. "But no run sauce."

"Yass'um," Effie Lou said, spooning bites into Jems' mouth. "He eatin' up jus' fine."

"A little Madeira would go quite nicely with this dessert, don't you think?" Winston suggested, as he swished his wine glass in the cleaning beaker beside his plate. Ada Mae poured small glasses of the sweet wine all around, then put the bottle back on the top shelf of the sideboard. "May I propose another toast?" Winston asked, holding his glass aloft.

"By all means," Amanda agreed.

"To a long and prosperous partnership."

"Amen to that, brother," Pitney said, downing her wine in one swallow. "Amen to that!"

June 28, 1821
Riverstop

Dear Lib,

Well that beats all! Our Katrina on the nest again! And nary a word did she peep afore they took off from here. I must be slipping. Not to see this one coming like last time. Before even she did. But now she knows what it feels like. Them first queezy waves. Guess she wanted to keep her peace till time was right to spill the beans.

So you and me will have us another grandpup to share. You tell that Simeon to keep his family up there with youens till this next babe gets born. Not to let his wife travel no more in her condition. If I had knowed I wouldda kept them to home. She took a chance to travel so early on like she done. But that is my Katrina. Always one to test out the thin ice.

If she gives you grief about staying up north you tell her there ain't no reason to hurry back down here. There be little boat traffic to speak of now. As the river already has dried up to no more than a trickle this season. Too shallow even to float a canoe. Zeke had to walk half way here this week pushing that scow of his. If you can credit that. Been awful dry. No rain for nigh onto 3 weeks now. Nobody comes in to eat at Riverstop but Harmon and Zeke. So I aim to close the doors for the rest of summer.

I have took me a notion, Lib. Which should come as no surprise to you. I have a burr in my blanket to go hunt for my Johannah. Besides which Zeke thinks I should not stay on here with Harvey spied moving up river. Zeke laid eyes on that trouble just a week past. This time down near Marietta. Getting closer to home all the time he is.

But Zeke will not hear of me going off anywheres on my own. He aims to come along to look after me. I say I need no lookin after. But he says he always had him a hankering to paddle up the Missouri. Take a look around. So that is where I go next. Up the Missouri with that crazy Scotsman. Guess I better learn to like the screech of bagpipes.

At first I was not too sure about leaving. Worrying over what Harvey was apt to do if he should come round while I am gone. But Harmon says he will take up here for a spell if I want. Claims he is tired of moving around so much and needs him some time to cool his heels. If you ask me, I think the man has dipped his wick in the wrong wax pot and has got his self in a peck of trouble. Wants to hide out till it blows over.

His offer does come at a helpful time for me. So I will leave my nephew to guard the place in my stead. If Harvey does turn up here he would find a peck of trouble from Harmon. Edie always did say he was the scrapper of all her boys.

You take good care of our little family, Lib. Make sure Katrina eats enough so she can knit that new babe together good and strong. Tell her Harmon will look after her chickens. And that I aim to go look for her sister. By hook or by crook I will find her.

If I run into that Christian of yours, I will ask if he wants to come along with Zeke and me. Mebbe he can talk her into coming back home if we can not. As I recall he was sweet on her once. But mayhap that was your Nate. Or was Johannah the one sweet on him? Too many years and too many children gone by to recall it all clear.

I will write to you as I am able, Lib. But I do not figger to hear from you. Do not know where you would send a post to me no how. Zeke and me hope to get back by late fall. Gives us five month to hunt up sign of my girl. Mebbe then I can come up youens way to help hatch out our new grandbabe. Would be so good to see you again, Lib. Have us a real good gab fest!

Keep your good thoughts out there for us. Together we will do our best to find the girl. I have to believe we will. Who knows? We might even run across your Levi somewheres! Lord only knows what tomfoolery that boy has stirred up by now!

Your foot loose friend,
Ellie Mae

P.S. I hope Zeke will not take any romantic notions into his head on this trip. So far he has kept all that nonsense to his own self. If he thinks he can sweet talk me into giving that furry face of his a smooch, he has him another think coming! After I got into so much trouble on account of Harvey, I do not aim to go smooching no man never again.

Chapter 6

Evangeline Louise Tedrow Bently lay propped against a stack of feather pillows on the réclamée, situated in the corner of the third-floor piazza, where the daybed-like settee could catch the slightest wisp of a breeze. Any breath of air came as welcome relief from the heat of Charleston in July.

"Cassie, I need a cool cloth for my head," Evangeline directed her personal maid. "Another glass of Bumbo, too. I have to keep my strength up as long as I can manage it," she said, handing her tumbler to the slim, dark woman. "Add extra rum to the next batch. This last glass tasted much too weak."

"Yass'um, Mizz Bently."

"I don't know how much longer I can hold on," Evangeline complained. She heaved a great sigh. "The gall that judge has... to keep my own daughter from me... after all these years. Simply *inexcusable!*" She shifted on the chaise trying to find a more comfortable position. "To deny a dying woman the grandchildren she's never even laid eyes on, for heaven sakes. How can anyone be so coldhearted?"

A short, buxom woman in her early fifties, Evangeline Bently had lingered at the edge of health for some months, claiming to be on the brink of crossing into the great beyond, due to a grave, "feminine complaint" she would reveal to no one. Doing nothing half way, she determined her exit from this earthly sphere would be as long and drawn-out as she could possibly manage.

It would serve Joseph right, for ignoring her feelings the way he always had. She'd suffered so much at the hands of the rumor-mongers! She'd like to see him endure half as much and not buckle under the weight of the humiliation. Six, long years, and still they whispered whenever she walked down King street. *There goes that woman who banished her own daughter,* she imagined the tongues of Charleston wagging behind her back.

The whole, sorry affair over Amanda's brutal attack, subsequent pregnancy, and hastily arranged marriage to her cousin's son haunted Evangeline still. Joseph's ruffians had to have been the ones responsible. She knew it to the depth of her bones. And now, on top of everything else, to be denied access to her very own family at their long-awaited home-coming? All because of Joseph's apparent blind greed? How could she continue to live with such disgrace?

"It's all his fault. *Everything!*" Evangeline grumbled to no one but the fan boy. Tutt stood stoically, waving his palmetto branch to keep the heavy air moving around her, uttering not a word.

Of course she held Joseph accountable for all the wrongs in their long and miserable marriage. She'd tried so hard to make it work—at least at first. Oh, if only he could understand what she'd been forced to suffer. *By the Good Lord, he should have to suffer right along with me.*

Truth be told, she'd done her best to bring about that very anguish.

Evangeline grew up in the prestigious social circles of Charleston's elite, thanks to the influence of her mother, Camellia Louise Tedrow, who persuaded her husband to help in founding the Saint Cecilia Society at its inception. She'd also been one of the select few to entertain George Washington at the Wednesday evening Ball, sponsored by the Society at the Exchange building, on his celebrated visit to Charleston in 1791.

It hadn't hurt that her father, Peter Harrington Tedrow, headed up Tedrow Shipping: one of the largest import-export businesses in the South. Yet, before Evangeline had consented to wed Captain Joseph Bently in the spring of 1790, she already felt her status in Charleston's hierarchy beginning to slip. This dubious fiancée, hand-picked by her father, no less, came with unimpressive background: the second son of a drinking, gambling planter, bred from ancestry supposedly tainted by savage blood, which would no doubt account for the rumored fratricide allegedly dogging his hasty escape out to sea.

Naturally, Evangeline felt that this less-than-desirable social standing reflected badly upon her own, so she took it upon herself to add "the Third" to Joseph's name (although he remained the first, and only, Joseph Alexander Bently of his lineage). She also insisted her shipping-magnate of a father improve her fiancée's financial prospects before she would even consider taking the Bently name as her own, which would then, understandably, enhance her status in the eyes of anyone remotely important in Charleston.

What she didn't know, was that her father already employed Joseph Bently and held him in highest esteem.

Like many an ambitious young man with empty pockets, Joseph had gone to sea early on, where he managed, in short order, to rise to second in command on a vessel owned by Tedrow Shipping. Joseph made quite an impression on Peter Tedrow, who'd been searching for just such an enterprising young man to marry his fussbudget of a daughter. Left to her own devices, Evangeline hadn't managed to spark the interest of a single, solitary suitor, despite the enticement of sizeable dowry and substantial inheritance earmarked to come her way.

So Father Tedrow made Bently an offer he could scarcely afford to refuse: in exchange for taking Evangeline off his hands, Tedrow would give the man three ships of his own to command (not to mention from which to reap hearty profit) on the condition that he carry the kind of cargo that would enrich Tedrow Shipping most—namely slaves.

Under the guise of merchant sea captain importing and exporting all manner of luxuries, Joseph carried on this clandestine importation for his father-in-law, who wished to keep his own hands clean and reputation above board, during the years the United States government had placed an embargo upon the slave trade.

The fact that Joseph had to put up with Evangeline as part of the deal scarcely deterred him, since he figured to spend but little time at home with her, anyway.

That is, until Father Tedrow unexpectedly dropped dead.

The slave rumor-mill had it that Tedrow met his end in the arms of a young quadroon, whom he'd kept in lavish comfort down in the warehouse district for the previous fifteen years. While the family would never begin to acknowledge such slander, no one else knew the ins and outs of this prosperous and influential man's dirty laundry better than Captain Joseph Alexander Bently—the Third.

In settling Peter Tedrow's estate, Bently handled matters with such tact and discretion, that no one of any standing had cause to suspect the slightest indiscretion, least of all the women of the family.

With Evangeline the only living issue of the Tedrow union, Joseph suddenly found himself at the helm of his father-in-law's shipping empire. Of course that position required his presence in the Charleston home office, which meant he had to spend less time at sea, and more time in the company of his wife.

Unfortunately, rather than bloom with the satisfaction of a husband more available to attend to her whims, Evangeline Louise turned into a cold, wheedling shrew, seldom satisfied with any part of her life—most especially that involving Joseph Alexander Bently, III. Although she'd managed to produce three, lovely daughters before Father Tedrow met his untimely end (and that seemed to be all the patriarch had required of her: progeny to live on after his demise), she refused to have anything more to do with the connubial bed after the birth of her last child, Eralynn Louise.

Evangeline took a handkerchief from the bosom of her light, cotton chemise and mopped at the perspiration running down her nose. "Where is that lazy girl with my Bumbo," she whined. Tutt continued fanning her with his palmetto leaf. "A person could expire completely and no one in this entire household would ever know it!" She shifted on the réclamée, untying the top of her bed jacket to allow the moving air better access to her clammy neckline.

A sudden commotion rising from the front portico caught Evangeline's ear. "What on earth is going on down there?"

86

Six-year-old Tutt stood in silence, still keeping his leaf in constant motion.

"Tutt, go find out who's making all that racket."

The black boy dropped his palmetto leaf and scurried down the stairs, where he found his grandfather greeting an assemblage at the front porch. A lovely lady, who looked remarkably like his mistress, stood at the door with two, identical little girls clinging to her skirts, chattering away to each other like magpies, in a language almost as unintelligible.

"Zeb! How good to see you again!" Amanda said, to the butler, who offered his arm to assist her through the entryway.

"Mizz 'Manda Jane! Dat really you?"

"It's me. In the flesh. And these are my daughters, Lillian and Camellia."

"Yo' Mama be in a stew when she find you home at last."

"How is she, Zeb?"

"She simmerin' in misery, Mizz 'Manda. Long time. Long, long time."

"I need to see her as soon as possible." Amanda turned her attention to the girls, trying to disentangle them from her skirts, while a stocky man holding a baby boy entered the house behind her.

"Michael Harrison," he said, reaching his hand out to Zeb, "and this is Jems."

Not accustomed to having a white man offer to shake hands, Zeb stood in stunned silence. Michael grabbed his hand and gave it a hearty pumping. "Pleased to make your acquaintance. Zeb was it?"

"Yass'suh. Zebeniah be my name." He pulled his hand back.

A dark gal in a bandanna bounded down the hall. "Mandy Jane! You comed home! Tutt, run out back an' fetch Mama Noreen. Go on now," she said, leaning down to give the boy a tender swat. "She gonna jump fo' joy when she see you fin'lly home!" said Ruth.

87

Tutt darted through the hall and out the back door, toward the cookhouse.

"Who was that?" Amanda asked Ruth.

"My boy, Tutt. I birthed him after you left."

Once Michael had released Zeb's hand and stepped into the entry hall, the butler painfully squatted down to reach eye level with the twins. "Look-alikes!" he remarked, gazing from one to the other in amazement. "Pete an' Re-Pete!"

"Where's Mother? Up in her room?" Amanda asked as she removed her bonnet and hung it on a hat hook beside the door. "You may take your bonnets off, girls. Hang them right there, beside mine. Could you take Jems' hat off, Michael? If you'd be so kind," she said with a decided edge to her voice.

Michael chuckled, ignoring her tone. The babe had already undone the ties and managed to extricate himself from his confining headgear in short order. Amanda turned just in time to witness Jems pitch his hat to the floor; she glared at Michael.

"I fetch it 'for it get stomped on." Ruth swooped in to pick it up. "My, my, he be a looker for sure."

"Are you speaking of me, or the baby?" Michael teased Ruth.

Amanda ignored him. "Is Cassie still Mother's personal maid?" she asked. "I need to speak with her."

At that moment Ruth's mother, Noreen, made her way down the back hall toward the front door, with Cassie fast on her heels, carrying the refilled glass of Bumbo for her mistress.

"My 'Manda Jane! Fin'ly she comed *home!*"

"Noreen!" Amanda ran to the bosom that had nurtured her all through childhood, claiming a smothering hug, long overdue.

"Stand back, now. Lemme set my eye on you," Noreen said, holding her by the shoulders and taking a long, hard look at the first child she'd been responsible to care for in the Bently household. "You a grown-up lady now. With comely babes o' yo' own."

"Noreen, meet Camellia, Lillian, and Jems," she said, pointing out each child in turn. "And that's Michael," she dismissed.

"Yo' man?"

"Heaven's no!"

"I'm just here to tote the trunks," Michael added with a testy smirk.

"Michael's my brother-in-law. My husband's brother."

"Our Papa went to heaven," Camellia spoke up.

"We planted him under the apple tree," Lillian added, not to be outdone.

"Oh my. A peck o' trouble a'ready you had?" Noreen patted Amanda in comfort.

"How is Mother doing... *really?*"

Cassie spoke up, "She gonna have my hide, I don't get this 'freshment up to her right quick. I 'most had to squeeze eggs outta them chickens my own self, so's I had enough to mix up this here toddy."

"Let me take it up and surprise her." Amanda reached for the glass. "You girls, stay here with your Uncle, until I find out whether Mother's up to having a troupe of noisy visitors."

"Don't mind me," Michael poked at her. "The girls and I can entertain Jems."

Amanda turned her back on him and headed upstairs, Cassie following right behind.

"Don't know how she gonna take layin' eyes on you, girl."

"Don't trouble yourself over it, Cassie. I'll handle it." *I hope I can*, she thought.

Over half-an-hour had passed since Evangeline sent Cassie to fetch her another drink, and she had herself worked into quite an agitated state at being left alone for so long. When Amanda rounded the corner to appear on the piazza, Evangeline liked to faint dead away at the sight of her estranged daughter standing before her.

"My Lord! *Amanda Jane!* Am I seeing things?"

"It's me, Mother. In the flesh."

"When? Wha… how did you ever get that judge to change his mind?"

"I didn't. I simply took it upon myself to come… regardless of what any judge or barrister says I can or cannot do."

"My, my… it would seem wilderness life has done you some good. Apparently you've grown a backbone."

"Not because I wanted to. I *had* to, to survive."

"Are you going to stand there holding that Bumbo all day?"

"Sorry. Here, Mother."

"I mixed it up real sweet this time, Ma'am," Cassie broke in, "just how you like."

Evangeline took a sip. "Where's the cold cloth for my head?"

"Lordy, Lordy… I go back an' fetch it right quick." Cassie made a hasty departure before Evangeline could scold her about forgetfulness.

"Pull that chair up, Amanda Jane. I have some things I need to say to you."

Before Amanda could sit down, Evangeline heaved a great sigh and held tight to her abdomen as if in great pain.

"What's wrong, Mother? What's this really all about?"

"I'm dying."

"Are you quite sure?"

"Quite." Evangeline pulled a hankie from the pocket of her bed jacket and dabbed at the perspiration on her forehead.

"What are your symptoms, if I may be so bold as to ask?"

"It's really none of your concern. But, if you must know," she lowered her head in a conspiratorial whisper, "I've had feminine bleeding since last winter. Nothing seems to stop it."

"What does Dr. Ballard have to say?"

"Unfortunately, Dr. Ballard has gone on to his reward."

"Well, surely there must be other physicians in this city who can attend you."

"I will *not* let that offensive quack who supposedly replaced Dr. Ballard come anywhere near my person. He is vile."

"Then, how do you know this affliction is fatal?"

"I just *know*. That should be sufficient for everyone."

"What does Father think?"

"I care little what your father thinks, unless it has to do with any provision he makes for Eralynn Louise after his demise."

"What about provision for Irene Margaret? Not to mention my own family?"

"You mean a whole plantation's not enough for you?"

"Hmm. I see where you're going with all this, and I–"

"No, I don't think that you do. When this ridiculous litigation finally comes to its end, you, no doubt, will end up a very wealthy woman. As I'm sure Olympia fully intended all along. She always did hold you closest to her heart... for what reason I scarcely can imagine." She took another sip of her enriched toddy. "Irene Margaret seems to have done quite well in marrying her prosperous sea captain, so I'm sure she'll be adequately provided for. That leaves only Eralynn Louise with no substantial means of support, unless Joseph should finally see fit to rectify that state of affairs."

"Doesn't she have any matrimonial prospects of her own?"

"She's taken with some destitute pirate, who apparently claims undying devotion to her. Nothing I, nor anyone else, can say will dissuade her from throwing away her life on such seedy liaison."

"She's smitten."

"Completely."

"And Father does not approve."

"Hardly."

"So, why won't he make provision for Eralynn, regardless of her romantic notions?"

"He's withholding his support until she decides to take her life more seriously and give up on this disreputable pauper. That's what he *claims*, in any case."

"Blackmail."

"Precisely."

"Which causes you, in turn, to use your own, scheming methods in trying to persuade him otherwise." Amanda looked her mother directly in the eye, and Evangeline's returning gaze did not falter.

"How *dare* you speak to your own mother in such a way!"

"When were you ever a real mother to any of us? Or even *try* to act the part."

"Well, I *never!*" Tears began to gather at the corners of Evangeline's eyes.

"Don't waste your hysterics. They'll no longer work on me."

Evangeline dabbed at her eyes with the hankie. "I refuse to listen to any more insults from a... a fallen woman."

"Have it your way." Amanda rose, then turned to leave.

Evangeline hesitated for just a moment. "No, wait... Please."

Amanda slowly turned back to face her mother.

"We've gotten off on the wrong foot. And I do want to make amends. I *need* to make amends."

Amanda took her seat once more, sitting quietly as she waited for Evangeline to continue.

"I know I didn't raise you girls in the way I probably should have." She lowered her eyes, twisting the hankie in her hand. "But you can't begin to understand the constraints I've had to endure. Living with a man who never loved me. Who cared for nothing but his own ambition."

"Slandering Father won't win you any points with me."

"All right. Forget I even mentioned him. The crux of the matter is this: I know I have but little time left, and I *do* want you to understand something. In my own way, I *have* tried, Amanda Jane. Knowing that may never go very far in appeasing your resentment for my apparent short-comings in raising you girls. But I do need to make peace with you before I die."

"You're convinced this is real, then."

"It *is* real. I'm running out of time."

"Oh, Mother, I don't want our animosity to continue, either. What do you suggest we do about it?"

"Why don't you bring those children up here to meet their grandmother? At least we can try a new beginning with them... in the little time left to us."

"Oh Mother, they're so beautiful! And so smart! They're the joy of my life!"

"What are you waiting for, then?"

* * * * *

The twins clamored up the steps, jabbering their private language the entire two flights. Michael, following behind the girls with Jems, had his hands full trying to contain a wiggling boy, who'd had his fill of being held. He wanted to *go*!

"Now, mind your manners when you meet Grandmother," Amanda reminded the girls, taking a moment to straighten crooked braids and brush crumbs off the pinafores covering their dresses, from the cookies Ruth had given them.

Michael rolled his eyes.

"Do you have a *problem*?" Amanda addressed him, her frustration showing.

"Don't mind me. I'm just here for the entertainment."

"Come along, girls." She ushered them around the corner of the stair landing, out onto the piazza.

"My *grandchildren*!" Evangeline extended her arms toward the girls, motioning for them to come toward her.

"Mother, this is Camellia Jane, and this is Lillian Jane, my twins." The girls stepped tentatively forward, eyes wide with wonder, taking in their surroundings. "Girls, this is Grandmother Bently."

"How old are you two big girls?" Evangeline asked in her kindest tone.

"I'm four years old. She's four, too," Camellia boldly answered, pointing at Lilly.

"How old are you?" Lilly spoke up in return.

"That, my dear children, is a question one never asks of a woman after she's reached her majority."

"What's maj... maj-*jor*... titty?" asked always curious Lillian.

Michael snickered, and Amanda gave him a hard look. She gathered herself and turned to answer her curious daughter. "That's when a person becomes an adult. And your grandmother's been a grown-up for quite some time. Now, why don't you two go sit on that chair next to Grandmother's chaise and show her what you brought for her?"

"I've got to put this boy down," Michael interrupted. "He won't last a bit longer in anyone's arms."

"My son, mother. Jeremiah Junior. He's almost one. And that's Michael. My husband's brother. Put him down on the floor, Michael. He'll be fine with this railing all around." Michael set the boy on his hands and knees, and Jems made a beeline for a pile of leaves on the other side of the veranda.

"You brought your husband along, I presume?"

"My Daddy's dead," Lillian spoke up. "We planted him under the apple tree next to my bruvvers."

Evangeline flashed an uncertain look at her daughter. "It would appear that I have a great deal of catching up to do."

Amanda stood up straight, took a deep breath, and nodded back at her mother in acknowledgement of a life-time's worth of suffering crammed into her six-year exile.

"A big tree busted his back," Camellia interjected. "It kilt Hank's Papa too." She pulled an acorn out of her pocket and handed it to her grandmother. "I brought you a nut from the tree what kilt 'em. Hank gave it to me. After they planted his Papa in the ground."

"My, what an interesting gift. I'll cherish it always." Evangeline carefully laid the acorn on the small table beside her day-bed.

"I brung you a nut, too," Lillian said. "But I painted a face on mine. Hank's new Papa says I'm a art-eest." She handed Evangeline her creation. "I brung a feather from Ol' Jake, too. He was our Daddy's big rooster. But a bobcat ate him."

"My Lord, I think you girls have had quite the adventures in your short lives thus far." Evangeline accepted the offerings with gratitude. "Might I be so bold as to ask you two for hugs?"

The girls flashed a worried look at their mother, and Amanda nodded to reassure them. They slithered down from their chair and moved hesitantly toward Evangeline, who reached forward for them. Both at once, they gave her the biggest hugs she'd ever felt from any child's arms.

Evangeline smiled in wonder. "You're two little angels," she breathed with a contented sigh, "come just in time to give this undeserving grandmother a second chance at learning to love."

* * * * *

Amanda let the girls visit only a short time, before she ushered her entourage back downstairs in order to let her mother rest. She could see the undeniable change in Evangeline's stamina after enduring only a few minutes of the children's interminable chatter. Her mother tired quickly. That, more than anything else convinced Amanda that this affliction was real. Amanda definitely needed to speak with her father. And with her sisters. Where were those two, anyway? They should be the ones here, looking after Mother, keeping the household running smoothly.

"Good thing I ignored that judge and came to see for myself," she told Michael.

"You feel better now you've seen her?" Michael asked. "You sure were on edge there for a while." Amanda and Michael sat on the overstuffed settee back down in the sitting room, while at their feet the girls entertained Jems on the floor.

"I'm sorry. I know I treated you dreadfully this morning," Amanda hung her head and sighed. "I just didn't know what to expect in coming here."

"Don't trouble your head over it. I mostly just ignored you."

"You did. That upset me even more, if you must know."

"Look, we've always been able to talk things through. Sometimes we just have to give each other a little 'wiggle' room, is all," Michael said, patting her hand.

"I have to speak with Noreen. She's the only one who'll really know what's going on around here. I can't see how Mother can keep this entire household running adequately, lying abed. Lord only knows where my sisters are and what it is they do around here. It doesn't appear to be anything at all!"

"Maybe you need to stay on for a while and set things to rights. Why don't I take the girls back to Wallingsford for a spell? That way you can focus on what needs doin' here. I reckon there's plenty of people about to help you with Jems between feedings."

"I don't know. Mother seems so taken with the girls. I've never seen her like that before... with anyone! It's really kind of spooky. I hardly know how to relate to her, she acts so different with them than she ever did with any of us."

"Well, what do you say, we find us some lunch, and then make up our minds? I'm so hungry, my backbone feels like it's rubbing blisters against my belly."

"If we stay here for a meal, I'll need to let Noreen know. Maybe we should go back to the hotel, so we're not a bother. Things here seem disturbed enough, without adding our confusion to this household."

At that moment, Ruth burst into the sitting room, where the Harrisons had made themselves comfortable. "Mizz 'Manda! Mama says y'all don't go runnin' off. She hab vittles fixed up right quick for the whole fambly. She-crab soup! Long time since we taste She-crab soup 'round here. Can't hardly wait!" Ruth bustled about, obviously unable to contain herself.

Amanda gave Michael an inquiring look, and he nodded.

"We'd love to stay," Amanda answered. "Maybe I can go out back and help. I'd love to talk to Noreen about Mother. And I have a ton of questions to ask about her recipes."

"Ress'pees? My lands, don't tell me you been cookin'?"

"Whom did you expect would feed my family?" Amanda asked with a tip of her head. "We have no servants out on the frontier, you know. Our own hands must do all that needs doing."

"My, My. Mizz 'Manda Jane! Doin' she own cookin'. Mama never gonna believe it!"

* * * * *

"What do I do with rice?" Amanda asked Noreen out in the cookhouse—a rustic building behind the main house where no white member of the Bently family had willingly set foot in her lifetime, as far as Amanda Jane could recollect. "I've never even seen rice in Ohio. We have corn or potatoes or biscuits to fill us up. Mostly cornmeal. Whenever we can get real wheat flour, I always make biscuits, though. I think they turn out quite nicely... if I do say so myself."

"Takes a fine hand t' turn out light biscuits. Fo' rice, measure out four handfuls in that big pot," Noreen instructed. "Pour in that jug o' water, an' put it on to bile till it swell up real good. Fo' my taste, I adds a pinch o' salt."

"So the amount of water to rice looks to be about two to one?"

"Yass'um. You gotta good eye."

"Do I stir while it cooks?"

"Just let it be. If you fuss over much, it gets all stuck up. Keep a eye out, now, an' when the water soak all up, pull dat pot off the fire an slap on a lid. Let it fluff up nice."

"Noreen, that She-crab soup you served at lunch was superb! And those crab cakes! I haven't tasted the like since I left home," Amanda complimented. "What's your secret?"

"Crab got to walk in de pot dey own self or dey ain't fit to cook."

"My lands, do you mean you have to cook it alive?"

"T'ain't no good daid!" Noreen said, putting the finishing touches on huckleberry pies she readied for the evening meal.

"Now tell me about shrimp and grits. It's been so long since I had a good plate of shrimp and grits," Amanda sighed.

"Lawsy, girl. You keep axin' an axin' till my head gonna up an' splode!"

"I'm sorry, Noreen. There's just so much I never learned that I really need to know," Amanda explained. "I have a family to feed and care for, and most of the time I feel so inadequate to the task. The good Lord only knows how much Jeremiah had to endure, trying to teach me the most basic of household chores." Amanda brushed a sudden tear from her cheek. "Sorry, sometimes it sneaks up when I least expect it."

"Grief tip-toes up behind when you ain' lookin'."

"I still can hardly believe he's gone. I'll think I hear footsteps on the porch and expect him to walk through the door carrying the morning's milk. Or I'll see his pipe on the mantle and think he's just set it down to go out and check the barn before bed."

"Takes time to ease grief, chil'. Long time."

"I do have a good man helping me now, in Jeremiah's brother," Amanda said. "And I know Michael is eager to marry me. But somehow I can't seem to get past the idea that I'd dishonor my husband's memory by loving someone else."

"Give it time." She set the pies in the reflector before the gigantic hearth. "Jus' remember, life still be fo' the livin'."

"How did you come to be so wise?"

"'Nough tribulation settles a restless spirit... in time." She took her rag to wipe up the pie mess from the butcher block. "Reckon you's had a wagon-load o' trouble a'ready. Else you never find so much sense."

"I have to admit, I've had a good deal to overcome," Amanda said. "I'd have never made it without Jeremiah's devotion."

"Yo sisters sure could use a dose of that sense."

"Where *are* those two? Don't they do anything around here?"

"What they fit to do, don' need doin'," the old cook said, shaking her head.

"Tell me what's really going on, Noreen? Where do those two keep themselves? Has Mother even *seen* a doctor? And where has Father been in all this?" Amanda wrung the dish cloth in her hands. "There appears to be so much out of control in this household, and only you and the other servants to keep it from unraveling completely."

"We does bes' we can."

"Why don't you sit down for a bit," Amanda pulled out a chair at the table, sitting underneath the only window at the far end of the cookshed. "You've got dinner well in hand, you could use a little rest... get off your feet for a spell."

Noreen gave Amanda a strange look, then tentatively lowered her bulk into the proffered chair. Amanda pulled the other chair over and sat at the table beside her.

"Yo' mama have her a conniption, if she know we be out here, a-settin' in dis kitchen."

"What Mother doesn't know won't hurt her," Amanda said, pouring two glasses of tea from the sweating pitcher sitting on the table. "Truth be told, I feel more at ease out here with you than I do over in that big house I grew up in. This looks so much like the cabin Jeremiah built us. It's peaceful. It feels familiar." She sat in silence for a moment, taking a sip of her tea. "Now tell me about Eralynn Louise and why Mother's so concerned about her."

"I got no call to go talkin' 'bout yo' fambly bi'ness."

"Come on, Noreen. You always know exactly what's going on around here. At least give me credit for that much," Amanda said with candor. "Why is Mother so focused on making Father set up an inheritance for Eralynn? Whether he does or does not approve of her current suitor should have little bearing on taking care of Eralynn after they're both gone, should it?"

"Reckon not. But yo' mama, she worried. On account of Eralynn's papa."

"What's Father got to do with this?"

"It what he *ain't* got t' do with it, you should be axin."

"You're talking riddles, Noreen."

"I ain't sayin' what don't need said." The tired cook took a long sip of her tea.

"You're not saying anything, far as I can tell," Amanda said in frustration.

"All I be sayin', is take a good, hard look at you three gals. Study on it. Then we talk some more."

* * * * *

Sixteen-year-old Eralynn Louise breezed through the front door, dropping her hat on the floor beneath the coat hooks.

"I fetch it 'for it gets stomped on," Zebeniah winced, as he stooped to pick up the hat to hang properly, the arthritis in his back completely ignored by the oblivious Eralynn.

"Is Father home yet? I have big news to tell him," she said, flouncing up the steps.

Eralynn's personal servant and guardian, Emmie, trudged in dutifully following her charge, shaking her head and complaining to no one in particular, as she carried her market basket in through the front door. "I swear, one these days that gal be the death o' me." Emmie mumbled more, but Zeb couldn't make out the rest.

"Hard time t'day?"

"That one give me a hard time every day." She plopped the sweetgrass basket down and stretched her neck and shoulders.

Zeb gave her a hard look. "What you thinkin', gal? Comin' in da fron' door like a gran' lady? You jus' axin' for trouble?" He poked his head outside and took a quick look both ways.

"Nobody aroun'. So, who gonna tattle? You?"

"You cain't act so high an' mighty. This here's no reg'lar day. Miss 'Manda done come back home."

"Manny's home! For real? She's here? Where?"

"Out back with my Noreen."

"You funnin' me?"

100

"That's where she be. Helpin' Noreen to cook dinner."

"Mandy? Cookin'? I don' believe it."

"Go see yo' own self, you think I ain' speakin' gospel."

Emmie recovered her basket and headed toward the back door, but before she reached it, Amanda and Noreen met her coming through the hallway by the butler's pantry just outside the dining room, as they came inside carrying initial preparations for the evening's coming dinner.

"My Manny! Dat really you?"

Amanda set her basket of clean, linen napkins on the sideboard and rushed to give Emmie a big hug. "I knew you'd still be here. No one else can look after this family the way you do."

"Stand back, let me set my eye on you," she looked Amanda up and down. "You skinny as a rail. We gotta fatten you up!"

"Don't be silly. I'm fine. I just have a hard time keeping on weight when I'm nursing a baby, is all."

"What? Don' tell me. You nursin' babies yo' own self? No fine lady I know ever do such a thing! We gotta find a wet-nurse right off! You can't be ruinin' yo' shape with dat chore."

"A *chore?* Oh, Emmie, how can you say that? It's no chore giving nutriment to my own child! I wouldn't have it any other way."

"I ain' gonna stand by an' see you ruin yo'se'f. Hear me?"

"Nonsense. *I'm* the only one who nurses Jems! He'll suckle from no stranger," she said, stomping her foot. "Lord willing, I WILL raise *this* boy up to manhood. I simply refuse to lose another son!"

Emmie stood silent, taking in what Amanda had really said. "Oh Manny, I's so sorry. I hab no idee my girl been through such heartache." Emmie gave Amanda a shy pat on the shoulder.

"You don't know the half of it. But I'm the one who's sorry, Emmie. I shouldn't have snapped at you that way. I'm afraid I get overly protective when it comes to my children."

101

"Way a mother should be, you axe me," Emmie said. "You ain' never learn that kind o' motherin' in this house, I can tell you straight out."

"I've had extraordinary teachers in that department," Amanda said, closing her eyes and taking a deep breath. "I'm quite certain I wouldn't even be alive, were it not for some of them."

"Well, where dis boy o' yours? I gots t' get my hands on him!"

"He's napping right now. My brother-in-law took him and the girls back to the hotel to put them down for the afternoon. They should be back here before too long."

"Ho-tel. What you doin' at some *Ho*-tel when we got fine rooms right here?"

Amanda started to explain as Emmie interrupted, "Hold on. Did you say girls? You got girls, too?"

"Twin girls. Camellia and Lillian."

"No! Don' tell me! You nursed twins yo' own se'f too?"

"All right, I won't tell you," Amanda smiled self-contentedly. "But I did."

"Manny, Manny, ain't you jus' full of su'prises!" Emmie shifted the basket to her other arm. "Lemme take these ve-ge-ta-bles out back, and I come he'p set up fo' dinner."

"Take your time. Sit down a bit and have a glass of tea first. You look completely done in." Amanda turned into the pantry to sort through the cupboards. "I can help Noreen set up in here."

The servant gave the back of Amanda's head the strangest look that said, *surely, you can't be serious.* Emmie shot an inquiring glance over to Noreen, who simply shrugged her shoulders and raised her eyebrows in response.

"Yo' Mama know you down here workin' like a servant?" Emmie called to Amanda.

"I need to talk to you about Mother," Amanda poked her head back out of the pantry. "From the look of things around here, there's a lot going on she doesn't know a thing about."

Noreen turned to busy herself counting out china, while Emmie made a hasty exit to the back cookhouse. Just then Eralynn came bounding down the hallway and rounded through the dining room door, nearly knocking Noreen off her feet. "I'm dying of thirst, Noreen. Where's the tea?"

"Have patience. It comin'. It comin." The old African worked hard at regaining her balance without dropping any of the dishes she held. "To an' fro. To an' fro. All I do, tote burdens to an' fro."

"I am not about to wait all day." Eralynn tapped her foot impatiently. "Go fetch that tea pitcher! And hurry up about it."

Amanda called from the butler's pantry, "Did I just hear what I *thought* I heard?"

"Who's said that?" Eralynn turned toward the pantry. "Who's in there?"

Amanda strolled out of the pantry holding a gold, damask tablecloth over her arm. "You *do* remember your big sister, Eralynn, do you not?"

"Amanda? *Amanda Jane!*" she squealed, throwing herself into her sister's arms. "I can't believe it... is it really you? When... where have... how long have you been here?"

"One question at a time! I've been back in Charleston for over a month. But I finally decided no judge was going to keep me from seeing my own family any longer. I arrived home today."

"Did Mother see you yet?"

"Yes, I've seen Mother. And I need some answers from you."

"Before you get all preachy with me, you need to know that Mother's been putting on this frail-health act for months, now."

"It's no act, Eralynn."

"Don't you believe it for a minute."

"Have you insisted she see a doctor? Has *anyone*?"

"Well, no. What's the point? You *know* how she is. Besides, I haven't had the time to deal with her complaints... good grief, what is that huge monstrosity you're wearing?" Eralynn came forward and tentatively fingered the treasured heirloom Amanda constantly wore at her throat.

"Grandmother's brooch. She gave it to me when I left Charleston."

"It looks gaudy on you, don't you think?" Eralynn stepped back to take a better look. "It's way too big for your tiny frame, sister. It'd look much better on someone with the correct bone structure to carry it off."

"Like you, for instance?"

"Well, look at us. I'm twice your size. My bosom would do justice to a regal piece like that. It just makes you look like a little girl playing dress-up!"

"Eralynn Louise, don't you think it's about time you started thinking of someone besides yourself, for a change?"

Dear Lucy,

My dearest friend, how is everyone back in Ohio? We miss you all so much. The girls talk of Hank constantly, wondering how he fares with "Hopper." And how your little Alice grows, I can only imagine. I wonder, how are you managing with no one but Netta Bailey close by for female companionship these past weeks? Please write and tell me all the neighborhood news. I am so overwhelmed with responsibilities here, I long for some lively, home-town gossip!

I hardly know where to begin, there is so much to tell of our adventure. We've been in Charleston and its environs for six weeks now, and still we have no resolution to this legal impasse over Grandmother's estate. I became so irritated with the unfairness of the Judge's restraining order, which has kept me from seeing my family all this time, that I finally took it upon myself to ignore this official nonsense and call upon my Mother's home in spite of threatened "judicial action" that could be taken.

Men and their grandiose ideas! Most of them know so little concerning real matters of life.

You cannot imagine the disorder I found in my old home. Mother abed for months, hardly able to run any kind of organized household herself. My sisters off every day, doing Lord only knows what. Which leaves the servants to their own devices in seeing to all the daily duties. Under the circumstances, they have managed to accomplish a great deal, to the best of their combined abilities, despite the lack of authoritative direction. At least Noreen, the faithful cook, has managed to keep the household fed through these unsettled months of Mother's illness.

But Lord help me, this place looks as though a hurricane has gone through! And if that kind of disorder were not enough to rectify, it appears that Mother's prized silver has been disappearing piece by piece. Not a soul claims to know a thing about it!

So far I have not been able to pry any useful information from either of my self-absorbed sisters. Whenever I can pin one down

105

long enough to ask a question or two, I get nothing but complaints from one about the other. I have managed to get this household running relatively smoothly again, now that I've moved our entourage into residence here when we are not out at Wallingsford. I refuse to stay any longer at that expensive hotel Mr. Hornsby contracted for us. They were charging us $1.50 a night for a single room! Can you imagine such extravagance?

Not only that, our esteemed barrister saw fit to engage two rooms for our continued use, whether we resided in town or not! Two! And each one bigger than my own cabin back home! That does not even include the expense for dining-room meals, at .25cents per person, per meal. Outrageous!

Oh Lucy, to think I used to live in such lavish ignorance! I don't have to tell you how hard we work all year long to earn enough hard money just to pay the yearly land taxes back in Ohio. Our Mr. Hornsby thinks nothing of throwing that much of my money away every week!

Lately I've been making the trip to Wallingsford every other week, to see to my responsibilities there and to learn as much as I can about the running of a plantation, besides trying to stay abreast of all the legal proceedings back here in Charleston. I thought that keeping one household running and its occupants fed in the wilderness was hard work. But now I find myself responsible for the management of two, very LARGE households, as well as overseeing what amounts to a small village of free people of color—not to mention directing the course of a heated legal battle with my own Father, no less!

Oh, Lucy, how I long for the simplicity of frontier living, when compared to the complicated layers of life down here. I have no one I can really talk to about any of this, other than Michael. And he has been more than useless to me of late, since he discovered the Jockey Club here in Charleston, and the Gentlemen's Cock Fighting Society back on Edisto. I never knew he could get so involved in wagering! He says I should relax and enjoy this windfall Grandmother left me. I tell him none of it really is—or ever will be—all mine.

I cannot talk to any of Mother's servants, because they feel I am accusing them when I ask questions about missing items in the household. When I try to broach the subject of the vanishing silver with my sisters, they simply toss their heads and say I'm worrying over trifles.

I have not had opportunity to utter a word about any of this to Father. So far he has managed to give wide berth to his own home, whenever I am in residence, so as not to arouse suspicion in the Judge, I suspect. Besides, it appears he would rather ignore the disarray of his household and remain comfortably ensconced in male luxury at his "Gentlemen's Smoking Club" downtown. He has not attended a single dinner here, since I've taken over household duties at home.

Oh Lucy, what ever happened to people treating one another with straight-forward honesty? All these intrigues and half-truths. I'm sick of it!

Forgive me, my friend, for ranting on so. Here I am, taking advantage of your kindhearted compassion, and truly I did not mean to do so. I must say, the salvation in this adventure has been watching Camellia's and Lillian's reactions to all the differences they discover down here.

These girls have completely won over the hearts of our House People. They follow my former maid, Emmie, around constantly. They're absolutely fascinated with her unusual hair. I don't know if you've ever been around many people of color, Lucy, but you must know how different their hair can be from ours: very tightly curled with a tendency to frizz, unless done up in tiny, intricate braids to keep it all under control, which Emmie does, and which has completely captured the girls' imaginations. They want me to fix their hair "just like Emmie's," which I have no intention of doing, even if I did know how to accomplish it.

So far they have been satisfied wearing bandannas over their hair, as does our servant Ruthie, who is about my own age. She has a six-year-old boy, Tutt, whom the girls pester relentlessly. But he seems to handle it well enough. When he gets too irritated with their chatter, he simply climbs the live-oak tree out back.

The twins have found the summer heat down here most extreme compared to Ohio's climate—so much so, that keeping them fully clothed has become quite the challenge. If Mother should happen to see them running around in nothing but a simple chemise, she threatens to swoon, unless we "get some decent clothes on those wild children at once!" Honestly, I remember how uncomfortable it felt to wear so many layers in this humid clime. Perhaps I'm being overly indulgent, but I see no harm in letting them play dressed (or rather un-dressed) so. Naturally, they wear suitable clothing when we must go out and about in public.

Immediately after our arrival, Mother did insist that I take the children shopping and buy them "proper attire." She was not overly impressed with the jumpers and pinafores I've made for them, although I am rather proud of my new sewing abilities and the articles of clothing I managed to turn out for my children. I did see her point, as what they require down here differs so from the needs we have up north.

What she said exactly, was "those children look like homeless orphans, Amanda Jane! When are you going to dress them properly?" We've all since become newly shod and attired as "befitting our station," in her opinion. Michael just laughed at all our feminine "fru-fra." I note that he did, however, acquire a new suit for himself (one befitting a dandy, in my opinion), as well as new hat, new boots, and a fancy cane to go with it.

Jems, soon to be one year, hardly knows he's anywhere other than where he should be. The house servants spoil him constantly whenever they can get their hands on him. I had been letting Michael see to the baby a good bit, especially during our times in residence at Wallingsford, as I'm always so involved going over account books and planning a multitude of tasks when we're there. That is until our stable master, Alvin, came carrying the boy up to the front porch one afternoon with the story that he had found Jems sitting underneath Winston's unruly stallion.

Can you imagine my consternation over the episode? When I asked Michael how Jems had managed to get away from his care and into the pen with a wild stallion, he just shrugged his shoulders and said, "What's so upsetting about that? I was right there talking to Winston the whole time. It's obvious to me the boy already has a way with horses."

Naturally, you can understand why I have not left Jems solely in Michael's care ever since. Men simply do not realize that it takes constant vigil to keep a crawling babe from escaping their keep and finding danger at every turn. Except for Jeremiah. He was always so good with babies, and now he's missing out completely on his son.

Oh, and here I go again, letting my mind get away with me. I find myself thinking of him more and more, not less and less. Is that natural, Lucy? To long so for what is lost?

Needs must I bring this already lengthy missive to a close. I finally convinced Mother to let a doctor examine her, and he's due to arrive within the hour.

Please give our best to everyone back home, Lucy. And thank Jonathan once again for all his hard work in keeping our homestead looked after while we're away. I can't tell you how dear you all are to us, and how greatly missed. I can, at least, look forward to seeing you all again, though only the Lord knows when that is likely to be!

Yours faithfully,
Amanda Jane

July 15, 1821
Fire Lands, Ohio

Dear Ellie,

I don't know if you are likely to receive this letter before you leave on your sojourn west to hunt for Johannah. But I had to try reaching you with the news that Simeon and Katrina have decided to remain with us until after the birth of their coming child.

I am doing my best to convince them that they had better stay on until spring at least, seeing as a December birth would not be conducive to safe travel with a newborn infant until after the weather breaks.

Zach has decided that with an extra set of strong arms available in Simeon for the next several months, he will begin building us a real house, at long last. You recall when he undertook such a plan previously, we ended up giving said dwelling to Nate and Ivy, as their need far outweighed ours at the time, besides which fact I was in no frame of mind to move, after losing our dear Leesha to influenza as we did that year. Were it not for your steadfast support through that dark time, I know not whether I could have recovered my will to go on without you, Ellie Mae. You know what a difficult time I had.

I must admit my excitement now, to help Zach plan for our new abode. My love says he will make a carbon copy of the house I cherished so back in Connecticutt. Even down to the intricately laid fireplace, which had a real oven included in its design. We need to find an expert mason to take on the project, however, as Zach says such an undertaking is far beyond his basic skills with stone. He much prefers working with wood, and is very good at all types of carpentry.

I intend to send this letter by special courier right away, so it at least has a chance of finding you before you are completely out of reach. Oh, Ellie, please be careful! I worry about you, even with your faithful Zeke MacTavish along, who so gallantly continues to look after you. Travel to the interior is so dangerous, with wild savages and all manner of bandits about. I scarcely allow myself even to think of Christian out there on his own, it distresses me so. But he is young and adventuresome, so much like my own Da. Trying to keep him from going further afield would be akin to pinning an ocean wave to the beach. It cannot be done, nor should it even be attempted.

All a mother can do is kiss such a son goodbye, and then send constant prayers aloft that the good Lord will keep him safe, eventually bringing him home to her once more.

Take care, my friend. Come back to us whole and sound, preferably in time to see our new grandchild make its entrance into this world, if you can manage it.

All my prayers are with you, El. Stay safe!
Faithfully yours, Libby

Chapter 7

Sisters

Mid July, Charleston

The morning after Dr. Anthony Jenkins had made his house call to examine Evangeline Louise Bently, Amanda determined to pin down both her sisters, before they fled the Tradd House for their separate amusements of the day.

Sitting at the dining table spooning grits into Jems, Amanda hailed Irene Margaret as she walked by the dining room door on her way to the foyer, already dressed to go out. "Wait, Irene. I need to talk to you for a moment."

"Can you make this quick, Amanda?" Irene turned back in consternation.

"We need to discuss some things concerning Mother and the running of this household."

"I don't have time for any of this now. I'm running late."

"This cannot wait any longer," she said, motioning her sister to a chair and pouring her a cup of tea. "Besides, you haven't eaten a thing. Make time for some breakfast, at least."

Irene acquiesced, accepting the tea and helping herself to biscuits and marmalade. "I don't see what the big fuss is about all of a sudden," she said, with half a mouthful. "Mother's been putting on this act of hers for months."

"I finally talked Mother into letting that new Dr. Jenkins examine her. He came yesterday afternoon," Amanda explained. She turned to house servant Ruth, waiting to clear things from the table. "I think Jems has had enough, Ruth. Would you take him?" Amanda released the baby from his chair and handed him to the eager girl in her red bandanna.

"I take dat boy any time you say. He a sweet one, he is."

"Thank you, Ruth. And would you go ask Emmie to roust Eralynn out of bed and get her down here? She needs to be in on this conversation, too." Amanda turned back to her own breakfast

112

and took a sip of cold tea. "Irene, you and Eralynn simply have to take more responsibility around here. Running this household is completely beyond Mother's capacity for the foreseeable future."

"It can't be *that* bad... can it?"

"Dr. Jenkins said she's lost a great deal of blood, if she's really been bleeding all these past months as she claims. And Cassie does confirm it, as she's been the one seeing to her care all this time." Amanda set down her empty tea cup. "The doctor said Mother's stamina has been greatly reduced because of the bleeding alone. But that's not her only problem."

"There's more? She really *is* ill?"

"It would appear she has a tumor of some sort growing in her midsection, but she would allow Dr. Jenkins to give her only a superficial examination. She simply refused anything more intrusive."

Eyes wide with disbelief, Irene shook her head. "I hardly know what to say. None of us gave a thought to actually taking her seriously."

"Well, it's past time you all do. Didn't you notice how pale she's become? How weak? Have you spent *any* time with her?"

Irene squirmed in her chair. "Oh, Amanda, how could we believe her... You *know* how she is. Besides, I'm so busy with my... work."

"Work?"

"Uhm... *volunteer* work. I do have other responsibilities you know nothing about."

"I understand you're married now, Irene. But since it appears you're still living here, I'd assumed your husband has no home of his own at the moment for you to attend to. Is that right?"

"He's a sea captain, Amanda Jane," Irene said with an indignant air. "He's ashore so seldom, it seems quite extravagant to maintain a separate abode for my exclusive use. I... ah, *he* thought it more prudent that I remain here, in Father's house... for the immediate future, that is."

"Well, if you intend to continue living on the beneficence of our parents, Irene, it's high time you cut back on your outside obligations and took on more responsibility around here. Mother needs your help... now, more than ever."

Just then Eralynn Louise shuffled into the dining room in her morning wrapper, rubbing sleepy eyes. "Why do *I* have to get out of bed at this ungodly hour?"

"It's past 9 a.m., Eralynn. Jems just had his second breakfast. You should have been up hours ago, helping with the running of this household.

"Oh heavenlydays, Amanda. That's what *servants* are for... they see to everything around here. Why do I need to do *anything*!"

"Eralynn, sit down."

Eralynn plopped unceremoniously into the proffered chair, laying her head across her arms as she leaned forward onto the table. "Wake me when you two are finished."

"Eralynn Louise! *Sit up this instant!*" Amanda shouted.

Not accustomed to hearing anyone shout at her, Eralynn straightened up with sudden, wide-eyed attentiveness.

"Mother needs you *both* to pay more attention to what's going on around this place. Until I got here, no one was planning meals, or daily chores, nor seasonal cleaning schedules. Everything has been disorganized confusion for months! Lord, Himself, only knows where half of Mother's silver has disappeared to," she said, fingering the flatware at her table setting. "Noreen has managed to keep everyone fed, but how she's done it with no direction and so little to work with is totally beyond me. It's high time you two took on the responsibilities Mother can no longer handle."

"She's really all that ill?" Eralynn whispered to Irene.

"She really *is* that ill," Amanda bluntly told her sisters.

"But she *can't* be–"

"She is," Amanda interrupted, taking her napkin from her lap, wiping her mouth, then folding it and putting it back on the table beside her used plate. "You two had better be making some plans about who is going to be responsible for what around here. I cannot remain indefinitely to keep this household running smoothly. I do have responsibilities of my own."

"*Wallingsford*, you mean," Eralynn said with a sneer.

"Yes, Wallingsford. More than 300 people look to me for their continued freedom and security, not to mention seeing to the needs of my own children."

"But I'm already so busy with 'The Society of the Daughters of the Founding Fathers.' We have planning meetings nearly every day for our weekly receptions," Eralynn whined. "My involvement is *vital* in helping to organize the fundraisers for all our charitable causes."

"All your parties and dances, you mean," Irene scoffed. "Ever since your coming out, I don't think you've missed a single social event in this entire city."

"Well, we *have* to make these things *enjoyable*, or no one would want to come bid on our doilies, or bed jackets, or picnic baskets, now, would they?" she countered. "Besides, *Mrs. Harington*," she spat, "you of the big, fancy wedding. What are *you* doing except making money for your own, selfish gain by teaching your stupid 'comportment and harpsichord lessons' all the time," Eralynn taunted back.

"Teaching?"

"Neveryoumind her," Irene interjected to cut off Amanda's query. "We're both just very involved elsewhere. That's all you need to know," she said, placing her napkin atop her butter knife.

"Well, *sisters*, it's high time you both got more involved right here, right now, in your own home! Mother's dying," she said with finality.

Her younger sisters sat, stunned.

"*Dy*-ing?"

"According to Dr. Jenkins, she hasn't got much longer to live."

"Does Father know?"

"Father hasn't been home long enough to change his socks," Amanda groused. "How in the world do you expect him to know *anything* that goes on around here?"

Bess, the middle-aged cleaning and laundry octoroon, wearing her identifying, single, large, hoop earring, came down the hallway with Camellia and Lillian glued to her heels. Bess carried a basket of clean linens balanced against her hip with one hand and held a feather-duster in the other. The twins, each carrying smaller versions of Bess's house-cleaning tool, followed along, wiping at every surface they could reach with their own, miniature dusters. As they passed the doorway, Lillian poked her head inside the dining room.

"We're cleaning!" she announced to Amanda proudly. "Miss Bess says we help good!"

"That's fine, darling. You girls keep helping, and stay out of trouble, you hear?"

"Yes, Mama." Lillian hurried to rejoin the others.

"You're making them *clean*?" Irene exclaimed.

"With the *servants*?" Eralynn shrieked. "Heavenlydays, Amanda! How can you expose a child to such an obnoxious task?"

"It would do both of you a world of good if you'd learn how to handle a few, practical, household chores yourselves."

No one noticed that during the little cleaning-parade interlude, Irene Margaret had slid her napkin-covered, solid-silver, butter knife discreetly into her purple-beaded reticule.

* * * * *

"Is there anything else I can get for you, Mother?" Amanda asked, as she freshened the water glass sitting on Evangeline's bedside table. "Are you hungry for anything? Some fruit, maybe? Or a glass of buttermilk?"

"No thank you, dear. I don't seem to have much of an appetite lately. But you're kind to fuss over me so." Evangeline pulled the sheet to her chin and heaved a great sigh.

"It's no bother. I'm just sorry it took something so serious to put us on more equal footing after all these years. I'm quite concerned, you know. I wish there were something else we could do to help you gain some strength. I hate seeing you like this."

"Has your father been home? Joseph needs to know this infirmity has not really been a sham, on my part. I'd like to talk to him when he comes in. Let him know what that Doctor of yours had to say."

"Dr. Jenkins is not my physician, Mother. But he does seem quite competent. I was impressed with his bed-side manner. I did check on his credentials before he came to call, just as you requested," she said, pushing back the curtains to allow more of a breeze to enter the bedroom.

"I know all that. I'm just tired of feeling so helpless all the time!"

"Maybe a little more eggnog will boost your stamina. Would you like to try that?"

"Oh, all right. But put a little rum in it. That seems to ease my discomfort more than anything else I've discovered."

Amanda pulled the door half way closed as she left her mother's room. Hurrying down the hallway carrying the empty water-pitcher, she paused at Eralynn Louise's bedroom, where the twins lay sprawled across the four-postered, canopy bed, absolutely enthralled as they watched their aunt change from one fancy gown to another in an effort to find the perfect dress to wear to this evening's scheduled "Entertainment."

"What do you think? This one? Or the red one?"

"I like red," Lillian informed her aunt. "It's pretty."

"I like that one, too, my darling. But it might be a bit too extravagant for an outdoor musicale. Should I try the blue one again? It does so much more for my eyes."

"I like blue," Camellia asserted. "Blue's my fav'wit."

"You girls aren't bothering your auntie, are you?" Amanda asked, sticking her head inside Eralynn's door.

117

"Oh, they're fine, Amanda Jane. They're helping me decide."

"Auntie Eralynn gave me this bootiful scarf!" Camellia boasted, waving the blue scarf so her mother could see. "My fav'wit color, Mama!"

"I don't like blue," Lillian fussed. "I like red. But she don't have a red one."

"She doesn't have one, Lillian. Well, don't make pests of yourselves, you hear? I'm going down to get your grandmother something to help her feel better. You be good girls, now."

"Yes, Mama," both girls said at once.

"Are you all right with these two in here, Eralynn?"

"I haven't had this much fun trying on dresses in ages. It's nice to have an audience!"

"I keep my eye on 'em, Mizz Manda," Emmie reassured. "They be jus' fine." Emmie stood at Eralynn's dressing room door, re-hanging the pile of costumes the fickle girl had already tried and rejected in her ongoing search for the perfect gown.

Amanda shook her head as she proceeded down the stairs, through the house, and out the back door toward the cookhouse. The compound laid out behind the Bently home on Tradd Street served to sustain the entire household and provide living quarters for all the family's servants. Kitchen gardens filled the area between the main residence and the cookhouse, where Noreen prepared the family's meals; she, her husband Zebeniah, their daughter Ruth and Ruth's small son Tutt, all lived in the two rooms above.

Beside that building a small carriage house contained the Bently's two, matched geldings, a family coach, and a small cart, which served for most of the household errands. Emmie and her son Pudge, the family's coachman, lived in the loft above. Pudge also cared for the horses and looked after the gardens. He had a young wife living two streets over, whom he managed to see on the rare occasions Joseph would issue a pass, allowing him to be out alone after the normal curfew for coloreds. Any Negro caught without a pass had to answer to the patrollers. For with the Negro

118

population of Charleston more than triple that of the whites, a constant fear of "rebellion" couldn't help but trouble the peaceful slumber of every, watchful slave-owner.

Bess had her own space in the tiny washhouse, situated behind the cookhouse and adjacent to the well, where she did all the household's laundry and kept mostly to herself. The other servants maintained their distance, considering her a "conjurer" and wielder of unknown power. The single, hoop earring she always wore reinforced her pirate-like appearance to the other servants. The fact that she had mixed blood and had come into the family's service through Joseph, only intensified her exclusion from the close-knit circle of the others, who'd all served Evangeline's family for years.

Most Charlestonians referred to "their people" as servants, rather than slaves, even though their status in the household did not improve a whit by that designation.

Amanda entered Noreen's kitchen and peeked into the soup pot bubbling over the hearth. "Mmmm. Smells good."

"Be done direc'ly. Put some good herbs in. Help perk up Mizz 'Vangeline, if she take a bit."

"She asked for some more eggnog with a portion of rum. I can mix that up," Amanda volunteered.

"Where Cassie at? *She* the one ought be seein' to Mizz Vangeline. Not you."

"I gave her the afternoon off. I told her to go out and enjoy this lovely day."

"You *what?*"

"Mother's been running her ragged, with her complaints and demands all these months. Cassie needed a break."

"Break? What you talkin' *break*? No slave get time off, gal. You daft? That one already got it too soft, livin' in the big house like some gran' lady."

"Cassie's at Mother's beck and call twenty-four hours a day. She has to step and fetch at her every whim. The least I can do is give her a little time to herself when I don't have other pressing matters pulling at me."

"No doubt 'bout it, gal. You done gone 'roun' da bend."

"Oh, Noreen. I wish I could give every one of you your freedom. Surely you know that by now. But with Father in control here, my hands are tied."

"I know, Manny. You a good girl. Always was." Noreen brushed the flour off her hands and laid a cloth over the lump of bread dough she'd been kneading. "Dat can rest a while."

"You should see my girls. They're up in Eralynn's room watching their aunt model dresses in front of the looking glass. It's so adorable," Amanda chatted as she stirred milk and eggs and spices together.

"There's one needs a useful task. Fancy dresses an' parties an' some-such. Humph!" Noreen muttered more under her breath.

"I've been studying her," Amanda commented to Noreen. "Eralynn. Now that she's grown, she doesn't look a bit like Irene or me, does she. Doesn't resemble our parents, either. That's what you were hinting at before, wasn't it."

"Could be."

"She had a different father, didn't she."

"Could be."

"Noreen. You know, don't you."

"Could be."

"You won't tell me?" Amanda stomped her foot in frustration.

"Can't tell you, Manny."

"Can't?"

"If I say one word, he take away my Ruth."

Amanda paled. "Oh, Noreen. I'm so sorry. I had no idea."

"I know," Noreen gave Amanda's shoulder a loving pat. "It outta yo' hands, Manny. You jus' keep 'em eyes open, now, hear?"

* * * * *

120

Irene Margaret gathered together all her books and papers, being careful to see that she left her room in perfect order. She wanted nothing to appear out of place. Amanda Jane had already gotten far too inquisitive around here. She wasn't about to leave any evidence lying about that would give her sister cause to question anything further about her life. Folding the harpsichord music in half, she placed it inside the *Lady's Companion Magazine*, which she planned to carry out the door when she left to teach her lessons later this morning.

Irene Margaret lived a lie, and she had no one to blame for it but herself.

She'd given up Cheney May, her own personal servant, three months earlier to keep her uptown landlord from throwing her out of the rented room in which she taught her lessons. She didn't really consider it a "sale" of human chattel, as such—more of an "exchange" on her part. Father had given her Cheney Mae when Irene celebrated her "coming out." Now she was trading that maid to her landlord as security for a room on Clifford Alley, just off Meeting Street, south of the Market, for the next three years.

Irene gave nary a thought to any of the repercussions for Cheney May in the transaction, as now Irene had a secure place to instruct young girls from middle-class families, aspiring to raise their prospects by snagging eligible bachelors from second or third or fourth sons of the landed gentry.

It was a common practice among working-class Charlestonians to have their young women learn comportment, needlework, dancing, and the like, in order to engage the attentions of eligible young men. A well-placed marriage could raise a girl of questionable status into a much higher echelon of society—and along with her, naturally, her entire family. Simply by learning the correct way to carry oneself and amuse said bachelors with intelligent exchange, any girl could have a chance in catching a suitable husband, at least so said the advertisements meant to lure them in.

Having already failed grandly in the making of her own match, Irene was doing her level best to keep body and soul together, without letting anyone in her family know the severe financial straits in which she now found herself. The union to her "rich sea captain" of a husband had turned into bitter disappointment, with the quiet annulment he'd insisted upon just three weeks after their nuptials, before he "shipped back out to sea."

Irene Margaret possessed far too much pride to confide her dire circumstances to anyone, especially after the grandiose spectacle of her own extravagant wedding a short five months before, at the height of Charleston's social season. She was doing her level best to "keep up appearances" by flaunting the newest fashions, and making sure she attended the most notable of society gatherings, where she talked incessantly about her absent, sea-captain husband, who, she said, kept sending her lavish gifts from exotic ports of call.

"There, that should satisfy any nosey sisters poking about," Irene mumbled to herself, straightening the folder in her arm and pulling the bedroom door shut. She hurried down the stairs and into the vestibule, looking back to be sure no one noticed her hasty departure.

At the same time Amanda Jane sat in the dining room, paging through the newspaper left sitting by her father's place at the table. Though he still had not made an appearance at his own home since Amanda arrived, the servants always placed his *South Charleston Gazette* beside the fork at his table setting, where he expected to find it every morning.

Casually looking through the editorials and advertisements, a small article on education for women caught Amanda Jane's eye:

Women's Education A Matter of Private Enterprise.

"Education of women should always be relative to men, to please, be useful to us, to make us love and esteem them, to educate us when young and take care of us when grown up. To advise, console, to render our lives easy and agreeable, these are the duties of women at all times," so says Rousseau as he recounts the merits of educating young women to take their appropriate places in a man's society...

Amanda could hardly believe what she had just read.

"Talk about self-centered conceit! That mindset has been shaping all of us far too long," she fussed to no one in particular, "though I'm sure few in these parts would find any fault with that outlook whatsoever."

"You talkin' t' me, Manny?" Ruth asked, as she cleared the table of used breakfast dishes.

"Oh, don't mind my blather, Ruth. I'm just a bit astonished by what I'm reading. Written by some man who obviously thinks that males are meant to dominate the world."

"They all think that."

"Well, stating it in a newspaper article where anyone can read such constraining ideas does nothing but perpetuate this kind of drivel," Amanda declared. Her eyes swept past the dubious article to private advertisements placed strategically around it.

Domestic Sciences Taught: preserving, pickling, pastry, wine-making, needlework of every kind. Justina T. Bradford. Kindly write to Box 27A for schedules and teaching credentials.

She glanced further down the page, where she stopped dead at an advertisement that jumped off the page as she read it.

Learn deportment and cultivate the art of conversation to be pleasing. Also teaching harpsichord, lute and elementary dancing. I. M. Harrington, 314-B Clifford Alley, Charleston.

"You don't suppose... I.M. That couldn't be Irene Margaret, could it? Teaching *deportment*, of all things." Amanda pushed the paper aside. "I need to get to the bottom of this."

August 18, 18 and 21
Port of Marietta

Dear Lib,

Well friend, me and Zeke made it far as Marietta afore we run into trouble.

Name of Harvey Thompson it was.

Shouldda knowed that sorry excuse for a man would turn back up. You recall Zeke told me he spied the turncoat at a tavern in these environs last time he come through this a-way. Figured the scoundrel would be long gone afore Zeke and me hit the Ohio River on this trip. But we did not have such good luck.

Come to find out Harvey was waiting for Zeke to show back up so he could pry news out of him about where I might be keeping myself. Still had it in his mind to take revenge for the death of his Theodore. Accident though it was. Even the judge agreed on that point. But not Harvey.

That brute had took up with a bad crowd in these parts. Claimed they was keeping mercantile men safe from river bandits. All they really did was bully shop keepers for money. If they did not pay up it was Harvey they needed protecting from.

Can not believe I once thought I loved that man. He turned into such a lout.

We was just coming off Zeke's scow at Marietta dock when Harvey spied us. Took him no more than a minute to see it was me standin there with Zeke. He made a run at Zeke and pushed him right into the drink. Then he grabbed me and handed me off to one of his goons.

That Scot come up fighting mad. Pulled him self back up on that dock and took Harvey on right there. You know how big Harvey is. At least two times the size of Zeke. Now Zeke may be short. But he is built like a bull. Arms size of tree trunks with all that river paddlin he does.

Harvey had four other brutes with him. Took two of em to hold on to me cuz I put up such a fuss. The other two joined Harvey to take down Zeke.

Now Lib I have to say it was a terrible sight to behold. Them critters beating on Zeke like there was no tomorrow. Zeke put up a good fight. Managed to push the smaller one into the water right off. Current washed that one down river a ways, on account of he could not swim. That left Harvey and one other hoodlum a-beating on Zeke.

Harvey never was one to fight fair. Pulled a knife on Zeke first thing. Other fella did too. Zeke had nothing to fight with xcept his wits. Saw a rope coiled there on the dock and threw it at the smaller feller. It tripped him up long enough for Zeke to lunge at Harvey's legs. Took him down hard. But as Harvey fell, he pushed that knife into the back of Zeke's shoulder.

Zeke managed to twist away and regain his feet afore Harvey did. Other fella was still trying to untwist his legs and arms from all that rope. Zeke grabbed for the anchor chain with his good arm and gave it a hard swing right at Harvey's head. Made a loud crack when he landed the blow.

Knocked the scoundrel out cold.

Zeke picked that anchor back up and started toward the two what was holding on to me. They took one look at Harvey. Another look at Zeke a-swingin that anchor. Then they dropped me to the wharf and high-tailed it outta there.

Marietta Sheriff showed up by that time with two of his Deputies. The Deputies took the rope tangled fella off to the whoosgow, along with the other fella they fished out of the drink. Sheriff tried to wake Harvey up with a bucket of water in his face. But he never did come to. Turns out that anchor punched a hole in back of Harvey's scull. Sent him right into the great beyond.

I can tell you true I do not know how that man could ever knock at them Pearly Gates asking to be let in. No doubt he has the gall. I would guess more likely he has gone down to hotter environs.

Got to say I was right proud of Zeke. But the long and short of it is he got his shoulder hurt real bad. So bad that the doc in these parts says he will never be able to paddle a boat again.

The doc told Zeke he should get him a paddle wheeler. Boy oh boy! You shouldda heard that Scot swear up a blue streak! Could not understand a word of his Scots talk. But I know how much Zeke hates them churning wonders. Claims they are not safe for ary a soul with a lick of sense.

Zeke says no knife stick can keep him off the river. He is pigheaded about saying he <u>will</u> paddle again. Once he heals up good. But by the look of that mess he calls a shoulder I do not see how he ever will, Lib. I am doing the best I can to nurse that crazy Scot back to health. But he is a trial. Never did know a man who was not a big baby when it come to illness or hurt.

So Lib, here we sit. Still in Marietta. We will not go any further on this trip to seek out word of my Johannah. Guess we will have to leave that task to your Christian. Pray he finds trace of where my girl has got to.

We will stay here till Zeke heals up enough to travel back up stream. Needs be I can paddle while he steers this tub with his good arm. But it will be considerable time till he can manage even that.

I worry for him, Lib. He is such a proud man. But he is a good man. And I feel my heart taking a giant leap. Lord help me. Here I go getting myself tangled up with another male critter!

Do not try to send any letters, Lib. I do not know how long we will stay round about these parts. Likely we would be gone by the time your post could find us here. Maybe in another month or so we can start back north toward Riverstop. Only time will tell.

Hope youens are all doing well up in them Fire Lands. Give those children of ours a big hug for me, Lib. Tell Katrina we can breathe easy now. No more looking over our shoulders for trouble to show up in the form of Harvey Thompson.

Thank the Lord! And pass the bandages!
Your friend, grateful to be alive.
Thanks to Zeke the river runner.
Ellie Mae MacTavish

Yep. We went an done it, Lib. Can hardly believe it my own self! And after I swore no more men's last names!

P.S. After we hitched up I come to find out Zeke is right well off to boot! Has him self a hearty stash put by in Muskingum bank here in Marietta. Now after so many years of scratching and scraping to make ends meet I find myself a wealthy woman! Boy. Just leave it to a Scotsman. Who knew?

Dear Amanda,

I have received the letter you wrote before leaving your ship the middle of May. From the look of it, that letter had an adventuresome journey getting here. It took 10 weeks to reach us in Justice from its starting point in Virginia. I did show the postmark to Netta Bailey, who proceeded to talk about her former life in that state with her Grandmother Rosanna. Her own Rosanna (now age five) seems a very introspective child. She says so little, it's hard to judge the personality unfolding in that one. Of course, she has little chance to get a word in edgewise when Netta gets wound up.

My own Hank at four and Netta's Rachael, also four, play well together when we have cause to call at the Bailey's. Rachael still merits Luther's nickname for her: The Screamer. Hank manages to tolerate her well enough. As for Rebecca, at nine months, it is entirely too early to tell what kind of personality shall develop in her. She and my Alice (now eight months) sit and play upon a blanket, entertaining one another to the exclusion of all else in their expanding worlds.

I feel it is quite necessary to expose the children to playmates of a like age whenever we can, for their own social outlet and growth, if nothing else. We do become tired of our own company for too long at a stretch. So we make the trip across the woods to Netta's on occasion. With her cousin Luella still in residence, we manage to have an enjoyable visit. Netta does, after all, stay abreast of happenings in the township, so catching up on neighborhood gossip is no difficulty with her in the community. No doubt it gives her something outside herself to focus upon, while Luther makes his sojourns far afield, leaving her home alone so much of the time.

As for the "real news" in these parts, you may be interested to know that we have a mystery going on in the neighboring settlement of Petersburg to the West of us. Remember the cooper and his wife who moved in down there a few years back?

The Simpsons? Their youngest son, the one they call "Snooks," has gone missing. Ever since the birth of their late-in-life surprise little girl, Ella Marie, the boy (now eight), has taken to exploring the woods around their home for hours at a time. Always he would reappear in time for supper.

But one day he failed to return at all. Nor did he come back by the following morning. When parents questioned their other children to see if he had imparted any information to anyone, as to the places he frequented, none of the older siblings could tell their parents a thing, except to say that, "he liked to play wild Indian with his invisible friend."

Al, the boy's father, immediately raised a search party from among the neighbors, who combed the area for the next two days. They turned up not a single clue as to the boy's where-abouts. Even Jonathan, who knows these woods inside and out, came up empty handed. Unfortunately Luther Bailey was deep in the forest at the time, otherwise I'm sure the boy would have been found immediately.

The curious coincidence in all this is that every evening, since the neighbors gave up their search for Snooks, along about suppertime, Rebecca finds a skinned squirrel hanging on her clothes line. Her recipe for squirrel fricassee happens to be little Snooks' favorite meal. So you can imagine Rebecca's consternation with the appearance of these squirrels every night, but no trace of her boy.

She has taken to leaving a pot of squirrel fricassee at the clothes post every evening; by morning she always finds the pot empty. If anyone should wait up to try to apprehend Snooks (for all assume it has been he leaving the squirrels), he will never emerge from the forest to claim the stew. So Rebecca has given up trying to pin down the boy. She simply leaves the food, calling out that she hopes when the weather turns cold, he'll at least decide to come in by the fire to keep himself warm.

Snooks, her little wild Indian.

The only other intelligence I have to impart has to do with Jonathan's nephew, Jason, and his family. Jason, you recall, is

Ellie Mae's oldest boy, who now has four children of his own, ages one, two, three, and nearly six. Mary Sue no doubt keeps plenty busy with so many little ones to look after.

Jason's old horse, RazorBack, has been with the family since before Ellie Mae and her first husband came out from Pennsylvania back in '03. That must make the horse in excess of 20 years old by now. Quite ancient for the kind of hard-working animal used in conquering this wilderness. Though Jason has a younger animal for break-out plowing, pulling trees, and the more strenuous of tasks required out here, he still uses RazorBack to pull an occasional cart or haul a load of hay. The children also love to ride the old beast, in spite of its rather unappealing name. They say well-padded the animal still sits comfortably enough.

Jonathan paid his nephew a visit two weeks ago Tuesday, to check on the family, (Jonathan is so good about that kind of thing, always looking out for "his own"); he came home with a sad, but most amusing tale.

It seems that Jason had old RazorBack hooked to a hay wagon, pulling a freshly dried load of hay to the barn. Six-year-old Josie happened to be riding on the back of the old horse at the time. Jason says she enjoys spending time with him, as does he enjoy her company while attending to his farm chores. At least it helps keep one child out from underfoot for Mary Sue, with three other small toddlers in her care.

Evidently on the way out of the hay field, the horse stepped in a hidden groundhog hole and went down hard, breaking a front leg as it fell. Josie, on his back at the time, also fell off, with the horse landing on top of her leg, breaking it, as well. Naturally, Jason had his hands full with a screaming child and a screaming horse. He managed to calm both child and beast, then ran to the house to fetch his rifle.

You know the necessary outcome for the horse, long-time family friend, though he be. Jason shot old RazorBack to put him out of his misery. Even though Jason had calmly explained the necessity for this unpleasant task to Josie, after having freed her from beneath the suffering animal, she sat there watching, as her father sent the horse to his eternal reward. Then, calm as you please she looked up at him and asked, "You gonna have to shoot me too?"

Jason says even in the midst of a crisis, children can manage to bring a kernel of comic relief—most especially Josie, as she is becoming known for her clever quips.

Having turned up just after Jason dispatched the horse, Jonathan helped Mary Sue to set and splint Josie's leg. Once again that man of mine coming to the aid of those in distress. How he always seems to know when others need his help, I cannot fathom to understand. I feel so fortunate to claim him as my own and be entrusted to his care for the rest of this earth journey.

Josie is recovering well from her accident. She will heal quickly, as young children usually do. Meanwhile, she gimps along behind her daddy on home-made crutches that Jason fashioned from forked, hickory branches. He says very little can keep his adventuresome girl down for long.

That about brings a close to my offerings of journalistic commentary from our little community and its surrounds. Jonathan and I are doing well, as are the children—both growing like weeds. Tell the twins that Hopper is growing, too. And that she has caught her first mouse. Just yesterday Hank came in the house and pulled it out of his pocket to show me.

Please take care of yourself, Amanda. I can only guess at the amount of responsibility you have on your plate right now. Just be sure to stay focused on what is really important in life. After all you have been through already, I know that you can do no other.

As for your description of fresh seafood and real coffee, you've made my mouth water! Being from the East myself, I also long for the kind of culinary selections we had available to us there, which so seldom find their way West of the Alleghenies. I look forward more to seeing you again soon, my friend, than I do to any gustatory treat.

Your forever friend, Lucy Johansen

Chapter 8

Mother's Surprise
Late August, Charleston

Tuesday, August 28th dawned hot, cloudy and oppressive. Even with the windows open their widest, very little breeze stirred its way into the house on Tradd Street. Late summer had brought its most unpleasant conditions to Charleston.

Amanda remained in her parents' home overseeing her mother's care. She worried, watching her decline as she got progressively weaker. She also began to see that the children's normal boisterous activity was becoming harder and harder for her mother to endure. So the previous week, Amanda had sent Michael and the girls back to Wallingsford on Edisto, where they, at least, could enjoy the sea breezes on that island in this hot season.

She instructed Michael to take the girls to Grandmother's summer house at "The Bay" in Edingsville, on the southeastern side of the island where planters' families spent the hottest days of summer along the beach. The girls could play in the ocean surf to stay cool, and perhaps even make some friends among the other youngsters accompanying their families to Edingsville's beach settlement. Amanda longed to join them herself, but she knew her mother needed her in Charleston.

Tutt, Ruth's six-year-old boy, stoically stood waving his palmetto fan over Evangeline Louise, in an effort to keep her comfortable. But nothing anyone did seemed to ease her distress on this day. She'd awakened long before dawn with a "funny" pain. Whenever Amanda questioned her as to its strength and location, Evangeline would only say, "I just hurt all over."

Her usual medicinal toddy did little to assuage her distress, nor did a second or third before noon. As the day wore on and the intensity of Evangeline's pain increased, Tutt was relieved of his fan duty, and Cassie, Amanda, and Ruth came and went from her bedroom with directions to fetch this, get rid of that, and "bring me something to make this agony go away!"

On yet another trip back upstairs with fresh water, Amanda met Cassie in the upper hall carrying a pan full of bloody rags, on her way back down.

"Mizz 'Manda, we needs more packin' rags. She bleedin' bad. Baddest I seen yet."

"I think it's time to send for Dr. Jenkins. Whether she wants us to, or not."

"Mebbe I get Bess t' make us up a conjure bag?"

"She needs more than Gullah charms, right now, Cassie. She needs medical attention," said Amanda. "Ruth, go tell Pudge to take the cart over and fetch Dr. Jenkins right away," she told the young woman in the bandanna, just now topping the steps with yet another toddy, as per Evangeline's latest request. "Here, I'll take that in to Mother. You hustle back down and find Pudge. Tell him we need the doctor here as soon as possible."

"I tell 'im."

"After you've sent Pudge on his way, you'd better go find Father, too," Amanda called to Ruth hurrying back down the stairs. "Tell him I need him to come home immediately."

"Want I should tell 'im Mizz 'Vangeline in dreadful misery?" she called back up.

"Don't say a word about Mother. Just tell him *I* need him here. *Now.* Understand?"

"Yass'um. I's goin'. I fetch 'im right home."

Amanda and Cassie continued with the bustle of activity, in their combined effort to ease Evangeline's distress. But after countless trips up and down stairs, back and forth to the kitchen for supplies, and in and out with waste buckets to dump in the backhouse and more bloody rags to drop at the washhouse, both women felt ready to collapse themselves, by the time Pudge returned with the esteemed, young doctor.

In the heat of the day, Dr. Jenkins omitted the traditional, long, black, frock-coat which proclaimed his exalted station as a physician, but the gold-topped cane and top hat remained with

133

him as undeniable symbols of his status. He handed said cane and top hat to Zebeniah when he entered the house on Tradd Street.

"Good day to ya, suh. Mizz 'Manda gon' be mighty glad you's come. Mighty glad. Mizz Bently in a bad, bad way."

"I shall best determine that for myself."

"Lemme take yo honor on up–"

"There's no need to subject those arthritic legs of yours to all those steps. I can see myself up. I remember the way."

"Yass'suh."

With medicinal bag in hand, the doctor rounded the staircase to ascend and met Amanda Jane on her way back down.

"Oh, Dr. Jenkins, I'm so glad you're here. We're at our wits' end around here trying to help mother. She's experiencing terrible pain today."

"Can you tell me anything more than 'terrible pain' Miss Amanda?"

"She won't let anyone touch her, except Cassie, of course. And she won't say where the pain is located nor exactly how it feels. She only says, 'I hurt all over,'" Amanda related. "The pain does seem to come and go, as she has a lull in her distress from time to time. But her bleeding has increased alarmingly."

"What you describe sounds almost to me like labor pains."

"Labor? How could she possibly be in labor? My mother's far past childbearing age, doctor."

"Since I did not have opportunity to examine her fully when I last called, I could only give an 'educated hypothesis' as to her true condition. Of course, a tumor of 'some sort' became the only possible conclusion I could draw, based solely upon what I could observe and what she, herself, divulged, you understand. But the situation could be entirely different altogether."

"Is there anything you can do to ease her pain?"

"I'd better take a closer look to see what I can determine. Perhaps her tumor has ruptured. If that's the case, we have little chance of staunching the flow without resorting to surgical means. Such a course of action brings its own risks, of course."

"I've called father home. We'll need his authority if you have to take extreme measures."

"Naturally."

"Come up this way," Amanda directed, ushering Dr. Jenkins past her and on, up the stairway.

He brushed her arm on the way by, "I'll need hot water and clean bandages..." he said, disappearing around the next landing.

Amanda continued on her way to the kitchen to ask Noreen for a pot of boiling water. Then she headed over to the washhouse to obtain more clean linens from Bess.

"Mizz 'Vangeline any better?" asked Bess. "I mix up special herbs fo' easin' de pain," she said, handing Amanda a little pouch.

"Thank you, Bess. I appreciate your concern. But Dr. Jenkins just arrived. I'm sure he'll see to whatever she needs."

"Don' you go trustin' no eddycate doctor, Mizz 'Manda. He cut your mama. Make her bleed. No good. No good at-all."

"Don't you worry your head over it, Bess. He'll get Mother turned around. I'm sure of it," Amanda said, accepting the basket of linens and heading back toward the house.

But Amanda wasn't sure. She had a strong foreboding this day would bring comfort to no one. Least of all, her mother. By the time she arrived back at Evangeline's bedroom door with hot water and linens in hand, Cassie was just exiting with another pan full of bloodied refuse.

"She in bad way, Manny. Bad, bad way."

Amanda pushed open the door, and Dr. Jenkins commanded her to put the hot water on the bedside table and hand the linens to Emmie, also pressed into service and now standing at his elbow. "Hold that light higher, woman," he instructed, "and hand me another towel. I need to mop more of this up so I can get a better look at what's going on."

Emmie did as instructed.

"Is there anything I can do, Doctor?" Amanda asked. Not hearing the least bit of protest from her mother alarmed Amanda even more than the spectacle unfolding at the end of the bed.

"Go wait for your father. I don't want you in here right now. Get that other black gal back here right away."

"Only if you're certain that I can't–"

"You shouldn't be seeing any of this."

"Doctor, I've already seen much more than you realize–"

"Go! *Now!*"

Amanda turned in a huff and walked into the hall, slamming the door behind her as she went.

Ruth met her at the bottom of the stairs. "Yo' papa say he come, soon's he finish up bui'ness with dat Factor man."

"I hope he gets here in time. From the look of things in there, I don't think Mother has much life left in her."

"She dat bad, Manny?"

Amanda caught her breath as a sob escaped her firm control. "Oh, Ruthie, I'm so worried!"

* * * * *

About three-quarters of an hour later, Joseph Alexander Bently the third, strode nonchalantly through the front door of the home he had not entered in the last month. "Zeb," he acknowledged the butler, handing him his hat.

"We'come home, Suh."

"I take it the women have the household in an uproar again, as usual?"

"Mizz 'Manda turrible upset, Suh. Doctor be upstairs with Mizz 'Vangeline now."

"Well, I guess I'd better deal with her once and for all, then. I had hoped to forestall any kind of confrontation, but I can see Amanda has managed to bring this entire situation to a head."

"Don' know what you goin' on fo' 'bout Mizz Manda, Suh. Mizz Vangeline up there bleedin' her life out!"

"She's what?"

"Ruthie say she close to passin' over."

"But I thought this whole thing was nothing but a huge sham! Another one of Evangeline's schemes to manipulate situations in which she has no right to interfere."

Having heard her father's voice in the vestibule, Amanda hurried in from the butler's pantry, where she'd been polishing her mother's silver, just to have something useful to do, to keep herself busy. She could no more sit and do nothing than her own Lillian could remain still for longer than two minutes at a time.

"Oh, Father. I'm so glad you got here. I haven't heard a thing out of Dr. Jenkins, and he's been up there with her for most of an hour, now. I just hope—"

"She's really dying? Evangeline?"

"I don't *know*! The doctor hasn't told us a thing since he went into her room. Just sends Emmie out for more water and more linens, and—"

"Amanda Jane, what's really going *on* around here? No beating about the bush."

"Mother's lost a great deal of blood. Dr. Jenkins thought it might be a ruptured tumor."

"Then she *hasn't* been pretending all this time?"

"No, Father. She hasn't."

"Why didn't she send for me?"

"She didn't think you'd believe her."

"Well, she's probably right on that account. The only reason I came now, was because the message said you needed me," he said, giving Amanda's shoulder a squeeze. "When did all this business begin?"

"Cassie says she started bleeding more than seven months ago. But it's only been the past several weeks that things have gotten so much worse."

"Good Lord!" He threw down the newspaper he carried and stomped up the stairs. Amanda hurried behind, working double-time to keep up with his long strides.

When they reached the second-floor landing, a sniffling Emmie was just emerging from Evangeline's bedroom. Through the open door they could see Dr. Jenkins standing beside the bed, wiping his hands on a bloody towel. He handed the towel to Cassie, who added it to the basin she held, then headed out the door herself, quite somber but uttering not a word.

"I'm sorry, Mr. Bently," the doctor said, following the servant out into the hall and discretely pulling the door shut behind himself. "I tried everything I could to save your wife and baby, but too many things went wrong all at once."

"Baby?"

"Yes, sir. Evidently she had a very abnormal pregnancy. Bled almost the entire nine months, which led her to believe she was growing a tumor of some sort, rather than a fetus. It also left her in a terribly weakened condition. By the end, she had absolutely no energy remaining to bring forth that unfortunate babe. I'm afraid I had to make some command decisions without your approval, in order to take swift action to try and save your wife, Mr. Bently. Seeing as the babe was so grossly deformed I thought it best to–"

"Baby."

"Yes, sir. You realize, of course, that I can't let you in there at the moment, she's in such a terrible state. It'll be much more fit for saying your good-byes, once the servants have her cleaned up and more presentable... disposed of the remaining detritus."

Joseph said not another word, but turned on his heel and headed back downstairs. He stomped to the vestibule, grabbed his hat from Zeb, and rushed out the front door, leaving Amanda and Dr. Jenkins in stunned silence on the second-floor landing.

* * * * *

That evening, out behind the Tradd House, the Negros stood solemnly beside a tiny grave at the edge of the herb garden, and

138

to the side of the washhouse. Since her father had not returned, Amanda made the decision to bury the pieces that remained of the unlucky babe here at home, away from the prying eyes of Charleston's gossipmongers. With Dr. Jenkins' consent, no documentation of a birth was ever recorded. The doctor's official record book stated that they buried "human refuse following a surgical procedure undertaken to save the life of Mrs. Joseph Alexander Bently, III, which ultimately failed to accomplish its intended purpose in the end."

"Po' unlucky babe," Cassie said, swaying to a silent melody only she could hear. Emmie blew her nose, and Ruth and Noreen held one another in a close embrace with Tutt between them, as Zeb, standing behind, rested his massive hands upon his family's shoulders in silent comfort.

Bess shook her head in disgust. "Done tol' our Manny that man be a butcher. Hands dat bring so much blood from de Debil. No good. No good a-tall."

"Hush, now," Noreen scolded. "This be no time for disrespec'." Being the only woman of the household older than Bess, Noreen had the confidence to reprimand the person everyone else avoided, for fear of invoking the retribution of her "conjuring charms."

"Miss 'Manda say it fo' true," Emmie said, of the words Amanda had spoken over the tiny grave, before she returned to the house. "This po' babe in happier place now, restin' in the arms of Jesus."

Tomorrow, Amanda Jane would also lay her mother to rest in the cemetery of St. Michael's.

* * * * *

The dawn of a new day.

Hazy. Humid. Oppressive.

Weapons: pistols at twenty yards. Joseph Alexander Bently, III, stood facing Douglas B. Hornsby, Barrister of the 1st Degree, in a duel to the death, upholding the long-standing code of the South. Even a man sworn to defend the law, once called out, had little choice but to defer to the time-honored tradition. After all, it was a matter of pride, of honor—Lord help them—of reputation.

The fact that Joseph had just lost a wife of thirty-one years had little bearing on his rationale for challenging Hornsby. That the barrister had cuckolded him—taking something that belonged to Bently—came closer to the truth of the situation. The evidence of this long-standing animosity now lay buried in a shallow grave at the back of Tradd House.

Bently felt he had no choice but to "call the man out."

His Second stood between them, giving both men the customary instruction. "I shall ask if both of you are ready," he said. "If neither of you answers, 'No,' then I shall say 'Fire.' Then, and only then will the Principals elevate their pistols and proceed to fire. Is that understood?"

Both contestants nodded their heads in agreement.

He continued, "If a party has not shot by the subsequent count of five, he loses his fire for that round, under the penalty which the Law of Honor imposes for infraction of said rule."

Hornsby and Bently stood glaring at one another, beads of sweat gathering across both brows.

"Ready?"

Both nodded again holding their collective breaths.

"Fire!"

* * * * *

"Mizz 'Manda?" Zeb called, poking his head into the dining room. "They's a gent' axin' fo' you at the door."

"It's awfully early in the morning for callers."

"Ain' no caller, Ma'am," Zeb said. "This here be 'fficial bui'ness. Won't hand his message to nobody but you."

"All right," Amanda said, laying her napkin aside and rising from her place at the table. "Ruthie, would you help Jems finish up? He's almost done with his breakfast. Make sure he cleans up all his grits."

"Yass'am. Don' worry your head 'bout this chil'. We do jus' fine. I take 'im out back t' play with Tutt, when he finish."

Amanda smoothed her skirts and walked resolutely toward the front door. Waiting inside the vestibule she found a man of medium stature, dressed in his finest, holding top hat in one hand, and an official-looking letter in the other.

"Mizz Amanda Jane Bently?"

"I am Mrs. Amanda Jane *Harrison*, sir. Bently was my maiden name."

"Silas Q. Thornhurst, at your service, Ma'am. I am your father's Factor... I handle all his financial affairs. Believe me, I'm terribly sorry to disturb your morning at such an early hour, but this dispatch could not wait." He handed Amanda the letter.

"Thank you," she hesitated, "I think."

"Perhaps you'd best sit down before you open this."

"Bad news, then?"

Mr. Thornhurst took Amanda's elbow and guided her into the parlor, where he placed her on the overstuffed, green settee sitting in the corner.

"I appreciate your indulgence, sir. But I've had to deal with my share of bad news before. Some most recently, in fact, as I have funeral arrangements to see to today."

"Please accept my condolences for your mother, Mizz Bently. I was sorry to hear of her untimely passing."

"Thank you. But you really don't need to mollycoddle me, sir. I'll be fine."

"I'd feel better remaining, until you've read through your letter, Ma'am. You may have need of my services, once you comprehend the full extent of its contents."

"All right, then." Amanda tore into the seal, unfolding the document. She read it over silently, as Thornhurst sat across from her on the rocker, no doubt waiting for her to swoon or keel over from shock, as he held his handkerchief at the ready.

29 August, 18 and 21
Charleston, SC

To Amanda Jane Bently, r.e. Harrison:

If you've received this missive, I, Joseph Alexander Bently, III, have not survived the completion of the last obligation to my family, undertaken with the sole purpose of defending its honor.

That being the case, you now face the daunting task of settling my affairs, as well as those of your mother. Her own estate, which pales in comparison to mine, will no doubt be handled by the father of her last two children, and the one who obviously has survived our challenge of moral rectitude...

Amanda sat bolt upright up in astonishment. She re-read that last sentence, to make sure she'd understood it correctly the first time. "He fought a duel?"

"Quite right, Ma'am. I stood as his Second."

"Now he's dead, too?" Though quite pale, Amanda continued on with the letter...

... To him will also fall the responsibility of seeing to the continued keep of Eralynn Louise (formerly Bently, now to be known by the surname "Hornsby"), from the present on into her majority five years hence, or until her marriage, whichever event should first occur. He shall arrange for proper papers to be drawn, in order to make her transfer of name legal and binding.

You, Amanda Jane, being of sound mind and level head, shall of necessity be the one who must convey this unsettling information to your sister—now known to you as half-sister.

I apologize profusely for the impersonal nature of this missive, but under the circumstances, I find it the only way to convey to you the necessary information concerning these matters. Please know that I always did what I though best for you and the other girls, even though a great many of those decisions will undoubtedly appear surprising to you now.

As for Irene Margaret, with her recent marriage into propertied family, she shall no doubt have adequate means with which to conduct her own affairs. She, naturally, will receive her token bequest, but the bulk of my estate now falls to you, as eldest of all my progeny, to hold in trust for your son, my only grandson and heir to the Bently line, Jeremiah Harrison, Jr.

My final wish is that you would add "Bently" as his middle name.

My factor, Silas Q. Thornhurst, can be trusted with any and all matters pertaining to my affairs, as can Dewitt Heston Park, my legal counsel. Please feel free to lean on their combined expertise to guide you through the jungle of official documentation you must now traverse. Without a husband of your own, you will no doubt need honorable men of plainspoken honesty to stand in your stead for all matters of legal intent. Whatever you do, dismiss any and all association with the so-called barrister Douglas B. Hornsby. He cannot be trusted.

You can, however, finally rest assured that your own inheritance from Grandmother Bently, consisting of Wallingsford and all its chattels, shall be saved any further legal entanglements, which my dispute over the judgment of Olympia's final change in documentation of her last will and testament has caused. With my demise, all contesting as to her state of mind at the time of her passing and the influence to which she was subjected by aforementioned Hornsby, now proves a moot point.

My intention in tying up Wallingsford with prolonged litigation was meant entirely as a way to safeguard it for you, Amanda Jane, and as a way to bring you home.

Hornsby had plans of taking over Wallingsford without ever revealing to you your bequest from Grandmother Bently. My contest forced his hand in finally notifying you, delayed though that notification turned out to be.

I'm proud of you, Amanda Jane, of how far you've managed to grow through the trials thus far placed in the path before you. I also ask your forgiveness, in making that path more difficult for you now. You've brought honor to the name of Bently. I pray you find the happiness that has eluded me. I hope you would also let my grandchildren know that I deeply regret not having had the opportunity to learn to know them better. Raise them with honor, my dear. I know you can do no other.

I love you, Amanda Jane. Never forget that...

Amanda shook her head in astonishment. "Father's gone. I can hardly believe it."

"I know it's a bit much to take in all at once, on top of what you already have to handle, Mizz Bently."

"Please, if you don't mind, I'd appreciate you addressing me as Mrs. Harrison."

"Of course. Forgive my blunder, Mrs. Harrison. I meant no offense, only honor, by using your father's name."

"Where is Fath–" she caught her breath. "Where is Father's body now?"

"Dr. Jenkins has him laid out at his dispensary, awaiting direction from you, as to how you wish to proceed. He suggests transferring your father to the mortuary as soon as possible, perhaps even burying your parents in a double grave this very day. The heat, you know."

"Tell him I'll send word within the hour," Amanda informed him. She also had to get word to Michael and the girls at Edingsville Bay on Edisto Island. She needed their arms around her now, the way she needed the comfort of no others.

Unofficially, news of the double tragedy and its repercussions was already making its rounds to the back doors of Charleston, by way of the ever-efficient "servant's grapevine."

Dearest Lucy,

Here I sit, on the porch of Grandmother's beach house, watching the children play in the rolling surf, and I can't help but wonder at how life can change so very quickly. At this time only one short year ago, you and I both struggled to go forward after the accident that took our husbands from us. We bore their last babies without them, and together we found the strength to persevere. I don't know how I could have done it all without you, my dear friend.

Now I struggle to grasp the full extent of losing both my parents at once—estranged for so long, though we'd been. It has all come as quite a shock. At the end of August, Mother died giving birth to what we had assumed was a slow-growing tumor of some sort, but which turned out to be a very deformed baby girl. Mother had so little strength left after all those previous months of constant blood loss, that the doctor had to resort to drastic measures to try and save her life at the expense of the child's. Regrettably, she did not survive despite his greatest efforts.

As far as anyone of import in this city knows, it <u>was</u> a tumor which took Mother's life. But as my closest confidant, I have told you the whole truth, Lucy, since I know you will keep that reve-lation between the two of us alone. My sisters begged me to conceal the truth of the matter from the wagging tongues of Charleston. Since they are the ones who must abide here, I gave in to their supplications, for at this juncture, I'm not entirely sure where I belong in the grand scheme of things.

The shock of mother's unsettling demise has been hard enough to bear, but unbeknownst to me, my father also lost his life fighting a duel the very next morning, before anyone in the household had even risen from their beds. What had been planned as a funeral for Mother on that day, turned into a double interment for both my parents. With the heat down here, expedi-ency governs all summer funerals in these environs.

146

Oh Lucy, I feel as though I've already spent half my life standing at the gravesides of loved ones. So much death, yet, constantly balanced out by ever new births. You and I both know how closely birth and death overlap—these, the sum and substance of ongoing life.

I cannot begin to fathom why Father chose to do what he did. I don't know if I will ever comprehend how a man could risk his entire lifetime for something as insignificant as pride. I suppose no woman ever could. It all seems such a waste to me. But with the strength of the Good Lord holding me up, and His constant blessings poured out to me in these little ones entrusted to my care, I must keep going forward.

I long to be with you, Lucy. To soak in the comfort of your grounding spirit. You, more than anyone, can understand the roil of conflicting emotions churning within me. When I get to feeling too morose, I need only listen to Camellia's and Lillian's shrieks of delight each time they're surprised by an unexpected ocean wave, or when they find a particularly interesting seashell and come running to show me. At those times, friend, I am renewed.

And Little Jems. Jeremiah's only son. His tottering steps give me nothing but delight. That boy has no idea what awaits him, as he matures into manhood. Right now, I am immensely grateful for that fact, for I intend to let him grow and discover his world as only a carefree child can do. Perhaps with the grounding of such a childhood, he will be able to handle the unusual responsibilities that will face him when he becomes an adult.

My father has left his entire estate to Jems, the only male heir in the Bently lineage. As his mother, I am to hold everything in trust, until he reaches his majority. The shipping lines, the import business, all the investments Father accrued. Everything. It's enough to make my head swim. That much responsibility alone makes me blanche at its magnitude. Yet, greater still, lies Wallingsford—my responsibility free and clear, with father's contest of the will now dismissed at his demise.

He's gone. And Mother's gone. And I have a small village that looks to me for its continued security.

Oh, Lucy, I hardly know which way to turn, so much demands attention of me all at once. I do ask Michael for guidance on occasion, but he's been no help whatsoever. He just tells me these decisions need to be mine. He holds back, I think, waiting for me to decide where, exactly, it is that I feel belong. I know he yearns to marry me and take us all back to Ohio. But at this juncture, I'm not sure <u>where</u> my home should lie. Wallingsford? Charleston? Ohio?

I feel rudderless on an angry sea, with no anchor to hold me fast. Michael stands on a distant shore waiting for me to turn my boat toward him, but the Wallingsford people beckon from a different shore, as do the responsibilities of Father's business concerns to hold in trust for Jems. All wave for me to plot my course toward their own their sheltering harbors, each with its own set of needs, wants, and expectations.

But enough of my whining. I am ever so grateful that both my sisters have been adequately endowed as a result of my parents' bequests. As far as I can determine, neither one need worry any further about her future. Mother's estate consisted of the house, its servants and contents, her dowry from Grandfather Tedrow (which is quite sizable in and of itself), and her line of race horses, which none of us knew a thing about. You can imagine our surprise at that revelation. Mother owned race horses!

It happens that my former barrister, Douglas B. Hornsby, owned the horses jointly with my mother. Mother's share of them, along with the house and all the servants, now belong to Eralynn Louise. She, as it turns out, is really <u>their</u> daughter. Which makes her my half-sister. All this time, and none of us ever knew, except perhaps Father, which in hindsight, is most obvious to me now. You can appreciate how this information has upset our whole world.

At last, I finally begin to understand why Mother treated Eralynn as her favorite all along.

Irene Margaret has been keeping herself quite removed from all this turmoil as much as is possible. She still seems to be hiding something the rest of us can only guess at. I suppose we must be patient with her until she's ready to trust Eralynn or I with her confidence. But as she had already married into a family of sizable means, her bequest consisted of all Mother's house-hold furnishings (which, in itself, amounts to quite a remarkable amount, as Mother collected only the very best of everything), all her jewelry, her art, and half of Mother's dowry, which is currently invested in government bonds. Father left Irene Margret with a stipend, as well, paid from the interest on two of his most lucrative investments, to be disbursed to her at yearly intervals.

After the funeral, I remained in Charleston just a few days to take care of the most pressing of concerns. But I quickly removed myself from my Mother's household (I should now say Eralynn's household), because I could hardly stand to listen to the constant bickering between my two sisters.

Eralynn thinks she should have been given the furnishings as well as the house. And Irene thinks she has the right to sell off anything she wishes, as they all belong to her. I could no longer abide the constant quarreling over what I consider trifles in comparison to what we all have lost.

So here I sit, soaking in the refreshing sea breezes at Grand-mother's beach house, letting the constancy of the ocean waves sooth my shattered emotions. Michael sits beside me, waiting for me to finish this missive, which has become entirely too long. But I hesitate breaking into his reverie, as he sits smoking Jeremiah's pipe. What now lies between us feels so unsettled. The ease we once felt with one another has vanished, and in its place, uncomfortable "prickles."

Pray for us, Lucy. We need your comfort, your wisdom, your grounding peace.

We all send our love to you and yours. The girls can't wait to tell Hank all they've discovered down here. At this point, I know not when we shall return to Ohio. So much still remains undone here. I don't know what Michael plans, but I feel his eagerness to leave this place, yet he hesitates to suggest it. I think he is just beginning to realize the magnitude of the responsibilities that face me—that demand so much of my time and attention.

The girls are sending Hank some of the special sea shells they've found on the beach here at Edingsville. I hope this parcel reaches you without too much delay, but I fear since this is a package rather than a simple letter, it may take longer to arrive than our previous posts. But I did so want to send you some real coffee, some Barbadian sugar, and a variety of fresh spices, that I am taking the chance this still might reach you by Christmas.

Give everyone back in Justice our greetings, Lucy. And to you and Jonathon, I wish only the very best. Kiss little Alice for me!

Missing you dreadfully,
Amanda Jane

Chapter 9

Michael's Quandary
September, Wallingsford

"You got any more of this peach brandy?" Michael asked Winston, as he sat with his heels propped on the porch rail outside the manager's office, his chair balanced on the back two legs. "I've got to admit I didn't think I was going to like this stuff, but you do make a tasty brew."

"Thank you. I've been experimenting with the recipe for some years, now. I think I've finally got it about right. Needs a bit of an adjustment to the aftertaste and then it'll be perfect."

"Don't know as I'd change a thing. Has a nice kick, just the way it is. Not a sissy drink at all, like I thought it would be."

"It takes a sophisticated pallet to appreciate the nuances of fine brandy, my friend." Winston rose from his chair next to Michael's and went inside his office to retrieve another decanter from the side cupboard. He removed the glass stopper, laid it aside, and went back outdoors to pour another drink into Michael's snifter.

"Thank you. You know, Winston, I didn't expect I'd like the south all that much, but I'm beginning to think it's not such a bad place after all. Even with all your heat down here."

"I don't imagine your wilderness is such a bad place, either. Even with all your cold up there."

"It has its good points. And its bad. About like any other place, I reckon. But I figure it don't much matter where you call home exactly, long as the people you love are there with you."

"You probably have a point."

"You got family, Winston?"

"Not any more. Most of my family was wiped out by the yellow fever about fifteen years back. A few years after I began working here, matter of fact. I don't think I could have born the loss, if it weren't for Mrs. Bently." Winston took a sip of his brandy and sat in silence for a few moments, as the colors of sunset broadened across the western horizon.

"For a long time I felt guilty I wasn't there to help when they all came down with the fever. But Mrs. Bently pointed out that if I had been, most likely I'd have died, too." Winston took a few puffs of his cigar, then exhaled long and slow. "I have to admit, she was probably right on that account."

"How old a man are you, Winston?"

"Forty three."

"You never married?"

"Nope. Haven't met the right woman, I guess. Or maybe I never really looked all that hard. Somehow, it just seemed like setting myself up for more loss, you know?"

"Yeah, I *do* know," Michael sat quietly, contemplating. "I lost my wife and baby a while back. Hurt terrible for a long time. Even went kind of wild for a while afterward there. But you know, if you go through life afraid to love again for fear of losing it, what's the point?"

"You could look at it that way, I suppose."

"'Sides, what else is there that's more important than the love of a man's family?"

"Property, prestige, power?"

"Yeah, but what's all that gonna get you in the end, 'cept a whole bunch of headaches? 'Specially if you got no one to leave it all to. An' when you're cold at night, what you gonna do... go hug a bag of money?"

"Well, I can't argue with that line of reasoning, now, can I?" Winston said. "But you know there are other alternatives for keeping a man warm at night."

"That might appeal to some, friend, but not to me," Michael said, taking his pipe and tobacco pouch from his pocket and going through the familiar motions of tamping the bowl full. "I'm a one-woman kind of man, when it comes to warming my bed." Michael motioned toward Winston's lighted cigar, and Winston held it over Michael's pipe, while he drew in a spark to light his own smoke.

"So you have no desire to remarry, then? After losing your own wife?"

"Didn't say that."

"Forgive my impertinence in asking, but where, exactly, do you stand with Mizz Amanda, then? Do you intend to marry her?"

"I been hoping to do just that... whenever she's ready," Michael said, taking a long draw on his pipe. "But life has turned her upside down so much in the last year or so. I'm not sure she knows what she wants, anymore."

"She's not cut out for wilderness living, you know."

"Yeah, I s'pose I always did know that. 'Specially after seeing the way she handles herself down here... in the kind o' life she was born to. It's even more obvious to me now."

"She should stay here. This is where she really belongs."

"Don't you reckon it's up to Mandy to decide where she belongs?"

"Perhaps. But maybe a little push in the right direction might make all the difference in helping her make up her mind."

* * * * *

Next day at Wallingsford, as the buzz of life went about its usual routine, Amanda came down late to breakfast. She'd slept so soundly after the return of their retinue from the beach house the day before, she hadn't even heard the children waken that morning—quite an unusual circumstance for her. Effie Lou already had them up, dressed, and breakfasted before Amanda had even begun to stir.

"You finally up, *Sister?*" Michael called from the sitting room after Jems had fussed for her when she passed by the door on her way to the dining room. Jems sat on the floor near him, playing with some of the stones and artifacts from the table beside the leather settee. Michael lay on the floor himself, with his head almost in the fireplace, scrutinizing its stonework.

153

"You lose something up the chimney?"

"I'm fascinated by the cantilever on this mantelpiece. Been trying to figure out how they laid it up."

"You're getting bored, aren't you."

"Not bored, exactly. Just gettin' the itch to work stone again. I miss it."

"I guess you didn't bargain on being stuck down here for so long, when we left home. I really didn't either."

"You thinkin' about heading back soon?"

"Oh, Michael, how *can* I? You've seen all I need to deal with down here."

"Yeah, I know."

"I don't see how I can even consider it any time before next spring at the earliest."

"Uuuu. Spring. That's a long way off. I was hoping to get winter wheat planted yet this fall. Get a jump on next year. We lost one whole season's worth of crops already."

"I hate to even suggest it, but maybe you should think about going back without us."

Michael sat up from his place on the floor and gave her a hard look. "You want me to leave you?"

"I didn't say that, *Brother*."

"What exactly did you say?"

"I just meant that maybe in the interest of all our objectives, you should go back to tend the farm... until I can see my way clear to leave."

"You're not thinkin' of staying on down here permanent, are you?"

"Winston did make mention of his thought that I should consider exactly that."

"Winston? I shouldda known," Michael muttered. "What *you* think should be most important, don't you reckon?"

"Oh, I don't know *what* I need to do. Or *where* I need to be," Amanda sighed, and sat down heavily on one of the side chairs flanking the fireplace. "All I *do* know is that I'm totally confused, and I have a mountain of responsibilities pulling at me down here, right now."

Michael stood and moved to the chair where Amanda sat. "Don't make any rash decisions right away, Mandy." He put his hand on her shoulder. "You've had too many upsets all at once. Just give it some time. I can wait."

At that moment, Winston stuck his head in the sitting room door, "Sorry to disturb y'all." He quickly took in the tender moment between Amanda and Michael. "It looks like there's a big storm brewing. I need all the help we can find to tie things down. This one might turn into a full-blown hurricane," he said by way of explanation. "Captain down at the landing said he just made it across open water before he ran into the leading winds. We'll have to work fast."

"I can help," Michael said. "Tell me what to do."

"Follow me. We'll get some of the workers started nailing up shutters."

Michael left Amanda sitting there, watching Jems shuffling and stacking his pile of stones. Occasionally, he'd fit an artifact into an indentation on the hearthstone that looked as though it could have been made to fit that very object.

"Come, Jems. We need to find the girls and tell Effie Lou and Ada Mae about the storm." She helped the boy stand, and held his hand as he toddled beside her into the dining room.

By the time the workers had secured all that could be effectively battened down outdoors, the women inside had everything of import toted upstairs where they hoped it would be safe from the storm surge that invariably accompanied such a storm. Winston had told them, "It's not the winds that do the worst damage, it's the flooding that comes after."

Being on a barrier island, they had little option for security from such inundation, other than retreating to the upper floors of

155

the big house, or to the rafters of the barns and storage sheds, should flood waters rise to such a height.

Most of the People's cabins had been built on storm supports, at their compound up behind the big peach barn, so they had as secure a spot as any on the plantation.

When Winston and Michael headed to the People's quarters to warn them of the coming storm, they found Pitney Bower already getting mothers to hustle babes and small children under cover, while she directed the remaining boys and men, not already out working, to gather up livestock and secure the animals in the storm sheds.

"You have one of your premonitions again, Pitney?" Winston asked the old woman.

"No signs. Just bones so sore, cain't hardly walk," she told them. "Means somethin' big blowin' in."

"Guess you've seen enough storms to know." Winston tipped his hat and the two men hurried on to the large peach barn, where efforts were underway to secure anything remotely apt to become airborne in the big blow.

"You do this very often?"

"What?"

"Nail down everything that could move before a rain?"

"You'll find what's coming is no ordinary rain, my friend. A storm of this magnitude can blow a full-grown man away, if he should be caught out in it without adequate cover."

"You joshin' me?"

"I wouldn't poke fun at a storm that can drive a cornstalk through a live-oak tree and make it look like it grew that way."

Michael gave Winston a skeptical look.

"Just telling what I've seen with my own eyes, friend."

"Guess I have to believe it's true. Hard for me to grasp such a power, though."

"Amen to that."

* * * * *

When the winds picked up, the strong force of the storm increased quickly. The people of Wallingsford hunkered into their respective places of cover for the duration. In spite of the more obvious security offered by the big house, the indoor help chose to ride out the storm in the shelters of their own homes, with the familiar security of their own families about them. Amanda told Effie Lou and Ada Mae not to worry about preparing any more provisions for the Harrison's use. She'd take care of fixing meals and looking after her own family, until the storm blew itself out.

And so, it rained. And it blew. And the winds howled so deafeningly, the twins sat underneath the dining room table with hands over their ears, trying to block out the sounds that were so unsettling. Jems hardly seemed to notice at all. He sat quietly alongside his sisters, playing with the stones and artifacts he'd carried in from the parlor.

"Come out from under there, now," Amanda directed. Jems dutifully crawled to his mother, but the twins stayed where they sat, feeling safer behind the long tablecloth that shut them out from the rest of the world.

"It's too scary!" Camellia answered.

"But we're right here, dears. You have nothing to fear from a storm. We're all inside, nice and warm and dry."

"It's too loud!" Lilly hollered, attempting to make herself heard above the whine of the wind and the pound of the rain.

"But mama has supper all ready. Come out, now, so we can all eat dinner."

"Noooooooo! Too scary!" both girls shrieked at once.

"Why don't we take dinner to 'em under there?" Michael suggested.

Amanda gave him the most unbelieving look. "You've got to be kidding."

"No! We can have us a storm picnic!" he said, as if the thought had just struck him. "Whaddya say?"

157

Amanda, ready to disregard the whole idea, actually stopped to think about it. At one time she'd have never considered doing such a thing. But with the happenings of the past few months crowded in on top of one another, she understood all too well, her twins' wish to hide from the world.

"All right. You count out bowls, spoons and mugs. I'll go get the stew pot. Look after Jems till I get back from the downstairs kitchen, would you, please?"

"Sure. No problem." He pushed the boy back under the table with his sisters and went to the sideboard to count out utensils.

In a few minutes, Amanda walked back up from the smaller, inside kitchen on the lowest floor, with stew pot in one hand, and milk pitcher in the other. Michael had a cloth spread underneath the table, with bowls, spoons and mugs set all around. He'd also pulled one end of the tablecloth up, so they had a window out to the lighted lamp he'd set on the floor beyond the table, where it wouldn't get knocked over.

Amanda handed the pot and pitcher to Michael, then crawled underneath the table herself, giggling as she did so. She settled at her place and dished stew all around. After she'd finished pouring milk into their mugs—half full, so as to avert unnecessary spills —Michael placed Jems beside Amanda and scooted over to his own spot under the table.

"Who wants to say grace?" Michael asked.

No one said a thing.

"All right. Reckon' I'll say a word, then." He closed his eyes, as Amanda had the girls fold their hands. "Dear Lord, we thank You for this dandy picnic, and for a place to stay warm and dry during this upsettin' storm. Please help the girls know that as long as we're all here together, they have nothing to fear." He gave a quick look around their impromptu picnic. "And thanks for this food and the hands that prepared it. Amen."

The girls picked up their spoons. Before they took a bite, they looked questioningly at their mother. "We really can eat under here?" Camellia asked, as if seeking confirmed permission.

"Yes, dears. We're having a floor picnic."

"We're *eating* under the *TABLE!*" Lilly hollered. "We're eating under the *ta*-ble... we're eating under the *ta*-ble," she sang over and over.

"That's enough, Lillian. It's time to eat your dinner."

They all sat enjoying Amanda's stew.

"Been a long time since we tasted your cooking," Michael said to Amanda. "Mighty good."

"Mmmmm, good, Mama," the girls echoed.

Jems sat with stew smeared all over his face, in his attempt to feed himself.

"Oh, Jems, look at you," Amanda fussed.

"Let him be. He's enjoying his, too," Michael smiled. "You got any bread?"

"Oh, I forgot to bring up the loaf I had set out. I'll go back and–"

"Don't disturb yourself," Michael told her. "It's not that important."

"But, it's just–"

"Stay put, Mandy. Let yourself enjoy the moment."

She settled back, and continued to eat her own stew. And the rain pounded louder, and the wind howled more discordantly, as the house shook in the force of the tempest.

Without warning, a loud bang made them all sit bolt upright.

"What on earth?" Amanda questioned.

"I'll go check." Michael crawled out from under the table. "You all stay right here. Don't go nowhere!" he smirked.

Amanda simply shook her head. Before Michael returned, the girls had finished cleaning out their bowls and Amanda sat spooning the last of Jems' dinner into him.

"Miss me?" Michael poked his head under the tablecloth, giving the girls a fright.

"Unka Mikey! Unka Mikey," the girls hollered.

"Oh, Michael, you gave us a start!" Amanda complained.

"Sorry. Didn't mean to." He crawled back under the table with them. "Come on in with us," he called.

"Someone's out there?"

Winston looked underneath.

"The bang we heard was Winston coming in the back door. Took all the might he had just to push it open. Wind sucked it closed so fast, it liked to bust right in two, it slammed shut so hard."

"What on earth were you doing out in *that?*" Amanda asked.

"Thought I'd better come in here with you folks a while. My quarters aren't proving all that weatherproof. Even with the storm shutters up."

"We're having a floor picnic," Lilly spoke up.

"Mama made stew!" Camellia added, not to be outdone.

"You're welcome to have some, Winston. If you'd care to join our silly diversion," Amanda offered.

"Well, I am hungry. I don't mind if I do." He squeezed himself under with the rest of them, trying valiantly to tuck his long legs out of the way. "Little snug under here."

"Everything all right out there?" Michael asked, reaching for another bowl from the table top where he'd left the extras.

"So far, so good," Winston answered. "Near's I could tell, everyone's safe, and all the shutters are holding. I'm afraid my roof is going to need some attention when this is all over, though. Thanks, Amanda," he said, taking a bite. "This is very tasty. You're a good cook."

"Thank you. You're lucky you never had to taste some of my first attempts."

"She's come a *l-o-n-g* way since then," Michael said with a solemn face.

Amanda reached over and gave his shoulder a smack.

"What was that for?"

"You *know* what it's for."

"I do?"

She gave him a hard glare.

"If you say so." Michael shrugged his shoulders and gave Winston a quizzical look. "She likes me, can't you tell?"

"Oh, you're impossible!" Amanda began to gather up dirty bowls and spoons. "I'll take these downstairs and bring up dessert." She backed out from under the table and pulled herself onto her feet. "I'll be right back. And keep an eye on Jems, will you *please?*"

"He'll be fine." Michael said. He and Winston began to talk, and the men got so caught up in their conversation, they paid little attention to the children, entertaining themselves at the other end of the table.

Amanda returned shortly, carrying the loaf of bread she'd forgotten previously, along with a crock of peach jam and pot of hot coffee. She handed it all under the table to Michael, then crawled back underneath, where she proceeded to slather slices of bread with jam for each person.

"Come, girls. Have your dessert, while the bread's still warm. You love Pitney's jam."

The girls crawled back to the picnic area and accepted their mother's offering.

"Where's Jems?" Amanda looked all around under the table, then gave Michael a hard look.

"He was just right here."

"I *told* you to keep an eye on him," Amanda groused.

"Don't get all huffy, I'll go find the boy." Michael untangled his legs and crawled out, expecting to return momentarily.

But he didn't. Time ticked by, and still no Michael, and no Jems.

"Maybe I'd better go help look," Winston offered.

Amanda agreed. After Winston had gone, she started to fuss. "I knew I shouldn't have left him with Michael. When that man starts talking he loses track of everything."

The men hunted all through the main floor. No sign of the boy in the dining room, nor sitting room. No trace below in the seldom-used, indoor kitchen, either. By the time the men had thoroughly scoured the downstairs, Amanda couldn't sit still a moment longer. She instructed the girls to "stay put" and headed upstairs to search through the bedrooms. Jems had just begun climbing steps, and Amanda knew he loved to sit in high places. She thought perhaps he'd climbed the stairs alone. She searched through the nursery, her room, Michael's room and the fourth bedroom presently unoccupied.

Nothing.

Michael met her on the landing. "Any luck?"

"He's nowhere up here! How could you lose him like this, Michael? I trusted you to watch him."

"I *was* watching him. He and the girls were playing with those stones of his an–"

"If I can't trust you to watch the children when I'm otherwise occupied, what good are you down here? You've become more than worthless to me, *Brother*."

"Well, you don't have to get so testy about a simple mistake–"

"Simple *mistake!*" Amanda began to shout. "This is Jeremiah's *son* we're talking about, Michael! My only *living* son." Panic began to rise in her voice. "There's a storm raging out there! What if he got out in that *hurricane?*"

"It's not likely he could have gotten outdoors, *Sister*. It took every ounce of strength Winston had just to open the door to come in!"

Amanda glared at him.

"All right. All right. Winston and I will go look on the porch and all around the house. If he *is* out there, he can't have gotten far."

"Oh, my son, my Jems! What have you done!"

Michael made a hasty retreat downstairs, collared Winston, and between them, the two men managed to pull open the door far enough to squeeze out before it slammed shut again. At its loud bang, Amanda nearly jumped out of her skin. She hurried back to the dining room and huddled together with her daughters, as much for her own comfort as for theirs.

Half-an-hour later, the men pushed their way back in the door and collapsed on the floor behind it, completely done in and soaked to the skin. Winston had lost his hat, and Michael had on only one shoe.

Amanda came running to the back door after she'd heard it slam shut. "Jems?"

"Nothing."

"Nooooo! Michael, my *baaaaa-by!*"

"Calm down, now, and let's think this thing through," Winston said, rising from his spot on the floor and gently touching her shoulder. "When you last saw him, what was he doing."

Amanda sniffed back a sob. "Playing with his stones under the far end of the table with the twins.

"Did you ask the girls if they saw where he went?"

"I never thought to."

"Why don't we go see if they can shed some light on this mystery of ours."

Michael began to rise from his spot on the floor, and Amanda gave him a glare.

"Don't you dare come near me, you... you... you *child loser!*"

"All right, all right," he said, putting out his hands in surrender. "I'll stay out of the way."

Amanda and Winston returned to the dining room.

"Camellia? Lillian?" Winston called. The girls came out from under the table at his authoritative call, as they would not for Amanda or Michael. "Did you see where your brother went?"

"He crawled out after Lilly pushed his stones away," Camellia tattled.

"He hurt me with that big one! I gived it back to him when he throwed it at me!"

"You gave it back when he threw it at you, Lillian."

"That's what I *said!*"

"What did he do then, Camellia," Winston asked in a calm, re-assuring tone of voice.

"He took his stones and crawled out."

"Did you look by the fireplace where he's been playing with his other stones?" Amanda asked.

"Michael hunted in there before I joined the search," Winston said.

"*Michael,*" Amanda huffed.

"You called?" Michael stuck his head in the dining room door, rubbing a dry cloth over his dripping hair.

"How well did you search the parlor?" Winston asked, reaching for the towel Michael offered him.

"Looked through the whole thing, under all the furniture, behind the drapes, up the chimney."

"Maybe we should take another look," Winston said with a quiet, even voice, in an effort to calm Amanda. They all trooped into the parlor and proceeded to tear the room apart looking for any sign of the babe. The girls sat on the hearth, where their mother told them to stay put.

"Anything?" Winston asked.

"Nothing," Amanda sighed, pulling cushions from chairs, then overturning them to check underneath.

"I hear Jems crying," Lilly said."

"You do? Where?"

"Back there," Camellia pointed behind the hearthstone.

"There? Are you sure?" Amanda pointed.

"Right down *there*," Lilly persisted.

Amanda put her ear to the floor next to the fireplace. "Oh, my Lord, I hear him! How in the world did he get himself stuck under the floorboards?" She began to panic. "Get him *out!* Winston, get him *OUT* of there!"

"I'll go get a crowbar and sledgehammer. We'll break 'im out."

"Don't hurt my *baaa-by!*" Amanda wailed.

"Now calm down here," Michael said, taking a step closer to the fireplace. "There has to be a simple explanation for how he got himself stuck back there in the first place. Let's take a closer look at this thing."

"I'll go for tools," Winston said, disappearing. Presently the back door slammed behind him.

As Michael studied the hearthstone, carefully feeling all around it, then behind it, he came to an extended break along the back of the stone. "Hmmm."

"What? *What?*" Amanda asked, the edge of panic beginning to sound in her voice once more.

Michael's hands went over the indentations at the front of the hearthstone, noting that a stone artifact had been carefully placed into each, fitting its hole perfectly. The last hole remained empty.

"See if you can find one of those stones that matches this shape," he told the girls.

They sorted through the pile of artifacts sitting on the floor beside the fireplace, searching for the same size and shape as the hole Michael pointed out.

"Does this fit?" Lillian asked.

Michael took the stone and placed it in the hole. "Not quite," he said, "but you're close. This one's just a little too short. You got a longer one with that bottom flange on it?"

"What's a 'flange'?" Camellia asked."

"A sort of doohickey that sticks out like this," he said, pointing out the projection on the end of her stone.

165

"Like this?" she asked, handing him a similar, larger stone.

"Just like that. Let's try it." Michael pressed the stone into the indentation, and, as if spring-loaded, the hearthstone began to slide forward, revealing a large hole underneath.

There sat Jems, ash-covered, tears streaking down soot-smeared face, and clutching a stone that matched the trigger stone exactly.

"Well, I'll be!" Michael shook his head in wonder. "A hidden compartment. How clever!"

"My *baaaa-by*!" Amanda shouted, scooping Jems up, out of the filthy hole. "How in the *world* did you get yourself stuck in there?" she asked the baby, clutching him tightly. She knew he couldn't answer, but she babbled on and on, releasing her anxiety in a flow of chatter.

Michael still sat studying the hearthstone, when Winston came back into the parlor, carrying an array of tools.

"You got him out!"

"Oh, my poor baby, just look at you," Amanda fussed, holding him out from herself and giving him a good looking over. The baby dropped the stone he still held. "You're covered with soot! I need to clean you up right now." She marched out the parlor door and headed up to the nursery.

Winston joined Michael where he still sat eyeing all the stones.

Camellia pointed out the last artifact neatly tucked into its respective hollow. "I found this one," she said, picking it back up. As she did so, the hearthstone began its slide back into place.

"Jems must have grabbed at that trigger stone when he fell inside," Michael said. "Closed the hole right back up with him in there. I reckon it must use a system of weights and counter-balances," he said. "Ingenious!"

Winston touched his shoulder. "Could you show me how that works again? I think I saw something shiny down there just before that stone slid shut."

"Hand me your stone again, would you Millie?" He accepted the artifact from Camellia and pushed it back into its nest. The hearthstone slid open once again. "Leave that stone in there for a bit. Don't take it back out yet, honey."

"All right, Unka Mikey."

Winston began to wipe aside the collected soot, revealing what looked like a journal of some sort with a shiny gold clasp. "What in the world?" He pulled out the small, leather-bound book, brushing it more carefully to reveal its full surface. "What do you suppose this could be?"

Michael ran his hand over it. "Looks like some kind of picture language on the front. A map of some sort, maybe?"

Winston shrugged. "Good a guess as any, I s'pose."

Amanda returned downstairs, carrying Jems, now all changed and scrubbed clean.

"Look what we got, Mama," Lilly said, pointing out the curious object. "Winston found a treasure!"

"Well, we don't know exactly what it is, darlin', but it sure must be something," Michael offered.

"Don't you speak to me, you... you child endangerer."

"But I *found* Jems for you! I'm the one who got him *out!*"

"Were it not for your neglect, he'd have never been lost in the first place!"

"But Mandy, be reasonabl–"

"Don't you 'Mandy' me, *Brother.* I'm Amanda Jane to you, and don't you ever forget it!" She marched from the parlor, carrying Jems and shepherding the girls before her. "I'm putting the children to bed. I'll deal with you in the morning."

Winston and Michael sat by the hearthstone, staring at each other in bewilderment, as the fading storm continued to blow itself out.

Dear Amanda,

We just received your letter from Charleston posted on 8 July. This one took 11 weeks to reach us. One week longer than the first, which you sent from Virginia. It is good to hear how the children are doing in their new surroundings. I understand how you would feel overwhelmed by the duties and responsibilities that face you there. Especially after a more simplified way of living up here. I have no doubt you can handle all that you must, Amanda. You've gained so much strength and wisdom thus far.

I've been going down to help Sadie as I can lately, since she's due to give birth within the next few weeks. Hank and little Tad, who's now three, play quite well together, and Sadie seems grateful for the distraction when we come. She says she's feeling much better with this pregnancy, as she has felt no need to walk with a cane, the way she did when she carried the little girl she lost last time. Nell. This pregnancy feels much the same as with Tad, she says, which gives her hope for a successful outcome at this birth.

I mentioned your frustration to her, concerning Michael's actions since your arrival, and as his sister, she had some interesting insight. Evidently when he gets discouraged or up- set, rather than become quiet and introspective the way Jeremy always did, Michael has the tendency to "act out," as Sadie put it. She said back home he would drink and gamble, on occasion. Most often during those times when he felt especially trapped by the restrictions of his apprenticeship and helpless to do anything about it.

Perhaps now he's feeling powerless to help you in your endeavors, and as a consequence has focused his time and attention elsewhere. Sadie says to give him a little space, and he'll eventually straighten himself out. According to her, he always does.

I must share with you the continuing saga of Snooks Simpson down in Petersburg. You recall I talked of his disappearance and the subsequent "mystery of the squirrels." Rebecca Simpson reports that her "wild Indian" son still leaves his meat offerings on the clothesline every night, although now they've expanded from squirrels to all manner of small game. Occasionally she also finds a well preserved fur. She says they've been tanned as well as any she's ever seen, which causes her to wonder how he ever managed to learn such a skill on his own.

With fall coming on, she worries that he'll not be warm enough out in the woods, once cold weather sets in hard. We have had two frosts thus far, so it's only a matter of time until a continuous fire will feel most welcome. Let's hope Snooks sees fit to give up being a wild boy and return to his home for the winter, if for no other reason than to ease his mother's mind.

In other news, it seems Clara (Guthrie) Hawkins had an incident with her skirts catching afire when she brushed too close to the hearth last week. You know how quickly a skirt can catch, when one gets the least bit careless about keeping it tucked back while cooking. Luckily Winifred, who sat at the table peeling apples, managed to grab the milk bucket and douse Clara's skirt before she became too badly burned. She ended up with only her ankles singed. Thankfully, nothing worse. She seemed more upset about ruining her dress than she did about her injuries.

You and I both know how quickly such a circumstance can escalate into terrible loss. Thankfully Clara and her coming babe both came through the experience without loss of life or limb. According to Winifred, Clara's due to give birth sometime after the first of the year.

Their little Tommy flourishes, being doted on by the four adults in residence. Winifred says at two, he's already talking up a storm, which seems quite advanced for a boy. Usually it's the girls who learn to speak so quickly. But I suppose Clara chatters non-stop to him, which has obviously paid off. The only problem with his quickness to repeat what he hears, is that Tommy tends to listen to Anson's swearing a bit too closely. As a result he has the saltiest language of any two-year-old I've ever heard. It would seem Anson has no control over his speech, since the effects of the stroke that left him partially paralyzed. But how they will manage to break Tommy of copying such remarks remains to be seen.

You wouldn't recognize my little Alice, she has grown so much since you left. She's crawling now, at nine months, and just beginning to pull herself up to her feet. Jonathan is so good with her. Whenever he's indoors, he most always seems to have Alice on his lap or in his arms. If he takes her outside, she rides atop his shoulder, giggling outrageously from her high perch. I think she has quite captivated his heart. When I watch them together, I continue to thank the Lord for Jonathan. Good as Henry tried to be with Hank, I shudder to think how he would have handled a little girl. Surely the Lord knows what He's doing, even when we can't see it for all the pain we must suffer. I don't know how I could have gotten through the anguish you and I faced just a short year past, without the strength of your support, Amanda Jane. Nor without Jonathan.

Please make sure you take time for yourself, amongst all your responsibilities down there. And do not despair, my friend. When we face difficulties, it's only human nature to long for what we once had, thinking life was better, easier, or simpler than what confronts us now. You will make it through these challenges too. And when you do, you can come home and tell me all about them.

I miss you, dear friend.

Yours, Lucy

P.S. Jonathan says to tell you both that your farm is doing just fine. The wheat harvest gave a good showing. And your cow freshened last month, having another little heifer calf. Hank named her Airabelle.

Dear Amanda,

Bet you are surprised to hear from me! I thought I should write to let you know about our little girl, Zoey. Born just this week. With the last hard year we all had, a little good news always comes as a welcome thing. Zoey Blue came into this world easy enough, as birthing goes. After my last troubling experience losing Nell, I have to say I am mighty glad she did. I don't mind telling you I was more than a little worried this time. But she came quick, without too much difficulty, just like Tad.

Willie always liked the name Zoey. Even though it is a strange one, I agreed to call her that. But we added the Blue, after she opened up her eyes and looked at us for the first time. She has the most striking eyes you ever saw on a baby. Nothing for it than to call her Zoey Blue. Her hair is a darker red than Tad's, more auburn colored. Not like his carrot top. That coloring and those eyes ought to make her something, when she comes of age. But right now, she is just a little bit of a thing. Not as tiny as your twins, but smaller than Tad was. Made for an easy enough birth all around.

Willie's Ma did manage to see this one come into the world, though she does not go about helping others anymore. So she was here for Zoey. She didn't have to help too much. And that was fine with her. Ma still has not gained back her confidence, although she did help Tad out not long ago when he got snake-bit. Lucky she was handy right then, sitting out on the porch snapping green beans, or I hate to think what could have happened to our boy. She saw the rattler, but was not quick enough to whack off its head before it hit. She tipped Tad over, made a fast cut over the bite, and sucked the poison right out before it could get a good hold.

Boy ended up with nothing more than a little swelling and a low fever from the whole thing. Thank the Lord and Ma's fast thinking. She saved his life, in my opinion, but she gave herself little credit. Said anyone with a lick of sense would do the same thing. Nothing noteworthy about it. Willie skinned out the snake and tanned the hide to make a belt for Tad, for when he gets older. Remind him of his good fortune in having a quick-witted grandma.

Ma lives over with Sam Justice, now, but she still spends a good many days here, with Willie and me. She and Sam had a quiet little ceremony about three months back down Mount Vernon way with Ranson Newell, Justice of the Peace in those parts. None of us can hardly believe they did it. But she is now Edith Justice, sure enough. Folks hereabouts still call her Ma Hawkins, though, as they have known her by that name for so long, it hardly seems right to call her anything else. But she flatly refuses to take up her doctoring or midwifing again. Says that younger hands need to handle such concerns now.

Well, I have danced around the telling of it long enough, but I need to let you know that Michael made it back here to Justice last week, safe and sound. I also have to say he is more upset than I ever have seen that man, as he commenced to plowing up fields even in the middle of cold weather setting in. Seems like some wild fever driving him to work so hard. I know when he acts like that, he is working out his anger or fear or grief, or whatever is eating at him. He won't say much when I ask what's wrong. Just gives me a faraway look then changes the subject.

He has been taking meals here with us, two or three evenings a week. Rest of the time nobody sees much of him. I gathered that you and he did not part on such good terms, Amanda. But don't be too hard on Michael. He really is a good man. He just goes a little crazy once in a while when he feels helpless, whatever the reason. He always does come back stronger once he works it all out.

He brought Freddie back to us right away when he got home. But Willie let Michael keep the gelding a while longer to work his fields, as Jeremy's old Patsy finally gave up the ghost this past summer. That old mare had more miles on her than any horse I ever knew. I like to think Jeremy's right glad to see his old horse again. Maybe is even riding my Nell and your boys around on her back up there in heaven! Michael says he will buy a new horse come spring, but not right now, as he has no hay put by this year for feeding out the winter.

Tad says to tell the twins "Hey" for him. He acts all puffed up, now that he is a big brother.

I hope you are happy down in that warm place, Amanda. I know how much you always hated the cold. Don't forget us up here. We hope to see you again come spring.

Best Regards, Sadie Harrison Hawkins,
your sister-in-law that was.

Chapter 10

Christmas Surprise
December 24, 1821, Cranberry Corners

"How much of this stuff you want cut up, Lib," Ellie Mae asked, as she sat peeling potatoes and turnips and slicing carrots for stew.

"You'd better add another large bowlful at least. We have quite the crowd to feed," Libby Howard answered, wiping hands on apron, after she'd finished filling the kettle to put on for tea. "I can hardly believe you're really here, Ellie! Do you realize it's been more than three years since we last sat in the same kitchen? Of course at the time, that particular kitchen had no roof over it and only barrels to sit on!" She scooted over to her best friend and gave her another impulsive hug.

"What was that for?" Ellie asked.

"Oh, I just can't help myself. It's so good to see you again."

"Reckon we have gone a mite too long without ary a hug," said Ellie. "Not to mention there's a good bit more o' me to hug, than last time."

"I don't see an extra pound on you anywhere, El. You look as slim as you did the day I first laid eyes on you at our cabin raising. My, how long ago has that been?"

"Five, six year? More 'r less. Lot of water gone over the dam since then."

"I shudder to think of the extra layers I've added in that time," Libby said, putting the kettle over the trivet atop a bed of coals on the hearth. "But Zach just smiles and tells me there's that much more of me to love." She took a moment to sit down at the table where Ellie Mae still worked cutting up vegetables. "And here you are, Mrs. Zeke MacTavish. Who'd have ever guessed such a turn of events?"

"Sure enough not me!" Ellie said, plopping another potato into the stew pot. "Never in all my born days have I gone an' done

174

something so rash as to say 'I do' to that crazy Scotsman. But betwixt you, me, and that hearthstone over there, I got to tell you, Lib, I'm mighty glad I did."

"He seems quite taken with you, Ellie. It's wonderful to see a man treat you so well, after that horrible experience you had at the hands of that... that... well, I can't even bring myself to utter his name!"

"Don't flusterbate yourself, Lib. He's a goner, sure as you're born." Ellie reached over to pat her dear friend in reassurance. "We don't have to trouble ourselves no more over the likes of Harvey Thompson."

"Please! I don't even want that name uttered under this roof! Cross yourself, quickly."

"I'd ruther spit an' say I'm glad I seen the end of that rascal," Ellie said, getting ready to spit. "But I wouldn't think o' dirtyin' up your floor over the likes of that varmint."

"Enough despondency. It's the holidays, and I'm surrounded by the people I love! What could be more wonderful than that?"

"Not much. Less'n my Johannah should come walkin' through that door. An' I kin tell you, I'd likely fall into a dead swoon, if'n she did."

"We can pray she's doing well, whatever she's about," Libby said with solemnity. "And say another prayer for Christian and Levi, too... wherever their adventures have taken those foot-loose sons of mine." Libby closed her eyes for a moment. "Would you like some tea, El? I could do with a little pick-me-up, myself."

"O' course! Nothin' better than takin' a cup of tea with my best friend in the whole world!"

"Oh, El, I wish you could have been here to listen to these girls of ours over the last few months. I hardly could contain myself at some of their conversations. Lizzie and Katrina sounded so much like you and I," Libby said, rising and going to the cupboard to take down her teapot and the last, two, remaining bone-china teacups in her possession. "It thrills me to see our daughters developing such a close friendship."

"Don't surprise me in the least," Ellie said, cutting up the last carrot in her bowl. "Them two know a good thing when they see it."

"And can you believe how much our little Simon has grown? Eighteen months and already he acts like a little man. It tickles me to watch him follow after my Elijah, copying everything his uncle does. An uncle at seven years! Naturally, Elijah carries on as if he's much too old to concern himself with toddlers. But I can see he's quite proud to have someone in the household look up to him for a change, even if it is only Simon." Libby put a measure of the real, English tea she saved for special occasions into her teapot, then pulled the kettle off the trivet and filled it with boiling water. "There, that can steep a bit." She sat back down for a few moments.

"Done with this bowlful," Ellie said, putting her knife aside. She picked up the stew pot, carried it to the fireplace, and hung it over the trammel hook, swinging it over the fire to cook. "What else you want done, Lib?"

"I thought perhaps we could make some pies for dessert. I still have some apples left. And I put up my own mincemeat this year to use for the holidays."

"You managed to get spices clear out here? Boy, I ain't had mincemeat since I was a young'un. My Aunt Nadine used to make her special recipe every Christmas."

"I don't recall you ever mentioning her before."

"She was my mother's oldest sister. Never had the uppity idees my own ma has. More down to earth like Edie," Ellie explained. "She took a shine to Edie right off. Taught her a whole lot about herbs and such, as I recall. Guess that's what started Edie out on the road to doctorin'."

"Your sister truly won't return to her healing practice?"

"Nope. Says she has lost the heart to watch anybody suffer ever again, if'n she can help it. Sadie's learnin' all her medicine ways now. Edie says she's a quick study, too. Picks things up real fast." Ellie trotted over to the dishpan and washed up the bowl and knife she'd been using. "Where d'you keep your lard and flour, Lib? I'll start in on pie dough, if you want."

"Let's have our tea first. It should be ready." Libby returned to the table with her teapot in one hand and the two cups in the other. "We'll still have plenty of time to put pies together and bake them, while the stew simmers. That big potful is going to take quite a while to cook through." She poured their cups full of the steaming brew, then both women took a seat at the table once more.

"What you reckon them men of ours is up to?"

"Knowing Zachary, he's showing your Zeke every inch of his mill." Libby took a sip, being careful to blow across the teacup so she didn't burn her tongue. "Honestly, I never saw a man so enamored with wood... spends every waking hour cutting, shaping or talking about wood. Nate handles most of the grinding duties up there, since Zach hardly ever leaves that saw blade." She sat her cup down a moment. "I do worry that he'll get hurt on that thing one of these days, but I simply cannot allow myself to think that way for long, or it would drive me absolutely crazy!"

"You gotta focus on the best, Lib. It's the only way."

At that moment, Zach and Zeke burst through the front door of the Howard cabin, stomping off snow, shedding coats and boots, and warming the atmosphere with their masculine high spirits.

"Je-*hospehat*, it's c-o-l-d out there! We need something to warm us up!" Zach called out.

"Mebbe the lassies 'll 'ave a hot toddy ready fer us... aye, lad?" Zeke gave Ellie a quick wink, as he shrugged out of his coat. It took a little finagling for him to ease his injured shoulder out of its sleeve.

"Looks like we caught 'em sitting down on the job," Zach said, walking over to give Libby the sack of flour he held. "You two catch up on all your gossip yet?"

"When I haven't seen my best friend in more than three years, we can't *begin* to do justice to all our news in only one afternoon," Libby answered. "Besides, we've been busy cooking for all you hungry people ever since Ezekiel and Eloise Maevis arrived."

"Eloise Mavi–??"

"Don't you *even* start in on me," Ellie warned Zach in a firm tone.

Zach gave Ellie a sly smirk, then said to his wife, "Nate sent over that bag of flour, fresh ground. Said to tell everyone Merry Christmas. He'll be over tomorrow to visit."

"Is Ivy doing all right? And baby Patience?"

"Said everything's just fine. According to Nate, Mrs. Cleghorn has a 'firm hold on the reins' over there."

"You should see that little babe, Ellie," Libby gushed. "She has the tiniest nose I've ever seen on a newborn, and such dainty fingers!"

"When did she whelp the young'un?"

"Three days ago. Ivy's mother came down a week ago to help out. She plans to stay on through the New Year, at least."

With the two men raising the noise level in the cabin, the others in residence began to shuffle out from their various places of napping and reading and conversation. Lizzie and a very pregnant Katrina had taken the opportunity to lie down with their babies for a brief, afternoon nap while the household remained relatively quiet. Now they came forth from the cabin addition— Lizzie carrying a squalling, six-month-old Liberty Lane, and Katrina leading little Simon on groggy feet. "He wakes up slowly," she explained to Zeke, who was giving the boy a good looking over.

"Such a fiery crown on that lad," said Zeke in his Scots brogue. "He'll make a hot-tempered river runner one day. Mark ma word."

Ellie took umbrage at his comment, "That boy's way too sweet t' turn into a river rat!"

"You callin' yer hoosband a river rat, lassie?"

At that juncture, Kit and Simeon came bundling down from the loft, where they'd been solving all the problems of the world between them. Elijah followed fast on their heels, determined not to be left out of the men's endeavors.

"How long till supper, Mother Howard?" Kit asked Libby.

"Ellie and I just put the stew on to cook, so it'll be at least two more hours till it's ready to eat," she answered.

"Then we have plenty of time," he nodded his head toward Simeon. "What say we break out the cards and stir us up a rousing game of hearts? We have enough for teams... make it really intra'stin. Whaddyea say? You in, Pa? Zeke?"

"I'm in!" Elijah shouted to be heard above all the hubbub.

"Girls? You want to get in on this tournament?" Kit asked Lizzie and Katrina, raising his voice to be heard above his howling daughter.

"You boys go ahead," Lizzie said, jiggling the babe in an attempt to quiet her down. "I have to feed Liberty first."

"Katrina?"

"Simon needs to cuddle a bit longer before he's fully awake," she said, snuggling the boy to her. "I'll give him a little snack. Lizzie and I can join you boys later."

The four men and Elijah trooped over to the cabin addition, where they pulled the extra table out from under the window and proceeded to grab chairs and benches enough to make seats for everyone joining their game.

"Would you put a pot of coffee on for us, Mother?" Zach called over to Libby.

"Certainly, my dear. Coming right up!"

"Hear that, Zach? We live to serve!" Ellie joked, finishing up her last sip of tea. "I'll start them pies, now, Lib. We got us a bunch of mangy man-critters to keep from starvin'."

A little over two hours later, the "hot card game" had still not lost a bit of its momentum.

"Got it!" Kit said, smacking his ace on the table and pulling in the cards of that round. "Skill wins out every time," he boasted, tongue in cheek. "Course it don't hurt to have a handful of hearts, neither."

"How is it you always get the good cards, Kit?" Elijah spoke up.

"Just lucky, I guess," Kit said with a wink toward his young brother-in-law.

"Ever notice how often it's on *his* deal those cards seem to show up all in one hand?" Simeon poked at him.

"Maybe we should examine that score sheet a little closer, hey *brother*," Kit poked back. "I recollect the one tallyin' up all them points ain't lost a single game, yet!"

"It sure does smell good over there, Mother," Simeon called to the kitchen. "We're getting mighty hungry in here!"

"There he goes again," Kit leaned over to Zach, "tryin' to change the subject. A guilty man's trick, if ever I saw one."

Sitting between the younger men, Zach smacked both boys on their backs. "Sure is good to have so much life in this house again, Mother," he called to Libby. "But he's right, we've worked up quite the appetite with all this card playing. Hope you got plenty of tucker for this gang."

Libby poked her head through the addition's door, "We'll have everything laid out in another quarter hour, boys. And don't you worry, there's ample amount to go around."

"You need any help in there, Mother Howard?" Katrina asked from her place at the game table, where she held Simon on what was left of her lap. He quietly played with the stack of cards sitting in front of her.

"Keep your seat, dear, we're doing just fine."

"You sure, Mother?" Lizzie chimed in.

"Ellie and I have everything well in hand. We'll let you girls clean up later."

* * * * *

By the end of the day, with supper dishes finished and tables pushed back against the walls, the eleven souls gathered around the hearth in the Howard cabin began to tell stories of Christmases past.

"Remember our first Christmas out here in this 'Hio country?" Zach said, "All we had to give each other that year was good wishes."

"I think the worst one came from Levi," said Simeon. "He wished that Leesha's beaver teeth would never kill anyone."

"I still can hardly believe our lovely girl is gone from us," Libby said, giving Zach a melancholy glance.

"At least we know she's not sufferin' now," he patted his wife's shoulder in comfort. "And I'm sure she wishes for us all to be happy."

"I liked the Christmas where Nate and Pa had a contest going to see who could make the most impressive toy," Simeon added. "I think Nate won that one, hands down."

"Whoa right there, son. Seems to me that my climbing bear took everybody's vote as the most inventive toy that year," Zach protested.

"I liked the bouncing man, best," Elijah piped up. "Maybe I should give it to Simon this year. I'm really too big for such toys now."

Libby smiled at her youngest son, trying to act so grown up among all these adults.

"I recall a Christmas we each had us a real orange to eat," Ellie told the group. "I never seen one before in all my days. O' course I was only seven or eight at the time," she explained. "Didn't know what to do with that blasted thing, neither. Couldn't figger it out for the longest time. Edie finally showed me how to peel it open and pull apart them little juicy fingers to eat. Got to say it tasted sweet and tart all at the same time."

"We Scots 'ave the custom o' puttin' candles in the winda' t' light the way of a stranger," said Zeke. "The Oidche Choinnle, or Night of Candles. Light the way fer th' Holy Fam'ly. Shopkeepers give 'em oot t' patrons, wishin' each one a 'Fire t' warm ya, an' a light t' guide ya'. Yule Candles, they calls 'em."

"Sounds like a nice idea," Katrina spoke up. "You got a candle to spare we could put in the window tonight, Mother Howard?"

"I believe I do," Libby answered. She started to rise from the seat beside her husband.

"Don't stir yourself, Mother. I'll get it," Lizzie said. "Extras still in the bottom of the pantry, right?" She walked to the other side of the cabin and rustled around on the lower shelf.

"Beside the tea towels, dear. Over to the left."

"Got it." Lizzie pulled a candle from the cupboard, lighted it at the hearth, then let a small amount of wax drip onto a saucer. She affixed the candle upright and placed it in the middle of the table sitting under the south-facing window. "Who knows, maybe it'll guide one of our long-lost brothers home," she said with a wistful smile.

"Anybody got a good story?" Simeon asked.

"How about the one of the babe born on this night," Katrina said, giving her husband a knowing smile.

"Before you sit back down, Lizzie, would you go get the Bible from on top of my trunk?" Libby asked her daughter.

Lizzie paddled to the bed corner separated from the rest of the cabin by a row of shelves, where she picked up the family Bible and brought it to her father. Zach opened the cherished tome and began to read, "Saint Luke, chapter two…

> *'And it came to pass in those days, that there went out a decree from Caesar Augustus, that all the world should be taxed…, And Joseph also went up from Galilee, out of the city of Nazareth, into Judea, unto the city of David, which is called Bethlehem, (because he was of the house and lineage of David,) to be taxed with Mary his espoused wife, being great with child. And so it was, that, while they were there, the days were accomplished that*

she should be delivered. And she brought forth her first-born son, and wrapped him in swaddling clothes, and laid him in a manger; because there was no room for them in the inn'..."

Zach continued on with the familiar story, as the friends and family about him listened intently, entranced by his rich, hypnotizing voice. No one noticed Katrina becoming more unsettled by the moment. But she continued to keep her peace.

"...'And suddenly there was with the angel a multitude of the heavenly host praising God, and saying, Glory to God in the highest, and on earth peace, good will toward men.'"

"I hate to interrupt this lovely story," Katrina finally spoke up. "But I do believe we're about to write another Christmas story of our own." She leaned into Simeon for a moment, waiting to catch her breath until the spasm passed. "If I'm not mistaken... and I don't believe that I am... we're about to meet a new little Howard this very night," she said.

"*Good Lord,* Katrina! You mean it?" Simeon jumped to his feet to help his wife rise.

"Please, don't let me disturb the rest of you," Katrina said. "Continue on with this lovely story, Father Howard. Lizzie and I can handle things in the other room just fine. Don't pay a bit of attention to us."

"You want Lib an' me t' come help?" asked Ellie.

"Not yet, Ma. We'll be fine for a while. We'll call you when this babe gets closer."

Lizzie rose and handed Liberty over to her mother, and she followed Simeon and Katrina into the cabin addition, where the rest of the stacked beds lined the walls.

"My, my, just look at those two," Libby smiled to her bosom friend. "I hardly can believe the change in my own Lizzie. Katrina talked her right through her fears when she gave birth to this little sweetheart, and Lizzie's been a completely different person ever since... so calm, and self-assured." She patted Liberty to quiet her back down, after being shifted into her grandmother's arms. "And before long we'll have another wee babe to cuddle."

"Cain't think of a better present than that!" Ellie squeezed the hand of her friend, while Zach picked back up with the original story of Christmas.

* * * * *

Nearly four hours later, with youngsters tucked into their respective beds for the night, the men still lounged over in the main cabin, smoking pipes and drinking the hot toddies Libby had mixed up for their Christmas Cheer.

"Wonderful libation t' top off th' evenin', lass" Zeke complimented his hostess.

"Tis a special recipe of my Da's," Libby explained in her father's brogue. "He was of the Irish, my Da."

"Achh, a goot Celt always kens how t' warm th' heart of a cold, winter's night."

"Mother?" Lizzie poked her head in from the other room. "I think maybe you and Ellie might want to come in here now," she said, motioning them over to herself. "This babe is looking mighty close."

"Oh, El!" Libby exclaimed, giving Ellie another hug.

"Come on, Lib. Let's go help hatch out this new one."

The men continued with their talk, as Kit and Simeon roasted chestnuts in a wire basket over the hot coals. From time to time, they'd toss hot ones back and forth, seeing if they could keep them in the air without burning any fingers, until they cooled down enough to eat. For the calmness that dominated the household, one would never guess that a woman lay in the adjoining room about to give birth.

In the cabin addition, Lizzie and Katrina carried on with their chatter, stopping momentarily whenever Katrina needed to concentrate on more pressing matters. By the time her final pushes forced all other concerns aside, the four women focused on none

184

else but the coming babe. In the midst of their attentiveness, not a single one heard the commotion that broke out in the other room.

"A few more pushes ought to do it," Lizzie coached. "Give it all you've got. You can do this."

A voice piped up from the doorway, "As I recall, Katrina, you used to tell me that Indian women thought nothing of giving birth. Just squatted down behind a tree and let nature take her course."

"Johannah?" Ellie stared at the tall girl taking up the doorway. "*Johannah!* My Lord, is it really you?"

"It's me, Ma. In the flesh!"

"Forgive me for not getting up to hug you, sister," Katrina leaned over on one elbow, "... but I have a... a bit more to do here, first..." she ended her puffed greeting with a big groan she could no longer contain. At the end of that last, big push, a boy babe hollered out his extreme displeasure at being so unceremoniously thrust into a cold, new world.

* * * * *

By the time the Howard household had settled in for the night, only a few hours remained until Christmas dawn. The new mother and babe rested in Simeon's arms on the larger bottom bed to one side of the cabin addition, with Johannah asleep in the smaller, stacked bed above. Zeke and Ellie snored loudly in the other, bottom bunk across the room, with Kit and Lizzie snuggled into the smaller bed above them.

Wandering sons, Christian and Levi, had bedded down in the loft of the original cabin with their baby brother, Elijah and little Simon, while Zach and Libby occupied their semi-private quarters in the shelved-off section of the main cabin below.

Just as everyone had finally dropped into a sound sleep, baby Liberty began to fuss in her cradle near the hearth. Immediately rousing at her daughter's cry, Lizzie eased her way around her slumbering husband, crawled down from the top bunk without disturbing Zeke or Ellie below, and retrieved her fussing daughter before she could break into a full-blown cry.

185

"You need anything?" came a loud whisper from Libby over in the corner.

"We're fine, Mother. Go back to sleep while you can," she whispered in return. Lizzie eased into the rocker still sitting beside the fire and nursed her precious babe while enjoying a rare moment of silent contentment. Most all her loved ones, safe, warm and accounted for under one roof. What could be more fulfilling?

No one in residence obtained much sleep that night, for just as the sun's rays peeked over the eastern horizon, Elijah and Simon came whooping down the loft steps rousing the entire household with their exuberance for the Yuletide holiday.

"Santa came!" Elijah hollered, pulling his stocking down from the mantle and digging into its contents to see what treats had been left him.

"I thought you were too big for such shenanigans," Levi teased his youngest brother, giving his hair a muss.

"No one's too big for treats!" Elijah countered, licking on a fat peppermint stick. "Besides, I'm just doing this for little Simon."

Eighteen-month-old Simon wandered around looking for his mama, not quite sure what all this excitement was really about. When he toddled into the addition and found Katrina and Simeon cuddling a tiny baby, he broke into a gigantic smile.

"Come on up here, big fella," Simeon pulled Simon up, onto the bed. "Meet your new baby brother, Matthew."

"Maffoo," he tried to repeat.

"Must be careful with the new baby," Katrina explained. "He's very small."

While the happy, little family cuddled and got acquainted with its newest member, Lizzie and Johannah worked together at preparing a breakfast for the enlarged group. Christian, Kit and Levi had gone outdoors to tend to the milking and other barn chores, so the oldest four people in residence took advantage of the rare opportunity to spend a bit more time relaxing in bed on a holiday morning. After the short night, it came as a welcome luxury.

"Come over here, woman," Zach pulled his wife to him in an all-encompassing hug.

"Zachary Howard, contain yourself!" Libby fussed. "We have a houseful of people in here!"

"I just want to hug my wife, Lib, there's nothing wrong with that." He gave her a pitiful, hang-dog look, and she burst out giggling, then snuggled in closer to enjoy their stolen moments.

"We hear you two carryin' on over there," Johannah poked fun from where she worked at a table pulled over to the hearth. The girls had laid out coffee and hot cinnamon buns for the early morning risers.

"Is your mother up and about yet?" Libby asked, now beginning to feel guilty at lying abed so long.

"She and Zeke are still snoring to beat the band over there," Johannah answered. "You two just relax and enjoy yourselves, hear?" She attended to her task of slicing up the few remaining apples to add to the big pot of porridge Lizzie had bubbling over the fire.

"This should be ready by the time the boys get back in from the barn," Lizzie said in a low voice. She dumped the bowlful of sliced apples in, added some precious cinnamon to the mix, and stirred their holiday breakfast to it keep from sticking to the pot. "You had a good idea, mixing in apples and spice," said Lizzie. "Makes it more of a treat."

"I used to do that for the fancy dining room on the steamboat," Johannah mentioned. "Those rich people always expect their eats tastier than plain folks."

"How long did you cook on a steamboat?"

"Oh, prob'ly eight, nine months. Got to see a lot of the Mississippi country during that time."

"You better not mention paddle wheelers around Zeke in there. Your mama says he hates 'em with a passion," Lizzie said.

"I saw it for myself, when Mother asked if they took a steamboat back up from Marietta, what with Zeke's hurt shoulder and all. Went off like an overloaded blunderbuss, he did! Couldn't understand a word he said, either."

"I sure am amazed at the all changes in the four years I been gone," Johannah said, washing her hands in the dishpan. "Ma killin' Theodore, and Zeke killin' Harvey. And now her married to that Scotsman, of all things. Boy, who'd have ever guessed?"

"Life does have a way of turning around on us. Yes it does," Lizzie said with a solemn nod.

When the boys returned from the barn, no one could stay in bed any longer with the rising noise level that accompanied their jocularity.

"Levi as a riverboat gambler! What a thought!" Kit teased. "Make sure you don't ever get mixed up in a card game with that one," he poked at Simeon, "that's all I gotta say."

"Where did you meet up with Johannah?" Simeon asked Levi.

"On the Memphis Messenger. Didn't even know she was aboard, till I was tryin' to get away from a couple fellas who took issue with the tone of my card playin', if ya get my drift," he said with a wink.

"As if there's ary a thing to question concernin' this one," Christian gave his younger brother a firm slap on the back.

"Well, I was headin' down the lower passageway with three hoodlums fast on my heels, when this tall gal stuck her head out o' the kitchen, pulled me inside and slammed the door shut behind me, before those scoundrels could round the curve in the hallway an' see where I'd got to," said Levi. "Turned out to be Johannah there," he nodded at his savior now sitting at the kitchen table.

"Couldda knocked me over with a feather when I saw who it was," Johannah smiled. "'Why, Levi Howard, what on earth are you doin' here?' says I," she mimicked her surprise.

"'Just making my way, best I can,' says I right back, with a low bow and a sweep of my fancy hat," Levi mimicked in return.

"When he finally realized who I was, we caught up on the happenin's of our last years of knocking around the country. Then between us we decided just maybe we ought to come on home for a spell," Johannah said.

"How did you run into this critter, then?" Kit poked Christian.

"He was making his way cuttin' wood for the steamboats coming up-river," Levi said. "When we pulled into St. Louis, who did we see standin' beside a woodpile on the docks, but my long, lost, toe-headed brother."

"You didn't even know who he was," Johannah teased. "But I recognized him right off."

Not one to waste words, Christian just nodded in agreement.

"When we told him we were on our way back to Ohio, he allowed as he might tag along," said Levi. "So here we all are, just in time for Christmas."

"Who put the light in the window last night?" Johannah asked.

"Lizzie did that," Katrina said, walking in slowly from the other room with the newborn infant in her arms.

"Well, it's a good thing, because these two so-called 'adventurers' couldn't find their way in a two-rowed pea-patch without some sign to navigate by," Johannah harassed. "Took me pointing out to 'em that most likely a light over yonder meant it must be the way to *somebody's* cabin. And bein' it was pushing midnight, we needed to get in out of the cold!"

"I always did say, put a bunch of hard-headed men together, an' nary a one of 'em know when to come in outta the cold," Ellie said, making her entrance into the morning.

Zeke, following behind, nodded his recognition to Levi, shook hands with both him and Christian, then he walked over to Johannah. "I'd ken this lassie anywhere," he said giving her a welcoming hug. "She's th' spittin' image of her mither."

Chapter 11

Wallingsford Christmas
Edisto Island, South Carolina
December 18, 1821

"Do we have any more roping?" Amanda asked the Plantation manager who was helping her hang pine swags along the front porch of the big house. "We're short about five or six feet, before we can finish up here."

"I'll go ask Pitney if her gals made up any more pine rope," Winston answered.

"Thank you so much for all your help," Amanda said, giving Winston an earnest smile. "I couldn't have reached those high spots without your long arms."

"No problem, my dear. Glad to be of assistance," he said with a tip of his hat. "Don't go away, I'll be right back." He stepped off the porch and headed around to the main kitchen building out behind the house.

Amanda stood there, looking over the orchard, missing Jeremiah, missing Michael, and wondering how she ever wound up here, of all places, to celebrate Christmas. Before she had a chance to brood for very long, Lilly and Millie came running up, chasing one another round and round her skirts.

"Girls, girls, slow down!"

"She took Dolly!" Camellia accused Lilly, who stayed just out of Millie's reach holding something tightly above her head.

"Stop right now!" Amanda took each girl by an arm. "Lillian Jane, did you take your sister's Dolly?"

"She tore my dolly's dress on purpose!" Lilly accused back.

"Enough! Hand Dolly back to your sister." Lilly complied. "Camellia Jane, did you tear her dolly's dress?"

"Yes, Ma'am. But she said hers was prettier than mine."

"That's no reason to lash out, Camellia. Tell her you're sorry."

190

Camellia kicked her feet, trying to avoid what she knew she must do.

"Go on, make amends."

"Sorry, Lilly."

"I'm sorry, too, Millie." The girls hugged one another, then clung to their mother's skirts.

"You two are missing home, aren't you."

"I want Unka Mikey!" Lilly whined.

"I want to see Hank," Millie added with as much emphasis.

"I know we've been away a very long time," Amanda soothed. "But Mama needs to stay here to see to the work Grandmother Bently left me. I know you have trouble understanding all that," she patted both heads, trying to give them some kind of assurance, "but for now, this is where we must stay for a while longer."

The girls gave Amanda a big hug, then ran off into the house, chattering as if nothing had upset their world just a few moments before. When they disappeared through the front door, Winston came out, holding another length of pine roping.

"They're in a hurry," he observed. "Pitney had this last piece left over from inside," Winston said, handing one end to Amanda. "When we finish up here, we're to go in to eat. Pitney said she would hold dinner no longer than 'half a-more hour'," he mimicked her enunciation.

Amanda laughed and applied herself to the task at hand.

"If you can finish up this last section, I'll go hang the mistletoe, since I can reach higher than you can," he winked. He picked up the sprig of mistletoe bound in a festive ribbon, moved a tall stool over just inside the front door, and worked at securing the kissing nosegay to the header above the doorway.

When Amanda finished fastening her last section of greenery, she headed for the front door, where Winston was just stepping down from his perch. Before she could walk through, he took her by the shoulders and gave her an unexpected kiss.

"Why... *Winston!*"

"Mistletoe!" he said, pointing upward. "Couldn't let that go to waste, now, could I?"

Amanda felt so flustered, she was at a complete loss for words. She hurried into the house, trying to gather herself as she headed for the dining room. She found Jems, already sitting in his chair, gnawing on a chicken leg, with Effie Lou just getting the twins seated at their places.

"You look red, Mama," Lillian observed.

"I'm a little warm, dear," Amanda told her daughter, as she settled herself onto her own chair at the head of the table, fussing with her skirts and napkin. Winston appeared a few moments later, removed his jacket and seated himself at Amanda's left, across the table from the girls.

"You little ladies look enchanting tonight," he complimented the twins, "just like your ravishing mother," he said, shaking out his napkin and laying it across his lap.

"Winston...," Amanda started. "I... I think after dinner we need to talk."

Winston laid a hand across Amanda's arm, "Of course, my dear. We have quite a lot to discuss," he said in an overly familiar tone of voice.

Amanda turned redder still, but to avoid upsetting the girls at the dinner table, she uttered not a word.

* * * * *

"How *dare* you take such liberties!" Amanda erupted at Winston down in the sitting room, after the girls and Jems finished their supper and had been tucked into bed for the night. "You should have more respect for my position than to assume that you can just–"

"Calm down, Amanda Jane," Winston tried to sooth her ruffled feathers. "I meant no disrespect whatsoever," he crooned. "On the contrary, I only took advantage of the holiday spirit to convey my deepest regard for you, my dear."

"But I had no idea... I mean, well... you never said a word to suggest that you felt any... any..."

"Affection? I suppose I did rather take you by surprise. For that, I do apologize. But you must admit, we've been in such close proximity, working and planning together for Wallingsford these past months, how do you expect me *not* to be enchanted by your lovely charms?"

"But I never even *thought* of such a thing, Winston," Amanda said in complete astonishment.

"Well, maybe you should."

"I'm so confused right now. Ever since Michael left in such a huff, I've felt terribly unsettled," she fretted. "And guilty. I'm the one who sent him off with such distressing feelings between us. It's just that I simply don't know what I should do, or where I belong, or whom I have any right to lean on any more."

"I have very broad shoulders, Amanda Jane. Why not lean on me?" he said, searching her eyes.

Amanda blushed once again. She took a deep breath and heaved out a sigh. "Winston, you'll have to give me some time to adjust to this turn. I've had so much to sort out... with losing my husband and my parents, trying to understand all that Grand-mother Bently left me to deal with, taking care of my fatherless children–"

"You have more than your share of burdens for such a deli-cate set of shoulders," he said, lightly touching said shoulders and turning her toward himself. "Let me help you, Amanda Jane. You don't need to carry all this alone." He pulled her to himself and wrapped his arms around her, holding her gently against his side.

She had a hard time relaxing into the embrace, but she looked up, taking in the wisdom of his weathered face and the sturdiness of the strong jawline. "I need some time, Winston," she whis-pered.

"Take all the time you need, my dear. I don't plan on going anywhere."

* * * * *

"Mista Winston, he say I'z ta bring you dis post right quick, Mizz 'Manda," the ten-year-old, curly-headed boy said with importance.

Amanda took the letter Buzzy handed to her from the latest mail delivery Winston had picked up from the steam packet that day. The packet made shuttle trips twice a week between Charleston and Edisto Island carrying passengers, cargo and mail.

"Thank you, Buzzy. You're a good boy." Amanda gave his nappy head a pat. "Go on out to the kitchen and tell Ada Mae I sent you to get a benne wafer."

The boy took off running, before "Mizz 'Manda" changed her mind.

"Hmmm, a letter from Irene. That seems rather odd," Amanda said to no one but herself. "Now why I the world would she be writing to me?"

"You ain't talkin' to spooks, again, is you Mizz 'Manda?" Effie Lou asked, hearing her speaking with no one else in the room as she walked past Amanda's small office situated behind the parlor.

"No, no, don't mind me, Effie. I have this habit of talking aloud to myself," she said half distracted. "It always irritates Michael terribly." She turned the letter over in her hand, examining the postmark. "I just received this letter from Irene Margaret, and I'm wondering what she could possibly be writing to me about."

"Well, you ain' gonna find out, less'n you open up that thing." Effie hurried on into the dining room, carrying her armload of clean dishes to put away in the breakfront cabinet.

Amanda took the bone-handled, flint knife lying on Grandmother's desk and slit open the letter's seal...

December 12, 1821
Tradd Street, Charleston

Dear Amanda Jane,

I realize Eralynn and I have barely communicated
with you since you left for Wallingsford, after Mother and

Father passed away. But I am writing now to ask an enormous favor of you.

Would you allow me to come and live at Grand-mother's Orchard? Of course, I realize her plantation now belongs to you, Amanda Jane. But at this juncture, I have absolutely nowhere else to turn.

Eralynn and I have come to a complete impasse, as far as our living arrangements are concerned here in Charleston—in her house. I can no longer tolerate the way she lords over me her "condescending benevolence" in allowing me "the favor" of occupying my own bedroom in the home we all grew up in, for heaven's sakes!

Naturally, she will listen to no advice from me as far as the running of the household or guiding of the servants is concerned. And Heaven forbid if I should even dare to make mention of any untoward behavior regarding a certain Cannon Burrell, her so-called "Pirate" who makes himself quite at home here, whenever his ship docks in port.

It has now come to the point that Eralynn even refuses to allow the servants to cook for me or to assist me in any way, as they also "all belong to her," she constantly reminds me. That Hornsby person, hardly ever checks on her at all, even though she will not come of age for quite some time yet. He's left her completely to her own devices with practically no guidance whatsoever.

Since Father's Factor controls the disbursement of our yearly stipend from his estate, I have few resources available to me for supplying even the simplest of my own needs for daily living. Eralynn withholds so much from me, I have been forced to sell more of Mother's silver (now my silver, I never fail to remind Eralynn) in order to have something on which to live. I must even buy my own foodstuffs, just to have something to eat!

Heavenly days, I've even been forced to learn how to cook for myself! Out in the <u>cookhouse</u>, of all places!! I can tell you, it has been a humiliating experience. Thankfully, Noreen has taken pity on me and been very helpful in teaching me a great deal, in spite of the way she laughs at my pitiful attempts.

But you should see my poor hands, Amanda Jane. I have burns and cracks all over them, which I can hardly display in their present condition to any of my harpsichord students. Yes, I had been taking students, as you surmised. I could not bring myself to admit such a fall of station to you, nor to anyone else of our social circle. I scarcely can bring myself to admit it to you now, but I am in such dire straits, I know not what else to do.

I'm alone, Amanda Jane. My marriage was annulled three weeks after our wedding, before Arlow returned to his ship and sailed out of my life forever. I never said a word to a soul. So you see, as things stand, I have no resources from my husband's "well-established" family, as everyone believes, for no longer do I even <u>have</u> a husband to keep me!

It hurts tremendously to tell you this. I must apologize for disclosing such unsettling news by way of an impersonal letter, but I knew if I didn't inform you in this manner, I should never be able to tell you face to face.

All those months, I was too embarrassed to breathe a word of it to Mother or Father, knowing that Mother, particularly, would be completely scandalized. I allowed them to continue thinking all was well between Capt. Harrington and myself. But the reality is that he's left me quite destitute.

While I lived on Father's beneficence (under the guise of saving money for a future household of our own when my captain returned), I took on young lady students in order to have enough money keep up appearances for all parties concerned, mainly Mother.

But with both of them gone, and Eralynn so out of control, it all seems quite pointless to me now.

I'm asking you to take pity on me, Amanda Jane. As the only one of my siblings who shared the same father, I have no one else to look to for help. If you won't allow me an extended stay at Wallingsford, may I at least spend the Christmas Holidays with you and your family, while I try to puzzle out what I should do? I hardly can stand living a minute longer in "Eralynn's House," as it has become totally intolerable here.

She and I <u>have</u> managed to come to an agreement concerning Mother's furnishings—which she desperately wants, in order to keep the house presentable for her ostentatious friends. If I consent to leave what remains and cease from selling off anything more to sustain myself, she's agreed to surrender Ruth and Tutt for seeing to my needs and relinquish all rights to me concerning their value…

"Oh my Lord, they intend to split up Noreen's family! How can they even *think* of doing such a thing?" Amanda fussed. She pushed away from her desk and hurried out the back door, down the steps, and around to Winston's office.

"Winston, you have to read this!" She shoved the letter at him, then proceeded to pace the floor while he quickly perused the gist of the message.

"Your sister's coming."

"How can I tell her not to?"

"You simply say 'No,' if you really don't want her here."

"But she has nowhere else to go!"

"You've led me to believe you don't have terribly warm feelings for either one of your sisters," he said with astute insight. "So what really has you so upset about all this, Amanda Jane?

"It's the last part, concerning Ruth and Tutt. My sisters intend to break up Noreen's family. Zeb and Noreen have lost so much already, I simply cannot allow that to happen to them again," Amanda said.

"Then don't. Bring them all out here, where we have our own way to safeguard these people."

"But how can I do that? They belong to Eralynn. Oh, I just hate this whole concept of owning people. They have feelings... desires. They have their own dreams. Believe me, I know what it's like to be forced into doing something you don't want to do. I wasn't 'sold' like a slave, but I know exactly how it felt to be used as barter goods. And quite helpless to do a thing to stop it,"

Amanda exhaled a huge sigh. "What can I do, Winston? You know we've talked this through before. With laws as they now stand, our hands are tied where my parents' slaves are concerned. Now Eralynn's slaves. Legally, I can't free any of them, no matter how much I'd like to do it. It's fortunate our own people had their freedom before these current manumission laws went into effect."

"You do have majority control over your Father's estate, until Jems comes of age. So use some pressure to make Eralynn realize she risks losing much more than a family of slaves, if she insists on going through with such a heartless deed," he said.

"You mean blackmail her into letting them go?"

"Think of it as simple bribery. Give her something she desires more, in exchange for letting the whole family come to live here on Wallingsford."

"Would you be willing to handle the negotiations in my stead, Winston? You're on much better footing with Mr. Hornsby than I am, at this juncture. And you do have a presence about you few women can resist... especially when you turn on your charms."

"I noticed they don't seem to be having much influence on you."

"We won't go down that road right now," Amanda smiled, giving his shoulder a pat. "But I would like you to escort Irene out here on the next steam packet run, if you wouldn't mind doing that for me. She can at least come for the Holidays, until we figure out what to do about Father's people... and Eralynn."

"You know I'd do anything for you, Amanda Jane. Just say the word, and I'm yours."

"Good grief, Winston. Turn it *off!*"

* * * * *

"Mama! Mama! Did Father Christmas come?" The twins came bounding into Amanda's room, with Jems tottering along behind. The girls had freed him from his crib, but he didn't understand all the excitement.

"It's way too early to be up and about!" Amanda complained, pulling the covers over her head, in an attempt to hide from the children. The twins pounced on top of her, with Jems crawling up after them. Amanda pulled all three into her arms, and they had a good, long snuggle.

"Where did you hear about Father Christmas?" Amanda asked her girls.

"Mister Winston told us," Millie volunteered.

"He brings presents!" Lilly added.

"Only for good girls," Camellia reminded her sister.

"I've been good!"

"Have not."

"Have too!"

"Enough! You've had your moments, I have to say, but you both are good girls."

"We want to see what Father Christmas brought!" They bounced on the bed, pulling back the covers, forcing Amanda out of her warm cocoon. "Come *on* Mama!"

"Maybe he didn't bring a thing," Amanda smiled.

"Oh, he did, he *did!* Come on, hurry!" both talked at once.

The Harrisons bustled down the steps and into the parlor, where Amanda had set up a small "Weinachtsbaum" for her children, so they'd know one of their father's Christmas traditions. They'd talked about Jeremiah for quite some time, while decorating the tree the night before.

"Look, look! *Presents!*" Lillian and Camellia ran to the tree and started pulling packages out from underneath.

"Wait a minute, you two. Don't you think we'd better see which packages actually belong to each of you before you tear into them?" Amanda asked. "Sit back, girls. Let me see what's written on the tags. Then you may take turns opening so we can all enjoy seeing what's inside."

As Amanda handed out gifts, Irene Margaret stumbled into the parlor in her morning wrapper, half asleep. "Good grief, who gets up this early in the morning?"

"Excited little girls, apparently," Amanda smiled at her sister.

"I heard all the commotion and thought the house was on fire, or something," Irene teased. She plopped onto the settee, which Amanda had moved to the side of the room in order to make more space for Jeremiah's Christmas Tree. In her mind, she determined that from now on, it would always be known as "Jeremiah's Tree" to help keep his memory alive for his children.

The girls could hardly stand the wait, as Amanda sorted gifts into piles. "There, those are yours, Camellia. And that stack belongs to you, Lillian. These are for Jems," she pulled a third stack of gifts to her feet where she sat on the floor, and put Jems on her lap to show him what to do. The boy needed no instruction whatsoever; he immediately tore into the package on top. "It would appear that Jems goes first!" she said with amusement.

Inside his parcel he found a little dog on wheels, with a string attached to pull it along as he walked. He wasted no time sitting still, but got to his feet and proceeded to drag the dog round and round the room, completely enamored with his new toy.

"Well, he's occupied. Why don't you open one, Camellia."

Millie took up a small gift and carefully pulled out a blue pinafore, holding it aloft. "Blue's my fav'wit!"

"That's lovely, sweetheart. I believe that one came from Aunt Irene Margaret," Amanda in-formed. "You'd better give Auntie a big thank-you hug."

Camellia got to her feet and dutifully administered the requisite embrace.

"My turn, my turn!" Lilly called with excitement.

"All right, you're next, Lillian. Why don't you open that one first," Amanda directed.

Lilly pulled a gift from her pile that looked very similar to the one Millie had just opened. Surprise of surprises, it was a pinafore that matched her sister's, but in a bright hue of Christmas red. "Oh, pretty! I like red the best!" Lilly boasted. "Mine's prettier!" She jumped up and gave Aunt Irene her own thank-you hug before being instructed to do so.

By that time, with more of the household bustling about, Effie Lou came walking into the parlor with a tray full of goodies for the Christmas celebrants: hot coffee for the adults, cambric tea for the children, and warm, sweet, pecan rolls for everyone.

Winston followed Effie Lou into the room, carrying a stack of gifts in his arms. "Merry Christmas, all!" he said with a wide smile. "I had a hunch this troupe would wake up early." He laid his gifts at the foot of the tree beside Amanda, giving her a huge smile as he did so. "Just a little something for the family," he said.

"Thank you, Winston. You really didn't have to, you know."

"I wanted to, my dear."

"Are *you* Father Christmas?" Lilly asked in awe.

"I'm just one of his helpers," Winston said with a smile, patting each little head. "There's something special there for both of you. Why don't you open them?"

"Here, girls," Amanda said, handing each one a large box.

The twins tore into the big packages, which revealed beautiful, porcelain-faced dolls dressed in frilly dresses. Lillian picked up her vision in pink, but Camellia was half afraid to touch her blue version of an identical doll.

"You can hold her, darling. Just be careful not to handle her too roughly, or her face might break." That warning did little to help Millie feel more confident in touching the delicate doll. She sat and simply stared at it, as she hugged her ragged Dolly closer.

"My goodness, Winston. Such expensive gifts!"

"I noticed those scruffy rag dolls the girls are always playing with and decided it was high time they had something more befitting the heirs of a plantation," he said with a smile. "That one's for Jems," he pointed to the other large gift.

"Come here, Jems," Amanda called, as the boy trotted to her, pulling his doggie behind. She put him on her lap again and handed him Winston's gift, which he promptly tore open without preamble. Amanda raised the lid of the box, uncovering a wooden puzzle in the shape of a horse, made just the right size for little hands. Jems dumped out the pieces and began to examine each one, seeming to know instinctively that he must fit them together to reassemble his horse.

"This is wonderful, Winston!"

"Thank you. I made it myself. That boy seems to like horses so much, I thought it might be just the thing for him. And we all know how much he enjoys fitting things together."

"You're too kind. Thank you. You've given thoughtful gifts.."

"My pleasure. That small one's for you, my dear," he said with a nod toward a tiny box left beside her. "But you might want to wait till you have a bit more privacy to open it."

"I'll let the children finish with the rest of theirs first. They're so excited, I don't want to keep them from their fun."

"It'll wait," he said, turning to give Irene a smile. "Here's a little something for you, too, Mrs. Harrington."

"Please, call me Irene," she said. "And if you don't mind, from now on I'd rather go by the surname of Bently," she announced.

"As you wish, Mizz Irene Bently," Winston said with a gratuitous smile. "Merry Christmas."

"Why, thank you! And I didn't even get you a thing!"

"No matter. It's just a small token for the holidays," he said. "Go ahead. Open it, if you wish."

Irene unwrapped the package, revealing a box of Swiss chocolates. "Oh, I haven't had chocolates in ages! How considerate! Thank you, Mr. Applebaum."

"It's Winston, to you, dear lady."

Irene blushed.

After the children had finished opening their remaining packages, Irene Margaret excused herself from the morning's festivities. "I'm going back to bed. In my opinion it's still way too early for breakfast."

With the children occupied in their play under the Weinachtsbaum, Amanda took Winston's gift and moved over to the settee, where she could open it away from inquisitive little eyes. He joined her there, waiting anxiously for her to unwrap the tiny package. She slowly lifted the lid as if something might jump out and bite her, then she gave a sudden gasp.

"Oh, my... Winston!"

"Before you say a word," he dropped to one knee, took the sapphire ring from where it nestled in the velvet-lined box and held it out to her, "will you do me the honor of becoming my wife, Amanda Jane? I know it may seem a bit sudden, but you can't honestly say you didn't see this coming now, can you?"

"No, ah, yes... I mean, yes, it is sudden, and no... I *didn't* see this coming! Oh, Winston!"

"Is that a yes?"

"No. It's not!"

"You're not ready. It's too soon, forgive me, Amanda... I'm just so taken with you, I couldn't wait to spring the question. You need time to adjust to these thoughts, I know," he babbled in an effort to keep his composure.

"Winston... " Amanda said softly, touching his arm. "I... I don't know if I'll ever be ready."

"Truly?"

"It's just that... I think my heart may lie elsewhere," she said, dropping her eyes.

203

"Well," he said, moving back to his seat next to her on the settee, "I can't say I'm surprised to hear it. But I also know you're still not all that certain, Amanda Jane. Please don't make your mind up too hastily," he said with a warm smile. "Don't say anything just yet."

"I... I really don't think I should accept this," she said, trying to hand the ring back to him.

"No, please. I want you to keep it. A woman as magnificent as you should have beautiful adornments, regardless of how you interpret its meaning," he flattered. "I want you to keep it... and promise me that you'll at least think about my proposal. You belong here at Wallingsford."

"Well... all right," she said, "I'll wear it on this hand," she acquiesced, sliding it carefully onto the third finger of her right hand, pulling the ring back and looking closely at the beautiful jewel set in platinum. "I'll think about it... for now."

* * * * *

The day after Christmas dawned clear and cold on Edisto Island. Lines of smoke rose from the People's cabins, as families huddled around fireplaces to stay warm in the rare, early morning temperature-dip below freezing. Winston came into the big house to start a fire in the parlor and found one already ablaze, with Amanda warming herself at the hearth.

"Who started the fire?" he asked.

"I did, of course. Who else did you think would do it?"

"I just assumed you wouldn't want to dirty your hands undertaking such a task," he said, stepping up beside her to warm his backside.

"My heavens, Winston. I've spent the last six years of my life cooking over a fire. Starting one feels second nature to me, now."

"I keep forgetting your rustic sojourn over these past years," he said. "Forgive me for underestimating you, my dear."

"I realize I'm rather a strange bird down here after all I've been through up North," she said, rubbing her hands together.

204

"I've had to learn many things no Southern Lady would be caught dead attempting to do for herself."

"I commend you, Amanda. No doubt you've weathered a great deal up in your wilderness."

"More than you could ever know, Winston," she said with a sigh. "But do you want to hear the craziest thing? I miss my tiny little cabin back home. And I miss the friends I made back there... strange as that may sound."

"It doesn't seem at all strange. You invested a great deal of yourself in making a life away from here. It's only natural to miss the place and the people."

"Thank you for understanding. I doubt my sisters ever will."

"They've just not endured their 'trials by fire' the way you have," he observed. "Give them time. Life will no doubt leave its bruises on them as it has on you. That's the only way true understanding ever begins to dawn on any of us, you know."

"You have a great deal of depth, Winston. I'm just beginning to see that in you." Amanda gave a shiver. "I can't seem to get warm today," she said, rubbing her arms. "Have you seen Pitney this morning? She's usually up here long before this. I hope she's all right. She did seem rather subdued after yesterday's Christmas celebration for all her people. I told her she'd been outside in the cold way too long, but she wouldn't hear of going in before the 'doin's was done', as she said."

"These temperatures cannot be helping her rheumatism one bit. I'll go up to her cabin and check on her, if you'd like," Winston offered.

"Oh, would you? I'd be grateful," she said. "How many winters do you suppose that dear woman has seen by now?"

"More than anyone I've ever known," he answered. "I'd guess at least 100... most likely quite a few more."

"Grandmother said Pitney was already a grown woman with several children, when they met at the Indian village."

"I know. She told me those stories, too."

205

"I can't imagine how difficult it must have been for them... trying to make a life in such harsh conditions."

"Ah, but you of all people *do* understand the difficulties," he noted. "You're the only one of your family who's gone through something similar."

"I suppose I have." Amanda stood in silence a few moments. "I just never thought of my life as anything remotely as difficult as Grandmother Bently's. Maybe in its own way, it has been."

"Enduring the same kind of bruises has given you all the understanding you need, Amanda Jane."

"I hope I can become half the woman my Grandmother was."

* * * * *

Pitney's cabin sat at the center of the People's village on Wallingsford. Whereas most plantation "slave rows" were just that, rows of rustic cabins built away from the immediate view of the main house, the worker's village at Wallingsford followed a design more akin to that of an Indian village—a meeting house facing the east, surrounded by spirals of individual dwellings. A community well sat at the center, adjacent to the meeting house and just down from Pitney's little cabin. When Winston knocked, one of Pitney's granddaughters opened the door.

"Mornin' Iddy," Winston said, tipping his hat. "Pitney hasn't come up to the house, and Miss Amanda was wondering if she was all right. Is she still here?"

"She be here," the sad-eyed woman replied. "Done took to her bed las' evenin'. Say she ain' never risin' up ag'in."

"Does she need a doctor?"

"No doc c'n fix what ailin' Mammaw Pitney," Iddy replied, opening the door wider for Winston to enter. He removed his hat and stepped toward the bed in the far corner, taking the chair Iddy directed him to.

"Pitney?"

The shriveled woman took a labored breath. "Owl flew at th' winda las' evenin'... means my time t' go."

"Pitney, surely–"

"She b'lieve in dat sign, Mista Winston," Iddy fussed. "Owl had blue eyes. She say de Plateye done sit on top her all night long. Cain't hardly catch a breath."

"Sounds more like heart failure to me. Heavy chest, hard to breathe."

"She waitin' on Jesus."

"Bring me Manny..." Pitney wheezed, reaching out to Winston. "Gots to tell–" She went into a coughing fit, unable to finish.

"This does not look good," Winston said. He rose and headed out the door, making a beeline for the big house.

Fifteen minutes later, Amanda sat at Pitney's bedside, holding the withered, old hand. "Pitney, you can't leave me now. I need you here. How can I ever hope to run this place without you to guide me?"

"No he'p fo' it, Manny. You strong... you be fine," Pitney wheezed. "But you gots to know–" Coughing stopped her again. "Woman Who Sings. I make her a promise ... t' hold de secret."

"Secret? What secret, Pitney," Amanda leaned in closer. "You're talking in riddles."

"Fo' the People... onliest one who knows be me." Pitney reached up and touched the mole behind Amanda's right ear. "Use yo' secon' sight, Manny. Look..." she began to choke. "Look in–" Her coughing became so difficult, she couldn't manage to continue speaking. With her last breath she managed to squeeze out, "Journal... Lillian's journal."

Tears slid down Amanda's cheeks and landed on the hand stilled now in death. "Rest, my dearest Pitney," she sighed. "You've more than earned it."

For the remainder of the day, everything on Wallingsford came to a standstill in honor of Pitney Doubleday Bower. Her extended family, which amounted to more than three-quarters of all the plantation's people, came by in small groups all afternoon long, bringing food, paying their respects, saying their good-byes.

At eventide, everyone gathered at the burying ground on a small rise, out behind the village.

The fenced-off part of the cemetery with the larger, stone markers sheltered the graves of Grandmother Bently, her Wallingsford parents and siblings, and her son Falling Leaf, along with his wife and their oldest son, Jamison. The remainder of the cemetery, outside the fence, served as final resting places for the free people of color, whose toil had made Wallingsford Plantation thrive.

Amanda insisted that they dig Pitney's grave within the iron fence, right beside Grandmother Bently's. No one questioned her decision to give the matriarch of Wallingsford's people a final resting place of highest honor. As the moon rose over the assemblage gathered to send Pitney on her final journey across time and space, the singing lasted long into the night, after Winston spoke his final words of commemoration. No one wanted to see the first shovel of dirt to fall.

Along about midnight, families with heavy hearts and yawning children began to disperse, one by one, heading back to their individual cabins. Amanda and Winston were the last people standing vigil, as several of Pitney's great-grandsons began to fill in her grave. Effie Lou had taken the Bently children inside to put to bed, long before the singing had stopped. Amanda stood shivering in the growing cold, still reluctant to leave.

"It's going to feel awfully strange. Wallingsford with no Pitney," she said in a subdued voice.

"She'll be sorely missed," Winton said, "...by everyone."

"What do you think she meant about Grandmother's journal? Do you know of any personal record Grandmother left?"

"Her plantation records are all that I'm aware of."

"You don't suppose it could be that book you found in the fireplace, do you?"

"I don't know. I looked it over briefly, after the storm. That drawing on the front must mean something, but I couldn't make heads or tails of it. Couldn't open the lock to take a look inside it, either. I put it up on my bookshelf, if you want to examine it yourself."

Amanda gave another shiver.

"Come on, it's time we got you inside. You're freezing to death," Winston said, guiding Amanda toward the iron gate. "You need a warm fire and a hot toddy."

Amanda did not argue, but simply allowed herself to be led back to the big house, where Effie Lou had the fireplace roaring and hot toddies at the ready.

Dec. 28, 1821
Justice, Vermillion Twp.

Dear Amanda,

Thank you <u>so</u> much for the wonderful surprise of coffee and sugar and spices! What a special treat! The aromatic package arrived just in time for Christmas—16 weeks from the time you posted it in early September. And with all you had to think about then, I can't believe you found time to think of us in the midst of your sorrow! You are the most considerate person I've ever known, Amanda Jane.

Jonathan and I send our deepest sympathy for the loss of your parents. I know how difficult losing a parent can be. I can only imagine what it must be like to lose both at once. My prayers are continually with you, my dear friend. You always can rely on that.

Jonathan and I celebrated a simple Christmas holiday, of which your gifts became our central treats. I made a cinnamon cake with some of the spices and sugar you sent, along with newly-ground flour that Jonathan had just brought home. We accompanied it with a pot of real, fresh-brewed coffee, sweetened with your Barbadian sugar. Oh, Amanda, I hardly can thank you enough for the wonderful luxury!

Hank was a bit hesitant to take his first bite of the spice cake, as he'd never tasted such a thing before. But once he discovered how delicious it was, he wolfed down two pieces before I realized he'd even helped himself to another! I had to stop him from reaching for a third helping, so we'd have some left to eat the next day.

With the coming of cold weather and snow, most of the neighbors stick close to home these days, so there's little in the way of community news to relate. However, I did hear that little Snooks (Rebecca's wild Indian) finally reappeared at the Simpson cabin in late November, dressed from head to foot in furs that he'd tanned himself and sewn into warm, winter garments. The whole family showed surprise at his prowess with simple supplies he'd gleaned from the forest.

210

Rebecca reported that Snooks agreed to stay in their cabin, warm himself by their fire, and eat an occasional meal with them only if the family would allow him to come and go as he must. He'd laid out an extensive trap line, he said, which he needed to check at regular intervals. He would not guarantee to stay throughout the entire winter. He already had a snug little lodge of his own constructed deep in the woods where he felt entirely at home, and since he felt quite self-sufficient on his own, he expected his parents to go along with the arrangement.

He did mention that a "native woodsman" of unknown tribe had taught him many of the skills he needed to learn in order to survive in the forest, which has helped to explain the entire mystery surrounding Snooks, wild-Indian child of Al and Rebecca Simpson and his supposed "invisible" friend. Who would guess that a boy just turned nine could already be so independent!

Hank sends his love to the twins, and a special thank-you for the interesting sea shells they sent to him. "Santa" put several of them into Hank's Christmas stocking, but as he's become a "big boy" now, he no longer believes in such things. He knew the shells had come from Millie and Lilly. He says to tell them he especially likes the starfish and the horse-shoe crab. I must say, the crab is most unusual. I've never seen the like, myself. It arrived mostly intact, with only a portion of it broken off. Packing the shells in Spanish moss as you did kept them all in relatively good shape for the entire journey.

Up to this point, I have not mentioned Michael, as I hesitate even to bring up the uneasiness that now lies between the two of you. But I should report that after working himself like a madman, trying to get land fit up for spring planting before the hard freeze set in, he plans to take himself up to the Fire Lands to work on a stone-laying project after the holidays. Apparently a friend of Ellie Mae's needs a special fireplace and oven laid up in a new-house construction, so Michael agreed to take on the job. He told Sadie he'd been itching to work stone again, and this undertaking came at a most opportune time for him, as he wasn't sure what he'd do with himself for an entire winter alone.

That about sums up the happenings in and around the big metropolis of Justice. We miss you and the children, Amanda Jane. Don't stay away too long! And please make sure you take care of yourself. I know you have so much pulling at you from every side right now. Just make sure you remain true to yourself, as you weigh the needs of everyone else around you; keep your focus on what is best for you and your children, my friend, wherever that may lead you.

Yours most faithfully, Lucy

New Year's Eve, 1821
Wallingsford

Dearest Lucy,

I hope this letter finds you and yours snug and secure for the coming winter, and that the holiday season has been kind to you. Would that we all could be together to celebrate the coming new year as we were last winter season. But needs must I remain where I am for the time being.

I sit here by the fire, on the eve of this passing year, wondering what 18 and 22 likely will bring us. We have seen so many changes recently past, I hesitate to contemplate what might be in store. I do know my task here will be made more difficult without the wisdom of Pitney Bower to oversee her Wallingsford domain. We lost her five days ago, the day after Christmas, and already the emptiness she's left seems unbearable. The best estimation anyone has put forth as to her actual age is 110. No doubt she saw more changes in her lifetime than any of us could even begin to imagine. She truly was a treasure who can never be replaced.

The children and I spent a wonderful Christmas here at Wallingsford, with my sister Irene Margaret in residence. The girls had a marvelous time opening what seemed to be a mountain of presents, as did Jems. It did not take him long to figure out how to unwrap packages to reveal the goodies inside.

Winston gave the children unbelievably extravagant gifts. And he gave me a stunning, sapphire ring, along with a most unexpected proposal. I had no inkling of his intent for such a turn in our relationship. As of yet, I have not given him an answer. To be completely honest, I don't know how I feel about the whole idea. I realize that Michael and I had an agreement to marry "sometime in the future" when I felt ready, but with all that has happened of late, I know not what to think nor how to feel about any of this.

I'm so confused, I don't know where my heart lies. All I do know is that I miss Jeremiah very much. Would that he could see how strong and lovely his children continue to grow.

Winston was intent that I attend an island New Year's party with him this evening at Seabrook Plantation. But I begged off this time. With the social season in full sway for the next two months, on the island as well as in Charleston, I know I cannot remain secluded here at Wallingsford indefinitely. And Winston is right: I do need to get out among society and "see to this business of living," once again. I cannot keep myself locked up here, pining for what was or what could have been—for all that I've lost.

I must not dwell on the past. I have to move forward.

The girls miss home terribly, but they have adjusted well to life down here. Children have the ability to adapt so quickly, it seems.

Thank you so much for your letter from September. It arrived here in early December and gave us quite a lift, learning all the news from home. I can just hear Clara fussing about ruining her dress. No doubt by now she's close to delivering her second baby, if she has not already done so. I pray all goes well through her confinement. And your little Alice, now one year old! Can it truly be a whole year since that precious little bundle arrived? I'm so happy you have Jonathan to help you with your children and to keep you all safe. I, too, wish for that feeling of safety and contentment. I pray the coming year will help me to see where my own security lies.

I shall bring this missive to a close, dear friend. I hope you and yours have a wonderful new year, and that it brings you nothing but happiness and prosperity.

Your faithful friend,
Amanda Jane

Chapter 12

End of 'The Season'
February, 1822, Saint Cecelia Ball
Charleston, South Carolina

Winston helped Amanda down from the sturdy, enclosed brougham in front of St. Andrews Hall on Broad Street, then waved the carriage on.

"I never thought I'd actually have the chance to attend a Saint Cecilia Ball, and here I am!"

"Don't tell me you've never been before."

"Never."

"Well, I'm honored to be the one escorting you, my dear. But I'm afraid the extravagant musicales The Society has been noted for are becoming a thing of the past," he explained. "Tonight I'm told we'll enjoy an evening of tamer music with an emphasis on socializing and formal dancing."

"That sounds divine!" Amanda breathed. "Do you have any idea how long it's been since I've attended a real dance?"

"How long?

"Eight years," she said. "Eight years that have held a lifetime."

"I bet you were the most beautiful girl at the ball."

"At only 14, I *was* still just a girl. I hadn't yet had my 'coming out,' so I was permitted to stay only until nine o'clock, when Mother had the servants whisk me away before the best part of the evening could begin," Amanda reminisced. *Mother. And I didn't even get to tell her goodbye.* Amanda still had a long way to go in coming to terms with that most strained of relationships. But she thanked her lucky stars she'd had the opportunity to find some peace with her mother at the last.

"Mother would be pleased as punch to see me here tonight," Amanda sighed. "With all that happened, she never did have the opportunity to introduce me into society, as she always planned. Now she'll never have the chance to see Eralynn's first Saint Cecelia Ball, either," Amanda mused. "Do you suppose Hornsby will see that she comes tonight?"

"I wouldn't place too many hopes on that scoundrel," Winston said. "I have to say I've been most disappointed in that man."

"I know you had your doubts about him all along, but it would appear Grandmother never questioned his objectives."

"For a while there he fooled a lot of people about his intent to take over Wallingsford. Me included," Winston said. "He managed to keep it well hidden from Olympia. Didn't slip once in his resolve to appear completely honest and above board ...until after she passed on, that is."

"I guess Father had his measure all along... for more than one reason, as it turned out."

"Well, thank goodness we can put all that behind us," Winston said. "And now, for the rest of this night, we shall think on nothing but our own celebration. Do you agree?"

"That's a wonderful idea."

They'd reached the entrance, where liveried servants held the doors for guests and took their wraps. Winston helped Amanda out of her golden pelisse and handed it over to a nearby servant. Further inside, others passed out glasses of champagne and escorted couples into the sparkling ballroom, festooned with hanging candles and greenery.

"Oh my," Amanda breathed. "It's so lovely!"

Winston swept her out, onto the dance floor as the orchestra struck up a waltz. Amanda's head spun, and she danced and laughed and watched other couples swirl by in three-quarter time.

"You look radiant in your golden frock," Winston said, flashing his most charming smile. "Right now I'd swear you were a young maiden at her very first ball."

"You're doing it again," she said, shaking her head. "Trying to use that maddening charm of yours on me."

"Is it working?"

They danced several twirls without saying a word. Then Amanda leaned forward and whispered, "I have to admit ...I think I *am* beginning to like it! You'd better be careful though, Winston. Tonight I'm liable to believe anything you tell me."

"Well hang on to that dance card of yours, Madam, because I don't intend to let another buck in this room sign up for a single turn around the floor with you," he said with a twirl and a flourish. "I aim to keep you occupied this whole evening long."

After the first set of dances, the orchestra struck up the Supper March, signaling the company to move toward the adjacent dining room, where tables laden with oysters, shrimp, duck, turkey, rice, greens and all manner of fancy desserts wafted their combined aromas into the candlelit night. Champagne flowed ceaselessly, and servants kept the crystal bowls of planters' punch filled to the brim, while feasting and dancing and the magic of the last ball of the season cast a dreamlike spell over Charleston's gentry.

In the midst of that enchantment, Amanda heard a familiar voice address her from behind. "Why, if it isn't Mizz Amanda Jane! Good evenin', Ma'am... Winston. Nice to see you two out and about in the big city!"

"Hornsby," Winston acknowledged in a flat tone.

Amanda took a big breath, then spoke. "I haven't seen Eralynn this evening. Didn't you bring her?"

"Craziest thing. She was so excited about coming to her first Saint Cecilia. Been fussing with dresses and bonnets and silk slippers and the like for weeks. But when I arrived at the Tradd House to escort her here tonight, she fled up the stairs to her room in tears and wouldn't come back down for any amount of coaxing."

"Whatever is the matter with her?"

"Damned if I... 'scuse me, Ma'am. I mean, I haven't the slightest idea. Every time I go over there lately, she seems to be in some kind of a tizzy," Hornsby said in an exasperated tone. "I

217

thought we had this evening all planned, but when I got there, she flatly refused to leave the house."

"That's not a bit like Eralynn," Amanda said with uneasiness. "She's always the first one ready for any kind of a party or entertainment. Something must be dreadfully wrong to keep her away from her first Saint Cecilia Ball." Amanda fussed with her beaded reticule, looking for a hankie. "Winston, I think I'd better go right over there to see what's got her so upset. I knew we should have stopped at Tradd House on the way in here tonight."

"It's already late, Amanda. What good will it do to cut your own evening short to hurry over there? She's probably sound asleep by now, anyway," Winston tried to reason. "Can't this wait till tomorrow? It is your first Saint Cecilia Ball, too, you know. Why ruin it by running off for what most likely amounts to some silly, female insecurity?"

Amanda gave him a hard look. "Really, Winston. This is my sister we're talking about. Doing something most definitely out of character. To me that indicates a real problem."

"Well, let's deal with it tomorrow, shall we? Do it for me, Amanda Jane, won't you?" Winston asked with a pleading look. "I didn't tell you this, but it's my first Saint Cecilia Ball, too. And I simply must dance the last dance with you. It is tradition, I'm told."

Amanda knew the long standing custom of saving the last dance for husbands or sweethearts, although she still could think of Winston in neither regard.

"Don't spoil it for us," he whispered in her ear.

Amanda shrugged her shoulders in acquiescence. "All right. We'll stay to the end and deal with Eralynn tomorrow. But I want you there with me when I talk to her. She behaves much better whenever there's a man of authority around."

"You can count on it, my dear," he said with a huge smile of accomplishment, sweeping her onto dance floor as the orchestra struck up the first strains of a quadrille.

* * * * *

Knowing Eralynn would undoubtedly sleep late in the morning, Amanda first paid a call at the office of her Factor, Silas Q. Thornhurst, originally retained by her father. She wanted a look at the current Tedrow Shipping records while Winston accompanied her on this trip, so he could help ask the right questions and interpret unfamiliar figures for her. A bell jingled above the door, as she opened it into the reception area of S.Q. Thorn-hurst, Esq.

She heard a woman's shouts come from the office to the rear.

"I won't stand for it," the feminine voice shrieked. "We have every right to stay where we are! It was promised!"

"Hush now. This is a professional workplace, not a scullery where you can shout at the top of your lungs," Thornhurst's self-possessed voice spoke in measured, even tones to try and calm the woman down. "I have important clients coming in and out of here. You must conduct yourself accordingly."

"Very well," she said, smacking something down on his desk. "We *will* discuss this again. And you'd better talk to her, *Mister Thorney*, or I guarantee you, *I* will!"

A smartly dressed young lady with a light, toasty complexion stomped from Thornhurst's office, flounced past Amanda and Winston sitting on high-backed leather chairs in the waiting area without noticing them, and slammed the door behind herself as she exited onto East Bay Street.

"That was not a happy person," Winston drawled.

Thornhurst appeared from his office, pulling at the front of his vest to straighten himself, then he held his hand out to take Amanda Jane's. "Welcome, Mrs. Harrison. I've been looking forward to seeing you again," Thornhurst smiled, pulling her to her feet and escorting her back to his polished, dark mahogany-paneled office. "You're looking simply lovely today, Ma'am."

"That young lady who just left didn't seem too pleased. Was it Mister Thorney, she called you?"

"Yes, well, most women have a great deal of trouble comprehending the logistics which drive business affairs. Of course that doesn't apply to you," he hastened to add. "She'll no doubt come to realize the necessity for some of the actions I've been forced to take, which have undoubtedly brought significant upset into her little world."

"Well, I don't claim to understand all the ins and outs of business dealings any better myself, sir. Which is exactly why I brought my plantation manager along with me today. Winston Applebaum," she introduced, nodding toward him, "Mr. Silas Thornhurst."

Thornhurst gave Winston's hand hardy shake, then ushered both to chairs situated across from his desk.

Thornhurst sat behind his desk, leaned forward and clasped his hands together. "What can I do for you today, my good woman?"

"We'd like to go over Father's business accounts, while we're in town. Winston's very good at keeping all the records for Wallingsford, and I've been wanting him to take a look at Father's books, if you don't mind. To help me better understand the full scope of what's being held in trust for Jems. Help me determine if there are any changes I should initiate on his behalf."

Thornhurst gave Winston a hard look. "Forgive my impertinence, but weren't you pretty tight with that Hornsby fellow for a while?"

"We worked together on quite a few Wallingsford matters for Mrs. Bently, yes," Winston answered. "But if you're worried about my becoming the same kind of turncoat Hornsby revealed himself to be, you have no worries on that score, sir."

"I didn't mean to imply that—"

"Winston's been my Grandmother's right-hand man for over twenty years. I don't believe he'd do a thing to endanger my interests nor jeopardize his situation at Wallingsford," Amanda said, giving him a knowing look. "I trust him implicitly."

"I meant no disrespect, believe me," Thornhurst hastened to reassure. "But as your father's confidante all these years, it's my duty to make sure that you, as his successor, have only the best of advisors to help you oversee your son's inheritance."

"We both understand that," Winston added. "And now we'd like to have a look at the books."

Thornhurst presently got Winston and Amanda settled at a large, library table in an adjoining room, with a stack of leather-bound account books covering the past year's worth of business for Tedrow Shipping interests.

"If you need anything more, just call," Thornhurst said. "I'll leave you two to browse things here, while I tend to some other matters. If you have any questions, I'll be right next door."

"Thank you. We appreciate all your help," Amanda gave him a glowing smile. "I don't know what Father would have done without you all these years, Mr. Thornhurst. And I'm grateful you've agreed to continue handling these business concerns for me."

"My pleasure, Mrs. Harrison, I assure you."

For the next two hours, Winston and Amanda worked their way through countless pages that listed bills of lading for imports and exports of all kinds, employees' salaries and benefits, monthly maintenance and upkeep of ships, warehouses, and investment properties, along with all manner of incidental receipts, statements and invoices from related business interests. Shortly after noon, both were feeling quite overwhelmed by the sheer scope of Tedrow Shipping.

"Would you like fresh coffee?" Thornhurst asked, sticking his head in the side room. "You both must be exhausted by now."

"I have to say, I'm quite stunned by the sheer magnitude of Father's enterprises," Amanda said with a sigh, stretching her neck and rising to stretch her back. "I'm going to need some sustenance, though, or I'm liable to wilt right away after so much intense study."

"Why don't you let me take you both to an early lunch," Thornhurst invited. "I'd be honored."

"That's very thoughtful. Winston? Is that all right with you?" Amanda deferred.

"Sounds like a grand idea," he said, also rising to stretch, then reaching for his frockcoat hanging across the back of his chair. "I'm famished."

"Would you like me to leave the books here for you, or are you finished inspecting them for today?" the Factor asked.

"I think you can put them away for now," Amanda answered. "I've got some other business to attend to this afternoon, so we won't have time to return to examine anything further today. But I think I've seen enough to begin to grasp the extent of my Father's interests. I feel better prepared to attend the stockholders meeting, now that I've acquainted myself with his records."

"You do realize, there's no need at all for you to attend such a boring meeting, don't you? I'm fully prepared to handle all that's necessary with the board. It's highly unusual for any woman to attend, as most ladies pay so little attention to the business dealings of their men," Thornhurst added.

"Oh, but I do intend to be there, sir. And with a whole list of questions to ask the board members, you can be sure of that."

"List? You have a list?"

"A small one. But we can talk about that another time. Right now, I'm starving."

* * * * *

Thornhurst hosted their lunch at The Mills Hotel a few blocks down the street, where the trio sat at his regular table enjoying today's specialties of fisherman's stew and oyster pie. They'd eaten in relative tranquility, with non-threatening conversation peppering the repast, and finally ordered a light dessert of sand-dollar cookies and sweet tea.

As they sat savoring the last of their meal, Amanda saw the same, dark-haired, toasty-skinned beauty, who'd stormed out of the factor's office earlier in the day. She now made her way over to their table in the corner. She wore a full apron covering the flounces of her fashionable dress and carried a silver tray which held their cookies and tea.

"Oh, Lord, here it comes," Thornhurst breathed more to himself than to the others at the table. "I should have known she'd save this hotel for last."

"*Mister* Thornhurst," the woman said, looking directly at him. "A light dessert for you and your little party," she said with a decided edge to her voice, setting the tray on the table and passing around the glasses of sweet tea. To Amanda and Winston she flashed her most winning smile. "My mother and I make specialty cakes and cookies for the best hotels in town, and we've built up quite a following of folks who seek out our sweet treats," she said. "Normally the waiters do the serving, but I thought today I'd bring them out for you myself, since I'd already finished my deliveries to the other hotels," she explained. "I hope you enjoy your dessert."

She took a step back, made no move to leave, but just stood there, waiting.

Thornhurst stammered for a moment, then cleared his throat. "Mrs. Harrison, I should... I mean, I, ah... *need* to introduce...," he turned to give the woman a glare, "Amanda Bently Harrison, meet Eleanore Bently Pierce."

Amanda, who had just taken a swallow of her tea, began to choke. Winston quickly took the glass she held and gave her a firm smack on the back. By the time Amanda caught her breath and composed herself, Eleanore had swooped to her side and ensconced herself in the fourth chair sitting at the table.

"Bently?" Amanda squeaked.

"Yes Ma'am. Bently. Helen Mercy Pierce is my mother, and Mr. Joseph Alexander Bently was my father, too."

Stunned, Amanda turned a deathly shade of white, before she could regain control. "Good Lord, I have another sister?"

"Yes, Ma'am. You have another sister. And *this* man," she tipped her head in the direction of Thornhurst, "is trying to keep me from my rightful inheritance... which is why I had to come to you," she said with hope in her voice. "Would you mind? Could we talk privately?"

223

The two women excused themselves and removed to a nearby powder room (no longer used for the purpose of the powdering of wigs, as was originally intended several decades earlier, but now a place of relaxation set aside for use by the women of a dinner party, while their men enjoyed brandy and cigars in the hotel's library). Amanda listened with rapt attention to the surprising story of Eleanore Bently Pierce.

Back when her Grandfather Tedrow had died in the arms of a young quadroon (unbeknownst to the women of the family, since Joseph Alexander Bently had handled matters with such discretion at his father-in-law's death), said quadroon, namely one Helen Mercy Pierce, never came to the attention of anyone of familial importance. In his position as executor of the Tedrow estate, Bently took a shine to the young woman himself, vowing to keep her safe and secure in the comfortable little home and lifestyle provided her by Amanda's Grandfather.

At that time Amanda's mother had already barred Joseph from her own bedroom, so, being the ever astute opportunist, he took advantage of the situation dropped right into his lap, so to speak, by Father Tedrow's untimely demise. Helen, by default, became Joseph's own concubine, and Eleanore, it turned out, the fruit of that unlikely union.

Eleanore, an octoroon herself, could easily pass for white, which, at her mother's insistence, she quite often did. Under the circumstances, Bently provided what he could for her by way of hiring tutors and giving her the best possible education to someone in her situation. But he never, ever, let his family know of her existence, keeping this last daughter far-removed from his "official heirs." All these years he'd been paying expenses for the up-keep of their little house, along with a small, monthly stipend. The women supplemented this boon with profits from their baking enterprise in order to live in modest comfort at the edge of the warehouse district, where many free people of color had settled.

Until Bently's unfortunate death, Eleanore had gone only by her mother's surname of Pierce. But she'd taken to adding Bently, of late, in an effort to help her claim what she believed to be rightfully theirs: namely the little house and its upkeep, given by Grandfather Tedrow to her mother, along with an additional allowance Bently had vowed to pass on to Eleanore upon his demise. But now, having determined that their ongoing maintenance was proving an unnecessary drain (not to mention embarrassment) to the Bently estate, the Factor had put their little house on the market and was insisting that they move to other quarters— preferably ones in another city altogether.

"So you see, I'm fighting for our home! Our own father promised it to me, and I see no reason why it should be taken away from us now."

"He's trying to sell it out from under you? That's absolutely appalling! I simply will not allow such a thing to happen. You can rest assured on that, Eleanore," Amanda said, patting her hand. "My Lord, I never dreamed I'd go to lunch and end up meeting a sister I never knew I had," she said, shaking her head in disbelief. "You must meet Irene and Eralynn, too. It's only right that you should."

"Oh, I don't think they're ready to know about me yet," she said with a wisdom well beyond her tender, fifteen years. "Papa always kept me well informed about their personalities and selfish ideas. I doubt they'd tolerate having a mixed-blood sister any better than most whites of Charleston would. But I am very glad I finally got to meet you, Amanda Jane. Papa always did speak quite highly of you."

* * * * *

Later that afternoon, Amanda walked into Tradd House wondering, once again, what trouble awaited her there.

"Mizz Manda! You a su'prise, you is!" Zeb said, pulling open the door when she knocked. "No one gibbed wannin' you wuz comin' t' town. Noreen gon' be powerful upset. You know she likes mekk'in fancy treats in yo' honor."

"You mean Eralynn didn't say a word to any of you that I was coming by?" Amanda asked in astonishment. "I had the hotel send a note over this morning, telling when I'd arrive."

"Dis here message come in da forenoon," he pointed to an envelope in the silver tray on the entry table. "It still be settin'. She ain' come down yet."

"What? You mean to tell me that girl hasn't stirred from her room today? It's nearly 3 p.m.!"

"No'um. She take t' sleepin' away mos' days now."

"We'll, I'm putting a stop to that nonsense right this minute," Amanda said, handing Zeb her bonnet and hastening toward the stairway.

Winston stepped through the front door behind her. "Perhaps I should make myself scarce, while the sisters sort this thing out," he said, tipping his head to Zeb.

"Mista Winston," Zeb said, taking his hat as well and stepping aside for the white man to pass. Winston strode back to the library, poured himself a brandy, and made himself comfortable with a book, after Amanda muttered her way up the steps.

"Sleeping away all hours of the day. Really!" She fussed down the second-floor hall to her sister's bedroom. "Eralynn Louise?" she called, pushing open the bedroom door. "What in the name of heaven are you doing still abed at this hour of the day?"

A lump on the mattress slowly turned toward her, peeked out from beneath the covers, then pulled them back over her head. "Go away and leave me alone."

Amanda stood only a moment, then marched to the bed and pulled aside the quilt, exposing the disheveled form of her sister. "Eralynn. Look at me. What is this all about?"

Eralynn glared up at Amanda, then burst into tears.

"Shhhhh," Amanda comforted, sitting on the edge of the bed and taking her sister into her arms. "We'll fix whatever's wrong. I'm here now. Tell me what's the matter."

"You can't fix this, Mandy," she hiccupped. "Nobody can."

Amanda handed Eralynn her handkerchief and instructed her to blow. Then she poured a glass of water from the carafe on the bedside table and handed her the tumbler. "Here, take a drink."

Eralynn did as told.

"Now take a deep breath and tell me why you've taken to your bed."

"I'm with child, Amanda," she said, and burst into tears again.

Amanda pulled her into a consoling hug, rocking easily as she held her sister, waiting for this newest round of tears to subside.

"You're sure?"

"I've missed four moon cycles."

"Have you felt any quickening yet?"

"The first time was two weeks ago."

"Oh, dear heart!" Amanda hugged her once more, patting gently as she cried from a seemingly endless supply of tears. When she stopped, Amanda asked. "Who's the father? Have you told him yet?"

"It's... it's my 'Pirate,' as Irene calls him... Lieutenant Cannon Burrell," she said, blowing her nose. "And yes... I *told* him. Once I knew for sure, I told him right away."

"Does he intend to do the honorable thing and marry you?"

"Oh, Amanda. He's *gone*! He told me he wasn't ready to be a father or a husband! Three days after I gave him the news, I found out he'd sailed on *The Essex* bound for Gi-*bral*-tar!" she wailed.

"You mean he's left you to face this all alone? Knowing you're under-aged and without parents?"

Eralynn nodded a scrunched-up face, trying valiantly not to give in to another round of weeping.

"Well, then. You're better off without that one. I can tell you that much," Amanda comforted. "We *can* work this out, Eralynn. Truly we can." She smoothed fly-away hair from her sister's eyes. "I know exactly how you feel right now, darling."

"How can *anyone* know how I feel!" she hollered. "I'm going to have a *ba*-by, Amanda! A *baby*, forheavensakes! What in the *world* am I going to do with a *BABY*?" She let her sobs give way to rising hysteria.

Amanda soundly slapped her sister's face to stop the emotional frenzy from escalating. "Eralynn Louise! Stop this right *now*!"

At the jolt of Amanda's slap, and with bugging eyes of shock and disbelief at her sister's action, Eralynn took in a deep breath and hiccupped. Her spiraling panic immediately ceased.

"I *do* know how you feel, sister, because I found myself in the same situation once."

"Unmarried and pregnant? *You*?"

"Yes. Me. Don't you remember when I had to go away? Didn't you ever wonder why?"

"But I never thought... I was so young... I... I never *considered* such a thing! Mother just told us Father sent you away for a time to grow up."

"In a manner of speaking, I suppose he did," Amanda said. "But it was Mother who did the sending... to get rid of the source for any gossip that might arise to tarnish her own sterling reputation in 'Charleston Society.' Father went along with her plan just to keep the peace."

"Oh, Amanda! Whatever did you do? How did you manage all alone?"

"I wasn't alone for long. Thanks to Jeremiah," she sighed, "the wonderful, patient man who rescued me," she said, closing her eyes for a moment, remembering her fear as she stood at the Harrison's doorway, clutching the letter she carried to her mother's distant cousin in Pennsylvania, as if it had been her only lifeline.

"Wouldn't the father marry you, either?"

"I didn't know who the father was," Amanda said with a huge sigh and a shudder. "I was raped by a gang of ruffians."

"Ohmylord! No!"

"Yes. And I managed to live through the consequences of that horrible experience. Just as you'll live through this, Eralynn. You *will*. But we need to come up with a plan." Amanda said, patting her sister's hands. "And I think I know just what we need to do."

Dear Libby,

Zeke and me got back to Riverstop safe and sound after our holiday time spent with youens. Lucky we got a break in the weather mid-January to give us good travel. Never can count on such during most winters. Found the place in tol'able shape, seeing it was Harmon looking after things all this time I been gone. But we got us a surprise. Was not just Harmon keeping watch over Riverstop, but also his wife and a new baby boy!

Who would ever guess such a thing out of Harmon!

Seems the oldest Simpson gal snagged Harmon right out from under Luella Witherspoon's nose. Luella is Netta Bailey's cousin, you recall. Last I knew, Harmon was paying court to her regular after his mail rounds. Everyone looked for him to pop the question right soon. But I had an idee that boy was up to something when he offered to look after Riverstop for me last summer. Warn't a bit like him to hold up in one place like that neither. Figgered he must be hiding out from something. Or someone.

Guess I called that one right. Turns out he got more than his foot caught in Lovinia Simpson's door, if you get my drift. She had that baby boy back in November. But it took her parents some time to get her to tell who the daddy was. When she finally named Harmon, Al Simpson ushered him right up to the Justice of the Peace at the end of his shotgun. Made sure that Justice tied a knot up good and tight twixt him and his Lovinia. They got them a cute baby boy name of Carson. Ask me, he looks the spittin image of Harmon. He could never deny that one no matter how hard he tried.

Now all the neighbors wonder if Luella will stay in these parts with Netta or likely head back to Virginnie where she come from. She says her heart is busted over that two-timing nephew of mine. But Netta is ready to pop any day with baby number four. And you know how Luther takes off to the woods for weeks at a time. So Luella can hardly up and leave that poor thing all alone in her ripe condition. Guess time will tell what happens with that heart-sick gal. Do not know as she would even look twice at another sweet talker in pants ever again.

While I am talking babies I should report that my nephew Tom and his Clara had them a little girl born late January. Name of Matilda. After Winifred Guthrie's Ma. Clara's Grandmaw that would be. Tom seems happy enough with a girl baby as he already has his boy in Tommy who now is three. That boy still swears like a river rat. Follows his Grandpa Anson everywhere and repeats everything coming out of that old man's dirty mouth. Clara has give up trying to break the boy of it. Says washing his mouth out with soap does nothing to stop him. Tommy takes to blowing bubbles when she does it just to make her mad.

I can see that one will be a corker. Already is!

Zeke and me have not decided what to do now that we found Harmon's little family living here at Riverstop. Harmon says he will not impose any longer on our space with his troubles. But I can not put them out with a new baby and no place to go. Harmon flat refuses to move in with the Simpson's. I hardly can blame him there. His Ma and Sam Justice have no room over by Sam's blacksmith shop neither.

When Simeon and Katrina come back here in spring with their two boys this place will bust out at the seams. Either we add on more room or we pick up and move else wheres our own selves. We have time to think on it, as we still have a good two month of bad weather to ride out before river traffic picks up.

Harmon is making noises about goin into the tin goods business himself. Says he knows of an old tinker with a wagon full of wares to sell. The man has the rheumatiz so bad in his hands he can hardly keep at his work for much longer. Now that Harmon has give up his mail route he says he better be thinkin of some way to support his new family. Private mail delivery hardly paid much to speak of no how. Just enough trade goods to keep a young buck like him in fine fettle. But nary enough for a family.

He never was much of one for the farmin life neither.

230

Maybe a travelin tinker would be just the thing for this foot loose nephew of mine. But that still leaves his wife and baby with no place to stay. Lovinia flat refuses to live a gypsy life. Says she will have a proper home for her son if it is the last thing she does!

I can see fireworks ready to break out betwixt those two. Mark my word!

Zeke happened to mention he hears travelers say how good the waters taste from that spring down there in Petersburg. People have took to calling it Mifflin Springs. After Mifflin Township where it is located. Lovinia says her mother gets water from that spring all the time as it bubbles up right close to their homestead. Says it is the softest water around. Zeke got her to talking about that little settlement where she lived, and the more they talked the more she got a bee in her bonnet about an idee she had thunk up some time ago.

Why not start a little Inn right there in Petersburg? Maybe call it Mifflin Inn after the Mifflin Springs right close by. She could cook and keep rooms for travelers. The new stagecoach line travels that a-way from Wooster to Mansfield right regular. Would make a handy stopping place for tired folks. She said her own folks get people stopping by their cabin all the time on their way through as it is. Maybe she could keep a place right there for their little family while Harmon drives his tinker route?

That Zeke. He can be a sneaky fella sometimes. And a real smart one too. Sure did defuse them fireworks right handy!

Welp, that is about all to report from these environs, Lib. Hope youens ride out the rest of winter in fine comfort. Thank you again for the hospitality of your whole family. We can not let three years pass by before we see each other again, my friend. If Johannah is still in your neck of the woods tell her we always have a place for her down here no matter how full our cabin may get! If she should decide to stay on in these parts that is. Take good care of our newest little pup until Simeon and Katrina hit the road for home.

Your always friend,
Ellie Mae

Chapter 13

Déjà vu
Early March 1822
Uniontown, Pennsylvania

Eralynn shuddered on the doorstep as she clutched the crumpled letter to her ample bosom. How on earth she ever let Amanda Jane talk her into this crazy idea she'd never know... let alone actually carry it this far. She gave a quick rap at the door. *Lordy, what AM I doing here?*

When the door suddenly opened, she took a startled breath.

"Can I help you, Miss?" asked the smiling woman patting the hiccupping babe at her shoulder.

Eralynn swallowed and set her resolve. "Does the name Jeremiah Harrison mean anything to you?"

"Why, that's my brother-in-law!"

"My sister is his widow," Eralynn said, thrusting the letter forward. "She sent me here to give you this. It explains everything."

"His widow? You mean Jeremiah's dead?"

"Apparently."

"Oh... ah, forgive my manners. Do come in. Please," Melinda Harrison stammered, as she stood aside to usher in the young lady. "I'm sorry, but I'm afraid you took me completely by surprise with this news of yours."

"It's Amanda Jane's news, not mine. You don't need to apologize to me," Eralynn said, taking a critical look around the room. "You don't mind if I sit down, do you? I'm feeling a little light headed." She plopped onto the dreadful-looking, brown, overstuffed chair sitting nearest the door.

"My lands, can I get you something? A drink? A cool towel? Have you traveled very far?"

"Intolerably far." As Eralynn pushed the cape from her shoulders and laid her head against the chair's high back, Melinda took in the telltale bulge at her visitor's waistline. "From South Carolina. Charleston, to be exact."

"Well, no wonder you're exhausted. You just rest while I put the baby down for his nap. I'll get you fixed right up with some refreshment." Melinda hurried through to the kitchen, where a shy toddler peeked around the doorframe at their unexpected company. "Pauline, come help Mommy put baby Peter down for sleep. You need to take a nap, too."

The toddler meekly complied, following her mother to the adjoining bedroom, where a crib and small, child's bed practically filled the space. After getting the children settled, Melinda scurried around in the kitchen, preparing a light snack for her guest. She carried the glass of sweet milk and plate of cookies into the parlor.

"Ginger cookies always helped settle my stomach when I carried my babies," Melinda said, handing the plate and glass to Eralynn.

Eralynn gave a weak smile, then took a long drink of the cold milk.

"I'll go fetch a cool cloth for your head, too."

"Don't bother. I'm feeling some better," she said, setting the glass on the nearby side-table, then taking a nibble from a cookie. "Travel never did agree with me. Now it's even worse."

"You just rest a bit Miss... ah, Mrs. ...my goodness, I don't even know your name!"

"Eralynn Louise Bent–" she sighed. "I mean Hornsby. You can just call me Eralynn."

"Welcome to our home. I hope I can make you feel comfortable here."

"Quite," Eralynn said, looking for something to wipe the sugar from her fingers, then running them over the arm of the chair. "My sister said she's never met you, but she did meet all the Harrison brothers several years back. When she came here to choose a husband."

"Choose a husband, you say?" Melinda gave a patronizing smile as she sat on the nearby sofa. "The way I heard this story, your sister arrived on the doorstep with a letter from my mother-in-law's second cousin expecting one of the boys here to come to her rescue... given her unseemly circumstances."

"Unseemly?"

"She was unmarried and pregnant, was she not?"

Eralynn took another nibble from a cookie. "I think you'd better take a look at that letter before either one of us says something she's apt to regret."

Melinda picked up the letter she'd set aside earlier and cracked opened the seal...

February 18, 1822
Tradd Street,
Charleston, South Carolina

To Paul and Melinda Harrison:

By way of introduction, I, Amanda Jane Harrison, widow of your brother Jeremiah, send my sister, Eralynn Louise Hornsby (formerly Bently), to you with a regrettable, though somewhat familiar request.

Were it not for my own circumstance seven years ago, I would never have met any of you nor become a member of your family. As it was, Jeremiah nobly took me to wife, thereby rescuing me from the most unfortunate condition of finding myself pregnant and unmarried, due to a dreadful incident entirely beyond my control.

I can tell you Jeremiah loved and cared for me in a way that no other man ever could have—or would have. We built a good life together on the Ohio frontier. But a terrible accident took him from me just 19 short months ago, when a tree fell on him and broke his back. After giving birth to his last child just a month after his death, a son, Jeremiah Jr., I found myself called back to South

Carolina to tend to a bequest from my own great-grand-mother.

During the ensuing months, my sisters and I lost both of our parents, due to circumstances I shall not go into here. The intent of this letter is to introduce you to my sister, Eralynn Louise, and offer a proposition to one of the remaining, unmarried Harrison brothers on my behalf.

Suffice it to say that my sister, Eralynn, now finds herself in a somewhat similar predicament to that which brought me to the Harrison doorstep myself. She, too, expects a child and has no husband to support her.

Knowing of Jeremiah's many brothers, I have taken the liberty of sending her to you, Paul, the oldest brother, and to your wife, Melinda, whom, I inferred from Michael, is likely the most competent person to deal with such a situation, given her involvement in setting his and Violet's relationship in motion in the not so distant past.

Eralynn needs a strong man beside her to guide her through the coming ordeal. She most assuredly needs someone to help her "grow up" and see to the response-bilities of raising a child. I am sending her on to the farm in Ohio, where I, myself, learned how to be a wife and mother, thanks to my dear Jeremiah's unflagging patience and unique capabilities.

Therefore, I, Amanda Jane Harrison, finding myself in the most fortunate of positions to even be able to effect such an offer, make the following proposal to whichever Harrison brother will take on the charge of wedding Eralynn Louise:

1) For the next two years you will live on and work my farm in Vermillion Township, Ohio, for the sum of two thousand dollars, to be drawn upon a bank account set up for your exclusive benefit—the funds of which will be yours to use as you see fit during that two-year period.

2) You will help Eralynn Louise raise her child in the environs of the Justice settlement, where you will undoubtedly find ample support from neighbors most willing to be of assistance to you both.

3) Upon completion of the two-year work agreement, an additional two thousand dollars will be deposited in said bank account, with which you will then have the opportunity to buy aforementioned farm, given first right of refusal, assuming that Michael Harrison himself has set aside his interest in the Ohio property. Should he decide to remain as overseer of my farm, you will be free to use the money to buy other land of your choosing.

4) If, after that initial two-year time period, you should find yourself unwilling or unable to continue in a partnership with Eralynn Louise, you will be free to dissolve that union and go your separate ways—Eralynn returning to Charleston with her child, and you making a new start.

In my estimation, this proposal amounts to a win-win situation for both parties, and, if my life be any inspiration at all, you have a good likelihood of coming through this two-year growth period ready to continue forward in a satisfactory married life together with a more lucrative start than most couples manage to obtain after a lifetime together.

Melinda let the letter drop to her lap. "Well, this is going to take some discussion and planning, I can see that."

"Naturally."

"You agreed to this 'proposal' of your sister's?"

"I'm here, aren't I? Besides, given my current predicament and the wagging tongues back in Charleston, I hardly have much choice in the matter."

"We always have a choice," Melinda answered. "Of course, we must be willing to accept the responsibilities and consequences that come with each choice we make, too."

"You sound just like Amanda."

"Well, tell me then, what do you really think about all this?"

"I think that if I hadn't lost my own husband a few months back, I wouldn't be in this fix."

"Oh, my dear, I had no idea you'd already been through so much at your tender age. What are you, 18, 19?"

"Seventeen, soon turn 18, if you must know."

"You can tell me all about it," Melinda said, reaching forward and taking Eralynn's hand in her own. "I'm more than willing to listen, if you feel the need to unburden yourself."

Eralynn let Melinda pat her hand consolingly. "My husband was a lieutenant in the merchant marine, and he was sent to sea on *The Essex* just two months after we married. Naturally with such a short time together, he had little opportunity to make ample provision for me, let alone a baby." She paused for full effect. "Six weeks after they set sail, I received word that his ship had gone down off the coast of Gibraltar." She pulled her hand away and covered her eyes.

"I can't believe he left you with a baby coming "

"I didn't *know* about the baby when he left. And now he'll *never* know," she howled, giving in to manufactured tears, though Melinda had no clue as to their deceitfulness.

"Well, you just leave this matter to me, Eralynn dear. I'll make sure that we see you and your baby are properly taken care of. Amanda Jane was right in sending you to us," she said, rising to her feet and folding the letter in half. "I'll talk to the boys this evening. We'll get it sorted out soon enough, don't you fret."

Eralynn sat back in the ugly chair and closed her eyes.

Just then a knock sounded at the rear of the house, and Melinda hurried through the kitchen to the mudroom, where she pulled open the back door to reveal a tall, black man in dark green livery standing there with hat in hand. His presence startled her so, she put her hand to her breast and took in a deep breath.

"I'z sorry t' *in*-trude Ma'am, but what y'all want I should do with Mizz Eralynn's trunks?"

"Good grief, who are you?"

"Pudge be my name, Ma'am. Mizz 'Manda charge me t' see Mizz Eralynn travel safe."

"My Lord, she never said a word about a travel companion. Why didn't you use the front door?"

"Ain' proper fo' servants t' come to th' front, Ma'am," he said, lowering his head. "I 'pologize fo' takin' up yo' time."

"You mean to tell me you've been sitting out there in the blustery cold this whole time?"

"I'z use t' waitin', Ma'am."

"Well for heavensakes, come right in here and have a cup of hot coffee to warm yourself up!"

"Oh, no'um. But thank yo' kindly jus' the same. I be seein' t' the hoss. I kin bed down out with the am'nals."

"Nonsense. You'll do no such thing! I won't have any company of mine staying in the barn with the horses."

"I ain' the *comp'ny*, Ma'am. I jus' tends the hoss an' totes the bags."

"Well, when you come to my house, you *are* company, sir," Melinda said, taking Pudge by the elbow and pulling him inside. "Now you sit yourself down at that table and let me get you something hot."

Pudge did as he was told, but his eyes kept darting around the room, and he had the uncomfortable demeanor of someone about to bolt for cover at the slightest provocation. Melinda poured a cup of hot coffee for Pudge and set it down in front him, then busied herself at the fireplace, as she swung the trammel back over the hot coals to warm up the pot of soup.

"Maybe Mrs. Hornsby would take a little broth, too," Melinda said, giving the pot a stir.

"Missus Hornsby? Who she be?"

"Why, your mistress in there. Eralynn Louise? She's exhausted from the trip."

Pudge just lowered his head and took a long drink of the coffee. "Thankee for this 'ere heav'nly brew," he said, suddenly careful to say nothing more about Eralynn. He eased himself away from the table and inched toward the back door. "I ain' never had fresh coffee. We jus' gets the dregs. Thankee kindly, Ma'am."

"But won't you have a bowl of soup, too?"

"No'um. I got to go see to the hoss."

"All right. I'm sure you'll find some of the boys out in the barn. They'll show you where to put your horse. But when you get finished out there, you come right back in here and have some of this soup, you hear?"

"Yass'um." He turned toward the door, then stopped. "You want I should bring Mizz Eralynn's trunks in here?"

"That would be fine for now. I'll find a place for you to put your things, too."

"Oh, I ain' got but one poke, Ma'am. We be jus' fine beddin' down out in the barn."

"You'll do no such thing! You'll sleep upstairs with all the other boys... wait... did you say 'we'?"

"Yass'um." Pudge fussed with his hat. "My ma, she be settin' out in dat buggy, where Mizz Eralynn tell us t' wait."

"You mean to tell me, she left a woman sitting out there in the cold, too?"

"She *own* us, Ma'am. When we told to wait, we wait."

"Well, you bring your mother right in here to me! I refuse to let either one of you stay out there in that cold barn!"

"Yass'um. I go fetch her." Pudge made a hasty escape while he had the opportunity.

Melinda shook her head in consternation, then gave the soup another stir. When she was satisfied with its progress, she headed back into the parlor to check on Eralynn, where she found her sound asleep, head tipped back, snoring softly. She took the crocheted afghan from the back of the sofa and eased it over the girl, so as not to disturb her any more than necessary.

Eralynn turned and snuggled into the blanket without waking.

"Getting one of the boys to take on this girl might prove quite the challenge," Melinda muttered to herself. "I can see that quite plainly already."

* * * * *

Melinda pulled the heavy drape across the window to close out the glaring sun, in order to keep the fabric on her prized parlor furniture from fading. *Ugly chair indeed,* she thought, fluffing up the cushions she'd quilted herself. *I hope John knows what he's gotten himself into.*

Early that morning Mr. and Mrs. John Harrison had pulled out in a heavily-loaded wagon heading west, toward Amanda Jane's Ohio farm—the one Jeremiah Harrison had established with his own sweat and tears. The oldest three of the remaining, unmarried Harrison brothers (already in their 30's) found it impossible to move hundreds of miles from their family roots, let alone even consider taking Eralynn Louise to wife, in spite of the very generous dowry she brought into the bargain. "The Brutes," as everyone called them, were all quite content being life-long bachelors working the homestead for their oldest brother Paul and leading their very predictable lives.

John, on the other hand, having recently turned 21 and eager to strike out on his own, could hardly let such a proposition pass him by. The youngest brother in the family line-up (sister Sadie being the only sibling younger than he), John found himself with few financial resources and small likelihood of ever acquiring enough money to buy any land of his own. This offer presented him with the perfect opportunity.

For John had plans.

He'd developed a strain of winter wheat that he wanted desperately to try producing on a larger scale. But brother Paul would allow him no more than an acre of the family farm on which to test his "wild experiments" with seed. A whole quarter-section of Ohio farmland sounded like a dream come true for John. The fact that Eralynn came with the deal put only a slight damper on his enthusiasm.

After careful consideration of Amanda's plan, John stepped forward to take Eralynn to wife—although that also felt like more of an experiment than a true marriage in his eyes. But he'd give it his best shot. He had nothing to stick around for at home—no real hope of ever having an interest in the family homestead, nor anyone pulling at the strings of his heart. Truth be told, he missed his sister Sadie more than anyone he felt any affection for around here, and with this move she'd be living close by. The whole thing sounded like the best solution for his future.

Melinda made short work of arranging for a Justice of the Peace to perform a swift wedding ceremony. She did not, however, offer the use of her own wedding veil to Eralynn, as she had to her cousin Violet, when that poor girl had hastily wed brother Michael in the parlor a few, short years before. After two days of Eralynn's whining demands, Melinda was more than ready to get this whole shindig over and done with and usher the newly mar ried couple out the door!

Oh, she'd miss John, no doubt about it. And she did wish him well on this misguided adventure. But in her eyes, the poor boy didn't stand a chance. While she kept that nagging doubt tucked deeply away in her own heart, she dutifully provided a lovely wedding celebration for the anxious couple, meager though it might appear to a spoiled southern girl; Eralynn had little constructive to say about the entire festivity.

Her last memory of their leave-taking saw Pudge at the reins of the large wagon, loaded to the gunnels with all of Eralynn's fru-fra. John had insisted she make room for his sacks of seed wheat, which she begrudgingly allowed him to pack inside her mattress cover. Eralynn sat sternly at Pudge's side on the wagon seat holding white-knuckled to the side gunnel, while Emmie, Pudge's mother, sat precariously on the wheat-stuffed mattress perched atop the load of trunks and travel supplies. John rode his roan gelding confidently ahead of the loaded wagon, whistling a tune to the beat of his horse's canter.

Lord help them, Melinda thought. *They're definitely going to need it!*

My Dear Ellie Mae,

How I long to see you again, though it's been since only January we had to relinquish the pleasure of your company. Would that you could have stayed on with us a bit longer, but I do understand your need to return after so long a time away from Riverstop. I also can appreciate your surprise at finding not one, but three people in residence upon your arrival home.

It would seem that Harmon has gotten himself into quite the predicament. No doubt we shall have to resort to alternative methods of exchanging our posts to one another from now on, if he truly intends to give up his independent mail route for the life of a traveling tinker. Although, depending upon his intended work area, I can't see why he wouldn't still be able to carry a few letters for us now and again. That is, assuming his new wife will allow him to travel this far north. It sounds as though she maintains a firm hold upon the reins of that union!

I wish them both well, as I do our Simeon and Katrina and their precious little boys. They began their trip back to you just yesterday, as the weather here has stabilized nicely, with most of the mud now hard-packed enough to assure easier travel.

I told Katrina to keep baby Matthew well wrapped throughout the entire journey. At not quite three months, he's a little treasure we cannot afford to lose. I would imagine they should complete their journey by Thursday of next week at the very latest, assuming they run into no troubles along the way. Unfortunately, I did not have this post ready to send with them when they left.

Nate and Ivy's little Patience progresses nicely, as well. They have recently discovered that baby number two can be quite a bit more resilient than they thought possible with baby number one. It seems Ivy caught two-year-old Annabelle trying to carry baby Patience from her cradle up to her own sleeping place in the loft. When Ivy questioned the child as to why she wanted the baby up there, Annabelle answered, "Me want to sweep wif my baby." Obviously, she meant "sleep."

It took Ivy quite some time to convince the child that a baby has no business up in a sleeping loft. But she did promise that Annabelle would be able to share a bed with her sister once the baby has learned to climb the steps by herself. That seemed to pacify the child for the time being.

When last I spoke with Ivy, she also had some startling news to relate, concerning her older sister Chastity. You recall she's the one who ran off with the stable boy and left our Nate standing at the altar, the very day that Ivy, in her wisdom, claimed Nate for herself, before he had a chance to bolt in heartbreak.

Naturally, she was quite concerned as to how Nate might react to her sister's return. She expected heavy grief from him when he finally did see her. But to her utter surprise, Nate showed no reaction to Chastity's presence whatsoever. In fact, he hardly took notice of the girl when they went for Sunday dinner at her parents' home the week of her return. Nate was so involved in helping Ivy to keep Annabelle from walking off with the baby, that he paid her sister practically no mind at all. Simply spoke a hurried greeting to her when they walked in the door, then hurried off to ride herd over little Annabelle, so Ivy could visit with her family.

Of course, Ivy felt overwhelming relief by his reaction, not to mention great encouragement as to her own importance in his life. I could have told her that. She's become indispensable to Nate. On the day they wed, I knew Ivy was the better choice of sisters.

Thankfully, Nate recognizes that himself, as well.

Apparently Chastity has come home to stay. Some time ago the stable boy left her penniless in Altoona, when he took up with a librarian who'd caught his fancy there. Evidently Chastity remained in that town for most of a year trying to make her own way by taking over the librarian's position. But she finally relinquished the task, when the board of directors unanimously agreed to let her go, after she'd jumbled their organizational system so badly, it was in complete disarray. They despaired of getting the books properly organized ever again.

Frankly, I was never convinced the girl could even read, myself!

I'm just happy to know that my son is content and completely taken with his own little family.

As far as news concerning the others in residence here with us over the holiday season recently past, only Johannah and Christian remain, for the time being. Levi made his departure in late January after you and Zeke left us. Levi has convinced himself that living on Mississippi river boats is the only life for him. I think the attempt at walking that paddlewheel on his first, stowaway trip to New Orleans excited him so, the challenge of making his way up and down the river has been in his blood ever since.

I just pray that mischief-maker of mine manages to keep himself out of any real trouble. And that one of these days he meets a woman who has the pluck and strength of character to handle the man that boy is turning into.

You no doubt will be interested to know that I believe sparks have been flying between our Christian and your Johannah. The reluctance of either one of them to leave here leads me to think that more may be transpiring between them than we know. I would have guessed my reserved wanderer of a son should have been the first to strike out after the holidays. Yet here he remains, sitting for hours on end talking with Johannah about everything imaginable.

I hardly can believe such loquacious behavior from my solitary boy. Of course, he said nary a word to Johannah, until after Levi took his leave from us. Ever since then, those two have been talking non-stop. It amazes me, friend. Perhaps you and I shall become related once again?? We can but hope!

My, my, this is turning into quite the missive. And I haven't even told you a thing about the new house, yet. Of course, you saw the shell of the construction when you visited with us over the holidays. But over these past few winter months, when little else could be accomplished outdoors, these men of mine have done a wonderful job with all the finish work inside. Floors,

245

woodwork, built-in cupboards, and real closets! It never ceases to amaze me how Zach can do such remarkable things with wood.

And thanks to you, Ellie, we have the most unique fireplace! You can hardly begin to imagine. Michael Harrison spent the past three months laying it up for us. We'd never have known of his expertise, were it not for the intelligence you relayed in the matter. Michael built us not only a wonderful fireplace that draws superbly well, but he also included a bake oven in the design, and, would you believe, a secret compartment!

Who would have ever thought such a thing possible! Zach is completely taken with the design. And Elijah cannot wait to make the final move, so he can hide something special in that secret compartment. Lord only knows what we're apt to find squirreled away in there in the years to come!

Zach says once the weather warms up, we'll move all our furniture and household goods over to the new house. I hardly can wait, Ellie. Next time you visit, we shall have tea in my new kitchen! Which really, is my old kitchen, as it is an exact replica of the one from my beloved home back in Connecticutt!

I am so blessed, my friend. To have had my entire family in residence for such a wonderful visit over the holidays, not to mention gaining two, new grandchildren! And now, here I am, looking forward to moving into my lovely, new home.

I hope all goes well at your end, El. Please let me know that Simeon's family arrived safely. And be sure to keep watch over those precious grandsons for me.

Your friend, truly excited about living once again,
Libby

April 12, 1822
Justice Settlement, Ohio

Amanda,

Oh, my dear friend, how wonderful to hear from you! I was taken completely by surprise when your sister Eralynn arrived here with another Harrison brother as husband. She relayed your lovely letter to me. I would never have known of its—or of her—arrival, had it not been for Netta Bailey's eagerness to share the news.

And never would I have expected Netta to call so soon after giving birth to her fourth child. (Another girl, Ruby. This birth happened so quickly, Sadie didn't have a chance to arrive for it. I should also mention that Clara and Tom had a little girl in January, by the name of Matilda. Sadie did make it in time to deliver that one.)

You know Netta, ever on top of the happenings in our little community. She brought Ruby along to show her off and left the other three girls, Rosanna, Rachael and Rebecca, at home with her cousin. Luella's still there, even though she's making noises about returning to Virginia, now that her "intended" has been stolen away from her. It seems since last I wrote, Harmon Hawkins, who'd been courting Luella all spring and summer, up and married the oldest Simpson girl from Petersburg just before Christmas.

Apparently it was a pretty rushed affair, after Lovinia Simpson gave birth to a baby boy and her parents finally got her to identify the father. They've named the baby Carson. I have not had the opportunity to see him as of yet, but Netta says he's a darling boy.

Those Simpsons have had quite the eventful year recently past, what with their Snooks disappearing into the woods, and Rebecca, herself, giving birth to a surprise baby girl, who, as it turned out, became "Aunt" Ella Marie at just ten months old! Netta said that Al took on an apprentice cooper a few months back, as well, since Snooks' has given up working at his father's side for a life in the woods.

247

After Netta's visit with all the news, I was most eager pay a call to your homestead to meet your sister. But Netta didn't leave till late in the afternoon, so I waited until the following morning to make my way across the woods between our properties, along with Jonathan and the children.

I must say, Amanda, I did not find your sister a bit like you, neither in family resemblance nor personality traits. And I was more than a little surprised to find she'd brought two Negro servants along with her. Netta never said a word about them, which leads me to believe she doesn't know of their presence here, as of yet. Otherwise she'd surely have mentioned it.

I took a bouquet of daffodils, a loaf of whole wheat bread, and some of my cup cheese along to welcome the new Harrison couple. Jonathan and Hank spent the entire visit out in the barn with John and Pudge, while Alice and I sat in the cabin with Eralynn and Emmie. Emmie was quite taken with my little sweetheart. I haven't mentioned that Alice runs everywhere now, and chatters continually in her unintelligible babble. Emmie scooped up my little one right away and kept her occupied while I tried to visit with your sister.

She immediately gave me your letter, Amanda. But I waited to read it until I got back home, as I didn't want to seem rude by ignoring your sister in order to do so right there, even though I was quite eager to hear what you had to say. No matter how hard I tried to find something of common interest to talk about with your sister, we had trouble coming up with a single subject we could discuss, other than the ordeal of her trip and her coming baby, about which she seemed quite hesitant to speak.

She did seem pleased with the flowers and bread, but had little to say about the cup cheese, other than turning her nose up at the smell. Emmie, on the other hand, was quite impressed with the fact that I'd made it myself and asked if I would mind teaching her how to do so. The little bit I interacted with the two Negro servants convinced me of their genuine excitement at having the opportunity to live and work in the North. Pudge told me of his young wife, living two streets over from the Bently house back in

Charleston, and of his intention to earn enough money to buy her freedom.

Only when I got home, did I have opportunity to read your letter and learn of what you had in mind for the servants, and for your sister and her new husband...

Lucy took Amanda's letter from out of her lap desk, opened it up, and read through it once again, to refresh her memory and feel closer to the friend she so missed...

February 18, 1822
Tradd Street,
Charleston, South Carolina

Dearest Lucy:

Oh my friend, so much has happened since I last wrote you on New Year's Eve, I hardly know where to begin. However, since Eralynn Louise has undoubtedly delivered this letter to you, I shall of necessity begin with her.

My sister finds herself in a terrible fix, so similar to my own of seven years past that it's almost scary. She expects a child sometime this summer and was abandoned by the father—left to raise this baby alone.

I was terrified when my own parents sent me away to bear my child of shame, even though they provided a farm on the Ohio frontier and arranged for a husband who would look after me and the baby. I've since come to understand my father's wisdom in doing such a thing. He forced me to grow up there, although it quite literally almost killed me on more than one occasion.

Since Eralynn is in need of just such growth herself, in order to become even remotely ready to raise a child of her own, I've convinced her to give the Ohio frontier an honest try in helping her to mature—a place where she can learn how to be a wife and mother without the constraints of Charleston's meddlesome society pulling at her.

249

Her newly revealed father, Douglas B. Hornsby, Grandmother's former barrister, readily agreed to this arrangement when I presented him with my idea. Frankly, I think he felt relieved at not having to deal with Eralynn's predicament himself.

So now, finding myself in the advantageous position of being able to offer another of the Harrison brothers a generous dowry to undertake looking after my sister and her child, I feel I'm giving both of them a chance at a new life.

At this writing I will not know which brother has chosen to take advantage of my proposal, but I leave it to you to welcome him and my sister to the Justice settlement, Lucy. I know you and Jonathan will be most accommodating in helping to make the new Harrisons feel welcome, as, I'm quite sure, everyone in the neighborhood will offer their help and support. No doubt Sadie will be delighted to have another brother living close by.

As for the Negros who've accompanied Eralynn, I also ask that you introduce them to the neighbors and give as much assistance as possible in helping them get established in the community.

Since Eralynn flatly refused to leave Charleston without at least two of her servants along to help her, I finally acquiesced to her wishes, under the condition that after two years of service on the Ohio farm, she grant them both their freedom. Pudge and his mother Emmie chose to take up this offer. The other household slaves Eralynn inherited from my mother will be looked after while she lives in Ohio. Eralynn has agreed to grant the rest their manumission papers after they have given five more years of service here in Charleston. For if, after the two years that I've required she remain in Ohio, Eralynn decides to return to Charleston, she will still have three years of the other servants' help, before she will be obliged to set them free as well.

I aim to hold her to this promise.

As far as running of the farm is concerned, I've given whichever Harrison brother takes up this challenge free access to sufficient funds that will cover their living expenses and pay the land taxes for the next two years. Since I know all the Harrisons are capable farmers, I have no qualms about leaving the land in their care. That will give Michael the freedom to pursue his vocation as a stone mason, if he chooses to do so. Should he decide to remain with the farm, I'm sure he and his brother can come to an agreement as to how the place should be worked.

I hesitate to think anything more about Michael, at this juncture. I know I miss him, even though we're at odds right now. Beyond that, I cannot allow my thoughts to dwell.

I think that about covers the subject of my sister Eralynn—other than asking that you do what you can to help her through the birth of her coming baby. How amenable she will be to that help, I cannot say. We both know the vagaries of child bed and their defining moments. I pray that Eralynn uses this experience to become a better person. She seems to sincerely want to, but whether she allows herself to do so, remains to be seen.

Now, on to a more pleasant, and surprising, topic. As you know, I grew up in the company of two sisters. However, while seeing to details of my father's estate, I recently discovered that I have another sister, whom I never knew existed! Eleanore Bently Pierce, daughter of quadroon Helen Mercy Pierce—my father's paramour (another startling discovery).

Eleanore and her mother have lived in a little cottage at the edge of the warehouse district, where a small community of free people of color reside. Quite some time ago my grandfather set Helen up in that house, and all these ensuing years Father had been paying for its maintenance and upkeep. It came to my attention a short time ago that Father's Factor had put that house up for sale, in a cost-cutting maneuver for the estate, which I knew absolutely nothing about.

Naturally, the prospect of losing their home greatly upset both women. In their predicament, Eleanore made up her mind to come to me for help, and in so doing revealed her existence as my sister.

Can you believe it, Lucy? I have another sister! I'm thrilled at the prospect of getting to know her, as she seems quite an energetic and hard-working girl of great intelligence. She and her mother run a small pastry business from their home, supplying specialty cakes and cookies for the best hotels in town.

So far, Eleanore hesitates in letting Irene or Eralynn know they have another sister, since, judging from what our father related to her about them both, she doesn't believe either one is ready to know about a mixed-blood relative, as of yet.

I happen to agree with her, so please, do not mention this to Eralynn, as I know you would never presume to do.

Because I could do nothing to stop the sale of Eleanore and her mother's house, I've had them moved into the Tradd Street house, now that neither Eralynn nor Irene any longer resides there. Irene has taken up residence out at Wallingsford and seems much happier since doing so.

She came to visit us at Christmas and simply stayed! I have to say, I'm coming to like her much better, now that she has ceased to pretend her life is something it was not. With no parents and no excuses as to a nonexistent husband, she's at last learning to find her own way—with our help, of course. Winston has given over several of his administrative tasks to her, here at Wallingsford, and she seems to be taking them to heart. I've been quite surprised by her competence and thoroughness.

The Pierces can hardly believe their change in circumstance, namely moving into the heart of Charleston. So far none of the neighbors has raised a single objection, for, as far as anyone of consequence knows, both women are white, since either one can pass as such. We're simply letting people assume they're distant Bently relatives. No one need comprehend any more than that.

The servants who remain at Tradd House get along with them just fine. Truth be told, I think they will all be good for one another, with the Pierces helping to acclimate the rest to the nuances of living a life of freedom, which they all will experience soon enough.

I'm proud of my newly discovered sister, for taking on the challenge of teaching our people how to handle their indepen-dence, when it finally comes to them. They've already begun reading classes, behind curtained windows, of course, given the laws against such activities for slaves down here. But I've encouraged them all to learn as much as possible in the next five years, to prepare themselves for making their own way in the world.

It took them all quite a while to make their decisions as to where they wished to spend the next two to five years, given that they've never had any say in their futures up to now. Zebeniah and his family have chosen to stay on at Tradd Street and help the Pierces look after the house, as has Cassie, formerly Mother's personal servant. Bess, the laundry mistress, has decided to join our community out at Wallingsford, since she never did feel accepted by the household servants in town. I think she'll be happy with us on Edisto Island. You know the decisions Emmie and Pudge have made.

That about brings my news to a close, other than catching you up on the children. The twins eagerly await their fifth birthday, and Jems spends most of his waking hours trying to figure out how everything works. Though he says but little yet, he does understand everything we say to him, even surprising me on occasion with the way he works things out for himself at such a tender age.

I wish you well in the task you face with my sister, Lucy. Please do not feel obligated to cater to her whims the way everyone in her life has, up to now. What she needs is your down-to-earth wisdom to help her through her coming ordeal.

Thank you again, dear friend, for your help and your understanding. I don't know what I'd do without a friend like you. Would that Eralynn could find just such a confidant herself.

Take care, Lucy. I hope the coming months bring us together again soon.

Yours,
Amanda Jane

Lucy refolded the letter and returned it to her lap desk. Taking up her quill, she resumed her own letter to Amanda Jane...

I so miss you, Amanda. I know you must continue to oversee all your responsibilities down there, but I can hardly wait to have you home again. You can't know the excitement I had going to your cabin, and then the letdown I felt when I realized your sister was nothing like you.

Come back to us soon, dear friend. Until you do, I'll undertake to help your sister as often as I can, and see to it that her people have as much acceptance as is possible in our small community. Maybe we should have a "doin's" to welcome them all here. After a long winter, I think everyone is ready for a get-together of some sort. I'll talk to Netta. No doubt she'll get the ball rolling.

She told me a new minister will be coming to town within the next month or two. This one plans to make his home here permanently, so the neighbors are talking about putting up a church building in Justice. That will be a first. Maybe a "church raising" is just what we need for an excuse to get everyone together!

Oh, and I almost forgot, Jonathan says that an official United States Post Office will be setting up in Uniontown this year! However, it seems since there's another Uniontown in the state that already has a post office, our Uniontown will have to change its name if they want official postal service. Word is the new name will be Ashland. Sounds like a burned out wasteland to me. Personally, I like the name Uniontown better. But then, I have little say in matters of governmental import.

Take care of yourself, Amanda Jane. We love you!
Your friend,
Lucy

Chapter 14

New Preacher
Early May, 1822
Justice Settlement, Vermillion Township

"Where you want I should put this basket?" Emma Putnam asked Lucy.

"Right on that table over in front of Sam's blacksmith shop. We're going to set the food out over there after the service," Lucy directed her simple friend. Emma waddled off with her picnic basket in hand; Frank Putnam followed slowly along behind his wife, after tripping over a rock in the path.

"He better watch where he's walkin'," Clara Hawkins said behind her hand. "He's blind as a bat in that bad eye."

"Long as nobody puts a gun in his hand, there's nothing wrong with Frank," Lucy responded. "He still has one good eye, you know."

"Does Emma look a might peek-ed to any of you?" Netta asked. "Seems like she's moving slower than usual. Maybe we should get Ma to take a look at her."

"You know Ma won't doctor anymore," Sadie answered.

"Well, maybe you better go see if she's feelin' all right then," Clara said to her sister-in-law. "My ma told me Emma hasn't been weavin' up much in the way of cloth goods lately, and that don't sound like her at-all."

"I'll talk to her after services and see whether she needs anything," Sadie responded.

"Oh, I'm so glad we're able to have this special Christening celebration today, with dinner on the ground afterwards and all," Netta chatted to the group of friends and neighbors gathering for the special service, which would not only welcome their new minister, the Reverend Brawley Gilmore, but dedicate all the babies born during this past winter and spring. That would be Tom and Clara Hawkins' Matilda, at four months, Harmon and

255

Lovinia Hawkins' Carson, six months, Willie and Sadie Hawkins' Zoey Blue, seven months old, as well as Luther and Netta Bailey's little Ruby, at just two months of age.

"I can't believe that after these last four years without a regular preacher, we're finally getting a minister of our very own!" Netta gushed. "You all know what happened to that last travelin' one, poor Rev. Longbottom? Who met a such terrible end in the river?" Netta babbled.

"We have no business going on about such things on this happy occasion." Lucy jumped in to cut her off. "Besides, we shouldn't let one bad apple spoil the whole barrel, when it comes to men of the cloth." She bounced little Alice on her lap. At seventeen months, the active little girl wanted nothing more than to get down on her feet and run. "Alice, be still, sweetheart. Here's your bunny. Now sit on mama's lap and play nice," Lucy crooned to her toddler, handing her a rag toy tied up in the shape of a crude-looking rabbit.

Sadie had little Zoey Blue asleep beside her in a basket that Ma Hawkins (now Mrs. Sam Justice) had made for her first living granddaughter. Clara's Matilda had a matching basket, as well, but Matilda sat with wide eyes on her mother's lap, happily sucking her thumb and watching the crowd gather on the benches set up in front of the shell of the cabin, which would soon become the home of their brand new church. Lovinia held Carson close, careful not to let the sun shine into his eyes, for she was certain they'd be damaged if he looked directly into that glaring orb.

Ma Hawkins shook her head in wonder at the array of babies with her daughters-in-law sitting there, tending to their needs.

"Quite the little group of grandbabes, you got, Edie," Sam leaned in to whisper to his wife of just nine months. Since Sam was nearly deaf himself, his whisper carried out to the entire congregation.

"Hard t' take in what all three o' my boys managed in just one year's time," Ma answered. "At this rate I'll have a whole passel of 'em soon enough!" She spoke directly into Sam's better ear, so he could make out what she said. After years of mixing up everything she'd say to him, he amazed her now, by listening intently to every word she spoke, seldom scrambling her meaning at all, the way he used to. Maybe now that he'd finally won her over after so many years of trying, he didn't have to go to such lengths to gain her attention any more.

Netta adjusted Ruby's blanket, trying to keep the baby's face protected from the morning breeze. "Rachael, Rebecca, behave yourselves," she scolded her two middle daughters (aged five and almost three) pushing against one another at their mother's side. Her six-year old sat quietly on the other side of Netta without a wiggle. "Why can't you two be good like Rosanna. Sit still, now."

Netta got her cousin Luella's attention, sitting on the other side of the squirming sisters, and Luella moved herself between the girls to put an end to the disturbance. Luella had been doing her best to ignore all the adults nearby, as she didn't even want to acknowledge the presence of Lovinia and Harmon sitting beside Tom and Clara. The fact that Luella had come at all today bore testimony to her sense of duty toward Netta and her family.

"You know I'm glad to help out with your girls, Netta," Luella leaned closer to tell her dearest cousin, "but I really don't feel I can stay on here much longer." She shot a heartbroken glance toward Harmon. "When Luther comes back this time, I aim to head back to Virginia."

"Oh, Luella, I wish you'd reconsider," Netta begged. "The girls and I would miss you so much! What will we ever do without you?"

Luella didn't say anything more, just smoothed at her dress and tried to direct her focus away from the newlywed Hawkins couple and their babe. But she wasn't having much success.

"Are your mother and father coming with their baby girl?" Clara asked her new sister-in-law Lovinia.

"I imagine they'll make the trip, being it's not all that far from Petersburg," Lovinia answered. "I know Mother wouldn't want to miss the opportunity to have Ella Marie baptized, not to mention seeing her very first grandchild baptized, too."

"You gonna take Alice up when the preacher calls for the new babes?" Clara asked Lucy.

"I'm afraid she'd make too much of a disturbance for everyone else," Lucy said. "This day's meant for the smallest ones, anyway."

"You don't want to have her baptized?" Lovinia asked in astonishment. "Aren't you afraid she'll go to hell if... heaven forbid...something should happen to her?"

"I believe the Lord takes care of his own, no matter what we do down here to convince ourselves we have any say in the matter," Lucy said, "though I doubt Henry would have thought so.

"What about Katrina's new babe? You think she's comin' to bring him?" Clara asked Sadie.

"I doubt if Aunt Ellie and Katrina's family will make a trip from clear down below Perrysville. That's a far trek to come just for services," Sadie answered.

"Well, it is an important service!" Lovinia protested.

"No one's denying that," Lucy said, trying to sooth Lovinia's feathers. "But not everybody feels as strongly about it as you do."

The men, who'd been talking over by the blacksmith shop, began to amble toward the benches, where their wives and families sat awaiting the start of the service. They filled in the empty spots next to their loved ones.

Netta looked around. "Oh, I hope Luther shows up pretty soon or he's gonna miss his own daughter's christening," she fussed. "I swear, it feels like that man's been gone since the day after Ruby was born!"

"Don't fret, Netta," Sadie comforted. "He'll get here in time... he always does."

At that moment, a cart pulled up beside the hitching post with a man driving who so resembled Jeremiah Harrison that it made all the neighbors take a second look, just to make sure they weren't seeing things. The stiff woman sitting at his side was definitely not Amanda Jane. With the novelty of two black people sitting in the back, no one mistook the little group for anyone they'd already met.

"Is that the new Harrison couple?" Clara asked, pointing toward the newcomers.

"That's Jeremy's youngest brother John, and his new wife Eralynn Louise," Lucy informed the group. "She's Amanda's sister."

"My, I'd have never guessed she was even related to Amanda, she looks so different from her," Clara said.

"We'd better go over and say hello... make them feel welcome." Sadie said as she stood, then turned back to Willie, who'd just sat down beside her with little four-year-old Tad in toe. "Keep an eye on Zoey Blue, would you, Willy? I'm going to go say hello to Eralynn and my brother before they sit down."

"Anything you say, my sweet," Willie said, giving his wife a big, goofy grin. "We'll be right here waiting for you."

"Why don't I come along," Lucy volunteered, handing the wiggling Alice off to Jonathan. "After all, I am the one who invited them to come today. Maybe it'll help them feel more comfortable to see another familiar face in this crowd."

Clara looked back and forth between the Harrison couple and the black people stepping out of the cart, trying to make up her mind whether to tag along or remain seated next to Tom, who'd just joined her with their three-year-old Tommy. "I think I'll wait till after the service to go speak to those people," she whispered.

Lovinia kept fussing with baby Carson so much, she didn't even notice any others joining the milling group, until her parents pulled up behind the Harrisons. She waved enthusiastically to get her mother's attention to come over and sit beside her. Harmon just eased closer to Willie and Tom, slumping down to conceal himself between his brothers, as best he could.

While the neighbors settled themselves and began to take their seats, the Reverend Brawley Gilmore spent the last few minutes inside the roofless church building preparing himself, before stepping out to face his new congregation. At the stroke of 10 a.m., he strode to the rustic pulpit, set up for the day in front of the benches on the cleared space before the incomplete church building. He signaled for the crowd to quiet down.

"Good morning, friends and neighbors!" he called in a loud voice.

Only a few members of the crowd responded with a cordial 'Good Morning' of their own.

"Oh, my goodness, let's try this again. *GOOD MORNING, Friends and Neighbors!!*"

Now that he had their full attention, a resounding *GOOD MORNING* came forth from the entire congregation.

"That's *so* much better! On this wonderful day the Lord has provided, let us open our service with heart-felt thanks. Shall we all bow our heads?" He waited a moment for the shuffle of preparation, then began in a strong, but controlled voice, "Heavenly Father, we gather before You in humble thanksgiving to offer our sincere gratitude for the bounty this land has poured out to us by the grace of Your ever-loving hand.

"We also thank you for the willing neighbors who have given of their toil and strength to begin construction on the very first church building to represent Your glory in this township. May You bless these people with Your continued care and keep them sheltered in the palm of Your hand. Be with us this day as we dedicate the precious new souls You've sent to grace our time on this earth, and help us all to encourage and support the new parents charged with their nurturing care. We ask these things in the name of He who died for us all, our Lord Jesus Christ. Amen, and *AMEN,*" he concluded in a booming voice.

"Let us rise and sing an opening hymn to get our praise juices flowing, shall we?"

At that directive, Winifred Guthrie began a squeaky rendition of *Shall We Gather At The River* on the pump organ, borrowed from Opal Ann Newell down Mount Vernon way for this special occasion. Though the unenthusiastic Winifred managed to pick out a melody with just one finger, everyone at least gave her credit for trying.

After the hymn drew to a close, it took a few moments for everyone to settle themselves back on the benches, and just as mothers got children stilled and quieted once again, the Reverend Gilmore called for the babies to be brought forward for dedication.

Netta fussed in a loud whisper to Luella, "I told you Luther wouldn't make it in time. Didn't I tell you?"

Reverend Gilmore called out in a strong voice, "The Lord said, 'Suffer the little children to come unto me, for of such is the kingdom of Heaven'."

It took a few moments for the parents to shuffle older children off to waiting neighbors or grandparents, while they made their way to the front with new babes in hand.

On her way up, Netta fretted to the other couples and directed them ahead of herself. "You all go first in line. Maybe Luther will show up by the time the Reverend gets to us."

As mothers jiggled fussing babes, and fathers shuffled their feet in embarrassed discomfort, the Reverend Gilmore made his way down the line, reciting a special Bible verse for each infant, spending a few moments naming and dedicating each one as he charged its parents to bring it up in the way of the Lord.

Lovinia and Harmon's Carson hardly stopped howling long enough for anyone to hear what the Reverend said to that nervous couple. Sadie and Willie's Zoey Blue spit up all over Rev. Gilmore as he passed her back to her mother. Clara and Tom's little Matilda simply stared with those huge eyes during the whole ceremony, thumb stuck firmly in her mouth. And the Simpson's sixteen-month-old Ella Marie, who'd walked forward by her own power, firmly smacked Rev. Gilmore in the nose when her turn for dedication came.

After a sincere apology from Al Simpson, holding tight to the recalcitrant child so the Reverend could finish dabbing her with water, he finally came to Netta and Luther Bailey's little Ruby.

"I'm so sorry, Reverend, but it appears that Luther hasn't made it back in time to be here with us," she said, looking all around the congregation, hoping against hope that her husband would still turn up. As she took in the surrounding faces, she noticed an unfamiliar young man walking in from the edge of the crowd with, of all people, Snooks Simpson at his side. The swarthy fellow strode forward with confidence and came to a stop beside Netta Bailey.

On his arm, he carried a percussion rifle with full, bird's-eye maple stock. It had the unmistakable carving of a feather on its butt end.

"That's Luther's gun," Netta said flatly. She pulled Ruby into a more protective embrace. "Who are you? And what are you doing with Luther's rifle?"

"Sorry to break up your doin's'," he said. "Name's Dan Bailey. And I come to tell you that Luther is dead."

Netta's eyes bugged out, she sucked in a deep breath, then fainted dead away. The Reverend caught both her and the baby before either one could hit the ground. At her collapse, Lucy quickly passed little Alice off to Jonathan and ran forward to assist her friend. Naturally, the entire congregation got to its feet, and all semblance of a religious service came to an abrupt halt.

By the time Netta revived, the Reverend had managed to shift her to a nearby bench, Lucy held baby Ruby, and Sadie came hurrying with a cup of water and a cool towel to bathe Netta's brow.

Slowly, and with deliberate care, Dan told what his dying father had charged him to tell his legal wife living in Justice.

It seems that Luther Bailey had, indeed, kept an Indian woman out in the deep woods all these years—Dan, himself, being the fruit of that union. That fact came as no surprise to the oldest men of the settlement, who'd long ago been sworn to secrecy, as far as the women of Justice were concerned—especially after Luther brought Netta, the sister of his dead partner Ned Pritchard, out to Ohio to look after, as he'd promised Ned he'd do. No one, however, knew the extent to which Luther had gone, to safeguard the life of one of the last Indians living in this part of the state— namely Dan's mother.

He told them Luther died protecting her. While Dan was out checking his trap lines with Snooks Simpson, six strangers came into Luther's camp, looking to "wipe out the last illegal redskins still living in the territory." They'd heard about Luther's squaw from a big-mouthed bully down river by the name of Harvey Thompson, though they had seen hide nor hair of that braggart in months.

Even though Luther was badly outnumbered, he still managed to take at least three of them down before going down himself. With multiple wounds he continued to fight the remaining three, but finally, with a great blow to the head, he lost consciousness.

They left Luther for dead.

He awoke some time later, barely able to move, to find his Indian wife lying at his side, scalped and quite lifeless. He continued to lose consciousness off and on for an undetermined amount of time, until Dan and Snooks turned up again.

Dan said he found Luther mostly dead, but still able to convey to the boy that he needed to go tell Netta that Luther had done his best to provide for the two women he'd taken a solemn vow to protect. He then extracted a promise from Dan to look after Netta and the girls for him, and to give him and his Indian mother a proper burial before they left for Justice. He also told Dan his treasured, bird's-eye rifle now belonged to him.

"I think it's pointless to try to finish our service now," Lucy said to the group gathered around Netta and Dan. "Maybe we'd better get these people busy setting out dinner, and decide what to do about all this after everyone settles down a bit."

"Why don't you get the food line started, and I'll stay here with Netta for a while," Sadie told Lucy, taking the baby. "Clara, it'd be a good idea if you go help your ma and Luella with Netta's girls. I think they've got their hands full trying to settle those three down, after hearing such disturbing news about their pa."

By the time Lucy had the crowd moving toward setting out the meal, the Reverend Gilmore had managed to get Netta moving around some and tending to her baby.

"That man must have a piece of sense," Ma said to Emma Putnam. "Never thought I'd see a man could handle Netta Bailey," she said, walking toward the food table. "Luther just took off when he couldn't deal with her no more." Ma handed her dinner basket to Lucy. "Here, girl. You go set this out for me. I don't aim to get in folks' way no more tryin' t' get things done. You can take charge of this doin's just fine."

With that simple statement, Edith Justice/a.k.a. Ma Hawkins passed the mantle of authority neatly from her own tired shoulders to those of Lucy Johansen, for she knew this particular young woman was up to handling community responsibilities from here on out.

May 20, 18 and 22
Justice Settlement, Ohio

Dear Lib,

By now you know that Katrina and Simeon made it home safe and sound to Riverstop by March's end. She told me she wrote a short note to you after they got back. To put your mind at ease. Good thing. As it has took me over long to get to writing this here letter to you. I could almost hear you stewing up a storm if you was waiting on word from me about their safety.

I got to say that having a man around again does not give me as much time to spend on what I want to do. Though Zeke does not make over many demands. Still he is a man. And you know how they can run your life when they have a mind to. It does come as a releef to know that I do not have to work so hard here at Riverstop no more. If I do not want to, that is. Now that Zeke has made me such a well fixed woman! I still have a hard time believing my good fortune in finally taking up with a respectable man for a change. One who WANTS to look after me!

First off I should mention that after Simeon and Katrina got back home, Harmon and Lovinia moved their selves up by her parents place. Harmon did buy that tinker's cart he spoke of. And Lovinia did open up the Inn she talked about running. Nice little stage coach stop right there in the heart of Petersburg. Calling it The Mifflin Inn, they are. I hear she is off to a good start with it, too. Her parents helped them get it set up for business.

Simeon and Katrina have no qualms about taking over our Riverstop business here on the Clearfork. And I aim to let them. Oh, I will help out now and again when we are around. But Zeke and me have decided to go visiting more in future. Sounds like a good plan to me! We do make a good travel pair.

This week we took ourselves over Justice way to pay a visit to my sister Edie and her Sam. Have been here with them 4 days now to catch up on all the news in these parts.

My Lord Lib, you will not believe what upsets has broke out round here! The worst of which is Luther Bailey went and got his

265

self kilt. Come as a big shock to Netta. As he died tryin to protect his Injun woman. Their son Dan come out of the woods to tell her the news. Right in the middle of a church service it was. When she seen him carryin Luther's gun, she dropped like a lead sinker. Out cold. Good thing that new preacher is fast on his feet. Edie said he managed to catch her afore she hit the ground.

Now Dan who is 17 years has stayed around to help look after Netta and the girls like he promised his dying pa he would do. Only trouble is he cannot hardly stand all the jabber and noise from that bunch of hens. So he moved his self out to the barn where he can have some peace.

Sam says Dan is a lot like Luther in that regard. Quiet. Works hard. Does not say ary a word, less it is important. I think Sam has took a shine to the boy. Is helping him get used to living round a settlement. It has got to be hard on the boy though. Losing both his ma and pa at once. Then to get saddled with blathery Netta to boot.

He does go off to check his trap lines regular. But Snooks helps out with that chore. So he ain't tied to it like he might be. Dan keeps Netta's larder full with tucker from the woods just like Luther done. Guess his pa taught him right. Do not know about his Injun ways. But then Luther seemed more Injun than white man most times anyway. So his son ain't much different.

Edie also told me that new preacher has made it his business to look in on Netta and the girls right regular. Figgers it is his God given duty to look after widows and their children. The man does not have a wife. So who knows what the good Lord might have in mind for those two? Myself, I think he took a shine to Netta. Lord only knows why! Maybe her spunk caught his fancy.

I still can hardly believe my hard hearted sister saying anything kind about a man. And this one a minister to boot! Which she never could stand. Not only that. But there she is, living right next door to a church house, of all places! Life continues to surprise me, Lib. Specially when it comes to sister Edie.

Speaking of surprises. Here is a doosey. Would you believe that after all these years of being childless Emma Putnam went and had her a baby? Quite the shock for everybody. Most of all for Emma. As she did not even know she was going to have a baby till she went into labor and there it come.

Edie says the only one around when Emma started to have pains was Netta. You can imagine how upset both them women would get each other. Netta's prone to get over excited about everything. And Emma being so simple she had no idea what was happening to her. Poor thing thought she was dying. For whoever would even think such a thing of Emma. Nearly 45 and never to carry a single babe. No one thought she even could!

You know how big that woman always was. Lately even bigger still. So who could tell a thing by looking at her? Netta never gave a thought to sending for Sadie when Emma started suffering so. Lucky for her Lucy happened by after paying a visit to the Harrison place. She saw right off what was happening and hurried Emma in to bed. Delivered her of a red faced, squalling baby girl not too long after.

Emma hardly knew what to do with the poor little thing. Sadie come after it was all over and helped out with the new babe for a while. Good thing Lucy thought to send Netta down to fetch her. I think Lucy did it in part to get Netta out of the way and give her a useful task, so Lucy could get Emma settled down.

You would think a woman who has four children of her own would be more level headed when it comes to child birth. But there is no accounting for Netta. Practical one minute. Fluttery the next. She is a might off balance right now anyway. What with losing Luther and all. So we give her the benefit of the doubt.

Well, you can imagine Frank Putnam's shock when he come home to find a new baby in the house. Would not believe it was theirs at first. Took him a long time to get his head round the fact that his Emma had give birth to a baby. His baby. Their baby girl.

When he finally held the little thing for the first time Sadie said he broke into the biggest grin you ever did see. Decided right then and there to name her Stella. As Emma had no better idea, that is what they are callin her. Stella Putnam. By the time Sadie went home they was doing right well with the little thing.

I must say Frank has took his share of joshing from the men over the whole business. Lots of jokes made at his expense on account of he never could see all that well. Teasing him about "Frank with the one eye who can't shoot straight" for all those years. Well clearly he shot straight in the right place at last!

Now for another piece of news. Since Frank now has him a baby to support he and Anson have decided to pitch in together to open them up a tavern. There ain't much Anson can do no more since his stroke left him but one side that works. One thing he can still do is sit and pour a drink. Mostly for himself! Frank has fixed up a old shed on Anson's place where the township men can gather together for manly refreshment. They took to calling it Anson's Shed.

Sam supplies the corn juice and what other hooch he can trade for. Anson pours the drinks. And Frank tallies up the bills and makes the change. Winifred even decided to make eats now and again for their customers. Just to keep Anson out of her hair.

Frank says he knew he better find something he could do to make extra money. Now that Emma can not weave up as much cloth goods as she used to. Seein she has that new baby to care for. That is a full time job for Emma.

I say it is about time those two old slackers did something useful for a change. Even if it does get a few township fellas pickled once in a while. With a new church in town it was only a matter of time till a tavern took root anyhow. Will give that new minister something to preach against, doncha know!

It is hard to imagine that just a few short years ago this place was a powerful wilderness. Much of it still is. But now here is little Justice turning into a regular town. Got them a blacksmith and a cooper. A new church and a new tavern. Even got a school teacher who just moved to the township. A Miss Sedelia Bushnell. Come here with her father just this May. Name of Sterling Bushnell. He bought the Thompson place. That would be me and Harvey's old farm. Glad to see it in better hands at last.

Sam has also took on a new apprentice blacksmith. Black man called Pudge. He come out with them new Harrisons. I have not yet told you of them. Seems another Harrison brother brung out his new bride to Jeremy's place. That would be Amanda Jane's sister to be exact. Sadie says Amanda is still down South Carolina way seeing to family concerns there. But she sent her sister up to the farm here in Ohio with Jeremy and Michael's youngest brother.

His name is John. That sister of Amanda's come with two black people in tow. Pudge and his mother Emmie. I can tell you it has turned many a head to see black faces hereabouts. They seem nice enough. I met them both here at Sam's. Talk a might funny. But you get used to that.

I think there is more of a story there than folks is telling. Or even know about. Maybe by the time I write again I will find out more so I can tell you.

Likely Zeke and me will leave here in a day or two to go visit with my son Jason and his Mary Sue and their children. Has been a while since I seen that bunch of grandbabes. Way they been going she likely could have another bun in the oven by now! I will let you know when I find out.

Until then take care of yourself Lib.

Your travelin fool of a friend,

Ellie Mae MacTavish.

Chapter 15

Amanda's Decision
Late June, 1822
Wallingsford, Edisto Island

Irene Margaret sat in Pitney's old chair on the expansive front porch at Wallingsford, humming a little tune, rocking comfortably, and snapping a bowl full of green beans, as she watched Amanda's girls playing happily with Buzzy and Tutt on the stone mushroom in the front turnaround.

"My don't you seem happy," Amanda said, walking out the front door with another pan of beans to join her sister in the domestic activity.

"I am happy, Amanda. I never thought I could be this happy!"

"What brought all this on?" Amanda asked, taking a chair beside her sister.

"Well, just look around! It's so peaceful here. And beautiful. And all these people honestly seem to care about each other. I never knew such a world could exist."

"Nice, isn't it. Nothing at all like Charleston."

"Oh, Amanda, I don't ever want to go back to all that hobknobbing, society nonsense. I love it here. It's so honest. And down to earth. Please don't make me go back there."

"Why would I do that?" she asked in surprise. "You've made yourself most helpful around here these past months. Pitching in with household work, taking over some of Winston's most tedious accounts. I have to say, I like this Irene you're becoming much better than the one I grew up with."

"I have changed, haven't I." She sat silently for a few moments, working at her beans. "I like this Irene better, too."

"I see no reason for you to leave here, if you've a mind to stay. So rest at ease on that account," Amanda said, working companionably beside her sister.

Just then Winston walked onto the porch with an account book in his hands. "Irene, I have a question about this last entry you made in the workers' ledger. Do you have a minute?"

"Oh, of course, Winston," she said, setting the bowl of beans aside on the porch as she rose from her rocking chair. I'll go back to your office with you and we can go over it together."

Amanda noticed the rosiness in Irene's cheeks, as Winston guided her off the porch and around behind the house. "Something's happening there," she whispered to herself. "I think Irene might be falling in love!"

"You talking t' haints ag'in, Mizz Manda?" Effie Lou asked, coming to the front porch herself with another bowl full of beans.

"No. I am *not* talking to haints. Or spooks, either!"

"Shore soun' like it to me."

"I was talking to myself, Effie, if you must know."

"Shucks, I does that all the time." Effie Lou noticed Irene's bowl of beans sitting aside on the porch. "Irene alr'edy give up on her chore?"

"Winston borrowed her for a little while. Something about going over workers accounts."

"Mmm hmmm," she said, shaking her nappy head. "I'za mind dem two mo' closer, Mizz 'Manda. They'ze spendin' way too much time out back in dat office, yo' ask me."

"You see it too? That she's falling in love?"

"That one done alr'edy fell head over heels, way I read it."

"Does he know it, do you think?"

"Who kin say what go through any man's haid when it come to love," Effie Lou said, shaking her own as she made short work of her bean-snapping task.

Ruth walked up the steps to the two hard at work on the porch, bringing another basket full of beans in from the garden. "I'za pick more beans fo' y'all," Ruth said, dumping her basket between the women. "Oh, Mizz 'Manda, ain' it nice out here? I'z so glad you brung me an' Tutt out with you from Cha'ston. Look how happy he be! Findin' a boy of an age to play," she said, adjusting her ever-present bandanna. "I never seen my boy have a chance to play b'fore," she said wiping a tear from her eye.

"Buzzy seems to have taken to Tutt, too," Amanda observed. "I think that pair will bear some watching."

"Oh, Mizz 'Manda, my Tutt a good boy, he is!"

"I never said he wasn't, Ruth. But you never know what mischief two such curious boys might think up between themselves."

"Lawsy, yo' got that right," Effie Lou jumped in the conversation. "We'ze all mighty glad y'all come out to Wallingsf'rd, Ruthie. I know you gonna like it so much you wanna stay," she said, putting more of the beans into her bowl. "'Sides, I seen that Earlie Hatchell makin' eyes at you, girl. You watch out fo' that one! He alw'ys lookin' t' trip up a pretty gal, if'n she give him any 'couragement at-tall."

Ruthie stood silent for a moment, considering, then gathered herself. "I go back yonder an' fill up this basket ag'in," she said, moving toward the front steps. "Sure feel funny comin' an' goin' by the front stoop. It surely do."

* * * * *

After finishing the morning's chores, tending to lunch duties, and getting Little Jems down for his afternoon nap, Amanda took the twins to her small office behind the parlor. She busied them drawing pictures, while she sat at her desk to begin another letter to Lucy...

June 21, 1822
Wallingsford, Edisto

My Dear Lucy:

Last week I received your letter from April 22, which reported that my sister Eralynn had arrived safely in Justice with her new husband, John. I recall meeting John as a boy of 14, when I married Jeremiah. But, of course, time changes us all.

Thank you so much for welcoming them. And for helping my sister adjust to such a different way of life. No doubt her baby should arrive shortly, if it has not already done so. I pray she is delivered safely of a healthy child...

Amanda tossed her quill down on the blotter. "Oh, I just can't do this right now," she said in frustration.

"Are you mad, Mama?" Camellia asked.

"No, darling. I'm not mad. Mother's just a bit upset by circumstances at the moment."

"Sercum...sterkum... what's sterkum-stances?"

"It means the way things are."

"What things?"

"Well, in this instance, I'm wishing I was the one back on our farm, instead of my sister Eralynn. I miss our cabin. I miss a simpler life. And I miss my friend Lucy."

"Me, too, Mommy. I wanna go home!" Lillian howled. "I miss Unka Mikey!"

"And Hank," said Camellia.

"And Hopper!" added Lillian.

"When can we go home? When? When can we?" both twins asked at once.

"Perhaps we should go outdoors for a while, get some fresh air," Amanda said, in an effort to distract the girls and change the subject. "I think I'd like a benne wafer. How 'bout you two? Let's go back to the cookhouse and see what Ada Mae has in the way of treats, shall we?"

Both girls raced out the back door, seeing which one could out-run the other to the treats jar.

"Oh, to have such energy," Amanda muttered.

Winston came up behind her and touched her shoulder; Amanda jumped as if she'd been shot.

"Oh my lord, Winston. Don't *do* that! You liked to scare the life right out of me!"

"Sorry. I thought you heard me step out of my office." He watched the twins squealing and pushing at one another in their rush for the cookhouse door. "Energetic, aren't they?"

"Oh, Winston, they're so eager to go home. I don't know how much longer I can distract them from the idea."

"Then why don't you go?"

"What? Leave here? Now? With all we have to do?"

"We've been handling things quite nicely. With Irene taking over so many of my more distasteful duties, it's freed me up to see to the more important things that need my undivided attention."

"Then you think I should go?"

"I think until you do, you won't know where you belong, Amanda," he said, looking deeply into her eyes. "You need to settle this thing between Michael and yourself once and for all."

"You've picked up on that, have you?"

"It doesn't take a genius to recognize the obvious. I know your heart doesn't belong to me, if that's what you're asking."

Amanda stood silently for a few moments.

"Winston... about Irene."

"I think you and I need to talk about that."

"Do you have feelings for her?"

"Let's just say that over these last months I've come to appreciate her better qualities," he said with consideration. "I'm not completely averse to the idea of considering a union with her."

"Truly? You're thinking of marriage? To Irene?"

"I know she's wildly in love with the *idea* of love and marriage and family," he said, removing his hat and wiping his brow. "She does believe she's in love with me at the moment. But I'm not convinced she has a clue as to what a union between a man and a woman really entails."

"Give her some time, Winston. She's had a lot of un-learning to do. I believe she'll come around. She's come such a long way already, since she's been here," Amanda said. "I just hope Eralynn gives herself a chance to mature the way Irene has."

"It's out of your hands, Amanda. You did all you could for both girls. Now it's up to them."

"I suppose you're right."

The twins came barging out the kitchen door, with benne wafers stuffed in each hand. "Here, Mother. I brung a wafer for you," said Camellia.

"And this one's for you, Mister Winston," Lillian shouted as they raced up onto the porch.

"Thankyousoverymuch, young ladies," Winston said with an exaggerated bow. He bit into the proffered goodie and downed it in two bites. "I think I'd better go hitch up the cart and take a ride to the landing to meet the mail packet. Anyone care to go along?"

"I do, I do!" both twins shouted at once.

"Is that all right with your mother?"

Amanda nodded her head in the affirmative. "Go on, you two. You need a diversion. I'm sure Winston will look after you." She gave him a penetrating stare. "You will make sure they keep all their appendages *inside* the cart, will you not?"

"No arms or legs sticking out. Got it!"

The girls gave their mother big hugs, then raced for the stables.

"We'll be back with the mail, directly," he said, replacing his hat and giving Amanda a slight bow. "Now go sit down and take a rest, while you have the opportunity."

* * * * *

An hour later the twins came running up, onto the porch waving letters in their hands.

"Mama, Mama, you got a letter from Aunt Sadie!" called Lilly.

275

"And this one came from Auntie Eleanore. Can we go see her tomorrow Mama? Can we?" Camellia asked her mother. Amanda roused herself from the short nap on the porch swing, which she'd managed to sneak in while the girls rode to the landing with Winston.

"Why don't we read what she's written us, before we go rushing off to Charleston, shall we?"

"I want to hear Aunt Sadie's letter!" Lilly shouted, shoving the letter she held toward Amanda's face. "Read this one first!"

"Settle down, girls," Amanda said, raising her arms in a leisurely stretch, and giving a long yawn. "Now come, sit yourselves down here next to Mama and we'll see what both your Aunties' have to say."

Amanda reached for Sadie's letter first and cracked open the seal...

April 17, 1822
Justice Settlement

Dear Amanda:

Hope you are faring well enough down Carolina way. I bet by now the girls are lots bigger. Tad and Zoey Blue sure are growing fast. Tad says to tell the twins hello for him and that he misses them. We all do.

I will not beat around the bush this time, as you most likely heard all the news from Lucy. I am writing to tell you about Michael. I know Lucy did not mention him to you, for she came over to talk to me about it.

We are all worried about him.

Michael spent this past winter up north working on a special fireplace for a friend of Aunt Ellie's. Also on a new courthouse in those parts. Stone helps settle him. Always did. He came back to your homestead late March to set things to rights before spring planting.

Then John and Eralynn arrived in April. I can tell you he was sure surprised to see those two. Not to mention seeing them together! We both were glad to have John out here in Ohio with us. Been too long since I have heard John's laugh. No one has a laugh like his. Except for Jeremy's. It sounded so good to hear my brother laugh, since we won't hear Jeremy's ever again.

After Michael helped John get familiar with the farm, and they got a start on sowing spring crops, Michael took himself over to Justice to help out with building the new church. Once they got log walls all set, it commenced to rain for the next week. So the men called a halt to the church project till the weather settles enough to roof it.

Michael went back home to the farm, but as your sister brought along so much help, Michael began to feel like a fifth wheel over there. It was then Eralynn happened to mention that the plantation manager down on your Wallingsford had given you a big ring for Christmas. Along with a proposal...

Lilly interrupted, "What is pro... pro-posal, Mama?"

"Never you mind about that, right now, Lillian," she answered her daughter. She continued reading in silence.

Michael went pretty much crazy after hearing that news. Broke up that rocker of yours, then took off over to Jonathan and Lucy's. Lucy said he was miserable. But after cooling down a might, he decided to head back up north for a while. Work some more on that courthouse.

Like I said, stone settles him. We have no idea what he is likely to do, once he finishes up with that job.

I do not know where things stand between you and your manager, Amanda, but I do know that Michael is empty without you.

Come home. He needs you. Find the truth about where your heart lies once and for all.

This comes from your straight talking sister-in-law,
Sadie Hawkins.

Amanda let the letter drop to her lap.

"What else does she say, Mama?" Lilly pestered. "Tell us!"

"Oh, nothing much. Just that they miss us all and can't wait till we go back home."

"Unka Mikey's sad," Lillian told her mother. "We hafta go home today."

"Well, it's not quite that simple, sweetheart. We can't just pick up and go without a lot of preparation. Mother has a great deal to do before we can even think about going back to Ohio."

"But I want to go home NOW!"

"Lillian Jane. You think carefully about using that tone with me," Amanda warned, giving her daughter a direct stare.

Lilly hung her head. "Yes, Mama. I'm sorry." She thought for a moment. "But Mama? We can go soon, can't we?"

"Soon, dear. Very soon."

That seemed to satisfy Lilly for the moment. She gave her mother a big hug.

"Here, Mama. Read Auntie Eleanor's letter," Camellia said, handing her the other one she'd been clutching.

"All right. We'll see what Eleanore has to say before I get back to work helping Ada Mae. We need to preserve the rest of those green beans today while they're still fresh." She took the second letter and cracked open its seal...

June 12, 1822
Tradd Street, Charleston

Dear Amanda:

I write as you asked, to keep you abreast of our situation here on Tradd Street. Mother and I continue to shake our heads in disbelief at the grandeur surrounding us, at the drastic change in our circumstances.

Again, we cannot begin to thank you enough for stepping in to help us.

Your people here have been quite accommodating to our needs. Never having servants before, I find it a bit overwhelming to adjust to so much help. But with the size of this marvelous house and extent of work entailed in its upkeep, I can see the need for many more hands to accomplish all that requires doing. We have managed to find a workable arrangement among us, as to the allocation of daily and weekly household tasks.

I believe it still surprises your people to have us work alongside them. But we are all beginning to gain one another's trust. Noreen has graciously allowed Mother and I to share her kitchen for the preparation of our cakes and pastries. She even helps out, on occasion, by making her own, special, pecan pie. We've seen that she receives all profits from the sale of that particular pastry. She's been amazed that anyone would actually pay her to produce such a thing!

Zebeniah and Noreen miss Ruth and Tutt immensely, but they understand her need to strike out on her own. At this late stage in their own lives, they feel quite content where they are, having had no desire to take up country living, as you well know. But at least they're thrilled that Ruth has had the chance to make up her own mind in the matter of her future, rather than having her sold away from them, as their older children were so many years ago. They still have no idea what became of those first three, where they may be living by now—if, indeed, they <u>are</u> still living.

My mother and Noreen have seemed to find much comfort in each other's company. I'm happy to see this new friendship blooming between them, as Mother's had so few friends near her own age over these past many years. Being a mix of two races, and little accepted by either, she's spent the majority of her life alone. Unfortunately, the only companionship and comfort she did manage to find was looked down upon by both.

I identify with her loneliness all too well. No doubt you can understand why she and I have developed such a close bond. I do need to tell you, Amanda, that our father always gave Mother and I what time and attention he could; I always felt he loved me.

The only other person left here in town with us now is Cassie. After Pudge and Emmie went up North, and Bess chose to live out at Wallingsford with you all, Cassie moved out to the carriage house by herself. She sees to her share of the work, but she doesn't say much to the rest of us here. She does appear to be a very determined student, most intent on learning how to read and do basic math.

Which brings me to our quandary. We all know how tricky our situation is, what with the laws in force banning the education of slaves. The fact that my mother and I are free does not lessen the danger it puts these people in, should they be discovered undertaking such activities.

However, that has not stopped us from pursuing the task of educating as many willing Negroes as we can. We slip our lessons in here and there as is possible during our daily routine and include any who "happen" to come to call on some assumed errand.

But it seems we have two rather inquisitive neighbors who've taken it upon themselves to find out the whys and wheres and whats of all those who make their way to our back doorstep. Mrs. Arianna Hinkle Gustanson, a widow lady who lives across the street, and her spinster sister, Miss Annabelle Hinkle, have been asking entirely too many questions to suit me.

I have attempted to appear as friendly and agreeable as I can, but their queries continue to become more and more pointed. Short of outright lies, I've sought to make myself as scarce as possible whenever they seem to be around. But it's getting harder and harder to avoid them.

They've even taken to coming right up to our door and pestering poor Zeb, when he answers at their persistent knocks.

God bless him, he's quite good at acting the ignorant butler. But even his good nature is beginning to wear thin.

I know it is an imposition even to ask, as you've done so much for us already. But would you consider coming in for a short visit and making a point of speaking with these women? (I hesitate to call them ladies.) See if you can alleviate their suspicions and put an end to their persistent meddling, before someone slips and they discover something they should not.

Thank you in advance, Amanda, for your help in this matter. I truly do not want anyone to get in trouble. I doubt neither Zeb nor Noreen could survive any time at all in the workhouse, should they be implicated in any wrongdoing here. I honestly don't know what consequences I might face in the matter, should it come to light. But I'm not overly worried about that. I've learned to talk my way out of many a troublesome situation already. No doubt I'll need to do so again in future.

I look forward to hearing from you, Amanda. Any advice you can offer in this matter would be most welcome. A visit would be grander still.

Again, thank you for your gracious kindness toward me and my mother. I'm glad that you finally told Irene Margaret about us, and that her reaction was one of tolerant acceptance. It's a relief to know she bears us no ill will and that she's finding happiness out there at Wallingsford with you. Please give her my best regards.

Your half-sister,
Eleanore Bently Pierce.

"Auntie Eleanore wants us to come!" Camellia squealed. "When can we go, Mama... when?"

"I'll talk to Winston and see if we can take a few days for Charleston next week. Perhaps we can do some shopping, while we're in town. I can hardly believe you've both outgrown your shoes already," Amanda said, giving the girls a squeeze. "Maybe we can buy some gifts for all our friends back in Ohio, too. Now go and play, you two. I need to get Jems up from his nap. I hear him thumping up there in the crib."

The girls scurried down the porch steps and out to the mushroom stone, where they scrambled on top and began to dance. "We're going to *Charl*-ston. We're going to *Charl*-ston!" they sing-songed while holding hands and spinning one another round and round."

"Don't you two come running to me when you fall off that stone and crack your heads," Amanda called on her way inside, "just be forewarned!"

Walking by on her way in from the garden, Ruth took notice of the girls, and Amanda's off-hand remark. "My, my, Manny. You comed a long way in lettin' them chillin's jus' be chillin's! Hardly can believe my own ears!"

Chapter 16

The Old Grandfather
Early July, 1822
Wallingsford, Edisto Island

The distinct touch of a feather stroked Amanda Jane's hand in the middle of the night.

She awoke with a start, to see a wise-looking Indian, in full ceremonial garb, standing at the foot of her bed.

She closed her eyes and shook her head, then opened them again.

Nothing.

"Good grief. I must be dreaming." She rubbed the back of her hand, where the feather's touch still lingered. "But that felt so *real*." She adjusted the covers, then snuggled back down into her bed, hugging the comforter to her chin.

She fell back into a fitful sleep.

The next morning, as she helped Ada Mae clean up the kitchen after breakfast, they chatted companionably while Amanda dried dishes. "I had the strangest dream last night," she mentioned off-handedly. "Have you ever been awakened by a feather stroking your hand before?"

"Don' reckon so," Ada Mae replied.

"It was the strangest sensation. And felt so real. I could have sworn someone woke me on purpose," she said, putting the dish she'd just dried atop the stack of clean plates. "I thought I saw an Indian standing by my bed, too. Really shook me up for a few minutes, there."

"Indian? In fancy skins an' fringe?"

"Why yes, have you seen him too?"

"Lawsy no! An' I hope t' never do!"

"Then how did you know what he looked like?"

"It be de Old Shaman, come t' give wa'nin'."

"Old Shaman? Warning? What are you talking about?"

"Pitney always say de Old Shaman 'pear to her when someone 'portant be comin'. Or be goin'. She tol' how he look."

"An old Shaman. My, goodness, who'd have thought."

"She never be wrong, neither. We best start cookin' up mo' food. Don' know what likely be in sto' for this day."

"I always knew about her premonitions... you say that same Indian would warn her?"

"Always," Ada Mae said, starting to stir up a big batch of biscuits. "Yo gran'mama al'w'ys tol' us you hab the gif', too, chile."

"What gift?"

"Of seein' be-on' the veil."

Amanda stood silently for a few moments. "I have had some unusual dreams before... some that felt very real, in fact," Amanda casually remarked. "You may not believe it, but I saw Grandmother Bently on the very day she died."

"I knowed it!" Ada Mae said, stirring hard at the dough in her bowl. "Pitney say she waitin' fo' one t' come who see de Old Shaman, too. I reckon you be dat one!"

"I'm not sure I feel at all comfortable being one to see such things," Amanda said, putting away the last of the dishes. "But if he came for a reason, I suppose we'd better prepare... just in case it *does* happen to be true." Amanda walked to the other side of the kitchen and pulled down a kettle. "Maybe I should start a pot of soup?"

"Best make it a big pot."

* * * * *

After working in the kitchen most of the morning with Ada Mae, Amanda took a break to go check on the children outside by Ruthie. She had a whole group of boys and girls busy on the front lawn, all catching beetles and grasshoppers.

"What are they doing?" Amanda asked.

284

"Seein' who catch de most bugs."

"Whatever on earth for?"

"Keep 'em busy! An' kill squash bugs an' grasshoppers an such. Keep 'em out de garden."

"Well, at least that's useful, I suppose... as long as it keeps the children out of trouble."

"They doin' fine, Manny."

The women watched the group scurrying over the grounds, whooping and hollering whenever one of them found a bug.

"They keepin' track. One gets de mos', gonna hab de bigges' treat when dey quit."

Amanda smiled, watching the group of nappy-headed, black children run and play with her own, whose light complexions stood out in stark contrast to the rest. Jems laughed his infections laugh while trying to keep up with the older ones, and Camellia giggled every time she touched a bug.

"Where's Lillian? I don't see her with the others."

"She wen' out back while ago, t' visit Aunt Tillie."

"Go to the outhouse, you mean?"

"Well, it soun' more 'spectable t' say she 'visit Aunt Tillie'."

"How long ago did she leave?"

"A while. Not long."

"Maybe I'd better go check on her."

"I mind deese chillin's a spell mo'. Then we gets some treats."

Amanda checked the outhouse and found no one. She went back to the kitchen to see if Lillian had gone over there, before heading back to the group out in front. No Lillian.

"Maybe she's in with Irene and Winston." Amanda headed toward the overseer's office beside the kitchen building. She gave a soft rap on the door, then pushed it open. "Is Lillian with you?"

"No. She's not here," Irene said.

"Have either of you seen her lately?"

"We haven't left here in the past hour. No sign of your girl around here, Amanda," Winston answered.

"Well, she's not out with the others, either, and I haven't found her anywhere out back. Maybe I'd better check in the house." Amanda turned and made her way in the back door, looking through each downstairs room as she went toward the front of the house, calling for her headstrong girl.

"Lillian! Lillian Jane? Are you in here?"

No answer.

Amanda continued on upstairs to the bedrooms, calling, searching, getting more agitated with each passing minute.

"Lillian Jane, you'd better show yourself before you get in big trouble, young lady!"

Still no Lilly.

After looking through the entire house and all the nearby out-buildings, Amanda became more and more alarmed. "It's not like her to disappear like this," she told Winston.

"Maybe we'd better look farther afield. Did you check the People's Village? See if she wandered over there?"

"Not yet."

"I'll go ask around, see if any of the workers have seen her," Winston said. "She has to be around here somewhere."

Another hour of searching turned up nothing. No one had seen any sign of the girl.

Amanda was beside herself with worry, what with all the alligators and poisonous snakes crawling around out there in the marsh swamps, and wildcats and wild hogs, and who knew what else lurking in the jungle woods. She wouldn't let herself even begin to think about ocean currents or rip tides or man-eating sharks, should her precious girl have wandered so far as the shoreline!

"Calm down, calm down, she must be here somewhere," Winston told her again.

"Mebbe a Boo Daddy done took her," Pitney's granddaughter Iddy told Ruthie. "Mammaw Pitney al'w'ys say dem Boo Daddies ca'ey off de chillin's when dey's res'less. Dey jus' waitin' t' grab a chile out wandrin' all 'lone."

"That's pure codswallup," Winston told the woman, turning her away to keep her out of ear-shot of Amanda Jane, who was over checking on Jems. "Don't you go scaring the other children with your stories of haints and spooks, now. We've got our hands full, just trying to keep Miss Amanda calmed down. We don't need to go getting the children all stirred up, too." He eased the woman over closer to the group of youngsters sitting on the grass, counting out their piles of bugs. "Why don't you all go over to the kitchen and see what Ada Mae has fixed in the way of treats?" he called.

The whole bunch rose as one and ran for the kitchen building.

"Has anyone checked with Alvin, over in the stable?" Irene asked.

"I didn't. Did you?" Amanda asked Winston.

"I sent him over to the landing a couple hours ago to meet the mail packet. He should be bringing the cart back any time, now. I'll talk to him when he gets here," Winston said. "By the way, has anyone thought to ask Camellia if she knows anything? As thick as those two usually are, maybe she can shed some light on this mystery."

Amanda hurried after the flock of children and followed them into the kitchen, where they all waited for Ada Mae to pass out hush puppies, cooling fresh from the pot.

"Tol' ya we'as gonna need lottsa tucker, Mizz 'Manda," she said. "'T'warn't a body comin'. But a body goin'!"

Amanda shivered, then took Millie's hand and pulled her outside where they could talk.

"Camellia, do you know where your sister is hiding?"

"She's not hiding, Mama."

"If she's not hiding, where *is* she?"

287

"Lilly's real upset about Unka Mikey," Millie said with a solemn look. "He's so sad."

"What does that have to do with Lillian disappearing?"

"She's not disappeared Mama. She goed to find Unka Mikey."

"She *what*?"

"I *told* her not to. But she said no more waiting. She had to go meet him."

"Ohmylord!" Amanda strove to calm herself. "Camellia, where *exactly* did she go?"

"On the boat."

"Boat? What boat?"

"The one that brings letters," she said. "Mama, can I go get my hush puppies now?"

"Yes, dear. Get your treat," she said, releasing her.

Amanda raced for Winston's office, panic beginning to get a firm hold over her emotions. After she reported her intelligence from Camellia, they both headed to the front steps to wait for Alvin's return. When he rounded the bend and headed down the lane, they ran to meet his cart.

"Y'all in a big hurry to go off some'eres?" Alvin asked, pulling the horse to a stop.

"You didn't take Lillian to the landing with you today, did you?"

"Why no'um. I'za gwan by my lonesome," he said in his slow drawl, handing Winston the mail pouch. "Dis be de onliest post de Cap'n, lef' y'all."

"You saw no sign of a little girl anywhere when you set out?"

"Jus' yo' gal playin' on de lawn."

"Not two girls?"

"No'um. Jus' one."

"You didn't think to look in the back of the cart before you left, did you?"

"No Suh. No shipment goin' t'day. Jus' de post."

Winston had gone around back to search the cart for himself. He pulled at the old burlap tarp and gave it a shake. A tattered doll's hat fell out, onto the lane.

"That belongs to Lillian's rag doll!" Amanda screeched.

"Looks like you had a stowaway, Alvin." Winston said, shaking his head.

"Lawsy be. I ain' seen a t'ing, Suh," he shook his head.

"She must have crawled in there when you weren't looking."

"But where she go?"

"That is the question of the day," Winston answered, throwing the tarp in a heap into the back of the cart. "Turn this thing around, Alvin. We're heading back to the landing to see if we can stop that Captain before he sets sail. I want to have a look over his boat."

Winston gave Amanda's arm a squeeze, then hopped aboard the cart. "Stay here. I'll be back."

Amanda stood watching the cart disappear under the canopy of live oak branches, hanging thick with Spanish moss.

Never had she felt more helpless and alone.

* * * * *

An agonizing hour went by before Amanda saw the cart return down the oyster-shell lane. Alvin pulled right up to the front door, where she and Irene waited.

"Where's Winston?" Amanda asked.

"He say tell y'all he sailin' over t' Charl'ston."

"He took the mail packet back? But wasn't Lillian on it?"

"De mail boat don' a'ready set sail fo' we got dere, Ma'am," Alvin told her. "Mista Winston, he took de skiff by his own se'f."

"You mean to tell me he left for Charleston alone?"

"Yass'um. Say he best make haste fo' dat chile fin' bigger trouble." Alvin gave the horse a click to start it toward the stable.

"Don' fret yo'se'f, Mizz 'Manda," he called over his shoulder, "Mista Winston be a good sailor. He bring Mizz Lilly back home."

The household went about its usual late afternoon and evening tasks, but Amanda could barely contain her anguish. After they finished supper, she readied Jems and Camellia for sleep, tucked them into bed, then went back downstairs to wait with Irene.

She paced the parlor. She paced the hall. She paced the porch, then doubled back to pace them over again.

"You're going to wear a path through here," Irene said on Amanda's third time through. "Why don't you sit down a while?"

"I can't sit still for worry," Amanda fussed. "What am I going to do if he doesn't find her?"

"You can't think that way right now. You need to think positive thoughts," Irene reassured.

"That's easy for you to say. She's not your child!"

"I love her too, you know." Irene lowered her head. "Just because I don't have children of my own, doesn't mean I can't feel the worry, too."

"Oh, I'm sorry. I don't mean to criticize your feelings. I'm so worried, I hardly know what to do with myself."

"Well if you can't sit, then why don't you take a walk in the orchard?"

"Good idea. Those peach trees always did calm me," Amanda said. "You'll keep an ear out for Jems, if he should fuss?"

"Yes, I'll keep watch over the children."

"You'd better. They're the only ones I have left!"

"Don't think that way…"

"I know, I know. Positive thoughts." Amanda headed back out the front door, continued down the steps and into Grandmother Bently's prized orchard, where the trees hung heavy with island peaches, nearly ripe for the picking.

Amanda wandered under the fragrant branches for quite some time, then found herself standing at the gate of the family graveyard. She opened it and went inside. Walking slowly around the stones, she inspected each one: Pitney Doubleday Bower, the newest grave in the plot; Oliver Jameson Wallingsford, founder of Wallingsford Plantation; Leaf Jameson Bently a.k.a. Falling Leaf, Great Grandmother's son; Amelia Casstleton Bently, Leaf's English wife; Jameson Oliver Bently, their oldest son, the uncle Amanda had never known; Olympia Lillian Wallingsford Bently. Great Grandmother. Alone she'd survived the deaths of all her other family members buried here.

"Oh, Grandmother, how did you manage to live through so much loss and pain? How did you do it?" Amanda beseeched as she fell to her knees beside Grandmother's grave. "How can I ever live through losing another child? I've lost too many already." Amanda gave in to her tears, sobbing through great gulps of air as she released her pent up emotion.

Through hiccups and deep breathing, her weeping began to ease. Slowly, she managed to regain a measure self-control. When she stopped crying altogether, she found herself lying on her back nearly underneath one side of Grandmother Bently's grave marker. She looked up and saw something sparkle in the rays of the setting sun.

"What on earth?"

She reached up and grasped an ancient-looking key, nestled in a little hollow carved in the overhang of the stone's side. Amanda scooted out from her spot and sat back up. "A key." She looked it over, turning it first one way, then the other. "A key? This couldn't be the key Grandmother spoke of in her will, could it? The Key to Bent Leaf's birthright? Could it really be an actual key?" She pushed herself up from her sitting position and regained her feet. "If it is that key, then what on earth does it open?"

Temporarily side-tracked from her worry over Lillian, Amanda made her way back to the plantation house to discuss this newest mystery with Irene.

* * * * *

The winds favored Winston's ride, and he made Charleston harbor inside three hours' time. He tied up the skiff at the Tedrow-Bently dock and hurried off to track down the captain of Edisto's mail packet.

He found Captain Eddington getting ready to disembark, before heading home to his dinner.

"Captain! Permission to come aboard, sir?" Winston called.

"Why, Winston. Whateva' you doin' in Charleston? I thought you wuz back on Edisto pickin' peaches!"

"We have a bit of a situation with one of Miss Amanda's girls, Captain. You didn't bring Miss Lillian with you over to Charleston today, did you?"

"I ain't seen hide nor hair of no little girls, suh. Just slaves an' degenerates."

"I have reason to believe Lillian may have stowed away on your ship today, Captain. You mind if I take a look around? See if we find any sign of her?"

"Come on up. Lucky you caught me 'fore I left for the day," said the captain. "What eg-zackly you lookin' for?"

"Anything that might indicate the transport of a little girl."

Winston and the Captain combed the mail packet from stem to stern, searching under boxes, lifting piles of ropes, looking underneath the mounds of folded sails.

Nothing.

"Maybe you should go talk to the Harbor Master, Bertram Peabody. He might know somethin'," said Captain Eddington.

"Thanks for the suggestion. I believe I will," answered Winston, on his way off the boat. At the foot of the gangplank he looked down and noticed a red ribbon sticking to a wooden splinter on the side of the wharf, fluttering in the breeze. He unhooked it. "You put this here, Eddington?"

"Nope. Not me. Got no call for hair bobbles... as you can see!" He raised his cap to uncover a bald pate.

"I think we may have found where Lilly came ashore," Winston said. "I'll go find Peabody. Maybe he's seen her. Thanks."

Winston walked down the docks toward the Exchange building, looking carefully up and down each wharf to check for any sighting of a little girl in a red pinafore. He saw people of light and dark skin, and every shade in between; people of all shapes and sizes, dressed in myriad colors of the rainbow, but no Lillian.

When he came to the Harbor Master's office, he walked into a flurry of commotion. Captains jostling for position at the counter, Factors with lists of lading in hand, pushing to the fore. He looked around to see if he could identify someone in charge, when his eye lighted on none other than Michael Harrison, standing in one of the ticket lines, not so patiently awaiting his turn.

"Michael! What in blazes are you doing in Charleston?" Winston bellowed from across the room, then rushed over to give his back a firm smack.

Immediately wary, Michael gave a hesitant smile. "Winston? Is Amanda with you?"

"Not this trip. She stayed back at Wallingsford with Irene and two of the children."

"Two? Where's number three?"

"That's what I'm here to find out," Winston said, pulling Michael out of line and outside the office, where they could hear one another without shouting. "We discovered Lillian stowed away on the mail packet this afternoon, and I sailed over to find her," he explained. "I'm glad to see you here. You can be a big help."

"Whatever possessed that little girl to run away to Charleston all by herself?"

"Apparently, she came looking for you!"

"Me?"

"That's what Camellia told her mother. She went to find Uncle Mikey."

"Good grief. I can just imagine Amanda's state by now."

"Worried sick. I left her thinking she'd lost another child."

"You sure Lilly's here?"

Winston held up a doll hat and hair-ribbon. "She's left a trail."

"All right. Let's think this through," Michael said. "If she came looking for me, where's the most logical place Lilly would think to find me?"

"When you came in with Amanda and the girls last year, where did you set sail from?"

"Philadelphia."

"Then, let's find out if any boats came in from Philadelphia in the last day," Winston said. "Where did you sail from this time?"

"Came from Baltimore this trip. Faster. Landed here late this morning. But I been standin' in that blasted ticket line for the past two hours, trying to get a boat ride over to Edisto." Michael said. "How would Lilly know which boat came from Philadelphia?"

"By reading the dock sheet posted at the wharf."

"She can *read*? Already?"

"Amanda and her half-sister have been teaching the twins for the past six months or so."

"I thought her half-sister was in Ohio."

"One of them is."

"*One* of them? You mean there's another one?"

"She just found out about her this past February. Long story. I'm sure she'll fill you in when you see her... You *have* come to see her, haven't you?"

"That's why I'm back down here."

"Good. She needs you, Michael. She just hasn't convinced herself of that fact, yet."

"But I though you two were getting married?"

"Well, I tried to walk her down that aisle, but the way she's dragged her feet about the whole thing made her intentions pretty clear," he said. "Besides, she never did say yes to my proposal."

"You're not sore?"

"Why should I be sore? I can't *make* someone else care for me, now, can I?"

"Reckon not," Michael said. "I do have to say, your attitude puts my mind at considerable ease. I came ready to do battle with you, if needs be, you know."

"Well, I'm relieved we won't have to fight for her, too," Winston answered. "Love is one of those funny things, Mike. Usually blindsides a person. There's no accounting for the leanings of the heart."

Just before sunset, the two men managed to collar one of the Harbor Master's clerks, who pointed them toward a wharf about one-half mile north of the Exchange building, where a steam ship from Philadelphia had docked earlier that afternoon. They made tracks to the specified pier, and began to question everyone in the area, as to whether they'd seen any trace of a little girl dressed in a red pinafore and stockings, with a red ribbon in only one of her braids.

After nearly giving up the search, they sat on an upturned dinghy to reconsider their options As they talked, Michael looked down and noticed a small hand coming from underneath the little boat, reaching toward his shoe. He squatted down and put his head low enough to look inside.

"Lilly? That you under there, Pipsqueak?"

Out squirmed a bedraggled little girl, dirty from head to toe, who shot straight into Michael's arms and held on for dear life.

"Unka Mikey! Unka Mikey! You *comed*!" She clung to him with a bear-like grip.

"Lilly, honey. Whatever gave you the notion to come looking for me by yourself? Don't you know it's dangerous for a little girl all alone?"

"But I wasn't alone."

"You weren't?"

"Nope."

"But I don't see a single soul around here. Who brought you to Charleston?"

"The Old Grandfather."

"Old Grandfather?"

"A old Indian man. In furs and fringes and feathers," Lilly said. "He told me you was coming today, Unka Mikey. Somebody had to meet you. Millie wouldn't do it. So I comed myself!"

"Why didn't you tell a grown-up, honey?"

"Grownups don't see Old Grandfather. 'Cept for a few. He told me so," she said with authority. "Old Grandfather watched over me the whole time."

"Is he here now?"

"Nope. He left when you sat down."

"Well, if that doesn't take the cake," Winston said with a shake of his head in utter disbelief. "Pitney always told us whenever an ancient, Indian Shaman would appear to her, someone important would be coming."

"Lilly, honey. Don't ever do something like this again, you hear me?" Michael told her.

"Unka Mikey?"

"What, sweetheart."

"Can we eat supper? I'm awful hungry. The food Old Grandfather gave me tasted like air."

Michael shook his head, and held the five-year-old close to his heart. "Lillian Jane, you're a treasure. You surely are."

* * * * *

In the middle of the night, Amanda again felt a feather stroke waken her. There stood the Shaman once more, with arms folded, looking her straight in the eye.

This time she did not blink. She spoke. "Someone's coming?"

He nodded.

"Lillian? Is she safe?"

296

He extended one arm and pointed toward the turnaround in front, then he disappeared.

Amanda didn't know whether to cry, or scream, or laugh hysterically. No way could she fall asleep again this night. She rose and headed down to the porch to sit vigil, until someone should return.

Wrapped in a tattered quilt, and holding a cup of hot tea, Amanda sat ensconced in Pitney's rocking chair, waiting... hoping... longing for news of some kind. As she rocked, she prayed, and occasionally she fell into a fitful doze with visions of snakes and alligators and a little girl's shredded red dress swirling in the ocean of her mind.

She jumped with a start when the first rays of the morning sun began to break over the eastern horizon. There stood the Old Shaman, beside the mushroom stone out front, beckoning silently for Amanda to come.

When she stood, the blanket fell away from her shoulders, and slowly, she walked toward the mysterious stone. The Old Shaman gave a reassuring smile, then evaporated into morning mist.

Amanda heard Jems call from his crib. A new day begun. Another day of waiting.

* * * * *

Along about noon, Amanda heard the crunch of wheels on the oyster-shell lane, and she raced outside. Winston barely brought the cart to a stop, before Lillian jumped down and bounded up the front steps, followed by none other than Michael Harrison.

"Mama! Mama! Unka Mikey's here! I *told* Millie he was coming!"

Amanda scooped up her wayward daughter and clutched Lillian to her breast.

"I can't breathe!" Lilly squeaked.

"Lillian Jane! Don't you ever, *EVER* do anything like that again!" Amanda gushed in relief. "You liked to scare me to *death*, when you disappeared, young lady!"

"I didn't disappeared," Lilly said, when Amanda stood her back on her feet. "I goed to meet Unka Mikey!"

Amanda looked into Michael's eyes with longing and relief. "Hello, *Brother*."

"Same to you, *Sister* of mine!" he answered, then stepped forward and folded her into his arms. "I'm never leaving you again, Mandy," he whispered into her ear. "Never."

"Can we go home now, Mama?" Lillian asked, pulling at Amanda's apron strings. Millie and Jems had joined the reunited group standing at the front door hugging Michael.

"Yes, dears. It's definitely time for us to go home."

Dear Ellie,

Scarcely can I believe my good fortune, Ellie Mae! Back in
May we moved into this lovely new house Zach built me, which
I like to think of as my old house, so much does it resemble the
beloved home I left back in Connecticutt these many years ago.
I have been so busy with the move and all the usual necessities
of living, I've had little time to put pen to paper this entire summer
to let you know how life fares for us in these environs.

Zach and I now have an entire bedroom for our own,
exclusive use! This marks the first time my husband and I have
had completely private quarters since we arrived in this territory.
Hardly do I know how to act, having so much space to ourselves.
Zach, however, seems to have no difficulty whatsoever in adjusting to this new-found extravagance, prancing around in such a
disrobed fashion I blush even to mention it here. He says he
sees no shame in wearing "the birthday suit God gave him." I
just smile, and draw him under the seclusion of our cozy quilt.

We left Kit and Lizzie and their little Liberty back in our old
cabin. Kit says they have quite the challenge in filling it to the
brim, the way we had done, but he does seem up to the task.
Lizzie just turns a lovely shade of red and keeps her peace.

As Elijah is the only other soul in residence with us here,
I find it quite ironic that we finally have all this space, and now
no longer need it! Oh to have had the luxury of three bedrooms
when we had beds hanging from the walls with so many bodies
to accommodate in our first, tiny home in these Fire Lands!

Ah, but life seems so full of ironies, does it not, dear friend?
The cabin we left rings with all the memories we made there—all
the little families given start from the haven of its refuge. I pray
Kit and Lizzie manage to fill it with many more of their own
(memories, I speak of here, not necessarily children. Although
we both know they do go hand-in-hand!).

I doubt not that our Elijah will do his best to fill the walls of
this new house with his own, unmistakable character. Even now,

he spends much time squirreling away "treasures" in the secret compartment of our lovely fireplace hearthstone. Lord only knows what some poor soul will think years from now, when he stumbles upon this little boy's store of riches.

I have yet to mention our Christian and your Johannah—two kindred spirits if ever I saw them—both adventurers at heart. Together they set out from here the end of May, after helping us to move all the heavy crates and furniture and household goods into our new abode. They spoke of traveling the great lake north to Canada, or perhaps taking the Missouri into unknown lands in the west. Lord only knows how far their daring spirits may carry them.

They did make a stealthy trip to visit Justice Purdy in the neighboring township, just two days before they left us. They returned the next day to tell their news, with grins stretching from ear to ear. Naturally, we insisted upon an impromptu celebration with Kit and Lizzie, and Nate and Ivy joining us. Though I had no time to bake a proper wedding cake, I did manage to stir up short cake, which we covered with what early berries Elijah could find.

We sent Christian and Johannah on their way with as many supplies as they had room to pack, on the little mule Johannah brought along when they came at Christmas time. I think she takes after you, Ellie, in the way she seems to love that mule, even naming him "Lucifer the Second," in honor of your own.

That about covers the extent of news from here, friend, other than hearing no word of our Levi's whereabouts. I pray that whirling dervish of mine keeps himself as far from trouble as he can, although trouble does seem to have a way of finding him, I fear.

Take good care of each other, El. I know Zeke will look after you better than you look after yourself. Perhaps in your newfound freedom to travel, you will find yourself coming up this way more often? We can but hope.

Until then, I remain your faithful friend,
Lib

300

10 August, 18 and 22
Wallingsford, Edisto

Dearest Lucy,

We're coming Home!! I hardly can wait to see you and the children, to see how they've all grown. I'm certain that quite a good deal has also changed around Justice, in more than a year's time.

As to the goings on here, there is much to relate. You most likely know by now that Michael left Ohio and returned to us here in Wallingsford, arriving the second week of July. But before his arrival we had quite the scare concerning Lillian, who disappeared for a time. If I related the full circumstances of her vanishing in this missive, I'm certain you would question my sanity—and have every right to do so! Suffice it to say that Lillian was found, safe and sound, on the very same day that Michael returned to us.

But Lucy, I believe I lost ten years from my life with worry over Lillian Jane! Lord only knows what could have happened to her, but no. I shan't go down that road. She's safe. That's all that matters now.

And by the end of next week we shall be on our way home! I sincerely hope this letter reaches you before we do. I imagine we should arrive in Justice by the end of September at the latest. Hopefully some time before that, if all goes well on the trip. I have much to finish packing yet, and some loose ends to tie up with my Father's businesses in Charleston, before our departure on Friday next. Michael made sure to buy our return tickets soon after he arrived.

Here at Wallingsford I have no doubt that things will be well looked after in my absence. Winston and Irene have taken over day-to-day responsibilities concerning all business and worker concerns here. I have given Winston full authority and have no qualms about leaving plantation affairs in his very capable hands. Since he is now my brother-in-law—yes, he married Irene in a quiet service at the Episcopal church here on the island—he has a more personal interest in all undertakings at Wallingsford.

301

I should also mention, that Michael and I tied the knot at the very same matrimonial service as Winston and Irene. A double ceremony with my sister! It was simple, but very lovely. We wore no fancy frills or lace, only tasteful dresses that suited our intimate setting. The people back at Wallingsford gave us quite the festive reception afterward. The girls and Jems are tickled beyond measure, now unsure as to whether they should continue calling Michael, "Uncle Mikey" or whether they should now call him "Papa."

I'm sure that problem will sort itself out in due time.

The only other piece of unfinished business before us involves Grandmother's Journal. I don't believe I've mentioned it to you before, but earlier we'd found a very old book in a hidden compartment of the fireplace here at Wallingsford. It had a rusty lock, which we had been unable to open, until I discovered a hidden key on Grandmother's grave stone.

Voilà! The key fit the journal—which turned out to be the very one Pitney tried to tell me about, as she lay on her death bed. The journal itself consisted of a detailed account of Grand-mother's time spent among the Chickasaw Indians. The stories she related there could nearly curl one's hair, should she have straight hair to begin with!

Within those pages I came to know a side of my Grand-mother I'd never before discovered. And Bent Leaf, her mate among "The People of the Forest," as they called themselves, as well as my great-grandfather, became much more real to me. I discovered that he, too, had a mole behind his right ear, as does Lillian, and do I. Apparently Grandmother took this sign to be the "soul marker" she spoke of in her last will and testament. I can only suppose she was correct in her assessment, given some of the astonishing goings-on that have transpired here over the past few months. I shall wait to tell you of those things, until we again meet, face to face, Lucy, as I doubt you'd believe me, should I try to relate them here.

The only mystery remaining involves a treasure of some sort, that Grandmother kept hidden to safeguard the welfare of her people, meaning the workers of Wallingsford. I always knew that raising peaches alone could not come close to covering all expenses of the huge enterprise this plantation involves. Nearly every other planter here on Edisto has made his fortune raising long-staple, sea island cotton, which entails quite the labor-intensive methods.

Grandmother let her people choose the products they would prefer to grow, coming up with several amongst themselves, the main one being the island peach. Knowing that crop would most likely fall short of keeping all the workers' families well supplied, she had some sort of treasure put by to insure the continued freedom of her people, should the work of their hands not sufficiently see to the supply of their needs.

Naturally, Grandmother also had a substantial inheritance from her own father, based upon the indigo and rice he originally grew here, and which she wisely invested over the years. As those investments grew, along with prudent husbandry of the plantation's crops on her part, her earnings made her a rich woman and have kept Wallingsford more than secure.

However, there is still the question as to this "hidden treasure" of Grandmother's, which she insisted remain so, in order to make sure there would always be back-up reserves stored away to take care of her people, should disaster ever befall.

Wallingsford rolls along quite nicely right now, and Grandmother's investments rest on firm footing, so there is no real need for this fortune of hers to be found. Naturally, it is a great mystery waiting to be solved. However, I leave the discovery of said treasure up to the resourcefulness of Winston and Irene, for I've already realized my own treasure in Michael.

And would you believe he hasn't stopped talking since he arrived! Travel stories, stone-laying stories, the agony he experienced waiting through a long winter and spring—he keeps me enthralled just hearing the timbre of his voice and watching the expressions on his face. I never fully understood how very much I missed him, until I got him back again.

I have no doubt Jeremiah would be most pleased for us all.

So, my dear Lucy, we're finally coming home! I can't wait to give you a real hug, my friend!

Until September, then.

Amanda Jane Harrison (once again!)

Chapter 17

Leave Taking
August 1822
Wallingsford, Edisto Island

"Mama? Can I take these shells for Tad?" Millie asked Amanda, while they worked at packing trunks for their trip home.

"All those? You have entirely too many to pack, Camellia," Amanda said. "You may choose five of the best shells for Tad. That will take up enough space."

"But Mama, I have so many pretty ones! I *have* to take this one... and this one... and these... and all those too!" Millie whined.

"All right, you may choose five for Tad, and five for yourself. But that's it. We have entirely too much to fit into this trunk for you and your sister as it is."

Millie struggled over her task of choosing the best sea shells in her collection. "But what will I do with all the rest?" she asked her mother.

"We'll leave them here."

"Can I give some to Tessie?"

"Of course you may, darling," she said, acknowledging Millie's friendship for Iddy's granddaughter. "Why don't you go take them down to her right now, and leave me alone so I can get this packing finished."

Camellia gathered up a pile of her seashells, making a pocket from the skirt of her pinafore in which to carry them. "Tessie loves the pink ones best. I'll give her all my pink ones, Mama."

"That's fine," Amanda said absentmindedly, as she sorted through a pile of the twins' out-grown clothing, trying to determine which things to take back to Ohio for Lucy and Sadie to use for their girls. She stopped and looked up as Millie started down the steps. "Camellia? Would you send Lillian back up here?"

"Yes, Mama," she called as she hurried below.

Lilly so feared letting Michael out of her sight, that she'd stuck to him like a cocklebur, since his arrival back at Wallingsford. Millie knew if she found Uncle Mikey, she'd find Lilly, too. It didn't take her long to track them down out in the stable with Alvin and send Lilly scampering back upstairs to their mother.

"Lillian, I need you to try on these shoes and see if they fit," Amanda directed her daughter. "Is your brother still out with Ruthie?"

"He's under the mushroom stone with Buzzy and Tutt," Lilly answered. "This one won't go on, Mama." She tossed the shoe back to her mother.

"Try on that other pair, please. I can't believe how fast you two have grown in the last few months!"

"Unka Mikey's teaching me to drive the cart!"

"He's *what?*"

"I'm big enough, Mama. He said so."

"Well, as long as you're very careful. But you must never, *ever* try to drive the cart all alone, you hear me, Lillian Jane?"

"Yes, Mama."

"Only when Michael's with you, understand?"

"Yes, Mama. Can I go back outside now?"

"Go. And please tell Papa Michael I'll need his assistance with these trunks."

Lilly raced down the steps and out the front door, stopping momentarily at the base of the mushroom stone, where Jems sat playing with a pile of his favorite artifacts, which he'd carried out from the living room fireplace.

"He's not 'posed to have those special rocks out here, Buzzy," Lilly said, pulling at Buzzy's shoulder. "You gotta take 'em back in the house!"

"Tutt's mama say he 'lowed, Missy," Buzzy argued with the outspoken twin.

"Cannot!"

"Kin to!"

Hearing the rising squabble, Ruth came to intervene.

"What got yo' chillins so flusterbated?"

"Jems can't bring those rocks out here!" Lilly stated with authority.

"I tells dis chile yo' say he kin," Buzzy replied to Ruth.

"He don' trouble a soul, playin' so fine 'neath dat stone," Ruth told both children. "Y'all let dat boy be."

Jems sat studying each artifact with his usual, single-minded concentration. Occasionally he'd place a particular rock into an indentation that corresponded to its exact shape and size in the base of the mushroom stone's pedestal.

"Mama won't like it," Lillian told Ruth.

"Pay it no mind, Mizz Lilly," Ruth said, giving Lillian's head a pat. "Run along, now, like a good chile."

Lillian rolled her eyes and heaved a great sigh, then headed back to the stable to find Uncle Mikey, to deliver her message as her mother had instructed.

By the time Michael reported to Amanda up in the nursery, she had the all children's trunks packed and ready to load.

"You called for me, my sweet?" Michael asked, leaning down to give Amanda a peck on the cheek.

She jumped, still not accustomed to more familiar contact with her new husband. "Sorry, you startled me," she said, turning a decided shade of red.

"Are you blushing?"

"No, I'm not blushing! I'm merely flushed from the heat up here and all this packing," Amanda rattled nervously.

"I made you blush," he chuckled, quite proud of himself.

Amanda slowly rose to her feet while dabbing at her forehead with a handkerchief. "I'm not used to such... such... familiarities between us, yet, is all," she breathed. "It's been quite a while since I've... well, *you* know."

"Yeah, it's been a while since I 'you knowed' myself!"

"Oh, Michael, you're hopeless!"

"Ain't hopelessness, darlin'," he said, enfolding her into a warm embrace. "It's pure love, plain and simple."

Amanda melted into his insistent kiss, beginning to lose herself in its intensity.

Lillian raced into the room and pulled at Michael's shirt sleeve, bringing the embrace to an abrupt halt.

"Unka Mikey! Unka Mikey, you gotta come quick!"

"What's wrong, Pipsqueak?"

"The big mushroom made a funny noise! You gotta come!"

Michael looked down at Amanda's face, filled with longing. "Hold that thought Mrs. H. I'll get back to you quick as I can!"

Slowly regaining control of her senses, Amanda rushed to follow Michael and Lillian down the steps and out onto the front lawn. Michael and Winston were already carefully studying the mushroom stone, one from the top, the other from below.

"What happened?"

"The children said this stone made a loud noise," Winston said, as Amanda moved toward him.

"You see anything up there?" Michael asked from where he lay underneath examining the bottom of the huge mushroom cap.

"A circular crack of some kind appears to have opened up, 'bout half way in, toward the center," Winston told him.

"I don't see much down here," Michael said. Jems sat beside him, staring at the last artifact he held, turning it over and over. "Jems, what you got there?" he asked the boy.

Jems pointed to the artifacts he'd lined up around the base of the mushroom, each snug in its own, matching groove. He placed the stone he held into the last, unfilled hollow. As he did so, the stone made it's loud groaning noise once again.

"Well, look what you did, little fella!" Michael said with pride. "You do that when the stone made noise before?"

Jems nodded his head in the affirmative, then gave a growl like the noise of the stone.

"Looks like you've uncovered another puzzle, my boy!" Michael looked at him proudly, then called up to Winston. "Anything happen up there when it made that noise just now?"

"I think that crack opened up a smidgeon more."

Michael crawled out from below the mushroom, pulling Jems by the hand behind him. "Here, take him back a bit," he directed Amanda. "Girls, you stand back, too."

After carefully examining the crack for himself, Michael grabbed the edges of the mushroom and gave a push. Nothing. He tried a twisting motion, which answered with a tiny grating noise.

"Winston, grab that other side. Let's see if anything happens when we both twist this thing."

The two men took hold of the circular stone and gave a firm shove clockwise.

Nothing.

"Try the other way," Michael said."

They pushed counter-clockwise, and the stone moved infinitesimally.

"Again. And put your back into it this time, man!" Michael goaded his new brother-in-law.

The two men pushed with all they had, and slowly, very slowly, the stone began to move. As it did, the crack on top opened ever wider.

"It's opening up!" Amanda shouted. "Whoever would have guessed such a thing?"

"Stop a minute," Michael said. "Let's take a good look before we push any farther."

The girls rushed up to see for themselves, but Michael stopped them.

"Stay back! This thing might take a notion to fall, and if it did, you'd get squashed like a bug!"

Amanda pulled the children back, keeping them close to her skirts.

Michael and Winston bent over the stone, Michael feeling around the opening with an experienced stone-mason's touch.

"I believe there's a hollow inside that base," he told Winston. "Take a look."

Winston checked the opening for himself. "Can't see a thing inside there. I'll go get a light." He hurried back to his office to retrieve a small lantern. While he was gone, Michael continued to push at the mushroom top, opening it up a tiny bit more with each heave he gave. By the time Winston returned with his light, Michael had the opening large enough to lower the lantern into the hole.

"Can you see anything?" Amanda called from the porch, where she and Irene had ushered the children to safety.

By now a small group of curious workers and children and wives had gathered to watch the goings-on, all giving opinions as to what the mushroom stone held.

From where he stood, Winston lowered the lantern as far as he could, looking up and down inside the stone's base. "I can't tell a thing. Just looks like rock to me."

"Let me take a look," Michael said, easing closer as Winston gave way. Michael squirmed himself flat to lie on top of the stone, lowering the lantern all the way to the bottom of the pedestal. When it hit bottom, he sat it down. "You got a poker or something I could use?"

"I'll go get one from the fireplace," Amanda answered, and turned to go inside. She met Ruthie stepping out of the parlor with the poker already in hand. Amanda hurried it down to Michael.

"Thanks," he said, giving her a quick peck. She reddened again, but he didn't see it, since he'd already scooted back atop the stone to return to his task. He scratched at the inside of the base, then raised the lantern once again.

"Well, I'll be!"

"What is it?"

"Take a look." Having determined the stone wasn't going anywhere, he pulled Amanda up beside himself, until she could manage to see down inside, noticing something shiny reflecting back in the lamplight.

"Silver?"

"Silver," he affirmed.

"You've got to be kidding!"

"Nope. Sure's you're born, that base is lined with solid silver," Michael said.

By the time Winston and Irene had each taken a long look, and all the children took their turns ogling the treasure, word had spread to the People's Village.

Grandmother's Treasure had been found.

Dear Lib,

Well Lib. I called it right when I said Mary Sue could be setting on the nest again. With number 5 this time. The poor girl had legs already swelled up like sausages when Zeke and me got here in June. So we had no course but to stay on to help out with the other 4. They look for this one to pop long about Christmas or a mite after. So I get another holiday grandbabe!

Zeke seems content enough here with three little boys to tussle. As they are just 2, 3, and 4 years, they are quite a handful. Harley, Jay and Toby that would be. He keeps them busy. Josie has turned into a good worker at 7 years. She stays inside more to help with house chores now that her ma ain't feeling so spry. She misses spending as much time outdoors with her daddy. My boy Jason. But she does not complain. She does her best to keep everybody laughing round here.

Her leg healed up fine after it got broke just a year ago. Guess you did not know about that. Now you do. She still limps some. But she makes a game out of it. Playing the clown. That is our Josie!

Jason looks after the farm just fine. You recall this place once belonged to me and Jason's daddy. Before he took off with that red-headed floozy down New Orleens way. Me and Jason worked it our own selves after that. He was not more than elbow high when he started doing a man's work. I have to say he turned into a right responsible daddy. Mighty proud of him I am.

I got news from Justice the other day when Harmon stopped by in his tinker's wagon. Found out his route brings him this way and then on East to Wooster. Also goes far West as Mansfield.

He said that new preacher went and married Netta Bailey about a month back. Harmon reckoned that fella musta took his vow to look after widows and orphans right serious. He also reckoned no one else was likely to step up to help that poor woman raise all those girls. Specially once Luella finally leaves as she keeps threatening to do. Harmon did not say much about her. Just changed the subject right quick to talk about Dan Bailey. Guess that boy still hangs around Justice. But he takes off to the woods for longer times now that Netta has her a new husband.

Turns out Netta is making a bang up preacher's wife. She keeps on top of anything that happens in the township anyway. So it ain't much of a change to turn all that news into a prayer chain! You ask me it just makes all the gossip sound more holy.

Speakin of gossip. That new Harrison gal. Amanda's sister? She had her a baby back in July. Little girl. Harmon did not know what they named the tyke. That slave woman Emmie done the deliverin. Good woman. I am told she knows lots about healing. So maybe twixt her and Sadie folks will have more help in these parts. Now that Edie has give up her doctoring ways for good.

Harmon brung a receipt for a cough remedy Emmie told him about. Mix up hyssop, hoar-hound, wild cherry bark and dog wood flowers with a equal amount of spirits. After it steeps for a time you can take it 3 to 4 times a day with honey or sugar.

He did not say what kind of spirits. But I reckon any strong corn juice would do.

Before Harmon left here he did happen to say that Lovinia just fell pregnant again with number 2. So it appears he does make it home now and again! She is sick as a dog real early this time. In fact so sick she has trouble cooking anything for the stage coach travelers. Guess her sister Dora has been helping out with work at the Inn of late. Harmon did not know when this baby is due. But he figgers her to pop some time in spring.

Not much else to pass on from here Lib. Other than to say Simeon and Katrina are doing a bang up job of running River-stop. The boys keep growing fast. Too fast! Simon is 2 now. And baby Matthew at 9 months crawls everywhere. Katrina says Simon keeps careful watch over the babe. Pulling him back from the fire if he gets too close. Takes his big brother chores to heart.

I was hoping Zeke and me could make our way up to youens for another Christmas visit. But we will stay on here till after this babe gets delivered. Most likely a spell after that, too. Mary Sue bounces back fast. But after 5 babes so close, her bounce ain't apt to be so swift as it was.

I am sure you will be merry in your new house for the holidays this year Lib. Make a toast with your special hot buttered rum for us!

Hope to see you later in spring,
Ellie Mae and Zeke

Chapter 18

Late September 1822
Justice, Vermillion Township

"You gonna eat that last griddle cake?" Lucy asked Jonathan, as she began clearing the table from their early morning meal. Baby Alice sat strapped in the high chair, mushing her pancake all over the table.

"I'll leave that 'un for Hank. He could use some more meat on his bones."

"Hank? You want that cake?"

"No, Mam. I can't eat no more," said the five-year-old.

"Well then," Jonathan said, slowly, "I'll roll it up an' put it in my pocket for later." He pushed his chair out from the table, stood with a stretch, then gave Lucy a quick hug, after shoving the pancake in his pocket. "I best get a start on chores."

"Are you going down to check my old place today?"

"Thought I might."

"You know, I've been thinking..."

"Makes me nervous when you get to thinkin,' woman." Jonathan teased, giving her a tickle.

"Michael and Amanda will be coming home soon. And what with their cabin already so full of John's family and Eralynn's servants and all, there sure won't be much room for Amanda's family, too," Lucy reflected. "Maybe we should see if they want to use my old cabin. What do you think?"

"I think you got a good idee, there, Luc."

"It's sat empty for so long, I know it'll need a good cleaning. Maybe I'll just go along with you when you head down that way. Give it a going over before they get here."

"Sounds like a plan!"

"Let me know when you want to leave. I'll have the children ready."

"Once I get the milkin' finished up, we can mosey our way south this forenoon, if ya like."

"We'll be ready."

* * * * *

On the first and third Tuesdays of every month, Netta Gilmore (formerly Bailey) took it upon herself to host a quilting bee for the newly formed Ladies' Circle of the Justice Methodist Church. As Pastor Gilmore's brand new wife, Netta felt it her "boundin' duty" to lead the women of the church in tasks that would uphold the virtue of wholesome Christian pursuits. Not to mention, that it served as a practical way to get everyone together for a nice, long visit without men.

This third Tuesday of September found a sizeable group gathered in Netta's large cabin for its bi-weekly gossip session around the requisite quilting frame at its center. In addition to Netta, her girls, and her cousin Luella (remaining still in Justice), attendees included Winifred Guthrie and her daughter Clara Hawkins, who brought along baby Matilda (8 mo.), Emma Putnam with her baby Stella (4 mo.), Rebecca Simpson and little Ella Marie (19 mo.) along with her 15-year-old Jessie, to keep watch over the babes and toddlers this day, and Sedelia Bushnell, the newly arrived school teacher to Vermillion Township.

"Is Lucy coming?" Clara asked, busy threading her needle, where she sat at one end of the quilting frame.

"She told me she might stop in for a while later, but she can't stay this time." Netta said. "She mentioned something about extra cleaning, or some such. I guess she decided it was time to house-clean at her old cabin. Told me she went down there last week to get a start. She even made new curtains and everything! I don't know what she's thinking, but she sure has been acting strange... even for Lucy!"

"She's not in the family way again, is she?" Clara asked. "That would explain a lot."

"She never mentioned anything about expecting," Netta said. "But, then, Lucy never was one to let on a whole lot about herself till it's obvious."

"What about Sadie?" Winifred asked, giving Emma a strange look. "Emma, what are you doing to that poor child over there?"

"Just rubbin' her head like Frank told me to. Says that keeps it from getting' flat on one side."

"You're more daft than I thought, if you listen to Frank for baby advice."

"She's such a beautiful baby, Emma," Rebecca complimented.

"Thank'ee. I ain't seen the like, if'n I do say so myself," Emma said, hugging little Stella tightly to her breast. "My little miracle."

"My Ruby's quite the miracle, too," Netta jumped in. "She's nothing like the other three at this stage... so quiet and solemn. Hardly ever makes a peep! I think Luther must have put the best of himself into this little wonder before he left us," she said, swaying back and forth with six-month-old Ruby in her arms.

"So what about Sadie?" Winifred asked again. "She comin' or not?"

"I don't look for her today," Netta said. "She sent word that she's swamped with garden produce, and she wants to get it put by while it's still fresh. Guess she's busy making pickles and chow-chow today. Ma's helping her."

"I made some corn relish t'other day," Emma said. "Frank always likes that."

"We made up a big batch of jam yesterday," Clara said. "Tom brought in a whole sack full of fox grapes. They make good jam, but it sure takes a lot of 'em."

"I'm looking forward to apple butter," Rebecca said, working steadily with her usual, tiny stitches. "Apple-butter-stirrin's my favorite time. Fresh, crisp fall air, smell of spices... nothing in the world like it."

"Lovinia any better, or is she still feelin' so poorly?" Winifred asked Rebecca.

"She's having a hard time of it with this one," Rebecca answered. "She wanted to come today, but she felt so dizzy, she decided it'd be best to stay put."

"Prob'ly a good call."

Luella sat in silence, appearing to focus on her stitching in order to avoid any interaction with Lovinia's mother. Losing Harmon to the woman's daughter still rankled beyond bearing, even though Rebecca had tried to make peace with Luella.

Rebecca directed her attention to Sedelia, sitting across from her. "What's your favorite time of year?" she asked the young woman no one knew much about, trying to pull her into the conversation."

"I like spring the best," Sedelia said, raising her head from her work. "Seeing flowers pop up after a long winter, hearing birds singing again when they come back."

"I love seein' my daffydills pushin' up after snow," Emma said. "Makes me smile."

"Sedelia, where did you move from?" Rebecca asked.

"Johnsonville. In New York. It's close to Buffalo? Papa wanted to come out here before land got any more expensive."

"Youens moved into that old Thompson place, dinchya?" Emma asked.

"Yes. It needed a lot of cleaning up. And a new roof. But we've managed to make it quite homey."

"Your Papa's a farmer, then?"

"Well, he always wanted to be. He's a silversmith by trade, but he told me he always felt he had farming in his blood."

"Silversmith? That's quite the skilled line of work," Rebecca replied.

"His Papa was a silversmith. And his Papa before him. He was expected to follow in the family footsteps."

"And your Ma? She in favor of this move?"

"Ma died a long time ago," Sedelia said, dropping her eyes. "Influenza took her back in 08."

"Sorry to hear it," Rebecca consoled. "You must've been pretty young. Are you the only child, then?"

"No, I have an older brother who took over Papa's silversmith works back in Johnsonville. He's already married and didn't want to leave New York."

"So now you're going to teach?"

"I'm just thrilled with the prospect!" Sedelia lit up with excitement. "I can't wait until harvest is finished, so we can get a good start before bad weather sets in," she said. "I brought out slates, and soapstone pencils, and new readers. I'm all ready for students!"

"When you aim to open up classes?" Winifred asked.

"I'm thinking by the middle of October. End of the month at the very latest. That should be ample time for the farmers to bring in enough crops to free up their older children for study."

"'Bout time we had some learnin' for youngens in these parts," Winifred said.

"I schooled all my children," Rebecca said. "Boys didn't take much to book learning, but the girls loved it," she nodded toward Jessie.

"I'm sending Rosanna and Rachael, soon as you ring that bell," Netta said. "It's so nice we got such a fine, new church building we can use for a schoolroom, too. Brawley says it's fitting we start a new church and new school in the same year."

"Who'da guessed you'd ever end up as a preacher's wife, Netta!" Clara said with a shake of her head. Matilda sat beside her in her basket, wide-eyed and smiling. No sign of napping yet.

"Certainly, not me!" Netta exclaimed. "This has been the most unsettled year I've ever lived through! Having a new baby, losing one husband, and gaining another! It makes my head spin, I can tell you that for sure!"

319

"You gettin' on all right with the Reverend?"

"Oh, Clara, he's amazing! He listens to everything I say! He even asks me questions and talks about his day... what he's thinking... I never experienced the like with Luther." She took a breath and held her hand over her breast. "God bless him. Luther, I mean... well, Brawley, too. God certainly did bless me when he sent that man to Justice, I can tell you true. I don't know what I'd have done, if he hadn't stepped up for the girls and me," she rattled on. "Course, Dan's helped out, best he could. But carryin' responsibility for a house full of girls and women is an awful lot to expect of such a young man. Luther taught him right, though. He surely did."

"Dan around now?"

"He took off to the woods last week. I expect he'll show up again in a day or two... just like his daddy used to do."

"I figger'd you'd have nothin' t' do with that boy... bein' as he's Luther's by that Injun an' all," Winifred stated.

"Why, you cannot mean that! He's Luther's only son, for-heavensakes! I'm proud he can carry on Luther's name."

"Netta, you're one of a kind," Clara exclaimed. "You surely are."

Just then the Rev. Brawley Gilmore stuck his head in the door. "You ladies doing well in here this lovely afternoon?"

"Just fine, Reverend," Emma offered.

"Got us a good group today," Netta jumped in. "We've made a lot of headway on our quilt project, too!"

"Who's this one for, if I may ask?"

"We thought it'd be nice to make one for the next new people who move to Justice. Have something pretty and practical to welcome them to the community."

"That's an admirable undertaking. I hope you ladies enjoy yourselves," he said, tipping his hat. "Netta, I'm going to be over at the church for a while, tending to a few chores. You want me to take any of the girls with me?"

"Of course, Brawley. Anything you say."

"I have a couple jobs Rosanna and Rachael could help with for an hour or two, if you don't mind."

"Girls, go on with your new Papa, now. Mind your manners," she instructed her two, older girls, who dutifully trooped out the door to follow Rev. Gilmore over to the church building.

"He's a rite good lookin' man, Netta," Clara tittered. "Bet he keeps you nice an' warm at night, too!"

Netta turned a deep shade of red. "Clara Hawkins, you should not say such things… and about a preacher, too!"

"He's still a man, ain't he?" Winifred added. "You ask me, they're all a bunch o' worthless shikepokes." She jabbed her needle with purpose. "Not a one of 'em worth their weight in sour owl shit."

"Winifred Guthrie! I should wash your mouth out with soap, I should!"

"Sorry, Netta. Forgot this was a church meetin'. I been listenin' to Anson's bad mouth way too long, now."

"How 'bout I fix us all a cup of tea? I think we could use some refreshment," Netta said, as she babbled away putting the tea pot on to steep, while the women continued to chat and stitch. Once the tea had reached its peak, Netta poured cups all around. Before they finished their hot drinks, a knock came at the door, and Netta pulled it open to reveal Lucy Johansen standing there with little Alice in her arms.

"Hello girls," Lucy greeted the quilting circle. "You're all looking well today!"

"Lucy! You came!" Clara spouted.

"I was passing by on the way from my old place back home to Jonathan's. Thought I'd stop in for a few minutes, at least."

"Netta said you're fixing it all up. You thinking of moving back down there?"

"No, I'm quite happy in Jonathan's cabin, now that he's added on more room."

"Then what's all this mopping and dusting business about?"

"I'm getting the house ready for Michael and Amanda Jane," Lucy said. "They're coming home!"

A cacophony of noise broke out as everyone tried to talk at once.

"She's coming back to Justice? When?" Clara asked, once the noise settled a bit.

"I got a letter from her a week ago, saying they'd arrive by the end of September. That means they should get here by next week!"

"But ain't they goin' to their own place?" Emma asked.

"With John and Eralynn and their people already there, where would they all sleep?" Lucy asked.

"Never thought about that."

"Anybody seen that new Harrison baby yet? She ain't brought it out to church. An' it's been over two month, now!" Winifred said.

"She does seem a little standoffish to me," said Clara. "Don't want to join in the way most folks do hereabouts."

"I'm sure it still feels very strange to her up here," Lucy said in her defense. "Remember how long it took Amanda to come out of her shell? It's no surprise her sister acts much the same. It's quite a drastic change from what they were used to down South, don't forget. Maybe once Amanda's back, we'll have more of an opportunity to get to know Eralynn."

"Oh, I can hardly wait to see the twins, and little Jems... Amanda, too, of course," Netta babbled. "The twins are the same age as my Rachael, you know," she mentioned to Luella.

"I take it this Amanda person is someone you haven't seen in a while?" Sedelia asked.

"Amanda Jane Harrison," Netta declared, "she's a little Southern gal who's been gone for ages, now. You don't know her whole story yet, but you'll find out soon enough. She had a hard time of it for... oh, a long while there. Lost two babies, then her husband,

and even went round the bend for a bit, too… if you know what I mean. But all that's past. She's turned into a right steadfast woman now."

"We ain't seen her in over a year," Winifred added. "Went back home to… to… some'eres in the Carolina's, warn't it?"

"Charleston," Lucy informed. "South Carolina."

"She an' that Michael ever get 'round to tyin' the knot?"

"They married just last month," Lucy said with glee, "so I was thinking… when they get back here, maybe we should have a sociable for them. What do you say?"

"Oh, that'd be wonderful! We haven't had a wedding party in ages!" Netta exclaimed. "Should we have it at the new church, doyouthink?"

"Well, that might be nice. But would the Reverend allow dancing in the church house?" Clara asked.

"My, I didn't think about that. I'll have to ask him," Netta said.

"We gotta have dancin'!" Clara pressed. "A weddin' party's no good at all without dancin'!"

"Oh, I have a wonderful idea!" Netta burst out. "Let's finish this quilt for Amanda and Michael! Give it to them for a wedding present!"

Heads nodded assent all around.

"I'll make my cherry bounce for the party," offered Lucy.

"And I'll stir up my special buttermilk cake," said Clara.

"I don't think cake and punch will go all that far. Maybe we should have a whole carry-in dinner. Make a real doin's out of it," Netta suggested.

As the women sat planning for a wedding party, a sharp knock sounded at the door. Netta pulled it open to reveal Snooks, standing there in his leather and furs, holding on to Dan's (once Luther's) rifle.

The minute Netta saw the rifle, she caught her breath. "Don't tell me. Dan's not dead, too!"

"No Ma'am. He's not dead," Snooks said with reassurance. "But he ain't in too good o' shape, at the moment," he pointed behind himself, to a drag he'd fashioned to pull Dan out of the deep forest back to Justice.

Netta hurried outside to assess the situation for herself, and Rebecca came forward to talk to her son. "What's happened?"

"Dan got his foot caught in a bear trap. I found him this forenoon when I was doin' my rounds. Looks like he laid there two, maybe three days."

Netta came running back inside. "Ohmylord, he's *dying* out there!" she hollered. "Someone go get Ma... I mean Sadie! We need help! *Right Away!*"

"Calm down, now, Ma'am. I don't reckon Dan'll expire for another day or so, at least," Snooks said, in an attempt to set her mind at ease.

The effort did little to alleviate her fear.

"You just keep him comf'ter'ble, an' I'll go fetch a doc."

"It's too far to go for any doctor. There's no time!" Netta flustered. "Go down to the Hawkins' place and fetch Sadie. Tell her she better bring Ma along, too. We're gonna need 'em both!"

Snooks set Dan's rifle behind the door, then turned and headed for the Hawkins', about a mile below Justice.

"Three days in a bear trap? Likely that foot'll have t' come off," Winifred said, in her usual doom-and-gloom fashion. "Be a downright miracle t' save it, now."

* * * * *

By the time Sadie and Ma arrived at Netta's, the quilting party had broken up. Netta already had her husband move Dan inside onto a makeshift cot they'd set up in the corner. Luella managed to remove what was left of Dan's moccasin and wash the injured foot to the best of her ability. Although she claimed to have a weak stomach, she accomplished that odious task without losing her lunch.

"It sure don't look good," Ma said, watching over Sadie's shoulder as her daughter-in-law examined the mangled appendage. Dan made no sound, but his face had taken on a pasty shade of gray, and his brow was covered with the sweat of fever.

Sadie pulled his pant leg away to see if any streaks of blood poisoning showed climbing up his limb yet. "Leg still looks good," Sadie said. "Don't know if we can save that foot, but those toes'll have to go for sure."

"What's this 'we' business, girl? You gotta do this your own self," Ma groused at her daughter-in-law. "I ain't got steady enough hands for this kind of doctorin', no more."

"All I need from you is your knowledge, Ma," Sadie said, "and your experience. I can handle the hands-on part… or in this case, toes-off part!"

"Very funny. But I don't think Dan is laughing," Netta said with a scowl.

"Dan gave a weak smile with a wave of his hand, then let his arm drop back onto the bed.

"What can I do, Mrs. Hawkins?" Rev. Gilmore asked. "Tell me what you'll need. I'll get it."

Sadie recited a list of supplies for the Reverend to gather up. While he was at his task, she had Netta making up some fever tea, Luella tearing bandages, and Ma mixing an analgesic to help numb the pain. Within half an hour, they had everything assembled and ready.

Ma had already managed to get a goodly amount of Sam's corn liquor into Dan. He was conscious, as he had been since his arrival, but now becoming more and more woozy from the effects of the moonshine, not to mention the delirium of fever.

"Pour some of that over his foot, too," Sadie directed Luella. "Rev. Gilmore, I'm gonna need you to hold on to his legs and keep 'em from moving. Put your weight into it if you have to," Sadie instructed the hefty man. "Snooks, you'll have to hold both his arms. Can you handle that?"

"No problem, Ma'am."

"I don't think I can watch this," Luella whined. "I really can't do this."

"Just pour some more corn juice over his foot, then you can go keep the girls busy and out of the way. Maybe you better take 'em upstairs."

"Fine. That I can handle," Luella said with relief.

"Netta, you got that knife in the fire? Keep it good and hot. Red as you can get it," Ma instructed. "Got to cauterize that tissue quick, once it's cut."

"We're ready," Sadie said. "I'll take the knife now, Netta."

Netta painstakingly walked to Sadie and handed her the searing knife. She grimaced and held her breath as Sadie poised it over the toes. *Ohmylord, This was not going to be pretty.*

With one hand holding the knife, Sadie reached her other hand out to Ma. "All right, hand me that hammer."

Before Netta knew what happened, Sadie had the toes off, the wound neatly singed, and Ma busily worked at covering the foot with her numbing powder.

While Sadie bandaged the foot, and Netta cleaned up the bloody remains, another knock sounded at the door. Lucy poked her head back inside. "Am I too late to help?"

"The deed's done," Sadie told her.

"Oh, I'm so sorry I didn't get back in time to help you," Lucy apologized. "After I took Alice home to Jonathan, I hurried back as quickly as I could. Guess I didn't hurry fast enough."

"No problem, Lucy. It went well enough but thanks anyway."

"Well, you're never going to believe who I ran into on the way in here," Lucy said with a wide smile. She threw open the door.

"Michael! Amanda! You're *home*!"

The family trooped inside, twins scurrying in to hug Rosanna and Rachael, but Jems and little Rebecca just stood and eyed each other warily.

"Ohmylord, Amanda! Is it really you?" Netta babbled. "You've missed so much that's happened around here, it's going to take *weeks* to catch you up on all the news!"

"Don't you fret, Netta. We'll have plenty of time for all that," Amanda said, giving her another hug.

"Well, take off your wraps and make yourselves to home. I got a nice big pot of stew all ready for supper, and you got here just in time." She turned to her husband and pulled him to her side. "Brawley, this is Amanda Harrison. Amanda, Pastor Brawley Gilmore, my new husband!" Netta crowed. "And you also got you a new husband! Lucy told us you two went and tied the knot. Who'd believe it? Both of us new married!"

As Netta chattered away to Brawley and Amanda, Michael walked over to Sadie. "Looks like you've had your hands full," he said to his sister, taking in the blood-stained apron and her patient in the corner, where Ma still sat, wiping at Dan's brow. "You doin' all right?"

"I'm fine," Sadie said. "Just had a little amputation to deal with."

"Willie and the children to home?"

"Yup. He's keeping the home fires burning while I tend to medic duty."

"How's John doin'?"

"He seems in all his glory, planting that new wheat strain of his," Sadie said, giving her brother another big hug. "He'll be glad to see you, I'm sure of that."

"How's it going over there with Amanda's sister?"

"Nobody's seen much of 'em. So far they tend to stick pretty close to home. But maybe that'll change now, with you and Amanda back here." Sadie walked over to Amanda and gave her a warm hug. "Welcome home, Sister! I was beginning to wonder if you'd ever come back!"

"How could I stay away, when this is where my heart is firmly planted?"

EPILOGUE

February, 1823
Justice, Vermillion Township

Mid February's lengthening days brought welcome sunshine to this bright afternoon. Amanda stood at the business end of yet another birthing bed, helping Lucy Johansen bring forth her third child—Jonathan's very first.

It brought back so many memories.

"One more push ought to do it, Lucy," Amanda encouraged the big-boned farmer's wife. Lucy gave it her all, and in a gush, a cry of new life echoed through the bedroom addition, into the main Johansen cabin.

"You have a son. And quite a vocal one, at that!"

Lucy heaved a great sigh and fell back on the bed to rest from this great labor of love. "Jonathan's going to be so pleased," she breathed. "I'm glad I could give him a boy."

"Have you talked about names?"

"Jonnie Jo. We'll call him Jonnie Jo, after his Daddy, but still a name of his own."

Amanda tended to cleaning up Lucy and the baby, then gently placed the newborn in Lucy's arms. "You ready for me to call Jonathan in?"

Lucy simply nodded, as tears streamed down her cheeks.

While Jonathan and Lucy welcomed their new son in the bedroom, Amanda excused herself to give them the privacy they deserved at this intimate moment. She walked into the main cabin, where Michael sat playing a game of pick-up-sticks with Hank and the twins, while Alice and Jems sat in a corner playing with puzzle pieces. Jems worked at putting them together; Alice simply chewed at the stray pieces he hadn't claimed, yet.

"Another babe, safely delivered," Michael said, as he pulled Amanda down beside him. "It's always a relief when they get here safe. I can't help but worry till they do."

"Well, you may as well get used to it, 'cause in about six months' time you're going to have to worry another one here," Amanda said, giving him a huge smile.

"You... you're... we're...?"

"Yes we are, my love. I hope I can give you a son, too."

"Lordy, I'll take anything! Long as you both live through it!" He said, giving her a crushing hug. "A babe. We're going to have a baby!" He shook his head in utter astonishment.

"Baby, baby, baby... we got a baby!" Alice babbled from the corner.

Jonathan sauntered back into the main cabin, giving Michael and Amanda the proudest smile they'd ever seen cross his face. "Got me a boy!" He broke into an even bigger grin. "Reckon we oughtta mosey over to Anson's Shed an' have us a celebration drink, now Mike, don't you?"

* * * * *

By the close of 1823, Frank Putnam and Anson Guthrie had poured up a great many celebratory drinks from behind the bar at their little tavern, for family and friends alike, to welcome another round of citizens into Vermillion Township.

And the Rev. Brawley Gilmore dutifully christened every one of them in the new church building sitting right next door, as the embers of new life continued to glow:

January: ....Tillie Kirtland, #5 to Jason and MarySue Kirtland;

February: ....JonnieJo, #3 to Lucy and #1 to Jonathan Johansen;

April:...............Rebecca Hawkins, #2 to Harmon and Lovinia Hawkins;

June:........... Brawley Gilmore, Jr., #5 to Netta and #1 to Rev. Gilmore;

July: ....Dudley Howard, #1 to Christian and #2 to Johannah;

August: ....Mikey Harrison, #6 to Amanda and #2 to Michael Harrison;

September: .... Mark Howard, #3 to Simeon and Katrina Howard;

October: .... Jimmie Hawkins, #4 to Sadie and Willie Hawkins;

November:....Jamison Coulter, #2 to Flora Jean and Wheatly Coulter.

ABOUT THE AUTHORS

Sheryl Drake Lawrence   MaryLee Marilee
(as Libby Howard)   *(as Ellie Mae)*

MaryLee Marilee, published humor columnist (15 years in The Holmes County Bargain Hunter), former editor & feature writer (Graphic Publications), motivational speaker, and most recently bed and breakfast owner, currently devotes her time to writing, while traveling the country in her little motorhome to visit children and grandchildren.

Sheryl Lawrence, office finance-coordinator, former English teacher, and short-story author, has published stories in "Girls To The Rescue" series, printed by Meadowbrook Press. Sheryl lives with her husband of 27 years, stays current with their many children and grandchildren, while keeping multiple offices organized and humming.

"We met in a creative-writing class nearly 30 years ago and haven't stopped talking since! We encourage and motivate one another at a time in history just as challenging, in its own way, as that of our frontier sisters."

**Contact the authors at www. Marylee@hearthstones.net
Or Sheryl@hearthstones.net**

Print and E-Books available at Amazon.com, Barnes&Noble.com or at **www.hearthstones.net**

Made in the USA
Lexington, KY
07 September 2017